In memory of my brother SGT Eric Justin Seims,
and my fellow soldiers SPC Jeremiah Schmunk,
SGT Damien Ficek, and SGT Jeffery Shaver.

You are gone, but not forgotten.

TABLE OF CONTENTS

PRELUDE

Dark Affairs

Victory City, formerly Denver, March 2096

GENERAL MURDOCH STALKED through his control room at the core of his compound. Holo screens displaying hundreds of different video feeds snaked in circles around a central control station. He glimpsed a video of himself flashing across the largest feed in the room. It was one that had been on a constant loop for the last twenty-four hours.

He glared at the old man on the screen: silver, tight-cropped hair cutting an edge in his dark skin and contrasting with his much darker green uniform. Weary crow's feet crept out from the corners of his eyes and his angular jaw set tight as the AP riddled him with questions.

A middle-aged female reporter with bright red hair recorded him with a pair of green, glowing contact lenses. "What do you have to say about Senator Cole's allegations that you continue to stall the transition of governmental control to the Senate?"

"No comment," he had said.

Another reporter motioned, and a drone camera the size of a hummingbird shifted so he'd be in the same frame as the general when he asked his accusatory question.

"Don't you think, General, that after thirteen years of martial rule the country deserves to become the democracy it was meant to be?"

He didn't get a chance to answer before another reporter piped in with more questions. His fingers squeezed together behind his back like a vise and he sneered at the overweight, sweaty, unkempt male reporter.

"General, is it true that you have been in negotiations with the Colonies? And that those negotiations are in direct violation of a Senate mandate?"

General Murdoch saw his own eyes flash red on the screen. The crowd started to murmur and took a collective step backwards.

He turned sharply and walked away from the podium, flanked on either side by his security detail. A salt-and-pepper-haired soldier with the same close-cropped hair, dark green uniform, and muscular build replaced him at the podium.

"That's all the time we have for questions today, folks. Thank you for coming out."

The screen flashed to another reporter who was standing outside the Senate building.

General Murdoch turned away from the feeds and shook his head as he continued to his ready room. A younger soldier at the main feeder controls nodded to him as he walked by, his look solid with approval.

Why can't they understand that I'm only doing what's best for the country?

The artificial intelligence sparked from the link that was embedded in his brain. *Would you like me to get the locations and credentials of the questioning reporters?*

The silent door to his ready room slid open as he got to it, and then slid closed just as silently after he passed through. He took a deep breath and headed to a tall, concrete stool at the center of the almost-empty room, where he could pull up his private feeds.

Give them to David, let him handle it.

Sending them now, sir.

Ungrateful, that's what they are. If they only knew how close we are. How soon we'll be damn near invincible again. Hell, they'd be praising our rule instead of trying to sabotage it.

Sir, you have a feed coming in on your secure server.

Patch it through.

He sat on his stool and let the holo feeds come up around him. A holographic keyboard popped up and his fingers raced over a set of symbols and keys. The feeds collapsed into one large screen and the single image of a black-robed figure appeared in front of him. The majority of the person's face was hidden in the shadow of a deep black hood, allowing only a set of pale lips to be visible.

"You better have something good to report, monk."

The monk's pale lips slid into a smile. "We have them."

ONE

Greeting Disaster

JOHN THREW HIMSELF BEHIND a half blown-apart wall, landing like a sack of rocks. Beads of sweat rolled down his face, his body raced to repair burns on his arms from the Canadian's Inferno rockets. He looked at his smoldering uniform and wondered what the hell he was still doing on the battle-worn streets of Old Montana.

The clanking of shrapnel surrounded him as the ground quaked under the barrage of more high-ordinance explosives hitting all around him. John chanced a quick look over the wall, and heavy red drops spattered across his face and into his mouth like a warm, copper-tasting maple syrup. One of his soldiers fell to the ground in front of him, his body riddled with shrapnel and bullet holes. John quickly returned fire with his rapid electric pulse rifle and kept firing over the wall as the approaching onslaught got closer and closer. He wanted to check on his wounded soldier, but knew it was pointless, so he just kept firing — firing at an enemy he knew he must kill, but he didn't know why. There was a small break in the fighting, so he looked down at the soldier's bloody, burnt face and fell back in horror. The young man's face was barely distinguishable, but John recognized his eyes, those almost golden hazel eyes, and what was left of his face. His son's face.

What's happening? How did Adam get here?

John grabbed his weapon, screaming in rage, and fired a burst of electric fire at his attackers with murderous intent. No matter how many came and how much killing he did, he couldn't stop firing. He pulled the lower trigger of his pulse rifle, which bellowed out a high-explosive anti-personnel round. It broke apart in the air, sending small, precision ordnance fragmenting out to kill the rest of the attackers in one fatal volley. John kept his weapon steady to his eye and swept through the piles of bodies. When the faces of the dead became clear, he froze, his blood turned to cement.

Hundreds of mutilated corpses lay in the blood-soaked mud, but they had only two faces. He lost his breath and collapsed as if one of his own rounds had just seared through his chest.

This can't be possible. How could this happen?

His hand reached out and crept across the faces of his dead wife and son, revealed over and over again amongst the heaps of bodies. The bodies started moving, convulsing, and bodies upon bodies erupted out from the piles. Bodies of people he recognized, family, friends, soldiers, and enemies. They fell on top of him, smothering him, shattering him with ear-piercing screams.

You killed them! You killed them all!

* * *

John Howe sat bolt upright in his bed, sweating and panting from his nightmare. He blinked his eyes rapidly to clear the fuzziness and took stock of himself. Fresh cedar-and-dew-filled air drifted into his nostrils as he breathed in through his nose and out through his mouth, slowing himself down, calming his body and mind. He scanned his surroundings, absorbing the rough texture of the bare log walls, the warm light coming in through the cracked windows, and the steps and railing that led down to the rest of his cabin, and allowed himself to settle back into reality.

He was in his room, their room, his and Elizabeth's. He was in his home, his own empty home for the past thirteen years. He reached over, leaning toward his bedside table, and straightened out the picture of his wife and son, which didn't need straightening. He ran his fingers over the face of his dark-skinned wife, her silky black hair showering her shoulders and sneaking over her eyes. She hovered behind their son, chin tucked into the nape of his neck by his right ear, arms stretched out far in front of them to take the self-shot picture. *Thirteen. He was thirteen when this picture was taken.* He had short black hair, spiking up and messy, *unruly just like mine,* over golden hazel eyes, *just like his mother's,* caramel skin, sharp chin, already a muscular build, the perfect mix of them both. *Good-looking kid, hot dame.*

I was one lucky SOB, Cam.

The implanted AI link sparked from deep within his mind, whirring him even more into the conscious world.

Remember when you wanted him to get blue eye mods, so they'd be the same color as yours?

Remember when you were going to stay out of my business?

Another bad dream, I see.

Not very many nights without one.

Maybe you should take Oliver up on his offer to dump your archives.

Thanks, Cam, I'll make sure to ignore that advice.

Big surprise coming from a man. Shall I start the exterior sweep?

Yes. That'll get you away from me for a bit.

I heard that.

You hear everything, darling.

Cam was the closest thing John had had to a wife since Elizabeth died. An AI implant fashioned as his internal female counterpart, Cam gave him a tactical advantage. A gift from the IRIS guys that he was ever so thankful for. The communications between the two only took a split second, completely imperceptible to anyone besides other CyOps, which was helpful in not making him look like a nutter who talked to himself.

He threw his legs over the side of his bed and shook his head side to side, cheeks and skull vibrating, reminding him to move. He slowed his breathing as he stared at his feet and wiggled his toes. The air was refreshingly cool, and gave him small goose bumps all over his naked body. The morning came sweeping in through the window and into his lungs, urging him to wake up, and reminding him that he would need to get the house and shed cleaned out and ready for spring. John arched his back, let his head roll on the top of his neck like a bowling ball, and stood up to shake the kinks out of his rusty joints. He walked over the cool floor to the stairs and softly kicked his German shepherd in the butt.

"Time to get up, Adam. We got rounds to do."

Adam yawned, stretched his front legs out in front of him as he shook his butt at John, and then strutted down the stairs and out his small door to go make his morning pissing stroll. John jogged down the steps after him, grabbed some old cargo pants off the drying rack and slipped them on, before heading over to stoke the fire in the wood stove and put a pot of water on to boil.

He smiled as he heard Adam trot back into the house.

"Done with the pisser already?"

Adam nudged up behind him and started pawing at his leg. "Bet you think you deserve some food, don't you, boy?"

Adam barked and sat, stretching his neck out long so that John could scratch the soft golden fur there.

"Coffee first."

John walked a few steps into his kitchen and reached into the cupboard for an old metal can that had COFFEE stenciled across it in bold black letters. He shook it, listening to the echo of a depleted bean supply. The side of his mouth lifted to a wry smile as he looked over at Adam.

"Almost out, bud. How could you let that happen?"

Adam's ears perked, and he tilted his head slightly to the left, his big hazel eyes sparkling with innocence.

"Don't look at me like that. This isn't my fault." John gathered up supplies to make his morning coffee. "We'll have to make a trip in to see Oliver sooner than we thought."

John's AI sparked again.

Perimeter check's done.

Thanks, Cam. Anything remarkable to report?

The dumb-dumb you call a mainframe has sensed a heat sig on the northern part of the complex. Probably just another glitch, but we're still arguing about it.

It's property, Cam, not a complex.

So you always say, and as I always say, per my programming it is a complex.

You're full of insight as always, Cam.

You're lucky you have me.

I'm not sure I would say that exactly.

You're welcome regardless, John.

Adam trotted over and started nudging John's leg with his nose. "I know, you feel left out, don't you, boy?"

Adam barked, putting his front paws up on the counter and then licking the coffee tin.

"You want to go see Oliver so you can refill on his treats, yes? He's much easier to get along with than Cam, isn't he?"

I take offense at that.

Sure you do, Cam.

Adam barked again as he dropped his paws off the counter and then trotted over to his water bowl, lapping at it as if he might drink the whole thing.

John made his coffee and then poured himself a cup, inhaling slowly as the steam from the black liquid worked its way from the cup to his nose. "That's what I'm talking about!"

I'll never understand you.

You're never supposed to.

Adam barked at him from his bucket of food, where he was waiting, impatient, tongue hanging out the side of his mouth, and tail wagging on the ground.

Adam understands me.

Makes sense.

Because we're both so highly evolved?

Adam circled around John for a moment, and then flopped down on his side as if he'd gotten bored, and started licking himself.

Yeah, you go with that theory.

John grinned, and then nudged Adam's butt with his foot so he'd stop. "All right, boy, alright. I'll dish you up."

He threw on a gray cotton shirt that had been hanging on the back of one of the kitchen chairs. His arm jerked to a stop as his finger snagged into something. He looked down at his finger sticking through a new hole in his sleeve.

Damn, looks like we'll need to make a stop at Ms. Trowley's for a new shirt, too.

Oh boy, going out on a limb with that, aren't you?

That's me. Johnny Dangerous.

That was really bad, John.

What? I thought it fit.

He scooped out some dried food from a bucket by the kitchen table and dumped it into Adam's bowl as Adam paced around him.

Really bad, John.

You're just jealous you don't have wits like mine.

Your wits are my wits, John.

John smiled as he watched Adam dig into his food.

I think they were mine first.

I believe if we research this you'd be surprised how dull you were before me.

Are you having one of those "I'm confused about my life as an AI implant" moments again? Because if you are, I'd rather you just go back to the mainframe for a while.

You would never say that to Adam.

That's it. Cam, go do another perimeter sweep.

John checked to make sure Adam was eating and then sat down at the kitchen table, threw on his boots, and laced them up.

If I could say no, I would.

But you can't.

He grabbed his coffee off the counter and headed to the middle of the kitchen. He looked around, knowing he was the only one in the room, but checking anyway, and then bent over, rolled the carpet off a large hatch in the floor, and headed down to his underground control center.

Fine, John. If you need me I will be in purgatory doing another pointless perimeter sweep.

Try to dump your archives while you're there.

Ouch, that hurts, John.

You can't feel, Cam.

Touché.

He went down the steep stairs, cranked his generator a few times, and started running through his systems checks. As he drank his coffee, he searched through the screens, making sure none of his sensors had been triggered during the night. *All clear, that's always good. Cam said Hank thinks there was a heat sig somewhere...* He scanned the small 3-D maps he had pulled up and flipped through the holo projections with his fingers. *There it is. Cam was right—probably a glitch.*

John set his coffee down by the workstation, unhooked his wrist computer from the main and put it on, then opened up the locker on the wall by the stairs and took out his chest rig, sliding it on over his shoulders and filling it with fully loaded magazines. His REP rifle clicked as he took it out of its rack and inspected the small digital readout on it, making sure it linked with his wrist comp. Satisfied that all his other REPs and pistols were in good order, he took a few steps over to where he kept his less sophisticated weapons—crossbows, knives, axes, and machetes—and ran his fingers across the various hilts and blades until they rested once again on his favorite, the machete. He slid it into the sheath on the back of his belt, linked his wrist comp to Hank one more time, making sure he had the grid marked where the heat sig came from, and then picked up his coffee and headed back up to the kitchen.

Cam. Are you ready?

Already on board.

"You coming, Adam, or you sitting this one out?"

Adam trotted up beside him and nudged his hand. John attached his rifle to a clip on his chest rig and grabbed his favorite zero-G football team's hat off the hook by the door and slapped in on his head.

"Let's go then, slow poke."

Still that crusty old Seahawks hat, huh?
Better times, Cam, better times.
Well, it needs washed.
Any new info on that heat sig?
Still there. Hank seems to think we should check it out.

He finished off his coffee in one big gulp, set the empty cup down on the porch rail, and took off toward the wood line that surrounded his house.

Might be worth a look.
Famous last words.

John had made this perimeter check of his home faithfully every morning since Day One, and then every morning after cease-fire. Every morning for the past thirteen years. Wasn't much left of the old country these days. Sure, there was a Western Colonies, a fraction of the old United States; and here, the Pacific Northwest Free Territories, where John and anyone else sick of *Great Leadership* lived in what used to be Washington State.

He had been a soldier during the great world conflicts. A specific type of soldier, CyOps, designed with genetic and technological enhancements so he could complete certain tasks normal soldiers weren't able to do. He excelled at those tasks, excelled too much. After Day One that all ended. The world ran out of money, out of the resources to fight each other on such a grand scale; they ran out of the ability to kill each other with the efficiency they were used to.

His team came home to a fractured country that was fighting and killing for the bits of rubble falling from the walls of the once-mighty nation. He was slated for leave, but he stayed with his unit and their leader, Colonel Murdoch. They were supposed to be trying to save the United States, but they lost sight of that goal, and instead turned the world into more of a nightmare.

He was sick of fighting, so he left and found his way through the broken country, determined to get home to his wife and son. He didn't make it in time. He found them dumped in a stack of trash by the shed. His family, treated like refuse that had gotten in the way of someone else's easy survival. He found a small squad of scavengers, former soldiers, who were unlucky enough to be looting his house. He slaughtered them, making messy work of it in his fury. He didn't know if they had killed his family or if someone else had. It didn't matter—they were there. He cleaned up, buried his wife and son, torched the dead bodies of the scavengers, and lay for weeks in his empty house before Cam made him move and eat, eat and move. She made him survive.

* * *

John snapped back to the real world when Adam nudged his leg and started sniffing the air and digging his paw into the ground.

Oh great, the boy wonder has found something.

What do you see, Cam?

An elk in the tree line fifty-six meters to the east.

John scanned the forest ahead until he heard a rustling in the bushes. Adam's fur rippled along his back, and he let out a deep throaty growl. John raised his rifle to his cheek and the laser scope came on, Cam linking with it at the same time to target the movement. John flicked his wrist toward the trees, and Adam sped in that direction with less noise than a whisper.

John waited, still as a statue. Eye trained. Weapon raised. Trigger finger loose. The trees and bushes rustled and John heard Adam growl, more like a large gray wolf than a shepherd. An elk came racing out of the underbrush, and John squeezed the trigger lighter than a feather, letting a single searing electric pulse fly through the horned giant's eyeball. Adam came running out just a split second behind the bull's tail, and leaped onto the freshly dead carcass.

John snickered. "I think you might be losing a step, buddy."

He's not the only one; seemed like you were spacing out.

Thanks for the encouragement, Cam.

Anytime. At least you don't have to resign yourself to early-morning perimeter sweeps and late-night dates with an overweight computer.

Don't worry, Cam, we'll always have each other.

Please don't remind of that.

Adam came up and tucked his head under John's hand, letting out a soft whimper and nudging him until he kneeled down and started scratching him behind his ears.

"I know boy, I know. I was just teasing you," John said. "Yes, you're a good boy, aren't you? Come on, let's get this giant back home."

Adam stretched his neck so John could scratch there too, tilting his head to lick John's cheek and chin. Then the dog turned to the tree line, abrupt and alert, a guttural growl forming in his throat, ears perked up as if he were hearing something much deeper in the woods. He stood up tall on all fours and put his nose high in the air, sniffing, and let out another growl, calling John to attention.

"What is it, boy?"

John stood back up and spotted what Adam had sensed. He followed a thin, white mist rising from the forest floor to the clouds above. Adam started to pace back and forth, sniffing the air, barking, and pawing at the ground.

John, it's the heat sig from earlier. I'm picking up four human sigs now instead of just one static one.

Can you scan them?

Mm, maybe you two are not the only ones losing a step. I should have seen this earlier.

Can you scan them, Cam?

Nothing past the body sigs. They must have a dampener with them.

Adam whined again.

"I see it, buddy, I see it." John took a deep breath and then let it out. He looked toward the smoke, then back toward the trail that led to their home. "Well, damn you two, our morning rounds are going to take a bit longer today. Go ahead, Adam. Go find 'em."

Adam took off swiftly and quietly through the trees with John following right behind him. John pulled out his machete, and cut through the brush as the elk had earlier. Adam would run ahead and then stop, sniffing the air to make sure they were heading the right way, wait for John, and then he would take off again. They kept forward like this for an hour, slicing their slow way through the woods.

How close are we, Cam?

Pretty close. It looks like Adam might be there, but he doesn't have his collar on so I can't be sure.

Just a glitch, huh?

None of us is perfect, John.

I want that in writing.

When John caught up to Adam, the dog was crouched on his belly, low to the ground on a small rock overlooking a clearing in the trees. John crawled to him, pinecones, rocks, and twigs mixing with the dirt to work up under his fingernails and into his clothes. He crept lower and lower to the ground up to the crest of the rock next to Adam and glared down at whoever was crazy enough to ruin his morning.

"Jippers," John said.

Two

Jippers

ADAM'S SNOUT CURLED, his lips rolling up to expose his sharp canines that showed ivory against his black fur. His body vibrated next to John as the killer instinct inside him fought its way to the surface.

John, be careful, these ones are loaded.

Can you tell what they have?

For starters, that's a hydro cell wagon, so they aren't your run-of-the-mill jippers. The man is armed with an electric whip and has a blaster on his back. I can't see inside the wagon, so that must be where the dampener is. Besides the man, there are two children out there; leaves one body unaccounted for.

And you said you were losing a step.

Don't try to make me feel better, John. It just feels dirty.

I love you too, Cam.

You're helpless.

Adam growled low again, and John put his forehead to Adam's.

"Yeah, tell me about it. Must not be able to read signs, huh?"

John scanned the small pasture and tree lines for other persons in the party.

Anything else, Cam?

Nothing that I can see.

John focused on the boy and girl huddled together by the fire, then moved his focus along the small camp past the fire to a heavily muscled man, who was throwing things out of a large chest. He was tall, with long, greasy black hair, tattoos all over, and a beard full of brass rings. He was also dirty, and John could swear that he smelled him from the trees.

"Let's get down there and show them where to go, Adam."

Adam licked John's face and trotted back down onto the path. They circled the clearing, sticking close to the cover of the tree line, and made their way around to the back of the jipper camp without so much as a broken twig or displaced leaf.

"You ate it," a deep, booming voice hollered from the clearing. "I know you did, you little whelp."

John stopped and held his hand out to steady Adam. He took a couple more creeping steps forward so he could hear better.

"Even if he did, what's the big deal?" A much different voice this time. A female voice, but smaller. The girl. "It isn't like either of you two needs it."

"You ungrateful little wench!" The burly man's voice boomed again, and heavy footsteps thumped the ground. Charging.

John stalked to the edge of the bushes to see what was happening. There was a thud, and he could hear feet grinding in the dirt like sandpaper on wood. Adam paced and whined behind him, as if he wanted to burst out and race through the trees at any minute. John turned and put his finger up to his lips, quieting Adam, and then leaned forward to get a better view.

"No!" A boy's voice screamed this time.

"Adam—"

John's whisper was cut off by the squeal of an electric whip and a child's screaming. He crept through the underbrush to the very edge of the trees. The young boy was being whipped by the jipper, curled up on the ground, writhing in pain and screaming.

John.

I know, Cam. Let me think.

"No. Please, I didn't know I was stealing." The boy was huddled against a half log on the ground, his arms raised up to shield himself. "Please, sir, no more."

The girl was on the ground, trying to push herself up. She looked over at her brother and jumped up into a dead sprint toward the whipping man.

"Leave him alone!"

John watched as the girl grabbed the massive man's free arm, digging her heels into the dirt and tugging as hard as she could to try and protect the boy. The huge man laughed at her and shrugged her off, sending her tumbling to the ground with little effort, while mocking her high-pitched voice as she fell.

"'Leave him alone.'" He laughed again. "He'll get exactly what he deserves, and then you'll get yours."

John.

Damn it, I know, Cam.

"STOP! Please. You're hurting him," the girl said. "He didn't mean anything by it. He was just hungry. Stop hurting him!"

"You shut your mouth, ungrateful rat. Our food ain't for you or your rat brother. It's for me and the missus. Now shut your rotten mouth, or yours will be twice as bad."

John set his jaw tight. The jipper had his whip up, ready to strike again. Before he could think about it, John stepped out of the trees, weapon raised to his cheek. Like clockwork, Cam linked with John's rifle, targeting the jipper with an accuracy that could nail a fly's ass to the wall a mile away. Adam stalked forward beside John, teeth still bare, a rolling growl making everyone in the small group stop everything and turn to face them.

"Whoa, whoa, whoa," John said. "I don't think that you want to do that."

The jipper snapped his head away from Adam and toward John, eyeing him with a snarl.

John, his opposite arm is damaged, old injury, still weak. He won't be able to grab his gun while he's holding the whip.

John kept his weapon trained on the man. Adam stayed by him, frozen with his haunches bent slightly, back angled, eyes focused on the man.

Good.

"What are you doing here?" John asked.

"We have no quarrel with you, mate. It would do you good to turn and leave us alone," the jipper said.

"Well, as tempting as that is, I can't do it. You see, you're on my land, and I don't take too kindly to people squatting on my land uninvited. I take even less kindly to people who beat the crap out of little kids."

John, the dampening field is moving toward us. It's coming out of the wagon.

The door to the wagon opened and a fat, round-faced woman came out, dressed in a worn, ratty black dress and a long, bright red velvet coat. She was carrying a bucket of fruit and bread, presumably for her and the whipping man, but dropped it suddenly when she saw John, letting the contents spill all over the ground.

The man ignored the woman and kept his snarling stare focused on John.

"What we do with our children and where we go is private business. If you didn't notice, we're jippers, mate, and we do as we please in these lands because no one owns them but the jippers."

He shifted the whip over his head with his wrist as if he hadn't decided whether to strike his new target or lash out again at the boy. He flinched just slightly when the girl used the opportunity to run to her brother and cover him, shielding him with her body.

Found some real winners this time, John.

Such slim pickings these days.

"Wow. Did you hear that, Adam?"

Adam tilted his head at John and perked his ears, then turned back toward the jipper man and growled.

"You're right," John said.

"Of course I'm right," the jipper man said.

"No, not you, idiot. You're most definitely wrong," John said. "Adam's right. We don't like you."

You think you might want to wrap this up sometime tonight, John?

I'm practicing. You always say I should work on my people skills.

And you always pick such wonderful times to listen to me.

"Mister, my patience is running out. If you don't leave, I'm gonna rip you and that damn dog to pieces."

"Wrong again. *My* patience has already run out. I own this land, not the jippers, not anyone else, and you're trespassing on it." John gestured to their wagon. "I don't much care where you go, but you will leave, and you'll leave without these children, or I'll shoot you dead right now."

Since when did you get so dramatic?

Too many books, I guess.

The large man roared with laughter. "Did you hear that, lover?"

"I heard him, dear." She raised her hands and started kneading them together in the air as if she were manipulating a fresh ball of dough. "Listen, mister, you ain't got no rights here. Must be crazy-thinking to order us around. You can't take them kids from us, no more 'n you could wipe my ass." The woman kept kneading the air with her hands. The children looked back and forth between the jippers and John and Adam.

Is she trying to cast a spell on you, John?

Or she's just hallucinating from her husband's stench.

Or she's an open-mind baby. She's a telepath, John. She is the dampening field.

John looked down at Adam, who shook his head from side to side, then growled and barked at the fat lady. John smiled and looked back at the jipper man, the cybernet behind his eyes turning his irises from blue to blood red.

"Uh, is she okay? It looks like she's having a seizure or something," John said.

"It's not working on these ones, lover. There must be a run on enhanced people in this area. I can't wait to be out of this place." She looked down at her hands and shook them off as if they were broken.

"And back to where people are more receptive to my charms. Will you just kill him and his stupid dog and be done with it?"

"Hey, now that's just not nice. Adam's not stupid because he doesn't respond to grade-school magic," John said. "Now I'll have to kill you just to defend his honor."

She might be right about the stupid part, actually.

Once again, so helpful, Cam. Why don't you be a doll and scan the wagon now that she's out of it.

Already on it.

"Ha! You're sure funny, little man. The wife's right. You ain't gonna kill me because you know that my whole tribe will come here and burn you to the ground, and that's magic you can't be immune to. So it looks like you're the one dying today."

The man brought the whip back farther over his head to strike at John. There was a loud hiss from the barrel of John's rifle, and the jipper's arm fell twitching on the ground, the whip still firm in the hand, the flesh where it had separated from the his body seared and steaming.

"Agh! What'd you do? My arm. My fucking arm!"

The man lunged toward John, but before he could get close, John fired another pulse. Another hiss, and this time the man dropped dead to the cool forest floor, a single steaming hole through his eye. Adam jumped over him to the children, guarding them with a vicious growl, postured to attack if the lady made a try for them.

"What'd you do? What'd you do?" The woman screamed and sobbed from the stairs. She tried to run at the kids, but Adam blocked her path, warning her again with a guttural growl. She glared at them and made her way to her dead husband instead.

Wagon's pretty high tech, John. These aren't your run-of-the-mill jippers. They're contractors.

Not anymore.

"Adam," John said.

At his command Adam sat on his hind legs, relaxed but aware as the woman made her way to the lifeless form of her husband and kneeled down beside him.

"What'd you do? You don't know what you done. You don't know who you're messing with." She sobbed and rocked back and forth, holding her dead husband's hand. "You'll pay for this, you'll pay."

John could feel the shocked stares of the boy and girl behind him as he stood silent and deadly. His eyes sparked red briefly as he trained his rifle on the woman.

"Like I was saying before: I don't care who you are, or why you're here, but you will get up and leave right now."

The woman wiped her eyes and looked to drag her husband to the trailer, aiming a deadly glare at John. He pulled his weapon closer into his shoulder, in position to fire again.

"He stays. He's mine now, and he'll stay there to warn anyone else that resting here is not an option. That the price is too high for squatting where you shouldn't squat, for picking a fight with the wrong person, and for spoiling my damn morning."

The jipper glared at him, and then started backing away, her hands held up in front of her. "You'll pay for this, techy. You don't know the pain that's coming your way."

She turned sharply and ran to her wagon, slamming the back door. A few seconds later the energy cell ignited, and she sped off through the woods.

John, she's using her comms right now; want me to intercept?

No. I have no intention of finding out where that rabbit hole leads.

That sounds like something you might regret.

Add it to my tab.

John let out a light, almost inaudible whistle and Adam came to him, nuzzling his head up against John's hand. He knelt down, weapon still slung across his chest in case he needed it again, and rubbed the thick fur behind Adam's ears.

"Good boy, Adam, good boy. Can you believe that lady tried to hex us? And she called you stupid." He let Adam lick his cheek. "You deserve a big treat when we slice up that bull."

Oh, please, he hardly did anything.

And you did?

I did more than he did.

Admit it, he's growing on you, isn't he?

Maybe a little.

Sucker.

Look who's talking.

Pay attention to the grid, will ya? Make sure that crazy bitch doesn't try to circle around.

Should I be expecting two extra in the house tonight?

No way.

Yeah, right, that's what you said about Adam, too.

Grid, Cam.

I'm on it. I'm on it.

"Excuse me," a small boy's voice said from behind them. "Excuse me, sir."

Adam barked, turning John's attention to the boy and girl by the fire.

He looked over the boy, who was sitting up now, his greasy hair partially covering his face like a mop. Long wet streams from his eyes had left lines in the dirt on his cheeks. His shirt was freshly stained red and torn to pieces from his beating, and he was looking at John bug-eyed and stunned.

"Uh, yeah, I guess you two are free now. So, best of luck." He started to walk off.

"But what are we going to do now?" the girl said.

John stopped and let out a deep sigh. Don't do it, John. Best to just keep walking. He ignored his own advice.

"Look, kid, I don't know what you're going to do now. I guess you can do whatever you want. I didn't really know what I was doing coming down here, and see how well that worked out. So just take this for what it's worth." He contorted his lips into a very fake smile. "You're free now, congratulations and you're welcome."

The kids looked up at him, both wet-eyed and dirty, their gaunt forms speckled by the orange light of the fire. The boy was wrapped tight in the protective guard of the girl's arms. A determined gaze steeled her face; she was trying to look anything but worried or scared.

There's fight in them, Cam. That's for sure.

John relaxed his shoulders and the grimace that he had thought was a smile disappeared. He remembered his son looking at him with almost the same expression when he needed help, but was too stubborn to ask for it.

Damn it.

They're just kids, John.

I know, Cam. I'm not blind.

He looked between the two and nodded his head, reluctantly coming to a sort of decision.

"Okay, you can stay camped out here tonight. There's a town about thirty miles from here that I could take you to in the morning. I know a guy there that might be willing to help a couple orphans."

John! They can't sleep out here.

No, Cam. No way.

John turned to leave for a third time and whistled for Adam. He took a few steps and sensed that Adam hadn't come up beside him yet, so he turned and stared at Adam, who was sitting stubbornly next to the kids.

He patted his leg and waved to him. "Adam, come on, buddy, it's time to go." He patted his thigh and whistled again, but Adam just lowered himself to the ground and whimpered. John let his head roll back and expelled a frustrated sigh.

See, even Adam is being more human than you.

What the hell am I supposed to do, Cam?

You know exactly what to do.

He turned toward the trail to his house, and then back to the kids and Adam, his face wrinkling as he forced himself to realize the only option he had.

Cam, we're going have two extra bodies tonight.

I knew it. Sucker.

He walked back and knelt by Adam, lifting the German shepherd's muzzle in his hand and letting him lick his chin.

"All right, old boy, just tonight, but they're out first thing in the morning."

Adam stood up on his front legs and barked excitedly, trotted over to nuzzle the injured boy until he stood, and then herded the kids toward John.

"Look, you can come stay the night, but don't get comfortable," John said. "I'll take you into town first thing in the morning and introduce you to Oliver. If anyone knows what to do with a couple of strays like you two, he does."

The boy walked over to John and grabbed his hand, putting his forehead on the back of it. "Thanks, mister."

John rolled his eyes and looked at the girl as he shook his hand free. "Okay, that's not weird."

John.

He cleared his throat and ran his hand under his hat to scratch at his scalp. "Um, good to meet you too, kid."

The girl stomped up to them, pulled the boy back away from John, and stepped in front of him.

"His name is Quinn, and that's his way of thanking you." She took a step closer to him and held out her hand. "My name is Sierra."

John reached out hesitantly, his rough fingers engulfing her much smaller, softer hand twice over, and shook it.

"John." He paused, waiting for something more. "No forehead thingy?"

"That's Quinn's deal, not mine."

"Good."

"Look, *John*. Thanks for everything, but I think we're just fine out here." She looked back at Quinn and nodded her head. "We should probably just stay. You being kind of a jerk, and us not knowing you at all."

See, they don't even want to come.

John, really?

Damn it.

Sierra pulled her head back a bit and studied him as if his eyes
had just changed color. "Are you talking to us?"

John looked at her, thought about saying something, but shook
his head instead as he started for the tree line.

What the hell am I doing? She's probably got brain damage.

Nice, John, real nice.

Well, do you want to get stuck with that?

John.

Fine.

"Try to keep up. If you lose sight of me, just follow Adam. He'll
show you the way to the house."

Sierra turned to Quinn and rolled her eyes. "Did you not hear us?
No way we're going with you."

John yelled back over his shoulder as he disappeared into the
trees. "You two coming or what?" He stopped just behind the tall
underbrush, watching and listening to them.

He saw Quinn look back at Sierra, who was glaring at the woods,
as if she were trying to find John and melt his brain with her stare.

Quinn waved his hands at her, and Sierra snapped out of her
momentary stubbornness, scanned around the campfire, and then
hurriedly gathered up what few supplies they had. It wasn't much:
a coat for Quinn, a blanket, and a big ratty knapsack with their other
possessions. Sierra did one last look around, stamped out the fire,
and then let her eyes settle on the body of the fat jipper man.

She ran over to him and kicked him in the gut. She smiled, and
kicked him again and again. Quinn raced over to her and put his
hand on her shoulder to pull her away.

John smiled to himself.

Lots of spark.

Just don't do anything to make her kick you like that.

No promises.

"Sierra, come on," Quinn said. "We'll get left behind."

She nodded to him, took a deep breath and wiped a sweaty clump
of thick brown hair off her face. She scanned the ground again and
spotted the jipper's electric whip, snatched it up and rolled it into

her knap sack. Then she grabbed Quinn's hand, and ran into the woods after him.

John smiled again.

Smart, too.

So, not brain damaged?

We'll see.

He turned away and started back up the trail. "Come on, Adam. Can't let them know we were hanging around for 'em."

*   *   *

The walk seemed to go faster than John anticipated, and he was surprised when they were already at the end of the long dirt road leading to his house. He stopped and turned back to face Sierra and Quinn, who were only a few paces behind him, and pointed up toward the hills.

"The house is up the road at the base of the hills. It's unlocked. Just head inside, but don't touch anything. I have to go fetch something that I left behind so I could save you two." He bent down and stared in Sierra's eyes. "Do you understand me? Just sit at the table and don't touch anything."

"I heard you the first time, and for the record, we didn't need you to save us. We were doing just fine." Sierra turned abruptly and grabbed her brother's hand. "Come, Quinn, let's go."

"Oh, right, it sure looked like you were doing just fine when that fat greasy jipper was whipping your brother."

You really put her in her place, didn't you?

You're not helping, Cam.

I think they're good for you.

You think too much.

Sierra rolled her eyes and huffed, then turned away from him and stormed up the road with her brother. Quinn broke free from her grip and ran to John, wrapping himself around his waist, and squeezed hard. His eyes were tight as if he were waiting for someone to try to pry them apart. John stood there, startled, confused. He looked down at his new attachment. He didn't need any attachments, let alone a boy-sized one.

"All right, kid, get out of here." He nudged Quinn away with a soft hand, and gestured to Sierra. "Take him with you, will ya, and remember, don't touch anything."

"Whatever." Sierra shook her head and went back to grab Quinn. "Come on, Quinn, let's leave the *hotshot* alone." She took her brother by his arm and pulled him down the drive.

John felt Adam nuzzle his cold nose up into his palm and whimper.

"Yeah, you want to go with them, don't you buddy? All right, go on then. You and Cam can make sure they don't touch anything."

Adam barked recognition and tore off after the two kids.

What the hell am I doing, Cam?

Good question.

Wait, this was your idea.

Oh, yeah. I think it'd be a good idea if I go up to the house. Keep tabs on Adam. Back in a jiff.

John let out a deep breath and followed the trail back to where the elk they had shot earlier should have been.

Wait, John. Might want to call this one a wash.

Cam flashed a heat sig that was two hundred meters in front of them onto John's HUD. A large feline quadruped stooped low beside the bull elk's carcass, bingeing on the organs it had just torn out.

Cougar.

Big one too.

So much for that idea.

There'll be more.

Not many.

He crouched down and scanned the tree line, pondering whether he should take on the cougar or call it a night.

Is the perimeter secure, Cam?

All locked up for the night. I expect you'll be back soon.

Yeah, I think this one's a lost cause. Adam and the runts staying out of trouble?

The house is still standing, if that's what you mean.

Just use your winning personality if they get out of line.

If that's your only plan, the house is screwed.

It works on Adam.

If I could get your dumb dog to listen to me, he would have stopped licking himself by now.

You haven't tried hard enough.

Just don't blame me if the house is a disaster when you get back.

When do I ever blame you, Cam?

When do you not blame me?

See you in a bit, Cam.

Anyone ever tell you you're hopeless?

You do, Cam, all the time.

THREE

Full House

JOHN FOLLOWED THE TRAIL back to where it snaked to a shed behind his house, grumbling to himself the whole time.

"'We didn't need you to save us,'" he mimicked in a whiny voice. "'Let's leave the *hotshot*.'"

He smiled just a little, remembering the twins, and the girl's readiness to try and make it on their own.

"Little brats."

He sat on a bench outside the shed for a while, staring at his house, tapping his foot on the ground, and fiddling with the scope on his rifle.

"Come on, Howe, too nervous to go inside your own house?" John glared through the lit windows. Shadows flickered: signs of life.

"Where the hell is Adam? Little turncoat, it didn't take him more than five minutes to dump me for a couple of younger models, did it? Well, I'm not sleeping out here, that's for damn sure."

Are you going to sit outside all night mumbling to yourself or are you coming in?

How bad is it, Cam?

Well, Adam is tearing the house apart while the children laugh and eat all your food.

Damn it, Cam, I told you to keep them out of shit.

What am I supposed to do? I'm stuck in the hawk box with dumb-dumb, remember?

He heard a loud bang followed by a high-pitched shriek from inside that shook him out of his own head and made him bolt to the house. He burst through the door and stalked into his now messy kitchen. He glowered at Sierra and Quinn as, smiling and laughing, they danced with Adam around a fallen shelf that had held most of John's pans. Pans that now lay on the floor, pans on the stove filled with food, and his favorite, pans that were being used as musical instruments in the hands of Quinn.

"What the hell is this?"

Sierra and Quinn spun around, wide-eyed and frozen, shocked out of the jig they were doing. Adam, as if sensing that John might throw the twins in the fire, went over and sat in front of them, proud and protective.

Cam's voice came out over the speakers in the room, which only magnified her voice in John's mind.

I told them not to touch anything, John, but Adam kept encouraging them.

You and Adam are the reason they're here in the first place.

"What's that annoying voice that keeps talking to us through the speakers?" Sierra asked. "Is there any way to shut it off?"

You're right, John. Take them back to the jippers.

Nice, Cam. A little late for that, don't you think?

John turned his attention back to the kids.

"I said don't touch anything. It was the only thing that I said. Don't touch anything." John turned to Adam, who lowered himself to the ground and covered his face with his paws. "How could you let them do this?"

"We just wanted to do something nice for you, to thank you for your help. I didn't even want to, Quinn did, and I told him you'd act this way."

"Nice for me? Using up my food and trashing my kitchen is nice for me?"

Sierra waved him off and started picking up their mess. "It's not like we weren't going to clean it up."

"I don't care if you were. I didn't want you to touch anything. I actually said that twice, and even Cam told you *don't touch anything*, remember?"

Sierra glared daggers at John while she helped Quinn pick up their mess.

"Whatever. There's no Cam person here, just Adam, us, and that weird computer thingy."

Okay, you can keep the boy, but the girl has to go.

Cam, not now.

"Cam might as well be me when I'm not here, no matter how she sounds coming from the speakers. And that doesn't change anything."

"*What. Ever*," Sierra said.

She glared straight at John one more time and then stormed into the extra room on the other side of the kitchen. Quinn looked between her and John and quickly put the pan he was using as a drum back on the now erect shelf.

"She only cooked dinner because I wanted to do something for you," Quinn said. "And I was the one who knocked down the shelf, not Sierra, so if you want to be mad, you should be mad at me."

Quinn patted Adam on his head, and then followed his sister into the room and shut the door.

Crazy kids you found, John? Whose idea was it again to bring them home?

Yours and Adam's.

I told you not to accept that dog from William.

You tell me a lot of things, Cam.

You want me to pull the screen up from the room?

Not now, Cam. I just want a minute of peace.

I'll check on them and run the loop in the room so they stay warm.

Thanks, Cam.

You did good today, John. They would be proud of you.

Cam, start the loop.
Starting the loop.

John sat in one of the chairs at the table and let out a deep breath. His eyes narrowed, and he sniffed the air a couple times, noticing for the first time the seasoned aroma. He looked over toward the steaming pots of food on the stove and inhaled sharply a couple more times. The glands in his throat tightened, and his mouth started to water. Adam trotted over and sat directly in front of him as he always did when he wanted John to do something that John had refused to do.

"What? Don't you think you're in enough trouble already, pal?"

Adam barked and nuzzled John's hand until he started petting him.

"What do you want me to do? I told them not to touch anything, and you and Cam were supposed to make sure they didn't."

Adam barked again, and John took in a deep breath and let it out.

"Anyone ever tell you you're pushy?" John asked. "I'll try it, but that doesn't mean that this makes it okay. I told them not to touch anything."

John made his way over to the stove and took the lid off the pot. He sniffed the mist sharp through his nostrils, once, twice, three times.

"Mm, doesn't smell like it'll kill us to try."

He searched the counter for a large wooden spoon and sneered a little as he picked it up from the small puddle of food it was lying in.

Messy.

And you're not?

He stirred it, sifting the spoon through the stew, trying to identify what they had used.

"All my best ingredients, damn it." He shook his head, reassuring himself that his complaints and attitude were valid. "It took months to gather up all of this, Adam."

He stirred again, and then took a spoonful and brought it up beneath his nose, letting the aroma continue to mist into his nostrils and tease his salivary glands.

He looked down at Adam, who was whimpering and wagging his tail in anticipation of his treat.

"Damn, that smells good though, doesn't it, boy? Probably won't hurt to taste it, see how bad they butchered our stores."

Be careful, John, you might end up feeling like an asshole if you actually like their cooking.

Not a problem, Cam. No way this turns out good.

Don't say I didn't warn you.

He took a little sip of the juices and was surprised at the wonderfully complex flavors that danced on his tongue. He blew on it slightly to cool it off a bit more and took a larger bite. This time his eyes opened wide as the meat melted in his mouth and the seasoned juices from the potatoes, carrots, and onion warmed his body. He was shaken out of his momentary stupor by Adam's whimpering and pawing at his leg.

Damn that's good.

Maybe there's more to those two than your first impression.

Really? It's just a few bites of food, Cam.

I'm just saying.

Stop saying, then.

John looked down and stared at a comically writhing Adam rolling around on the ground, whimpering as if he hadn't been fed in weeks.

"Okay, boy, calm down, calm down. I'll get you some."

John scooped the stew into a small bowl and put it by the table for Adam to start wolfing down. Then he got another bowl, started dishing himself up, and felt a pang of guilt.

Damn it.

Told you.

Like you knew it would be so good.

I had my suspicions.

Sure, Cam.

Are you going to be the adult here, or are you going to continue your run on pubescence today?

"Are you two going to come out and eat or are you going to sit in there sulking and let all this food you mangled go to waste?"

I knew you still had it in you.

Have I ever told you how grateful I am to have you with me, forever, constantly with me, never alone, ever? Have I told you that?

The feeling is more than mutual.

Good.

The door slowly creaked open and Quinn came out first.

"We're real sorry. We just wanted to do something nice for you and Adam," Quinn said. "For helping us and all."

"Shut up, Quinn," Sierra said. "He's just a jerk. You don't need to apologize to jerks."

I am very sympathetic toward those two again for some reason.

You're bipolar, Cam.

I can't be bipolar, John.

I'm telling you. You're bipolar.

Sierra came over to the table, nudging past Quinn and over to the stove, where she dished up a bowl of stew for each of them. John took a loaf of bread out of the breadbox, tore off a large piece, and tossed it to the other end of the table where Sierra and Quinn had taken up purchase away from him. He lingered for a minute, and then took a seat at the table to eat his portion of the stew and put together the puzzle that his day had turned into.

They ate in silence for a while, John's ears ringing from the thick air of an uncomfortable situation.

You're not being a very good host, John.

He wrinkled his lips into a crusty smile and tried to spark up a mealtime conversation.

"Where'd you learn to cook?"

You look constipated.

Be a dear and shut up for bit, Cam?

"She learned from our first set of guardians," Quinn said. "An old monk and his wife. They taught her how."

I would, but you need me on this op.

Fine, but can you at least be quiet for a bit?

Mum's the word.

"I thought monks didn't have wives."

I feel so much better already.

"He wasn't a monk anymore. I think it's because he fell in love with her or something like that and they kicked him out for it."

Sierra kicked Quinn's leg under the table. "Shut up, Quinn. Sorry, he doesn't know what he's talking about, really."

John took in both of their expressions and decided to pry a little more.

"So what'd you two do to your monks that made them give you up to Mr. and Mrs. Wonderful?"

Quinn slurped down a spoonful of his stew and kept talking without moving his head as he brought up another spoonful. "Nothing. We were kidnapped."

Sierra glared at him and pinched the back of his arm. "Quinn, shut up, really. Jeez."

John had to force himself not to smile as he watched Sierra and Quinn's interaction. He worked on his own stew, feeling a distant, peculiar pang in his chest.

You're enjoying yourself.

No, I'm not. It's probably gas.

You are enjoying yourself. I can tell.

"Sweet sister you got there."

Quinn rubbed his arm before wolfing down another bite. "Yep, she's all mine."

"Lucky you."

Sierra turned back toward John, a lemon-squeezed smile creasing the dirt on her face. "We lived with Jean and Sam Ortiz after the cease-fire. I'm not sure about our real parents, but the Ortizes got us from the meat market."

Part of John shuddered with revulsion. He knew about the massively overflowing meat markets that had been passed off as orphanages. Places that tried to house the parentless children after Day One. It was an impossible task, and years after Day One, during the cease-fire agreements, it was even worse. In the end, they were handing out children to just about anyone who would take them.

"We asked the Ortizes about our parents, but they didn't know them either. They just felt bad for us or something, and got us before the orphanage deans started working for the slavers."

"I really liked Jean and Sam," Quinn said.

Sierra rubbed her hands through his hair, digging the tips of her fingers gently into his scalp.

"I know, Q, I did too."

"Life was actually pretty normal." Sierra looked to Quinn, studying his face for a moment, and then looked back down at her clasped hands. "Well, as normal as life can be around here. The Ortizes were really good to us."

Sierra and Quinn got quiet for minute, as if they were lost somewhere, someplace, where things were better.

John, maybe you shouldn't push them.

I'm not, I'm just being a good host, remember?

Not exactly what I meant. Tread lightly for a change.

Noted, Cam, treading lightly.

"What happened?"

"Jippers," Sierra said, "raided our town in the middle of the night. Sam and Jean tried to save us but that just got them killed and us stuck with the dumb-dumbs. We thought maybe we were finally going to get traded at that last town, but it didn't happen."

That last bit intrigued John a little more.

"You were at Tree Top?"

"Not sure. Only reason we even knew we were in a town was because we woke up early and heard the fat man and his crazy wife trying to haggle with the locals."

"What were they trading?"

John stuck his head over his bowl and sucked down another bite of his stew.

Sierra wrinkled her brow, narrowing her hawkish eyes at him. "Why do you care about this anyway? You're just going to dump us off first thing tomorrow."

"You're right, I am." John stood up from the table harshly and started walking away. He paused, turned around, grabbed his bowl of stew to take with him, and then took off again. "And I don't care."

I think that went well.

That was real light, John.

I was never good at subtle interrogation.

No one would ever guess.

John heard sniffling behind him and stopped by the wood stove. He squeezed his eyes tight, took a deep breath, and then turned around, almost afraid he'd see some ghostly figure. Quinn's eyes had started to water, and his shoulders collapsed as if someone had just asked him to carry an elephant. Sierra pulled Quinn a little closer and gave him a hug.

"Something wrong, kid?"

Oh, real sympathetic sounding, John.

"Something wrong?" Sierra asked. "Really?"

This is why I should've kept walking.

No, you should've kept walking because you suck at this.

"I'm fine." The boy sniffed back some snot and tears. "I'm just tired, is all."

Adam, aware of the tension, jumped his front paws onto Quinn's lap and stretched his neck up to try and clean the boy's cheeks with his long tongue.

"Adam, gross." Quinn pulled his head back and wrinkled his nose, nudging him away.

John, caught off guard for a brief moment, let a chuckle escape, his tight lips forming a small smile even as the boy wiped Adam's slobber from his cheek. "He does that sometimes."

He looked at Adam, who had maneuvered like a ninja around Quinn's feet, lying on his back so Quinn and Sierra would get down and start rubbing his belly, his hind legs jerking in satisfaction.

"He really has no shame," John said.

Are you sure William said this was the smartest dog he'd ever trained?

He gets whatever he wants from all of us, doesn't he?

The jury's still out.

Adam whined and looked up at him with innocent eyes, legs stretched up in the air, tongue hanging out of his mouth.

No shame at all.

Sierra and Quinn laughed some more and Adam rolled over, inviting them to scratch him behind his ears and along his back while he yawned as someone would after a long day's work.

"Where'd you get such an awesome dog?" Quinn asked.

"A friend. I thought he was helping me out, but the longer I've had him, the more I think my friend was playing some kind of practical joke on me."

Adam hopped up on his hind legs and leaped over to John, barking, then put his front paws up on John's shoulders and licked his face. Sierra and Quinn's eyes went wide at the sight of his fully stretched-out height.

"Well, sometimes I wonder, boy," John said. "Now go easy, you're gonna make me spill my stew."

"I thought you didn't like the stew," Sierra said.

John pushed Adam's head to the side and sneered back at Sierra. "I don't."

Busted.

Real helpful, Cam. Flip the lights a little so I have to go check the generator, and get me out of this mess, will you?

Nope, you're on your own.

Glad you never left me hanging like this in the middle of a firefight.

You're welcome.

"Adam doesn't look that big until he jumps on you like that," Quinn said. "He looks like he could be as tall as you."

"Yeah, he's pretty sneaky that way," John said.

"Does he understand what you say?" Sierra asked.

"He understands when he wants to." John scratched behind Adam's ear and gently nudged him back down to the ground. "Isn't that right, boy?"

Adam let out a huff and then trotted back over to Quinn and Sierra, sat in front of them, and stretched out on the ground. As if that were their cue, Quinn and Sierra started scratching and petting him again.

"Well, you sure do got these two pegged, don't you, boy?" John said.

"We really like him," Quinn said.

Cam, run a scan on the kids.

What am I checking for?

Where the hell their wounds went.

John squinted at Sierra and Quinn as he sucked down another bite. "You two always heal fast?"

Sierra and Quinn looked at each other, both waiting for the other to answer.

John, I can't find anything. I'd never guess these were the kids we rescued.

Me either.

"I...we don't really know," Sierra looked down at Adam, running her fingers up and down through his thick fur.

"Never mind." John shook his head and put his bowl up to his mouth to slurp some of the juice out, and then brought it back down. "I don't want to know."

The room got quiet except for the settling of the house and the croaking toads outside. Quinn and Sierra sat with their heads down and fiddled with Adam's ears while John stood by the stove and finished off his stew, taking in the uncomfortable silence occupying his kitchen.

"Why'd you name him Adam?"

Well, it was good while it lasted.

Flick the damn lights, Cam.

Cam squeezed the power grid and the lights sputtered. Adam got up from letting them scratch him and sat in front of them on his hind legs, tail wagging, ears perked, eyes at attention.

"Looks like our generator needs a rest, so time for bed," John said. "Clean up your mess. Make it quick." He looked straight at Sierra. "We'll need to have an early morning if I hope to be rid of you two and still be able to get back here before the end of the week."

John put his bowl in the sink and walked toward his stairs, stopping at the bottom.

"Stay with them, Adam," he said. "Keep them safe."

Tuck them in, please, Cam, would you?

We got it, John. I'll turn the feed on in your room.

Thanks, Cam.

He went upstairs and watched the vid that Cam patched into his room. Sierra and Quinn had finished their stew and bread, and had started cleaning up the kitchen.

"I like him," Quinn said. "He's cranky, but I think it's because he's getting old."

"It's because he's an asshole, Quinn, that's why. He isn't any better than the fat jippers. He doesn't want us around, and I don't want to stick around."

"Maybe it's because you're so mean. Maybe that's why he wants us gone. Maybe if you were nice, he'd let us stay with him." Quinn threw a wet rag on the table and then ran to the bedroom.

"Quinn. Quinn, wait!" He heard Sierra go after him, but Quinn must have ignored her. The door to the bedroom slammed shut. John could hear the old door creaking as she leaned against it and tried to talk some sense into him.

"I'm sorry, Quinn, but it's true. We're leaving in the morning and we're not coming back. How did you think this would turn out, Q?" The door reopened and Quinn let Sierra into the spare room, shutting the door softly behind her.

The lights went out and John rolled over in his bed, putting a pillow over his head to drown them out.

What the hell did I get myself into?

FOUR

One Big Happy Family

JOHN WOKE UP TO THE THICK-TEXTURED feeling of Adam lapping his face. He rolled over, eyes still closed, and scratched under Adam's chin.

"Adam. Get out of my face. It's too early, jeez."

He nudged Adam gently back to the floor so he could sit up and kick his legs off the side of the bed.

Good morning, John.

Cam. Did I sleep the whole night?

Yes.

Weird. I feel so groggy.

Groggy? That's not too difficult to understand, considering the events that transpired yesterday.

What are you talking about, Cam?

Oh, you are groggy. This is going to be fun.

Why are you always so weird?

Good luck this morning, hotshot.

Uh, thanks. Good luck to you too, weirdo.

Adam jumped up on the bed and circled John, prodding him, pushing off him with his front paws. He crossed over John's lap and started working on the other side. He worked his way around the bed, pushing on his sides, on his back, nudging John mid-back with the top of his head.

"All right, boy, all right, that's enough, I'm getting up. You and Cam both, total psychos this morning."

He reached out, catching Adam off kilter, and wrapped his arms around the dog's chest, wrestling him down to the mattress.

"Gotcha." John kept him pinned with one arm and used his other arm to bury Adam's face in one of his pillows. "Ha, you're getting too slow, boy."

Adam wiggled his way out of John's grasp and jumped out of reach, turning around just enough to bark at him.

"What, you've had enough already?"

Adam barked again at him and then trotted toward the stairs. He turned one last time, letting out a small whimper before descending to the kitchen.

Jeez, you two are high maintenance this morning.

He's your dog.

You only hear what you want to hear, don't you?

Depends.

John stood up at the edge of his bed and worked out the kinks that always wove their way into his body during the night. He took a short step toward his bedside table and straightened out the picture of his wife and son that didn't need straightening. Then he followed his annoying dog down to the kitchen.

John froze as he got to the bottom of the stairs, eyes narrowed, staring at the table where Quinn and Sierra were sitting, eating breakfast. Adam wiggled around him and trotted over to sniff around the kitchen floor for fallen food trophies.

Told you this was going to be fun.

So it wasn't just a bad dream, huh?

It's way better.

At least they cleaned up.

Quinn and Sierra had stopped eating and were keeping their eyes on the table after their first glance at John. He looked back and forth between them, the events of the last twenty-four hours flashing forward through his head, causing his brain to ache as if he'd been without caffeine for days.

"Umm, we made coffee," Sierra said, still not daring to look up from the table.

"Oh, thanks."

John went over to the clothes he had on the drying rack and grabbed his holey button-up shirt and some pants, slipping them on quickly.

"Why were you in your underwear?" Quinn asked.

Sierra's face turned beet red. "Shut up, Quinn, you're making it worse."

Oh, this is fun.

Shut up, Cam, and start the sweep.

So worth it.

Cam, now.

I'm going, but this was the best morning I've had in a long time.

"It's my house, kid. I'm in my underwear a lot and I don't get visitors, so it's never mattered before. Why are you eating my food and wasting my coffee?"

Sierra finally looked at him, her face still shades of red. "We were hungry and you were still snoring. Oh, and you're welcome."

John looked at the food on the table. The fresh, salty-sweet smell of biscuits, syrup, bacon, and eggs finally made it to his nose. He looked over to the stove at the fresh pot there, and then over to the counter to a steaming cup of coffee. He walked over, hesitant, suspicious, and stuck his face over the mug to smell the last of his best coffee.

It's going to cost me more than a case of wine to get more coffee this early in the season. Shit.

He picked up his mug and brought it up under his nose, letting the aroma creep into his nostrils and through his olfactory system, sparking his senses to life.

Damn that's good.

Can we keep them, John?

How's the sweep?

Sweep? I bet they do sweep. I mean they cook, they clean, they make a mean cup of joe. They definitely make morning so much more interesting.

Cam?

You're so anti-social. All clear, no heat sigs, no creepers, nothing's been tripped, all clear.

Thanks, Cam; now secure the mainframe and make sure we're all locked up before our trip.

Mainframe! I can't believe you call Hank a mainframe.

I've heard it before, Cam. Now dump and jump, lock us up tight, and get back, so we can hit the road.

Fine. I'm going.

He took another sip of his coffee with his eyes closed and stood there, enjoying the black-brown juice coursing through his system and the peace that came with it. A peace that didn't last long.

"Well, are you just going to stand there looking like a retard, or are you going to tell me how it is?" Sierra asked.

John's jaw tensed. He took another sip and let the warmth settle again before he answered.

"It's okay. Not bad for being made by you."

Sierra glared at him. "Whatever. When are we leaving?"

John set his coffee down and stuffed his mouth with a biscuit. "As soon as I'm done eating this food I told you several times not to touch," he said around a partially stuffed cheek.

He grabbed a plate off the counter, filled it up, and headed toward the stairs.

"I'm going up to eat this in peace, and pack. The trip will take us a couple of days. Get whatever shit you have, so we can get started." John looked at Adam. "Come on, boy, let's get ready, so we can get rid of the brat twins and have the house to ourselves again."

John started up the stairs and then stopped to look back at Adam, who hadn't budged from his spot next to Quinn.

"Suit yourself, you little turncoat."

Up in his loft, John scarfed down the delicious breakfast that Sierra and Quinn had made and sipped on the best cup of coffee he'd had in years. Sierra and Quinn were laughing as they finished up their breakfast and tossed scraps to Adam, who barked and pranced playfully around the kitchen with surprising agility. John threw some extra clothes in his pack and looked down at the kids. He smiled, letting himself enjoy the patch of happiness for a moment. He shook his head, steeled his resolve, and straightened himself out.

Definitely not that good a cup of coffee.

Your loss, John.

"Hey, stop stalling them, Adam. They need to pack up their crap, so we can hit the road."

Sierra waved her hands in front of her and patted her knapsack. "We are packed, John."

Of course they're packed.

Nice, John, real nice.

You ready to go, Cam?

All ready, John.

Guess I should bring some extra stuff, just in case, right?

You're warming up to them, aren't you?

Fat chance.

Sure, tell yourself whatever you have to, big guy.

Open the barn.

It's already open.

Well, go do something, anything besides haggle with me about a couple kids.

It's all done. I'm dumped, Hank is geared for lockdown, and the control room is ready for you to seal up.

Good. Real good, Cam.

John measured up Sierra and Quinn with a couple of quick glances and then walked over to pull out a dusty chest from the corner of his loft. He opened it, pulled some folded pants and shirts out of it, and stuffed them in his pack.

Wow, that was a big move for you, John.

Cam, when was the last I saw them?

July fourteenth, 2082.

It's been a long damn time.

Are you okay, John?

Yeah, let's just get this over with?

Fine by me.

John went back downstairs and tossed a couple of packs he had made while he was upstairs to Quinn and Sierra. "Here, those are extra go-bags—food, water, first aid, thermal flares, spare heating packs. Should be enough to get you guys through the next couple of days."

Quinn eyed the bag he'd just caught as if it were a precious heirloom handed down from generation to generation, finally finding its way to him.

"Thanks." He nudged Sierra's arm and raised his eyebrows at her.

Sierra rolled her eyes at him and looked over her own bag. "Thanks, I guess." She leaned into Quinn. "Probably just rotting old rags and moldy food anyway."

"More than what you had, so don't mention it. Stable's in the back behind the shed. Adam will take you there."

Quinn and Sierra threw their packs on and followed Adam to the door. "What are you going to do?"

"Just go. I'll be right behind you."

Adam circled around Quinn and Sierra, prodding them out the door and toward the stable. Once they were gone, John lifted the hatch to his control center and jumped down. He opened up the locker and grabbed some full pulse mags and a few thermal grenades, replaced his wrist computer with one that was powered up so Cam would be able to dump when she needed to, and stuffed a map and compass into his pack just in case.

Probably won't need any of this, just a quick trip, then we're home free.

Yeah, right, John. The way this journey has started, I wouldn't count on it.

Better take some extra thermal flares just in case.

Good idea.

John grabbed the flares and a couple charged bio-cells for his wrist pad, and locked the control center up tight. He grabbed his worn-out Seahawks cap, slapped it on his head, and went out to meet Adam and the kids in the stable.

The stalls creaked open with the sound of old westerns and folk-
lore that was almost completely forgotten. Straw and dirt filled the
misty barn air as he led three horses from their stalls and saddled
them before taking them out to meet Sierra and Quinn. He handed
the reins of a black-maned, cocoa-brown Arabian to Sierra.

"Her name's Betsy," he said. "She hasn't ridden with anyone
besides me, so go easy with her."

Sierra walked up and put her hand under Betsy's mouth.

"I know how to take care of horses. The Ortizes had an inn and a
boarding stable. They taught Quinn and me how to take care them."

She took Betsy by the mane and removed her bridle and reins.

"We won't need the saddle either, will we, beautiful?"

Sierra put her cheek to Betsy's neck and ran her hands soothingly
through her mane. She moved down her body slowly to unbuckle
the saddle and pushed it off, then went back up and rubbed her
cheek against Betsy's.

"Yes, you are beautiful, and yes, he is a bit of a dolt, isn't he?"

"What was that about?" John asked. "Did you just tell my horse
that I'm a dolt?"

Sierra picked up the gear and headed into the stable.

"You sure you can do without the gear?"

Sierra just ignored him.

"OK. Good thing Betsy likes to stick close. Just remember, if you
fall off, you're on your own."

Quinn came up alongside John with Adam trotting right on his
heels.

"I think Adam likes me."

John narrowed his eyes, set his jaw.

Why didn't I just mind my own business?

You should have listened to me, John.

I did listen to you.

That's what I'm saying.

This is going to be such a long trip.

*We needed a good outing, but maybe you're right. We should probably
leave Adam here. It's just too much right now.*

Nice try, Cam. We're all going. One big happy family.
Yeah, big happy family on a forced road march to Tree Top.
I don't see you walking, Cam.
It's implied, which is just as exhausting.
I must've missed that somewhere in your manual.
That hurts, John, deep, real deep.

"All right, enough jerking around. Get on the horses, we're leaving now," John said.

He looked at Adam, who was licking Quinn's face, and then at Betsy, and rolled his eyes.

"Even the turncoat. Maybe I can trade all of you to Oliver."

Adam left Quinn and trotted over to John. He tucked his head under John's hand, prodding it with the tip of his wet nose, and whined.

"Too little, too late, pal. You're lucky I'm taking you at all. Cam wanted us to leave you."

Adam barked loud and jumped up, putting his paws on John's chest.

"Don't worry, boy, we're not leaving you, but I was serious about the trading bit, so you better remember who feeds you."

Adam hopped down and started pacing around as if he were inspecting everyone to make sure they were ready for the trip.

Sierra rolled her eyes at them and turned back to Betsy. She ran her hand down the coarse bridge between Betsy's eyes, down to her velvet nose, and then up through her mane again and down her neck. Betsy bowed her head low and Sierra slid on with so little effort, John couldn't help being impressed.

"Here." John gave another set of reins to Quinn. "Her name's Mazzy. Want me to take the rigging off like the horse whisperer over there?"

"No. I like my saddle, please," Quinn said.

"Good, now mount up. We need to go."

Quinn jumped on his horse and John double-checked the two. Once he was sure everything was right, he squatted in front of Adam and whispered something into his ear. Adam took off into the tree line. John stood up and mounted his large, storm-gray horse.

"What's Adam doing?" Quinn asked.

"Overwatch."

"What's overwatch?"

John let out a deep breath.

This is going to be a long trip.

Big happy family, remember?

Maybe I can trade you in for a younger model when we get to Tree Top.

You wouldn't like the younger models, all sassy and needy. No class at all.

I might like that.

You'd miss me.

I can't imagine what I'd do without you.

That's what I'm saying.

"Don't worry about it, kid. He's just going to watch our backs while we travel."

"Why do we need our backs watched?"

"Did you forget about the jippers already, Q?" Sierra asked.

"Oh yeah, right. What's your horse's name, John?"

"Shadow."

"That's a cool name. Why'd you name him that?"

John turned to Sierra. "Will he be like this the whole trip?"

"Only to you." She clicked her tongue twice against her teeth and sped Betsy up in front of them.

That's just what I need, more input.

If you don't like it, just shut them out.

Like I do you.

Oh yeah, I guess that won't work.

"She's always moody," Quinn said.

"Who, Cam?"

Quinn wrinkled his nose at him. "No. Sierra. Why'd you say Cam?"

"Oh yeah, Sierra. Right."

"You're weird sometimes."

John let out an exasperated breath. "Look, kid, I understand you want to talk and all, but right now I need to focus on our little trip, okay?"

"I understand."

"I knew you would, kid."

"So why'd you name him Shadow?" Quinn asked.

Shit.

"He's a special shade of dark, like a shadow."

Quinn looked disappointed and then smiled, as if he were forcing encouragement over to John.

"That's still pretty cool."

"I'm glad you think so," John said. "Now, remember two seconds ago when I said you should stay quiet?"

"Yeah, I'm pretty good at it, right?"

"I'm not sure I would use those exact words."

"Is Shadow a stallion? Do you let him breed with other horses? Sam and Jean used to breed horses for people. They would come from all over the place for their horses."

"Sounds really interesting, kid," John said. "Hey, listen, I'm gonna go check the trail up ahead. You should probably stay with your sister. Help keep her safe, okay?"

Quinn gave John a sturdy salute and rode over by Sierra while John galloped ahead.

"Good work, Q."

"Why? What'd I do?"

"Don't worry about it. You're just really good at being you."

"Thanks, Sis."

John rode ahead for the rest of the trip, keeping a safe distance from Quinn's questions and Sierra's sneers. Adam came back once in a while, barking and pawing at the ground in the language that only he and John knew. John would give him a bit of jerky and get down to play around with him for a bit. When Adam was bored with John, he would come back and pretend to chase Quinn, then he would head off back to the tree line, and they would mount up and hit the trail again.

We've been lucky. Road's been clear this whole time.

Lucky is a bit of an understatement. We haven't seen anyone at all the whole trip. No beggars, squatters, thievers, or jippers. Nothing.

Most would take that as a good sign, Cam.

We're not most people, John.

You're right.

Has Adam seen anything?

No, not a peep of anything unusual.

That's unusual.

"John, are we close yet?" Quinn asked.

"Seriously, kid? We've only been riding four hours."

"Oh. It seems like it's been longer."

"Well, we're not close yet," John said. "In fact, at this pace we'll have to make camp and finish up the ride tomorrow."

"Why don't you have a hydro vehicle like the jipper had?"

See, John, now there's a smart thought.

"Because hydro cells don't grow on trees and horses are cheaper."

Sometimes being cheap actually doesn't pay off like you think it would. There is such a thing as being too cheap.

Well, I'm so sorry, Cam. I'm sorry I decided to use the power that it would have taken for the trip to keep Hank up and running and supply the house with electricity for us to live.

Mm, duly noted.

Quinn wrinkled his nose at John.

"Why would you think that hydro cells grow on trees?"

"Sierra, why don't you hold a conversation with your brother for a while so I can actually concentrate on where the hell we're going?"

Sierra sneered. "I'm not his mother. You don't have to answer all his questions if you don't want to."

John turned back to Quinn.

"I know hydro cells don't grow on trees, Quinn," John said. "Horses are cheaper and easier to come by these days, that's all."

"Oh. Why didn't you just say that?"

"I did."

Quinn looked at Sierra, crossed his eyes, and stuck his tongue out, making Sierra laugh.

"What was that about?"

"Nothing, John. I think Q was just having a seizure from all the brilliant information he gets from you."

I know how that feels.

Whose side are you on, Cam?

Yours, of course.

Yeah, right.

"Whatever," John said. "I think there's a good place to rest up the road, and we can wait for Adam. Maybe he can you keep you better company."

They stopped on the side of the trail by a row of half-torn-down houses engulfed by branches, ivy, and brush. The trees crept through the old homes and up the edge of the trail, towering over them. Long shadows spun around them as the clockwork sun wound its way to the west.

On the other side of the trail, the dull roar of a river could be heard from somewhere behind the layers of soldiered trees. Remnants of an old road snuck out from the layers of earth covering it. It popped up in large concrete patches, leading down to an even older bridge covered with moss and rust. Past that, just over the trees, tops of crumbling, earth-worn buildings could be seen. A ghost town, one of many that dotted the ever-changing landscape. A pile of cars and junk formed a ruined makeshift barricade at the center of the bridge, and a huge chunk was gone from the middle of it.

Broken roads, broken buildings, broken homes, broken dreams, broken everything. Everything now covered in earth. Green, brown, orange, and rusty earth splashed yellow from the descending sun.

Quinn pointed to the town. "What's that place down there? Is that Tree Top?"

"No, kid, it's not. It's a ghost town. Scraps left over of what used to be, what hasn't been in a long time."

Sierra walked up to a rusted, fallen-down sign and kicked off the leaves.

"What's Leavenworth?"

Leavenworth. The name triggered a buried memory in John, a memory from so long ago that it was as rusted and buried as the sign that Sierra was reading. He had brought Elizabeth here with

Adam before he left, before he left and never came back; and when he did come back, Leavenworth was much like him, a ghost.

It's been a long time, hasn't it, Cam.

A long time, John, but not long enough.

Barely made it out.

Let's just steer clear.

Good idea.

Early on after Day One, people tried to stay organized and stay settled in their towns and cities, but without infrastructure, corruption grew faster than dreams. Like weeds through concrete, the crazies had spread, strangling any hope of rebuilding. Any hope of dreams. People fled the cities, and anyone who stayed learned fast that they should have left the towns, even the small towns, with the first waves of re-settlers. Because if you stayed, what followed was worse than taking the road. Staying meant raids, psychotics, disease, slavery, and torture. It meant a life worse than death.

John's thoughts were broke by Sierra waving her hand in front of his face.

"Um, hello, anyone home?"

"What?"

"You went like totally zombie on us there for a minute. You okay?"

John looked back toward the road leading to the forgotten town.

Clearly it has not been long enough, John.

Clearly.

"I'm fine. We don't have too much farther to go tonight."

"Where we going tonight?" Sierra asked. "Can't we just go down there to one of those buildings?"

John whistled loud and long and looked toward the tree line, ignoring her question.

"So are you going to answer me?"

"Answer what?"

Sierra kicked a rock at him and stormed off. "You're such a jerk sometimes."

John looked over at Quinn, who was playing on a pile of rocks by the road.

"What's her problem?"

Quinn shrugged. "She's a girl. They're all weird like that, I think. Are we going to that town? That'd be so cool."

I might actually like this kid.

We should probably travel through the night to get rid of them.

Funny how quickly you change your tune.

I'm only thinking of you, John.

Sure.

"No. We're going someplace else. Not as cozy, but it will keep us warm and out of sight."

"Why do we have to be out of sight?"

"Believe me, kid, you want to stay out of sight."

Quinn and Sierra led the horses off the road and settled on a fallen tree to share one of the rations John had given them.

Sierra looked to the bushes low under the trees on her right, squinting her eyes and bending low to see through the thick forest bed.

"Did you hear that, Q?"

"Hear what?"

She grabbed his shirt and pointed him toward the underbrush. "Listen."

They sat, eyes concentrated, ears toward the bush, and listened.

"I don't hear anything, Sis."

"Quiet, Q. Jeez. I almost heard it again."

"Well, whatever it was, it's gone now. Probably just a squirrel or something."

She listened for another second and then shrugged her shoulders, and they went back to eating. A single bronze-orange-brown leaf floated on the air in front of her. She watched it surf its way down to her to her lap as she chewed on the leathery rations.

John had settled on a boulder under a tree a few yards from them. He watched the twins on the log and waited. He barely saw Adam slithering low and silent behind them until he was close enough. Then he jumped out behind them and started barking. Sierra shrieked, and she and Quinn bolted off the log, tossing their food and running toward the trail. John rolled with laughter, almost falling off his perch.

Priceless. Simply priceless.

You two are hopeless.

"Adam! You scared the crap of me," Sierra said.

He sniffed around Sierra and jumped up, putting his front paws on Sierra's shoulders and licking her.

"Good one, Adam," Quinn said. "You really got her."

"*Good one?* Really, Q? Like you didn't jump."

"At least I didn't shriek like I was getting thrown off a cliff."

"Paybacks suck, Q. Just remember that."

"I'm quivering with fear."

She petted Adam's head until he got down. The dog went over to Quinn and repeated his antics there.

"Adam," John said, "before you lick Quinn's face off, do you want to tell me if the coast is clear, pal?"

Adam barked once and scratched the ground twice, then pointed his nose toward Leavenworth.

Coast is clear, Cam, but he's caught someone's scent.

Now that sounds a bit more normal.

We should be good as long as we stay clear of the actual town.

Are you thinking the cabin?

It should still be safe.

When we get closer I can scan the tracers you left before we go in. Make sure we didn't pick up any Goldilocks.

See, I told you they were worth it.

You get it right every once in a while.

Thanks, Cam.

I still think you're a scrooge.

John scratched Adam behind his ears. Adam squinted tight and raised his nose to the sky so John could get under his chin too. He whimpered and thumped John's big hands with his paw a couple times, tilting his head toward Quinn.

"Go ahead boy, go play. You did real good today."

Adam barked, took off toward Quinn, and prodded him until he got up and started playing with him.

It's nice, you know.

What's nice?

You smiling. Don't worry, John, no one caught you.

I wasn't smiling.

You just forgot what a genuine smile feels like.

Funny, I didn't notice.

Go figure.

"Where was he this whole time?" Sierra asked.

"Lots of questions running through you two."

"Is that too intimidating for you?"

John shrugged. "He was scouting out the road, woods, river bank, that town, anything he thought he should, really."

"He can do all that?" Quinn asked.

"He's really smart."

"Must have been taught by someone besides you, then," Sierra said.

"You ever heard of manners?"

Sierra glared at him and then casually got back onto Betsy.

Quinn came up behind him and slapped him on the back. "Told you girls are weird."

"Everyone's weird, kid," John said. "That's why I stay away from people."

John got on his horse and led the small band down a winding trail that led to a shallow spot in the river where they could cross and pick up the trail on the other side. The temperature was dropping fast, and Sierra and Quinn shivered as they started into the chilly glacial run-off.

"Where are you leading us again?" Sierra asked. "And why do we have to go into this incredibly cold river when we could just go over the perfectly passable bridge?"

"Because this *horrible* old river is better than getting spotted on the bridge by psychopaths and thieves who watch towns like this."

"What would they possibly watch this crap-hole for?"

"For idiots who cross wide-open bridges and announce their presence by being loud and annoying."

Quinn smirked at her. "Duh, Sierra."

"Oh yeah, right, like you knew we'd have to cross here, Quinn."

"Everyone does, Sierra."

Adam paced the other side of the riverbank and started barking at them to break up their squabbling and hurry up.

"Wait, how'd he...wasn't he just over here with us?"

John smiled at her. "Like I said, he's a smart dog."

He does have his tricks, doesn't he?

Are you jealous?

I'm just saying that he does okay sometimes.

I think you're jealous.

Keep dreaming.

John clicked his tongue against the back of his teeth twice and tapped Shadow's sides with his heels, encouraging him to move away from the kids and into the water.

Adam barked at them again. Quinn reined up on his horse and followed John into the river.

"Come on, Sierra. What are you, chicken?"

Sierra glared at him. "You won't be acting so brave when I catch up to you on the other side, Q."

Quinn smiled and waved to taunt her forward. "Whatever, Sis."

Quinn tried to copy what John had done by clicking his tongue and patting his horse's sides with his heels. Mazzy's hoof slipped; she lurched forward and got spooked. Quinn grabbed the reins and pulled back hard to try and bring Mazzy under control, but all it did was spook her more. She jumped into the deep and took off toward the far bank, moving so fast that Quinn lost his grip and went tumbling backward into the rolling white caps of the frigid water.

"Quinn!" Sierra screamed.

She took off after him but wasn't close enough to beat the fingers of the river grabbing him, stealing him away. John registered her faint scream over the sound of the river and turned just as Mazzy passed him, racing up his side of the riverbank.

John, Quinn's in the river.

How far?

Already eighty meters, and going fast.

Shit.

Adam bolted past him and down the trail, following Quinn's movement in the water, trying to find a place to go in. John turned and saw Quinn's small head bobbing down the river, and Sierra getting ready to go in after him.

"NO! Get your ass to the bank," John said.

He shouted something into Shadow's ear and they sprinted alongside the river after Quinn.

Do you still have him, Cam?

I've got him, John. He's nearing two hundred meters.

Don't lose him, Cam.

I won't.

John could still see Quinn's head moving up and down with the rising and falling white caps. The river was taking him into the boulders and speeding him toward a large drop off. John lowered himself close into the saddle and urged more speed.

You're almost to him, John. There's a pool by the bank in twenty meters. You can get there and get him if you go now.

"Adam, NOW."

Adam turned sharp toward the river and leaped from a rock into the white-tipped water. He paddled hard, muscles stretching and rippling under his heavy coat as he worked toward Quinn. He got close and thrust forward, grabbing him by his shirt, holding it tight between his teeth. His jaw locked, and he paddled even harder against the current. Adam tried tugging Quinn to shore, but they were held like quick sand by the swift water.

John, the current is too strong. Adam can't pull him to shore.

Damn it.

His heart is about to stop, John. You need to get him out now.

Damn it.

Quinn's head was sunk down in the water, and when he bobbed to the surface he was a lifeless, pale blue. John released a securing strap off his saddle and loosed the large rope that was there. He pulled the reins tight, secured the rope with a carabineer to himself and to his saddle, and plunged Shadow into the icy flow. When he got close enough, he jumped into the water toward Quinn's rolling body, gripped by a defiant Adam. The water smashed against him like a pillow of sharpened icicles smothering his face, but he bore down, plowed through the numbing needles, and grabbed Quinn by his foot. He pulled himself closer and strapped the rope around Quinn so Shadow could pull them in.

"I got him, boy. I got him," John said to Adam. "Now let's get him back to shore."

John shouted, and Shadow started to reel them into the shallows. He dug his feet into the riverbed, his enhanced muscles bulging, pushing them forward with each step. Sierra was in knee-deep, helping Shadow fight against the strength of the river and bring them up to the bank. When they were close enough, John stood up in the water, his cybernet sparking his eyes red, making him look even more fierce and determined. Muscles rippling, massive arms clung to a listless Quinn as Shadow pulled them step by step out of the water. He let Quinn down gently to the ground and checked whether he was breathing. Quinn's cold form was almost peaceful looking against the rocks, mud, and twigs that scattered on the trail along the river. John pounded hard on Quinn's chest and watched. Nothing. He pounded again and started thrusting upward on Quinn's chest with his hands. Four, five, six times it took before Quinn started coughing violently and breathing weakly.

Sierra fell onto her brother, smothering him under their cold, wet clothes. "Quinn!"

John rolled him onto his side and then collapsed onto the rocks next to Quinn's shivering body. Adam, soaked and shaggy, came over and started licking John's face. John nudged him toward Quinn.

"Go to Quinn, boy. Try to warm him up."

Adam knelt beside them and started licking Quinn's hand and whimpering.

That was a little too close, Cam.

You think?

John lifted his heavy arms and ran them through his soaked hair. They froze on top of his head as his eyes widened with shock and his stomach churned with realization.

My hat!

Oh shit.

I lost my goddamn hat.

It could have been worse, John.

How?

John rolled over and took stock of the twins.

Really, John?

Let's just get our bearings, Cam. We need to regroup fast.

On it. You better check out the kid.

"What were you thinking, Quinn?" Sierra asked.

Quinn coughed a bit and then sat up and pushed her away.

"Get off me. What are you trying to do, kill me? I'm just fine. Jeez."

Adam nudged Quinn's face with his nose and started licking the cold river water off him.

"Just fine? You don't look just fine. You look like a freezing wet boy who just about spent the rest of his life sinking to the bottom of that river, that's what."

"I wasn't going to die. John and Adam are with us."

"Oh, and that just makes so much sense."

I think they'll make it, Cam.

Once again I get no credit whatsoever.

Well, Adam did jump in the river and stop him from getting farther downstream.

Oh, Adam, he's so dreamy. Ugh, he's so stupid.

Thanks, Cam. You're just wonderful. We couldn't have done it without you.

That's a start.

We have to find some cover, Cam. Temperature's dropping fast. We won't make it to the cabin.

I'm on it.

John rolled up on his arms and got up off the ground, scanning their surroundings.

"Will you two shut up and give me some peace for just a second?" He let out a deep breath and looked up toward the sky and the disappearing sunset.

"We need to make it to someplace we can get him into some dry clothes, and sleep for the night, and we need to get there before the temperature drops anymore. So quit bickering. As soon as I get the horses back we're leaving."

Quinn glared at Sierra. "I was fine. I was just waiting to be swept closer to shore."

"Whatever, Quinn. I'm sure you were going to get to shore unconscious, too."

John rounded up an anxious Shadow, Mazzy, and Betsy, who were digging their hooves in the ground, nervous, waiting to leave the darkening riverbank. When he got back, the kids were ready to go. He mounted Shadow and started down the trail, blowing a melodic whistle to Adam, who dutifully nudged Quinn and Sierra over to the horses. He barked at them until Sierra got onto Betsy.

"You're both welcome, by the way," John said. "Lost my favorite hat for you. You understand?" He turned and stared at them. "Of course you don't."

John patted Shadow's sides with his heels and quickened his pace down the trail. Sierra and Quinn looked at each other and then let their heads hang a little. Sierra spoke first.

"You can ride with me, Quinn. We'll lead Mazzy behind us, okay?"

"Thanks, Sis."

"No worries, Q. I'm glad you didn't die."

"Me too."

They rode the rest of the way up the trail behind John, a small drizzle working its way down from the sky, through the trees, and onto all of them. Adam, the only one with any energy, brought up the rear alongside Mazzy, keeping a close eye on Sierra and Quinn. It was quiet except for the noise of the horses' hooves on the dirt and rock. No one, not even Cam, was in the talking mood. The temperature was dropping and the twins couldn't stop their teeth from chattering long enough to talk anyway.

John, I found a couple of structurally sound buildings that seem clear from my scans. They should do for the night.

How clear?

Clear enough to get all of us out of the cold, and someplace dry where you can get warmed up.

Sounds like a start.

John scanned up to the town of Leavenworth and closed his eyes hard to help him clear his thoughts.

"We're not making it to the cabin tonight. We'll have to stay up there."

Sierra frowned at him. "I thought you said it wasn't safe there."

"It's not, but we don't have a choice. We'll get up there and set up camp so we don't freeze to death."

John slid off his horse and went back to check on Quinn. The boy lay in front of Sierra, his head limp in the thick of Betsy's mane, again looking a little too peaceful. John reached out and put his hand on the boy's forehead. He was soaking wet, freezing cold to touch, and shivering uncontrollably.

"We have to hurry, John," Sierra said. "I don't think he's doing so well."

I agree, John. Quinn's internal temperature is still dropping. He's too wet to be out here much longer.

Damn it. Show me the building, Cam.

Cam showed John an overlay of the town and marked the building that she thought best with a flashing green icon.

And you say it's all clear?

As far as I can tell, it is our best option.

Okay, Cam. Lead the way.

Quinn opened his eyes a little and managed a weak, sardonic smile. "I'm okay, John. I can make it."

"I know, kid, but you won't have to. Cam spotted a good building right up the road, okay?"

"Whatever you say, John."

John led the rest of the way on foot, heading to a three-story structure that Cam had pointed out. It was hard to see in the dark, but it had an out-building close by that could house the horses, and it was far enough away from the other buildings in this part of town that they could set up in it without being noticed.

Hopefully we're the only tourists in Leavenworth tonight.

Hopefully. The way your luck's been, I wouldn't count on it.

Thanks for the positive energy.

Anything I can do to help.

Is the boy okay?

He won't be much longer if we don't get him warmed up. John, if he gets an infection?

I know, Cam, I know. Let's just get settled in and go from there. If we get spotted, we'll have more than a lung infection to worry about.

FIVE

Leavenworth

JOHN LED THE GROUP BEHIND the large warehouse, which overlooked a row of buildings and houses long since swallowed by the forest and the river. Leaving Adam and the twins in a shed with the horses, he went inside to clear the warehouse.

What do you see, Cam?

Still clear. It looks like there might be some sort of subterranean structure, but it's a little hazy right now.

Hazy?

Don't worry, scaredy-cat, I'll protect you.

John pulled the boards away from the back door and jerked it open.

Mm, I'm surprised the door's still on the hinges.

I pick only the best for us.

The corner of John's mouth drew up into a smile as he swept the large room with the light on the barrel of his REP. Shimmering reflections bounced back at him from silver cylindrical vats as tall as the warehouse, stacked like soldiers in line for inspection.

You got anything behind those fermenters?

Nothing.

This place is amazing. Must have been built right before all hell broke loose.
Explains why the windows aren't broken; they're graphene.
Jeez, those guys made a fortune off that stuff.
He shone the light on some stairs leading down to another level.
Can you scan in there?
It looks empty, but it's really hazy, John. I can't be certain.
I'll come back to it later.
John crept up the metal-grated stairs and to the back of a rusted bar. He swept the room with his light, and then took another staircase to the top floor.
Alright, this will do.
You're welcome.
I didn't thank you.
But you were going to.
Gee, you're the best, Cam.
He turned the light off and jogged back to get Adam and the twins, whistling three quiet bursts as he got close. Adam came running to him.

John knelt down and scratched under his chin while Adam chased his hand with his tongue. "Good boy, good boy, I know. Just a little scout and we'll be done."

Adam licked his hand one more time and then disappeared into the night. After scanning the area again, John made his way into the shed.
How're they doing, Cam?
Sierra's fine, I'm not so sure about Quinn.
We'll get them inside, get a full scan on him.
John secured the horses to an uncovered beam in the shed, and then got a soggy Quinn and Sierra up and heading toward the door.

The children followed him out the door along the muddy, weed-covered path to the warehouse. He settled them in on the top floor, one large room under a high ceiling with graphene windows on all four sides, which provided a mostly clear line of sight in all directions. The structure was still close to the river but far enough away that anyone curious enough to sneak up on them would have a hard go at it.

Adam came back from his scouting, growled low to John, and scratched a long line in the dirt-caked cement floor with his paw. John reached down to scratch behind his ear and slipped him a small round treat from his pocket.

"Good job, boy. We'll all have to keep our eyes peeled, okay?"

Adam barked twice, letting him know that he understood, and went back down to the main floor to stand guard while John set Sierra and Quinn up in the center of the room. They nestled close to each other, looking like Raggedy Anne and Andy dolls. Their teeth chattered unintelligible Morse code sounds, and Braille-worthy bumps spread over their exposed skin. John kicked over the junk in the room: rotted tables, chairs, and debris. He grabbed what he could and piled it up until he had made a small half-circle behind them so they'd have something to lean against, and then lit a thermal flare, putting it at the focal point of the curve.

Sierra and Quinn let out a sigh of relief and scooted as close as they could with their hands out in front of them, as if trying to encourage the heat from the flare to creep up and into their bodies.

Anything I should be worried about yet, Cam?

You'll have to check out the basement eventually, but other than that, should be safe for now.

It can wait, then.

John, Quinn won't last long out here if he starts showing signs.

I'm doing the best I can.

I know you are. I'll alert you if anything changes.

Good.

John turned toward the kids. "Sierra, I have to go out, check the horses' cover, and get some of our things. You got Quinn, okay?"

"I don't need any help," Quinn said. "I'm just cold's all."

"Don't worry, John, I got him. We'll warm up soon. Q, here, get a little closer to the heat."

She helped Quinn lean into to the heat and propped him up against one of the tables.

"I know, Sis. John will take good care of us, you wait and see."

"I love you, Q, but sometimes you can be a real sap. Just stop trying to help, and relax, will ya?"

Quinn let a whispered chuckle escape from his lungs and coughed. "I love you too." He grunted and tried to get up, but fell back against Sierra's arms.

"Look, kid. We all know you're tough," John said, "but listen to your sister, will ya? Get warm, rest, let us take care of the small stuff. I'll send Adam up, you can help take care of him. Deal?"

Quinn managed a weak smile. "Deal."

We need to hide the horses, John. There's something out there that's messing with my grid searches.

I'm on it.

"I'll be right back. Stay out of sight, stay quiet."

*   *   *

After checking that there were enough hayclone pellets for the horses and sliding the shed door shut, he did another sweep outside, then went back upstairs to check on their quick camp. He threw his wet pack down and sat rubbing his hands by the fire to warm them up.

"It's raining harder," he said. "Hopefully the roof holds up."

Adam tilted his head up and out from its nestled hiding place in Quinn's lap and trotted over to John, nudging his hand with his head, prodding it toward Quinn.

Sierra looked at him, big, wet, bloodshot eyes sunken into a dirt-layered face.

She's scared.

She should be.

She needs some encouragement, John.

Not one of my best strengths.

Try harder.

"Quinn's not doing so good, John. He can barely stay awake, and he still hasn't stopped shivering."

John put his hands on Quinn's cheeks and put his ear down to his mouth to feel his breath. The kid looked pathetic: pale, sweating, shivering, limp.

What do you think, Cam?

He's running a fever. Heart rate's faster, shallow breathing. He's got all the signs, John.

River fever?

Even with phages he'll be hard pressed to last the night.

"Will he be okay?"

"I wish I knew, kid. I've got some medicine that might help until we can get him to Tree Top, but that's about the best I can do."

"He'll be okay. He's special, like me."

"I'm sure he is."

"There's someone there who can help him?"

"They have a healer, Jane. She owes me favor. If anyone can help him, she can."

The look on Sierra's face softened, and her shoulders relaxed a little. She wiped the tears from her face, leaving streaks through the dirt.

"Thank you, John. I really mean it. Thank you. Thank you for everything."

"Don't mention it, kid."

John patted Adam on the head and gave him another treat from his pocket.

"You better go take a look outside, buddy," John said. "We'll take turns, okay?"

Adam barked and headed down the stairs to start his patrol.

Do you think Jane can help?

If anyone can, it's her.

Will he make it?

Your guess is as good as mine, Cam. I'll snoop around downstairs when I'm done here and see what I can find. Maybe I'll stumble onto something that's useful.

"What was the growly, foot-pawing in the dirt thing Adam did earlier?" Sierra asked.

"He's tracking a group. Probably thieves. That's his way of letting me know." John moved over beside Quinn and took out a small black container from one of his chest pouches. "There's no one in sight, so hopefully we just missed them and they've moved on." He popped the lid off and dropped a small vial, alcohol pad, and paper clip-sized auto injector into his hand.

Sierra scooted closer and eyed the purple viscous liquid swirling in the vial. "What's that?"

John clipped the vial into the auto injector.

"Phages. They'll help fight whatever infection he picked up in the river. This is going to pinch a little, kid."

Quinn tried a smile again. "I trust you, John."

He cleaned a small spot on Quinn's arm, and injected the purple liquid. Quinn flinched, and then took a deep breath.

"'s not so bad."

Sierra watched from beside him. He could tell she was trying not blink her bloodshot eyes, concentrating to see if Quinn reacted at all.

"Is it working?"

John put his hand on her shoulder and gave her a reassuring nod. "It'll take a while, and even then it will only keep him from getting worse. Should buy us some time, though."

He got up, walked over and grabbed his bag from the pile of supplies he had brought in, took a small bundle out of his pack, and tossed it to Sierra.

"Here you go. You need to wake him up. Get him out of those wet clothes and get him into these. They're my son's, so they might be a little too big, but they should do."

"Thank you," Sierra said. "Your son, is he…"

John stared at the floor, bare, blank, and dirty. Just like his expression. "He's dead."

"Oh, I'm sorry. I'm so sorry, John."

John looked back at her, his expression still bare, the lines in his face tight. "Don't be. Just get him changed."

"Thank you for the clothes."

"You're welcome. There's an extra set for you too, so you should switch out as soon as you're done taking care of the kid. Adam and I will handle everything else. Deal?"

"Deal."

Quinn looked up at them. He was having a hard time holding his head on top of his neck, but he tried anyway. "We'll be fine, John. We've been a hell of a lot worse."

John grinned. "I thought you being so near death, you'd talk less."

"We're all near death at some point," Quinn said.

Sierra rolled her eyes and got ready to help Quinn change.

"I'm okay, Sierra, you don't have to..."

Quinn tried to sit up but fell back against the table.

"Stop trying to be tougher than you are, Q, and let me help you."

Quinn looked as if he might want to argue with her, but didn't have the strength.

"All right, I'm gonna finish scouting. I think this place used to be a brewery or something. I saw some old equipment and a bar downstairs that I should probably check out."

"We'll be okay, John. I got this." Sierra went to work on Quinn.

"You should be careful. If you keep being polite and nice, it might become permanent."

"Whatever. I'll holler if I need your help with anything else besides my attitude."

John tried not to smile as he headed downstairs to pick through the pile of debris around the bar. He kicked around for bit before he hit something that made a metal twang, and squatted down to look at what his foot had found. He wiped through the layers of dust and garbage with his hand: it was a cool blue sheet-metal sign with Icicle Brewing still legible in stenciled white.

Wish I would have found this place a long time ago.

Remember, John, we're looking for anything that might help Quinn, not you.

A strong pint might be the best thing for him right now.

I'm sure you don't have any other motives.

You don't have to worry about my motives, Cam. This place is dry as a turnip. I can't believe I never came here.

Last time you were here, you weren't exactly sightseeing.

You notice anything that resembles medical supplies anywhere?

Nothing. Beer isn't the only thing this place is dry of.

He looked through the cupboards and then poked around on the main floor and in the tank room at the back of the building. Not finding anything useful, he headed over to the stairs that led down to the basement.

What do you think?

Only one way to find out.

Ladies first?

Funny, John.

What can I say, I have my gifts.

I still can't see much. Looks like the door's locked. There is a ton of equipment in there, but past that I can't tell. It's static.

Probably conditioning tanks. The insulation used to regulate the room temp might be what's screwing with your scans.

Age before beauty then.

We missed our calling, Cam. We've got some real talent here.

Speak for yourself, I'm in my prime.

John smirked and started down the stairs. He raised his pulse rifle up and flicked on the light again. The eerie yellow glow shone on the door at the bottom, and John inched down the cement stairs toward it. As he got closer, he could see that the door was secured from this side. He ran his hand along door, door jam, doorknob, and over the bright silver deadbolts.

John, these bolts are brand new. Maybe installed in the last twelve hours, tops.

"Damn it!"

John turned around and raced back up the stairs.

"John," Sierra screamed.

He rounded the next set of stairs, his heart pounding.

"Quinn, Sierra!"

"JOHN!"

John, the whole building just went dark.

Can you see anything?

Not until we're closer. We're being blocked.

John drove through his last step, leaping up and landing on the bar floor. He rounded the corner to head up the next flight of stairs and hollered again.

"Quinn, Sierra!"

John, get down.

The blast hit him like a flaming tornado and sent him flying back through the bar.

Chunks of brick and wood landed around him. He rolled into the wall, ears ringing and vision blurry, and staggered back to his feet in time to see the outline of something huge in front of him. His eyes turned red as boosters coursed through his body, readying him for fighting.

Is that close enough, Cam?

BACK, he's exo-armored.

A giant mechanical hand grabbed him and slammed him against the wall. He crashed to the floor, sending more piles of debris down on him. The mechanical assailant picked him up again with giant hands and chucked him up the stairs. He landed with a thud, splinters and clumps of metal falling on him. High-pitched ringing screamed through his head as he tried to regroup. A thud jolted up his spine as the armored assailant cleared the stairs and landed next to him.

JOHN, LEFT, NOW.

John rolled, just in time to avoid a chest-sized foot crashing into the floor. He shook off the buzzing in his head and grabbed whatever he could on his attacker, and threw the hulking mass back down the stairs.

"John, watch out," Sierra squeaked.

Cam.

Two closing on your six, John, MOVE.

He'd turned to run to the kids when an electric shock seared through him. Another armored thug came from behind, grabbed him, and swung him across the room. John hit the wall on the far side and fell to the floor with a thunderous convulsion.

Way too slow, Cam.

He rolled over and pushed himself up to one knee, wiping his mouth with the back of his hand, smearing blood all over it. More blood speckled the floor as it dropped from his mouth. His nano-tech went into overdrive and used his reserves to start boosting his stamina, pumping the adrenalin through his body to get him back in the fight.

Tell me about it. You want to wake up and do some fighting, or should I just shut down now and kill us both?

How many?

Two armored, another floating, but scan's limited to this room.

The kids?

Alive, but they have them.

Cam flashed an image of the twins on John's HUD.

Shit.

"LEAVE US ALONE," Sierra screamed.

Her body lurched backward as if she had been punched in the stomach, and a burst of energy swept through the room. Pops and whirring hisses came from the exo-armor suits, and they started powering down. Sierra's eyes rolled backward in her head, and she crumpled to the floor next to her pack. One of the people in the bogged-down suits started cursing.

Whoa, what was that, John?

No, idea. We still up?

Yes.

Sierra okay?

Yes.

Then who cares what that was, get us a scan.

In a rough growl, someone said, "Damn piece of crap won't move. It's froze up again, Gyver. Where'd you get these things? Piece o' Crap Mart?"

Gyver?

Oh, great.

"Don't blame the suit," said a raspy female voice. "It's top of the line military, and it cost a fortune. You better pray you didn't break it."

John squinted to see through the dirt and dust. Two black and green shapes shimmered into view against the messy scene, a spindly figure of a woman on a hover board, and a seven-foot-tall hulk in powered-up exo armor. The two kept arguing, giving John a second to regroup.

Cam, show me Sierra and Quinn.

Right by Gyver's goon.

Cam switched the field of vision so John could see all of the heat sigs. Quinn and Sierra lay in a heap between the two bickering thieves, breathing and unconscious. There was a loud creaking noise as the other member of the group came up the stairs and into Cam's overlay.

Suits must be working again. That didn't last long, Cam.

How did that even happen?

Don't know, don't really care. Give me some options.

The window. Make a break for it. Come back for the kids after we have a plan.

Next option.

Distract them, get the jipper whip from Sierra's bag, and kill them now.

Option two, please.

Wise choice.

Find me their weak points, get me something I can work with.

On it.

Gyver hovered in the air, halfway squatted on a saucer-shaped board, her feet strapped into metallic knee-high boots controlling its movements. She made a weaving advance toward John, her snake-like lips pressed into a smile as if she were some floating hobgoblin. As she inched closer he could make out a gray face, mechanical eye, and a salty odor that was all too familiar. The memory of why she had that mechanical eye and needed a hover board sparked a grin, a grin that faded once he saw the set of gray-green US military fatigues she was wearing.

"Well, I'll be damned," Gyver said. "John Howe in the flesh, a tad more scruffy than I remember. Years been hard on you, John? Oh, I really, really hope they have been."

Whip's too far.

I didn't say it be easy, John. Do you really want to listen to this all night?

Gyver turned to face the two giants.

"It's our lucky day, boys. We found ourselves what you might call a big fish."

"It's nice to see you again too, Gyver," John said, "and I'm glad you have your legs back under you."

"You thought a little thing like a broken back was going to keep me down? I've connections now, John. They fixed me right up, good as new."

"Except for the hover board."

She snarled, and John waved her away. He stood up and dusted off his arms and legs. Gyver leaned backward, just out of his reach.

"Whoa, slow down now, super soldier. You're not as young and spry as you used to be. You don't want to pull a muscle now." Gyver smiled. "I have big plans in mind for you."

"Big plans, from you? Now that's something I might actually want to stick around to see."

John kept his expression sardonic, his eyes scanning over her and her companions so Cam could check for vulnerabilities.

John, that's a crystalline carbon-tubed hover board with stabilizing boots. She's got new biotech all over her upper body and back. Pretty damn high speed, but still back-table compared to us.

Sum it up for me, Cam.

Cam highlighted Gyver's boots on John's heads-up display.

Her legs are probably her weakest point.

I can work with that.

"Always so quick witted, John. Always so brash," Gyver said. "You're not the same man you used to be. That John wouldn't have been caught dead cowering here in this wreck. I, on the other hand, have finally found my full potential."

"Full potential? You still look like the same piece of shit who got her ass kicked by me last time." John winked at her. "Wait, something is different. Did you get a sex change? You almost look like a woman."

Gyver hissed and charged at him but recovered herself before getting too close. Her one pale eye narrowed, and she wiggled her finger back and forth at him.

"Nice try, John, get me all riled up so I get close enough for you to try some bold maneuver and save the day." Gyver smirked. "Well, not today, my friend. Maybe the old me, but not this one."

"You're still a fucking jerk-off."

Gyver gestured toward Sierra and Quinn. "Now, now, John, that's no way to talk in front of corruptible children like these."

Gyver kept the smirk on her face and hovered away from John, over to Sierra. She pulled Sierra's head up by her hair and slapped her until her eyes opened.

"Wake up, little princess."

I'm going to kill her, Cam.

As long as you don't get us killed too.

Sierra screamed and backed into one of the giant exo goons, who picked her up and dangled her out in front of him as if he had a mouse by the tail.

Sierra's eyes widened in horror. "What the hell are you?"

"We're going to be your new guardians for a while," Gyver said. "So play nice."

"Screw you!" Sierra said.

"Out of the mouths of babes. See what a negative impact you've already had on them? Poor kids." Gyver hovered in close to her again and ran her spider-like fingers through Sierra's hair, grabbing as Sierra tried to flinch away. "I think they might do better with some time spent around a more positive influence."

John, the exo-armor frames are pretty damn indestructible. Graphene tubed, nanotech running the gears, EMP resistant, and damn REP cannons on each arm.

Give me some bad news, will ya.

The operators seem really stupid, and probably ugly, too.

Cam.

Battery packs are exposed on the rear of each leg. Ammo for their REPs is easy-access on the back of the frame.

Got it. Whip, batteries, ammo.

Do try not to get your head squished by their giant hands.

Always the optimist, aren't you?

"Fuck you, shit bag," Sierra started kicking the man on the chest as hard as she could with both legs.

"Agh, knock it off, you little twerp." He squinted his eyes as if getting swarmed by mosquitoes. "You got a death wish or something?"

Gyver snarled, hovered up close to Sierra, and knocked her out with a quick fist across her jaw.

"Bob, can't you even control a little girl? Just set her down." Sierra hit the floor with a thud. "What the hell do I pay you and your brother for?"

The giant replied in a deep, slow voice.

"Sorry, boss. She's just a kid."

She slapped the giant on his undersized helmet, making it sit off centered on his huge head.

See, told you they're stupid.

Should make the match a bit more even.

They still might have the advantage there.

Since you're obviously getting bored, want to find me an exit?

I did already: the window, remember?

How did we ever make it home alive?

Me.

Keep telling yourself that.

Gyver's lips slithered into a thin ear-to-ear smile.

"Who's smiling now, Captain John?"

"You won't be wearing that smile for long, Gyver."

"You know what, John? I've been waiting a long time to kill you."

She's still talking. What a putz.

John, please do not let her kill us. I wouldn't survive the embarrassment.

We're not dying today.

I figured. Still, it's an awful thought.

"Still sore about me breaking your back, huh?"

The two giants wearing the exo suits started laughing.

"Shut up, you morons, or I'll send you right back to that sniveling mother of yours."

The giants went quiet, and Gyver hovered over to John. She squatted down on her board to get face to face with him, forgetting to keep a safe distance this time.

Gotcha.

Oh, finally. Can you make her stop talking?

"Do I look paralyzed to you, John?"

"No. We'll have to do something about that."

John kicked the hover board out from underneath her, sending her flying forward into him. He grabbed Gyver by the throat in midair, twisting her around, and slammed the back of her head into the wall behind him. He pulled her out of the wall and threw her limp body at the two dummies. Using the hover board to propel himself off the wall, he blasted into her airborne body, rocketing them both toward the stooge named Bob. They hit hard, sending all of them toppling to the ground before anyone could react.

They're clumsy, not used to the battle suits. Nice.

Whip.

John reached out as he dove for Sierra's knapsack and grabbed the whip out of it.

Battery pack, John.

Can't reach it.

Damn it, John.

Too late, the other one's on me.

John heard thunderous steps coming in fast, so he spun off the side of Bob's suit. A huge metal fist came crashing down, missing John by a split second, instead collapsing the armor. Sparks went flying into the air along with an array of curses from the Bob twins.

John, batteries!

John flipped the charge switch and snapped the whip's electric core out. The blue-white surging cable shot like a lightning bolt toward the batteries on Bob's suit, wrapping around them and sending an explosion of sparks and electricity through his exo armor, leaving him helpless as a beetle on its back.

"You asshole! When I get out of this suit, I'm gonna kill you," Bob said. "Tear 'em in half, Zack!"

They both have names. Top-heavy and dumb.

Bob and Zack, cute.

His blasters are heating up, John.

Electric whip in the ammo?

Good idea. Trap the whip core, make the ammo go boom.

"I'm gonna rip you apart, Tiny," Zack said.

"Don't blow yourself up trying to kill me, Zack Attack." John flipped the electric charge back on, but didn't extend the whip core.

Zack came in fast. Using that momentum, John grabbed onto Zack's suit, swinging up and over Zack's head. He gripped the exo armor's frame hard and pushed the whip as far into the suit's ammo case as he could, then let himself fall off the giant man, rolling to his feet when he hit the ground. He broke into a run and raced to the far wall of the room. The thug clumped after him, shaking the room with each step and firing rapid, chain-linked bursts of high-energy explosives at John.

John, you have to get him away from here before he blows up the building.

Window?

Have a safe flight.

John leaped through one of the windows, rolled hard onto the broken concrete outside the brewery, and burst into a run. The giant landed behind him with a deafening thud, firing unsteady shots.

Still too close for comfort.

Almost there, just a little further.

John, you're still too close.

Just a little bit further.

John sprinted down the broken road, zigzagging to avoid Zack getting a lock on him.

Still too close to him, John.

No worries, Cam. Any second…

Five seconds to be exact.

You're right, too close.

Heart pounding, ears ringing, John dug deep and used his adrenaline to burst through his final few steps, desperate to get some distance from the blast. A thundering wave from the explosion threw him forward. The whip had finally heated enough to ignite, exploding the ammunition that was left in the reserve pack on Zack's suit. John hit the ground hard and rolled until he was on his back. He stayed there for a second, glad he was still breathing, before propping himself up on his elbows to watch the giant exo suit melt into an orange glow.

"Zack, I told you not to blow yourself up over it."

Did you just trash-talk Zack Attack?

Let's not remember that.

Oh no, that's going into the data bank.

You're so kind, Cam.

John, the dampening is gone. I can see.

Report.

Kids are breathing, Sierra is with Quinn. Gyver's unconscious but alive. Bob's still screaming. Zack is barely alive, maybe an hour to DOA.

Where's Adam?

No reading yet, John.

Damn.

He got up and jogged back to the building, stopping briefly to check and make sure that Zack was charcoaled. His body lay motionless a few feet away from his destroyed exo-armor suit.

He's still alive. Asshole tried to crawl away from it before it completely incinerated.

Dumb ass.

Tough dumb ass though.

John ran back into the badly damaged brewery and jumped up the stairs to where Gyver, Bob, and the twins were. Bob was still screaming and trying unsuccessfully to bang his way out of his armor with his head. Gyver was lying in a pool of her own blood and drool. Behind them Sierra was tending an unconscious Quinn, still looking a little shocked at what had just transpired.

Shit.

John, we should get the kids downstairs.

You don't think they'll like what comes next?

John strode over to Quinn, picked him up and wrapped him tight in his arms as he ran down to the main floor. He laid him in the closest corner of the tank room and took off his jacket, placing it under Quinn's head. Sierra came down behind them, and curled up next to Quinn on the floor.

"Stay here. I have to go tie up the Apple Dumpling Gang, and check for Adam, okay?"

"The Apple who?"

"Never mind, just stay here, okay?"

"Okay."

JOHN. BEHIND YOU.

He felt a searing pain in the back of his head. He grimaced and fell, barely registering the crimson dripping onto the floor.

"Who's the dumb-ass now, dumb-ass?"

I am.

Damn it, John...

Forget it. What's he got, Cam?

Sling shot, bricks.

John snarled and turned around. Zack was standing in what was left of the doorway, charbroiled and maniacal. He was holding an oversized slingshot loaded with a new brick, and had it pointed right at John.

Who uses bricks?

The dumb-dumb twins.

Can you find my REP?

Front left, five meters.

John rolled forward and the brick went rocketing by him, just missing his head. He grabbed his REP and brought it up to fire, but he didn't get a chance.

Zack screamed and let the sling shot fall to the floor as he fell onto his belly, arms flung behind his head in panic to protect himself. A fierce, growling Adam was at his back, his thick jaw set into the side of Zack's throat. Zack tried to grab, to push, to get out of Adam's unbreakable hold, tried frantically to get a hand in place to staunch the geyser of blood that surged out of him. Adam finished him off by jerking his head back and forth, ripping the skin, muscles, and tendons away from Zack's corpse.

John collapsed onto his ass and leaned up against the wall, letting the rifle rest in his lap.

"About time you showed up," he said to Adam. "Took your sweet damn time, didn't you?"

Oh, here we go. The prodigal son returns to save the day and get all the credit.

Don't be jealous, Cam. We've all lost a step.

We would have been fine without him.

Adam tilted his bloody head and barked twice before trotting up to John. He put his nose in John's hand, nuzzling it affectionately, the blood still warm as it dripped off him and onto John.

"*I don't know, Cam. I think we owe the day to Adam. Such a good boy, aren't you, Adam.*"

We should have left him at home.

I think we we're lucky to have him today. Damn lucky.

Maybe. Doesn't mean I have to start liking him.

I wouldn't think of it.

Adam barked at him again.

"I know, I know, boy. We love you too," John said. "Come on, no time to rest yet. Let's check on the kids, huh?"

Adam let out another bark and trotted over to Sierra and Quinn. He went to Quinn first and started licking his face. When he was satisfied that Quinn was alive enough, he nuzzled Sierra, who was just starting to rouse out her stupor.

"Take care of them, boy. I have to clear the upstairs, okay?"

Adam barked loud and then sat at their feet. Nothing would get past him.

John left his new ragtag family and stalked upstairs to see whether anyone had decided to wake up. He found Bob still struggling to get out of his armor and an unconscious Gyver still limp next to him.

"What do you want, prick?" Bob tried to spit on John, but it only fell back in his face.

"Well, I can already tell that Gyver had the pick of the litter when she found you two."

"Fuck you, asshole."

John put his foot on the broken armor, and pressed hard on the guy's chest, squeezing the breath out of him.

"Shut up and listen, jerk-off. Your brother's dead. Your boss is down for the count, and you're on the short list to be next. So you can see from personal experience that I'm not one for bullshit."

Bob started to sob. "No, NO. You're lying. You're lying. Not Zack, not my little brother, no."

"What were you doing here?"

"Not little Zack. It can't be true."

"What are you doing here, Bob?"

"Not Zack. Mom's gonna kill me."

All Bob could do was wail.

Useless.

Not like they were a fountain of information before we dismantled them.

Good point.

John brought his boot down on Bob's face. The sobbing stopped, and Bob slumped against the back of his exo armor quietly. John went over to check on Gyver. He kicked her to see if she'd wake up, but she was still unconscious. He tied Gyver to Bob's exo armor and went back downstairs, his limp already gone, his nano friends whittling down the injuries; healing his torn tissue, broken ribs, and bruised lungs.

Quinn was lying with his head in Sierra's lap. He looked as peaceful as when they had pulled him out of the river, as if he might already be too peaceful for help. Adam tried to do his part by licking Quinn's forehead; it didn't do much except smear Zack's blood around on him. Sierra stared blankly at them both and played with Quinn's hair. She was looking pretty ghostly herself. The heaviness of the last two days was catching up with all of them.

Damn.

Quite the scene, huh?

Never again.

Famous last words.

I mean it. Never again, Cam.

"Sierra," John said.

She didn't move from holding her brother's head in her lap.

"Sierra."

Sierra stirred a little and looked up at John with watering emerald green eyes.

"Will he be okay?"

Quinn stirred, and opened his eyes. He held his hand up and patted his sister's cheek, a crease of a smile showing between his cheeks.

"I'm not that easy to get rid of."

John couldn't help smiling in relief. "Can you keep that stubborn streak of yours up?"

"Does a jipper whip hurt?"

"I think you might just make it, kid."

Sierra wiped the tears from her eyes and smiled at both of them. "He'll make it. He's special like me. He'll make it."

"I'm sure he will, kid. We're not going anywhere tonight, so here." John took out his last thermal flare and tossed it to Sierra. "Gather up some wood, shelves, tables, anything you can find, turn them over and light it. Should give you two plenty of heat to warm up a bit."

"What are you going to do?"

"I'm going to find out what those assholes were doing here, and why that door to the cellar has a fresh lock on it. Adam will stay with you. I doubt I could get him to leave your side right now anyways."

He headed toward the stairs to go back up and start his interrogation, but he stopped when he heard Sierra's voice.

"John?"

He paused and turned to face her.

"Thank you."

"Don't mention it, kid."

He turned and headed upstairs, years of training coming back to him.

Like riding a bike huh, Cam?

More like beating someone with a bike.

Six

Old Friends

Too much internal damage from the fight, John. Nothing you could have done.

Didn't get very much out of him.

Don't think you would have even if he hadn't been dying.

We'll have to get it from Gyver.

Won't be a long wait, Medusa's starting to move.

Gyver woke up coughing, gagging, and trying to spit as John held her mouth opened and poured another bottle of ice-cold water into her. She shook the water off her face and wiggled her wrists around, making a clanking sound from the chain wrapped around them. She tried to kick at John, but she was still tied up to the metal exoskeleton that held the bloodied, lifeless form of Bob.

"You going to talk yet, cupcake?"

"I'm gonna kill you, you son of a bitch," Gyver said.

"You might not be able to see clearly enough, but right now I'm literally shaking with fear."

She sprayed out a combination of blood and spit onto his shirt.

"You know, it's a good thing I'm getting a new shirt soon."

"Screw you."

John let out a long, slow sigh and sat back into a chair. "I think we got off on the wrong foot here, Gyver. Let's start over. Let bygones be bygones."

"I don't have to listen to this crap," Gyver said. "You do what you have to, John, and see where that gets you."

"Tempting. But I have some business with you first."

"I'm not afraid of you."

"You should be, Gyver. You really, really should be."

"I'm not telling you anything."

"I guess I don't have to ask you any questions. It was just a courtesy. I could just have Cam extract the information."

Gyver's eyes widened, and what little color there was in her cheeks paled. For the first time since their tussle, she actually looked scared.

"Listen, John, I'll make you a deal. You give me the two kids, and I let you walk out of here. Let bygones be bygones, just like you said. I won't even mention any of this to the Seamstress."

"Eew, very mysterious sounding, and tempting too, but I'm gonna pass."

"God. What is it with you, John? You don't even like those kids."

"Yeah, but I like them more than I like you."

"You're a dead man, John. You have no idea how dead you are."

John got up and paced around her for a second, letting her stew.

"Let me put it this way, Gyver. You're not going to die here. Not like Bob and Zack at least. I'm going to let you live. I'm going to suck the will out of you, along with any information I want, then I'm going to leave you here and let your new boss—*the Seamstress*—I'm going to let whoever that is take care of you."

"Ha, you won't kill me? Yeah, right. I don't believe you."

"Suit yourself."

"I'm connected now, John. I can get you whatever you want. How else do you think I got this kind of equipment, this kind of firepower?"

"I'll know exactly where you got that kind of firepower soon enough. With or without your help."

"I should've had the Bobs kill you sooner."

"Yeah, you didn't pick the brightest people for exo-controllers."

"Slim pickings to find loyalists in these damn parts."

"Loyalists?"

"The world's changing, John. Events are in motion that are bigger than this, bigger than you and me, bigger than anyone up here can fight," Gyver said. "Do what you want to me, but the people I work for will find you, kill you, and still get those kids."

"What's so special about Sierra and Quinn? Why don't you just go to the meat market?"

"You have no idea what you've gotten yourself into, do you? Get out while you have the chance, John. This isn't your fight."

"You made it my fight."

"You're pathetic."

"Looks who's talking."

Well, this has been fun, but can we move on now, John?

Almost, Cam. If I can get her to slip up we might not have to go in.

Okay, but this is getting nauseating.

"You're so screwed, John. No way I'm talking anymore."

"Seems to me like you're doing plenty of talking."

Gyver lunged against her restraints, only to get pulled back down on the limbs of the exo armor, horror on her face as she met Bob's lifeless eyes.

"I...I don't know anything."

"Bullshit."

"John, I don't." Gyver's expression hardened. "I got my payday, John. Got a map grid to pick up those two bozos, and a couple of old pictures of some kids we were supposed find. Now I'm here. That's all I know."

Do you think she's telling the truth?

No.

She's scared of something worse than you, John. That much is evident.

Must be one bad mother pulling the strings then.

Do you think we can find out what she's hiding without killing her?

I'm working on it, Cam.

"Gyver, you're holding back something. I can tell. I have a certain knack for things like this; I'll find out what I want to know. Easy way, hard way, it's all fine by me."

John took a small earpiece out of a pouch on his chest and put it on above Gyver's ear, clicking it into the cyber port there that linked to her biotech.

"John, don't," Gyver said.

"Your choice, Gyver."

Gyver glared at him and then spit on his boots.

Do it, Cam.

Are you sure?

Do it.

Cam partially dislodged herself from her link with John and transmitted over the small connection in Gyver's mind that John had made with the biotech link. She started sifting through the small defenses that Gyver had put up to protect herself from something like this, quick work for an AI like Cam.

To make sure nothing was missed she dug deep until she hit Gyver's childhood, her life as a teenager, high school, the years of recession that led to the last war, Day One, and then eventually cease-fire. Gyver screamed in anguish as the memories were forced back to the forefront of her mind.

Found it, John.

Show it to me.

Cam flashed John the memories she had found. Gyver getting a coded message to find the kids. Directions to the nearest US outpost, where she got her gear and the exo-armor suits. A contract giving her a commission in the military, and governorship over any territory she could turn. The small mountain cabin she found the Bob twins in. Pictures of Sierra and Quinn flashed onto the screen, and then the memories started to fizzle.

John, I'm losing the connection.

What's happening?

Her biotech is black market. It can't handle an intrusion like this. If I continue I'm going to fry her brain.

Shut it down, Cam.

Are you sure?

Shut it down.

Gyver blasted out a breath of air, her chest rising and falling heavy and irregular. Her head rolled back on her shoulders and her whole body convulsed until she slumped over, unconscious. John threw some more ice-cold water on her and she woke up writhing against her bonds.

"We're not done that easy, Gyver."

"Fuck you, John."

"Have it your way."

"You can't do anything to me. You can't do anything compared to who I work for."

John picked up another bucket filled with river water and dumped it on her.

"Agh, enough already."

"Who do you work for?"

"Screw you."

"Why do you want the kids?"

"Screw you."

"What are you doing here?"

"The United States is forming up again, John. They've struck a deal with the Colonies. They'll be one country again soon."

John slammed his fist against Gyver's temple, and her head fell limp again.

I thought you said you had a knack for this.

I lost my patience.

The United States, huh?

Re-forming even.

What'd you think?

Obviously she's delusional. It would take something huge to get all the territories and colonies to unite.

How do explain everything we saw then?

I don't know yet.

We're missing something.

We're always missing something.

John grabbed his REP rifle and went downstairs to check on Adam, Sierra, and Quinn. He kicked Quinn's foot a couple times—nothing. He frowned, knelt down, grabbed Quinn's foot hard, and shook it to get him to stir. He had been sleeping so hard that John thought maybe he'd died, and they hadn't noticed. He let out a breath when he realized the kid was still alive. Adam watched John closely and lifted his head, ears perked, waiting to see what he would do next. It didn't look as if Adam had moved more than two feet from the kid's side since John had gone upstairs.

"You're doing good, kid. Just a little longer, okay?"

Quinn nodded his head up and down without opening his eyes. Adam watched him for a minute and then yawned and moved his head back onto Quinn's chest.

"Did they tell you anything?" Sierra asked.

"No. How're you holding up?"

"I don't know." She shrugged. "I think I'm okay, but Quinn's getting worse. We need to get him some help soon."

Cam?

His infection is spreading. If it continues like this he won't make it to Tree Top.

We need to catch a break.

Good luck with that.

Sierra scanned the room in bewilderment before looking back at John.

"How did you do all this? How did you kill them all?"

"What was it you said about you and your brother, you're *special*? Let's just say we're all a little special in our own way. Listen, I have to get into that room downstairs and check it out. I need you to go upstairs, get all of the gear, and bring it down here. Can you do that?"

"Yes."

"Get inside my pack and grab my med kit out. It's a small bag with a big red cross. Got it?"

"Got it."

John handed her his handgun.

"Here, probably won't need it, but just in case. Have you used one of those before?"

"A few times, to scare off coyotes on Sam and Jean's property. I've never had to shoot at anyone, though."

"Don't worry about it too much. If you have to shoot it to protect yourself, you'll figure it out."

"Do you think I'll have to shoot one of them?"

"You won't have to worry. Only one's alive, and I don't expect she'll be waking up anytime soon."

John headed for the cellar stairs, and Sierra caught his arm.

"Be careful, John," she said.

John winked at her and then waved her off.

"If there's anything I was ever good at kid, it's this."

Let's try this again, Cam.

Back to square one.

No interruptions this time.

I think they're getting attached to you, John.

Cam, can we talk about this later?

I'm just saying that having them around might not be such a bad thing.

Didn't you just want to try and get rid of them faster?

I said that about Adam, too.

I thought you didn't like Adam.

I don't.

Cam, you confuse the hell out of me sometimes.

Ditto.

He went down the stairs to the cellar and quickly scanned the door again. He blasted the locks off and hammered it open with his foot. Leading himself into the room slowly with his weapon, he followed the light shining off the side barrel, moving it methodically from corner to corner until it lit the center of the room. The light hit the gleam of a metal chair, and John stopped to scan it again. In the middle of the dark, dank room was a single chair. A small, motionless form tied to the chair slumped forward, a long, dark mess of braided hair obscuring its face.

I didn't expect to find that down here.

Is it alive?

Yes, malnourished, but alive.

Human?

Female, in fact.

Oh, great.

Watch it, John.

Sorry, Cam, but I think I'm maxed out on the women I can deal with at one time here.

Funny.

John closed toward the female form, still leading with his rifle. He scanned the room again as he got nearer, checking for traps and snares. He kicked the chair she was tied to. Nothing. No movement. He kicked again and she let out a small grunt.

What do you think, Cam?

No reason to stop being the Good Samaritan now.

Damn.

John slung his weapon and got down to cut the straps that held her to the chair.

John, they're already sliced.

The small female launched herself forward and tackled him to the floor. She punched her skull into his forehead and grappled with feral strength to try and break free from his thick arms. John fended off her blows and rolled her over, his red eyes flashing as he brought his knife up out of his boot and angled himself on top of her. He put the blade of the knife against her throat and used his other hand to hold her head still.

"Stop fighting or I'll open up your goddamn throat," John said.

The woman stilled and looked up at John with squinted eyes.

"John?"

John leaned back, almost frozen at the sound of her voice, and let his eyes adjust to the dim light. He slid off her and picked up his REP, shining the light into the woman's face. Her caramel skin was lined with scrapes and bruises, cheekbone and jawline sharp-edged and sunken in from dehydration. Long knife marks on the nape of her neck shone just slightly in the light under dirt and dry, flaking blood. Her shaggy, crusted brunette hair was pulled back into some sort of braid, and even though it was dirty, it still shone like silk in places. He traced her slender, hardened form with his eyes until he met hers. Crackled, crystal blue eyes that John could never forget.

"Sage?"

SEVEN

The Seamstress

SHELVES CREAKED AND HANGARS squeaked as an old lady climbed up and balanced herself on the ladder, digging through the many piles and racks of fabric in the small, yellow-tinged workroom.

"Aha."

Having found what she was looking for, she climbed down with a bundle of gray-green cloth tucked under her arm, went over to her work bench, slumped down behind the sewing machine, and started lining the fabric up with the edge marker. She jerked her shoulders back and let out a tiny gasp, as if she had just pinched her finger between needle and feeder plate, sensing a familiar pinging inside her head.

Damn thing, still startles the shit out of me after all this time.

I can change the tone, ma'am.

They're all startling.

Her hair reflected like lightning bolts on the chrome sewing machine as she moved it aside to uncover a small compartment containing her holo deck. She adjusted the bun that pulled her hair tight against the back of her head and pressed her palm down on it. A green-hued holo screen popped up, with a tall, solid-looking blonde-haired man in green-grey fatigues at the center of it.

"Gyver's not here, ma'am. We've scouted around the meeting area several times now, and there's no sign of her."

"Have you tried to bring her up on the net?"

"Nothing. It's like she dropped off the grid."

"I take it you haven't found any children and a greasy jipper couple wandering around out there either."

"No, ma'am."

"Well, keep searching, Sergeant. If you can't find her, I at least want some answers before you get back."

"When we find her, do you want us to bring her to you?"

"Gods, no, keep her with you, find out what you can, and then report directly to me."

"Roger that, ma'am."

The holo feed blinked out and the old lady sighed and rubbed the bridge of her nose.

I have to get out of this place.

It'll be much harder if General Murdoch finds out about your little side venture.

It was clear to me that I was his contingency, in case the monastery should fail. They were bound to fail, so there was no harm in jumping before being told.

Understood, ma'am.

There was a jingle at the service entrance and the old lady slid the countertop over the holo deck and moved her sewing machine back into place. She adjusted herself and then looked out through the door to her lobby, smiling at one of her regulars coming in to acquire one of her more fashionable services.

EIGHT

Sage

"SAGE? WHAT THE HELL are you doing here?"

He reached down, offering his hand to her. She hesitated at first, so John reached his hand a little closer, encouraging her to take it with raised eyebrows and a softened gaze.

"I'm not going to hurt you, Sage."

She set her jaw and grabbed his hand, squeezing his club-sized fist hard as if she were trying to show him she could still put up a fight. He pulled her up slowly, helped her sit back in the chair, and then backed away. Sage kept her gaze on him, eyes narrow, untrusting, unsure. He kept his eyes on her for the same reasons.

"What are you doing here?"

"I could ask you the same question," Sage said.

John scanned her with his light again, not quite believing yet that she was real. He traced her long braid with his eyes as she flipped it over her shoulder. She looked almost like an illusion in this light, but she was very, very real.

"Are you just going to stand there gawking, or are you going to say something?"

"You look like shit."

"Good to see you too, John."

"How'd you get here?"

"John…"

"What the hell is going on here, Sage?"

"Whoa, slow down. I'm not ready for questions yet, John. I can barely think right now. How about starting off with, 'Are you okay, Sage? Do you need some water, Sage?' How about that?"

"How about I'm fucking sore from getting my ass kicked, and I'd like some goddamn answers, Sage?"

Sage took in a deep breath, pushed on her forehead hard with the palm of her hand and let out a breath as if she had come to some resolution.

"Water first."

John shook his head and stormed out of the room and up to the bar.

Talk about blast from the past.

I've had enough of the past today.

I wonder who else we'll see again on this trip.

We've already seen too many people.

Maybe we'll run into Dr. Wilcox and his circus.

Not funny, Cam.

Those grizzlies of his are so awesome.

No circus, Cam, no Dr. Wilcox. No one else from here on out.

Party pooper.

"What's going on down there?" Sierra asked.

John stomped past her and rifled through his pack for his water bottle, ignoring Sierra's interrogating gaze.

"Keep these two safe for a bit longer, Adam. I'll be downstairs."

Adam looked up from his post by Quinn and barked his understanding.

"Wait, what's going on, John? What'd you find down there?"

"I don't know yet. Things either got more complicated, or we just lucked out. I'll know more soon, but I have to get back downstairs. Stay here, okay?"

"But…"

"Stay here."

John stormed back down the stairs and into the cellar.

Sage blew a small thatch of hair out of her face and looked up at John as he came into the room. She eyed the water in his hand and leaned back in the chair, stretching her chest and rubbing the soreness out of her shoulder.

"Glad you're seeing reason these days, John."

He tossed her the water and pulled another chair out of the corner, turning it to face Sage and taking a seat.

"Now," John said, "your turn."

"All work and no play. I guess some things don't change, do they?"

See, you are a party pooper.

Cam, run a scan.

Only checking for injuries, right?

And surprises.

"Cut the crap, Sage. I'm tired, pissed off, and incapable of bullshit right now."

Sage winced a little as she gulped down some more water.

"Where's the wonder trio?"

"The Bob twins? Dead. Gyver's sleeping it off. She'll wish she was dead when she wakes up."

John followed Sage's eyes as she looked down at her hands. She fiddled with the bottle cap for a few seconds, tightening it and loosening it.

"What're you doing here with them, Sage?"

"They caught me a couple of days ago," she said, still twisting the lid to the water bottle, tight, and then loose, over and over. "I've been holed up here ever since."

She took the lid off and took another gulp of water, swished it around in her mouth, and spit out some blood on the ground. She looked right at John, her expression worried. Worry that she was trying to hide beneath a cocky smile.

She's getting ready to lie me.

Did you think that she wouldn't?

I was hoping.

You always hope when it comes to her.

I'm a sucker for difficult women.

Point taken.

"I was hunting about three miles north of here when those two dumb-dumbs came crashing through the woods." Her knuckles whitened against the water bottle, one hand looking as if she were trying to crush the metal bottle, the other twisting the lid back on and then off again. "Scaring everything away and busting up the forest in their clumsy exo armor."

She took a deep breath, relaxing her hands, and stared down at the water bottle, still fiddling with the lid, tight, loose, tight, loose.

"That's when Gyver showed up. She's been on that damn hover board ever since you broke her back." She chuckled, more like a nervous reflex than a genuine act of joy. "She really hates you, John, more than most."

"I'm heartbroken," John said. "What happened when they found you?"

"Snatched me up and brought me here."

"Why? What did they want with you?"

"John, do we really have to talk about this right now?'

"Do you have someplace pressing to be?"

"They weren't after me. I was just opportunity knocking, I think. They've had me down here since they nabbed me." Sage's hands loosened the lid again and she sucked back another long swig of water. She tightened the lid back on and then returned to her nervous, white-knuckle twisting, tight, loose, tight, loose. "Those idiots fought over me the whole time, but Gyver wouldn't let them touch me. Told them she had something special in mind for me. Something about using me to reel in a big fish for her new boss."

"The Seamstress?"

She drew her lips up into a dorky smile, and another nervous chuckle escaped. "Yeah, sounds real scary, huh?"

John, she's pretty beat up, some bruised ribs, lots of superficial abrasions, but that seems to be the worst of it.

Anything else, Cam?

You mean is she hiding anything sinister that she might use to kill us all?

Something like that.

No.

"Sounds like you got more out of Gyver than I did," Sage said.

John leaned in close to her, forcing her to look right into his eyes. The cybernet behind his iris flashed from red back to his normal blue, letting her know she was safe. Their breath lingered together in the air for a second, making it the only other sound in the cellar besides the grinding twist of the bottle cap in her hands. He grabbed the water bottle, sliding his fingers over hers and breaking her tense movements. Her fingers loosened and she let him take it away from her.

"It's safe, Sage. Keep talking."

Sage breathed heavily. Eyes still trained on his, she brushed a few thick hairs out of her face, and then rolled her eyes and looked away from him. "She kept saying that they were rounding up loyalists or something. Gyver was at least smart enough not to talk too much, not to me at least."

Maybe you should go a little easy on her, John.

I'll think about it.

"What about the other two?"

"That's a different story," Sage said. "They thought I was just a dumb-ass cave woman, so they talked in front of me all the time. They didn't know much, though."

"What did they know?"

"Listen, why do you care, John? I mean, I'm thankful for you being here and getting me out of a shit hole, but what do you have to do with this? What are you even doing here?"

John swallowed down a big gulp of the water and then handed it back to her. She held the bottle upside down over her mouth and sucked down the last few drops.

"Oh jeez, John, thanks for saving all the water for me."

You're so generous.

You said go easy.

I had different methods in mind.

Same, same.

"You first. What did they know?"

"They were real excited about their new toys. They rambled on and on about how Mom would be proud that they were part of the new US territorial militia. Whatever that is. Gyver was getting funding from someone high up in the United States military, that much is clear."

"The United States? Are you sure?"

"That's what Gyver's goons said."

"US scouts haven't been out here for years."

"I know, but it gets even better. Those two went on about how they'd be set up nice, that they'd get whatever they want once Gyver's in charge. Can you imagine Gyver in charge of anything?"

"John, is everything okay?" Sierra's skinny form crouched at the top of the stairs, bending forward, one hand on the railing and one hand on the floor for support. She leaned forward a little more, moving her head side to side, eyes squinted, peering down into the darkness to try and find them. "Are you down there with someone?"

Sage sneered at John and then looked back up the stairs at Sierra.

"You're not alone?"

"No, I'm not, and before you ask, no, I don't want to talk about it." John reached into one of the pockets on his chest rig, pulled a jerky strip out, and tossed it to Sage. "Here, chew on this while I go take care of her."

"Oh, goodie."

You're such a gentleman.

I try.

John walked the few steps back to the door so Sierra could see him.

Do you think we can get her to help Quinn?

I hope.

"Yeah, I'm fine. I'm just down here with," he turned and looked at Sage, "with an old friend."

Sage rolled her eyes and gnawed on the leathery jerky.

I thought you weren't going to hope with her again.

I thought you didn't like Adam or the twins.

Damn. Foiled again.

"Oh, okay," Sierra said, her voice paused, but she didn't move. "John?"

"What is it, kid?"

"Do you think Quinn and I can have something eat? We're kind of starving."

"There's more?" Sage stood up out of the chair.

"There's a lot more. It's been a really long day."

John turned toward Sierra. "I'll be right up. Did you get my med kit out of my bag?"

"Yeah, but what's going on?"

"I'll explain in a minute. There's food in the front pouch right next to where the med kit was; help yourself."

John looked back to Sage and smiled as he heard Sierra scurrying away.

"I need your help."

"Sounds like you need a lot more than my help," Sage said.

"I think you owe me, Sage."

"Oh, for stumbling on me in this cellar?"

"For more than that."

Sage stared him for a second and then waved toward the stairs.

"Lead the way."

I knew she would help.

Sure you did.

John and Sage marched up the stairs to where he had left the kids. Sierra was back with Quinn, who was now sitting up, resting his back against the wall and holding a piece of jerky out in front of him as if it were a slug. Adam's head rested on the boy's lap, eyeing the jerky, waiting for the inevitable bite he would get out of Quinn.

He saw Sage and raised his head up just enough to bark to her. Sage rushed over to him, getting down on her knees and massaging the sides of his neck. He craned his head up and gave her an approving lap on her cheek.

"Adam, hey there, boy. I haven't seen you in so long." Sage moved her hands around him. "Is he okay? John, he's covered in blood."

Adam barked again. He put his front paw on her legs and started licking her face.

"Adam's fine. It's not his blood. Down, boy, down. Leave Sage alone for now."

Sage scratched above Adam's hind leg, one of the only clean spots he had left, and helped both of them ignore John.

"That's a good boy, Adam," Sage said. "Did you kill some bad guys? Yes, you did. Good boy, Adam."

"If you two are done, Sage," John said, looking from Sage to Adam. "I need Adam to check outside and make sure the horses are still alive."

Adam licked Sage's face one more time and then got up, looking over at John as if he were irritated with the interruption.

"What? Now that Sage is here you think you get to give me shit, too?"

Adam barked at him and nudged past him, his snout in the air as he trotted out the door.

"I see your training has been real strict."

What a little snoot. You should've kicked him, John.

"Focus, Sage. Can you check out the boy?"

Cam, just run the boy's bios so I can give them to Sage.

Already on it.

Sage walked over and knelt in front of Quinn, leaning in close and putting her hands up to touch him. "May I?"

Quinn shrugged and stuffed the last bit of meat into his mouth.

She ran her hands over his forehead, put her cheeks to his, and then leaned back over his face, squeezing his cheeks, looking into his mouth.

Cam flashed John Quinn's BIO signs on his HUD. The abnormal readings brought a heaviness that he hadn't expected to feel.

"Cam says his core is thirty-eight Celsius, heart rate is one-twenty, and his lungs are inflamed. Only reason they're not full of fluid right now is the phages I gave him."

Sage leaned back and wiped the loose strands of hair off her face. "Good, that's something I can work with."

John, if we don't hurry…

I know, Cam.

Quinn narrowed his eyes at them. "I don't feel that bad."

"John, what are you talking about? Why is she touching my brother like that? I thought you said he'd be okay."

"And he will be. She's a healer, Sierra. She can help."

"What's going on? How do you know all of what you just said?"

"It's a long story, kid. One we don't have time for now." John gestured over to the pile of belongings. "Did you get everything down here?"

"They're over there," Sierra said.

"Good. What do you need, Sage?"

Sage gave them an irritated look. "Peace and quiet to start, some warm water, cloths, blankets, a little space, and any chocolate that you may have."

"Chocolate?" Sierra said.

"I'm starving."

Quinn raised his eyebrows. "Me too."

Sage reached for John's brown pouch that had the red cross on it. "Do you have more phages and the basic herbs I told you to always keep with you?"

"Yes."

"Then the kid might stand a chance, but I won't know for sure until I get a full run on him. Go scrounge up what I asked for and then give me some time to work."

"No way I'm leaving my brother," Sierra said.

Quinn smiled at her, and winked. "I'm okay, Sis, really."

"He's safe here, Sierra," John said. "Come help me get the stuff she needs."

She turned her head, looking back at her brother and then at John. John reached out and put his hand on her shoulder. Not hard, but gentle, consoling.

"Come on, kid, nothing we can do here except hinder her. She might be rough around the edges, but we can trust her."

Sage glared at John and then turned, softening her gaze at Sierra.

"I'll see what I can do for him, but you need to back off. I'll take good care of your brother, I promise."

Quinn nodded his head. "Yeah, I'm just fine. This nice lady will take care of me."

Sierra blinked her eyes and wiped some tears away with the sleeve of her dirty shirt. "You're a dork, Q." She looked at them both one more time and then turned on her heel and walked over to her belongings.

"John," Sage said, "it's good to see you again."

"Yeah, whatever. Just fix the kid and we'll be square."

"John."

"Not now, Sage. It's been a long day. My head is spinning. I ache all over like I haven't ached in years. I'm in a town I never wanted to see again, with two dead bodies, an idiot jerk-off, a sick kid and his bull-headed sister, and you. And to top it off we're in a brewery that's been out of beer since God knows when."

Sage drew up another vial of phages into an auto injector and gave Quinn another dose, then took some of the packages out of John's pouch and started pulling small cubes from them, adding them into a mixing bag, and then kneading the contents together. She looked up and gave John a wink.

"I wouldn't say *completely* out of beer."

NINE

Tree Top

JOHN LAY ON ONE OF THE wooden benches by the bar with his head on his folded-up jacket, an empty pint glass on the ground next to him.

"How many barrels do you think are down there?"

"More than we can drink, and too much to carry out of here," Sage said. "We'll have to re-lock the door to the cellar and try to come back for them later."

"It's really awful sour beer, you know."

"You still drank plenty of it."

You two are helpless.

Helpless, but not hopeless, Cam.

Oh, please.

Sage gestured to Sierra and Quinn, who were both asleep in the other room, two humps on the ground silhouetted by the low-burning fire, with Adam, a third hump, curled up at their feet.

"I didn't take you for a family man anymore, John."

"I'm not."

"So how the hell did you end up with those two?"

"I guess it's just my ongoing good luck. And Cam, I mostly blame Cam."

It was Adam's idea too, John. Besides, I think you're starting to like them.

I like them enough to make sure they get to Oliver safe.

"Tell Cam hi for me. I feel like I share a certain baptism by fire with her."

It's all right. Act like a tough guy. I know better.

So does Sage. I'm ambushed.

We could've been best friends if it hadn't been for you, John.

"She says goodnight, Sage."

Time for bed, Cam.

Whatever, grandpa.

"Goodnight? It's morning already, it'll be light soon."

"Goodnight, Sage," John said. "Wake me up when it's light out."

"There're other things we could do besides sleep, John."

"No, there aren't, Sage."

Oh boy, this is getting awkward.

Don't worry, Cam, I'm as strong as an oak.

Sage tiptoed over to him and straddled his waist, pressing down on him, gentle, but firm. She tucked her hips in and squeezed him, trapping him under her, leaning so close to his face that he could feel the static from her lips and taste her honey-scented breath in his mouth. Straightening up, she arched her back as she slipped her raggedy shirt off, digging her sit bones into his thighs enough to make him groan.

"Are you sure there's nothing else we can do?" She brought her hands to his chest and started unbuttoning his shirt, sliding it open like pages of a book.

John's eyes narrowed as he sat up, pushed her naked breasts against his chest and then leaned closer, tracing his lips with her tongue.

Damn.

Must be a baby oak.

* * *

"John," Sierra said. He didn't budge, so she shook his shoulders. "John."

Still nothing. She smirked and tried for a more direct approach. She raised her arm up high to slap his face. Her arm stalled in the air as it came down, caught in John's massive hand.

"Stop," he said.

"Well, wake up when I'm shaking you then," she said. "It's like midmorning already. That woman, Sage, is gone. Quinn's awake, slightly better too, but he doesn't look like he's all the way with us yet, and he keeps asking if Mazzy's okay. It's getting real annoying."

John smiled. "Sage is gone, huh? Imagine that."

"Are you listening to me?"

John sat up, crawled out of his sack, and started rifling through his pack, which had also served as his pillow. He took out a bar to eat and then pulled out a pocketbook-sized green metal box.

"First things first. Coffee," John said.

Sierra rolled her eyes and kicked over a box to sit on.

Good morning, sunshine. So glad to see you're up. I'm surprised you didn't use up all your energy being as strong as an oak.

Good morning, Cam. How's it look out there?

All clear so far. There's no dampening field, so I can see a couple of miles into the woods. Nothing dangerous out as far as I can see.

Nice.

Can we have a brief discussion about last night, and how weird that is for me when you do that?

Do what?

Sex.

Listen, Cam, you could have gone to the wrist pad and stayed there.

It's like a coffin.

Then it's sex.

Thank God it's not very often.

"Adam," John said.

Adam got up, trotted over by him, and bent his head down so John could rub behind his ears and massage his neck. John narrowed his eyes and ran his fingers through again, surprised how smooth and fluffy Adam's fur felt. "He's clean."

"I found some rainwater leaking into one of the giant sinks in the cellar, so I gave him a bath while you and Sage caught up over those sour beers."

"Thanks, Sierra," John said and massaged Adam a bit more. "You look sharp, boy. You were a big help last night, weren't you?"

Adam let out a couple of triumphant barks, and Sierra laughed.

"All right, Adam, you know what to do, boy. Just once around this morning, okay?"

Adam licked John's face and headed outside through a flap that John had made for him in the repaired door during the night.

"Where's he going?" Sierra asked.

"Perimeter check."

"How does he know to do that?"

"That question requires an answer I'm not ready to share yet," John said. "Why don't you go get the kid up and then start breaking down camp?"

"What are you going to do?"

"Enjoy the relative peace while I make coffee and breakfast."

"Whatever." Sierra looked over at Quinn. "What are you going to do after that?"

Yeah, what are we going to do, John?

"I'll have to figure out something to do with Gyver, burn the dead Bob twins that Sage and I threw out back, and get whatever I can salvage off the battle suits."

Sierra wrinkled her nose and sneered at him. "You're going to burn them?"

"What'd you think we'd do with them?"

Sierra thought about it for a second and then shrugged her shoulders, moving on to her next subject.

"What about Sage?"

"What about her?"

"Is she coming back? Obviously she's a friend, so who is she?"

"I don't know if she's coming back. Why are you asking so many questions? Remember when I said *relative peace*?"

"No, I don't." She slipped a black cylinder about the size of a marker out of her pocket and gave it to him. "Here, she left this for you."

John took the cylinder and popped the top off, letting a rolled-up cream paper slide out into his hand.

> *John,*
>
> *I can't stay—big surprise, huh. I did all I could for the boy. He'll be okay for about twelve hours and then the infection in his lungs will set back in, and with a vengeance too. He will need a strong healer and a place to lie low for a couple of days. Jane's the healer at Tree Top. You remember Jane, right? He should be fine if you can get him there.*
>
> *Give Adam a kiss for me. I miss that furry guy.*
>
> *Sage.*
>
> *P.S. Thanks for the after-hours last night.*

"Did she leave?" Sierra asked.

"Don't you have anything better to do?"

"No. I'm bored."

"Go be bored someplace else."

"Are you two lovers?"

"Lovers? Jesus, Sierra."

"Well, it's just a question."

John lowered his head and looked at her, narrowing his eyes and setting his jaw. "Camp?"

Sierra let out an annoyed sigh, and turned to leave, shaking her head as if she thought John were crazy. "I got it. Wake up Q, break down camp."

I might actually go nuts on this trip, Cam.

Don't blame us. You made your own bed.

Next time you suggest that we help someone, will you also flash me these memories so that I remember to ignore you?

I have no idea what you're talking about.

That's what I thought.

Sierra went into the other room and started putting her sleeping bag away before helping Quinn get up. John pulled a quart-sized silver cylinder out of his green metal box and twisted it in half. He poured some water in one half of it and some black coffee grounds in the other, then twisted them back together and hit a red button on the top. It hissed for a couple of seconds, and then the small button turned green. He twisted it back open and took the side that had the black grounds off, setting it by his pack. He scanned the mess of a building, and peeked back at the kids, smiling to himself as he cupped the steaming coffee under his nose and watched them pack.

Almost seems normal, in weird sort of way.

Yeah, real normal.

John chuckled to himself as he watched Sierra come back to the bar room.

"What're you laughing at?' She leaned on the counter next to him.

"Nothing. You close to being packed?" John closed his eyes and sipped on his coffee, and then opened them back up ever so slightly to see whether she was still staring at him. She was.

This will take some getting used to.

What, your magic powers—closing your eyes to ignore someone and making them disappear—aren't working?

Exactly.

That never really works, John. It just makes you look like an idiot.

Jeez, what's up with you this morning?

Really? Do we have to go through this again?

Please, no.

Fine, then you'll have to make do with my attitude for now.

Lucky me.

"So?"

"So what, kid?"

"How's the coffee? Is it better than mine?"

"Is your brother up?"

Sierra rolled her eyes and slumped off to finish helping get Quinn up.

John smiled to himself and went back to enjoying the few minutes of peace he had just created for himself. He surveyed the wrecked door that he'd boarded up late in the night and watched the sun's rays sneak through the cracks, entangling the space with webs of light.

A breeze rustled outside and carried notes over the soft, low tone of the nearby river. Birds chirped early morning sun songs as they darted around their nests high in the roof of the brewery and the surrounding trees. John turned around and watched Sierra stumbling through the room, getting hers and Quinn's things together. He saw Quinn getting up, slow but alive, and felt a pang in his chest.

Guess I should make them some food, huh?

Yes, I think kids still eat something called food these days.

I get it, Cam. I'm not good at this. Can we move on now?

Maybe.

You're the best, Cam.

I know.

He reached into his saddlebag, scrounged some rations out of it along with a heat bag, and started making breakfast.

* * *

The timers on the heat bag turned green right as John finished his breakfast bar. Sierra and Quinn staggered out to the main bar and dropped off their packs. Quinn looked as if he were sleepwalking, but John couldn't help smiling at how good the kid looked compared to last night.

"Here." He tossed some rations to Sierra and Quinn, who eyed the packaging hesitantly.

"What're these?" Sierra sneered at the package as she read the label out loud. "Breakfast Omelet?"

"Mine says Biscuits and Gravy." Quinn seemed to be forcing a weary smile. "Can they do that?"

"They tried. Listen, food's not perfect, but it's warm. It'll do the job for now," John said. "I have to finish cleaning the mess up here as best I can, and then try to find where Gyver was camped out. Think you two can handle being alone for a bit?"

"We've been alone before, John," Sierra said.

"I take it that means yes."

"Yes."

Adam trotted into the building, circling around the room as if he were missing something important, and then settled in by John's feet, nuzzling his hand.

"Hey, boy, all clear outside? Horses okay?"

Adam barked once and pawed at the ground.

"Good boy, Adam, good boy." John scratched him behind his ears. After Adam was satisfied, he pranced around John on his hind legs, waiting for John to feed him the jerky strip he had taken out of his pocket. "Can you help get these two kids ready, boy? I have some business to finish up." He looked at Sierra. "Check the horses, will you? Get them prepped and ready to go?" She nodded, no sass for once, and John tossed Adam the jerky.

Adam chomped down his treat and then trotted over to Quinn. He barked, jumping up, and pushing off of him with his front paws until Quinn put his food down and started wrestling with him.

"Big help you are these days, Adam."

"John."

Quinn's voice caught John by surprise. He hadn't heard Quinn speak more than a couple of times since they had gotten here, and even then it was in a weak, raspy voice. He was surprised how glad he was that the boy was sounding better.

"What is it, kid?"

"I'm sorry I almost got us all killed," Quinn said. "Twice."

"Forget about it. I'm sure that Sierra and Adam, maybe even Mazzy, are just glad that you're alive."

John took a sip of his coffee, smiled, and then went outside. He got to where he and Sage had dumped the exo suits and the Bob twins, salvaged a hydro cell, some ammo, and then prepped the bodies for the bonfire. When he was done, he stacked the gear for loading, and then followed the giant tracks left from Gyver's crew back to the garage they had camped in.

Not much here, Cam.

Guess they didn't need much.

There's some food and ammo at least. They must've been packing most of what they had with them.

There was a clunk and then a whirring from the corner. John spun around, training his rifle like a second set of eyes on the noise. A four legged robot that looked like a giant, carbon-fiber Doberman came forward from the shadows and rocked its head to the side, its limited decision-making apparatus kicking in. Two rapid electric pulse cannons raised on its shoulders and pointed straight at John's chest.

"Whoa, easy there, little fella."

The robot's pulse cannons came on line and started to spin to life.

Cam.

I'm jumping to it now.

Once inside, Cam started re-routing and changing its programming and recognition software. She rebooted it within seconds of coming into contact with it, changing its command syntax to allow her to control it. The guns rolled down to its sides, back into their concealed compartments.

That's much better.

You're welcome.

What's your read on it?

IBEC, Intelligent Bionic Equipment Carrier. Top of the line remod. The frame's a bit old, but the software, hardware, and weapons upgrades are all up to date and pretty friggin' fantastic.

Are you two going to start dating, or can we see if this thing will follow our commands?

I would never cheat on Hank, the cheapest mainframe date on earth.

John did a once-over inspection of the IBEC. The majority of Gyver's gear was still mounted on it.

Plenty of food and water, fuel cells, ammo. Score.

Maybe you're the one who needs a moment.

John let out a whistle as he ran his hands along the IBEC frame.

Maybe I do. Gyver, Gyver, Gyver, where did you get all these toys?

John finished checking the load on the IBEC and made sure that Cam had downloaded all the specs she would need from it to maintain control, and then headed back to the brewery.

*   *   *

Adam was out in the weed-clogged streets, entertaining Quinn and Sierra with a game of hide-and-go-seek when John finally made it back with the IBEC. Adam spotted them before the kids did and trotted over to meet him, jumping up and pushing off him to try and get him to join in the game. Sierra and Quinn quickly followed, gawking at the new addition to their small band of travelers. The horses stood patiently in the shade of the building, munching new grass where they could find it.

Look at Adam. All fun and games while we're always left to do the heavy lifting.

If you could jump into his mind, you'd probably be doing the same thing right now.

Never. I have my pride.

Yes, at least you have that, Cam.

As they got closer, the IBEC stopped and planted its legs firm into the ground. Its cannons whirred to life again as its head moved quickly between the twins and Adam, lighting them up with its laser targeting system.

CAM.

Damn it.

Adam jumped into a protective stance in front of the twins, as if he were going to try and block any rounds that came their way, but before it fired the IBEC's cannons stopped spinning and rolled back into its sides.

Oops. Sorry about that.

That was too close, Cam.

I didn't see its backup security mode when I was in there. It's not like you gave me time to do a full workup on it yet.

Adam was still in his protective stance in front of the kids, who were more wide-eyed with shock than excited.

I don't want that to happen again.

No worries. It won't do anything without orders from us from now on. Hopefully.

If you can't control it, I'll make you stay with it for the rest of the trip.

It won't happen again.

"What the hell?" Sierra's voice shook.

John turned his attention to the twins. "Little glitch."

"Little glitch? What if it would've blasted us to dust?"

"Mm, that's an interesting thought," John said. "But it didn't. IBEC is just having a hard time learning who its boss is," John said.

"And who's its boss?"

"Me, who else?"

"I don't feel much safer."

Sierra and Quinn crept cautiously toward the IBEC, Adam staying close beside them. They circled around it as the IBEC's head rotated to follow them.

"What is it?" Quinn said.

"An IBEC. Basically a robotic ibex that can carry a bunch of extra gear and is smart enough to follow instructions." He looked at Sierra, who glared at him. "Well, most of the time."

"Is that why he was going to shoot us?"

"I said most of the time, didn't I?"

"Are those guns?"

John grinned, thankful for the interruption. "Not just guns, kid, big fun guns."

"That is totally rad!"

Just what we need. Another boy who loves guns.

I need all the help I can get around here. A little more testosterone is more than welcome.

Oh, goodie.

John smiled big before he could catch himself. "I think they're cool too."

"If you two boys are done drooling, can you explain how those idiots got all this stuff?"

I'm with her.

Big surprise.

"Good question, but let's just hope we're lucky enough to never find out."

"Why don't we want to find out?" Sierra asked.

"Believe me, kid, we've done enough finding out to last us the rest of this crappy little adventure."

John quickly inspected the animals and the IBEC, and then checked over his traveling companions.

John pointed at Quinn. "Is he okay to ride?"

"I'm fine," Quinn said. "And I'm right here, you don't have act like I'm not."

Quinn shared a quick smile with John, and then hopped on Mazzy and started down the trail.

"Shouldn't we wait and see if Sage is coming back?"

"She's not."

Sierra started to protest, but John cut her off.

"And we have to go before Gyver's friends, if she has any, come looking for her."

John got on his horse and started off down the road, with Sierra and Adam close behind.

"Did you kill her?"

"Kill who?"

"Gyver."

John smiled wide and pictured Gyver screaming her brains out, locked tight in one of the empty brewery's giant fermenters with a water bladder, a throbbing headache, and some horrid-tasting protein bark.

"No, but she won't bother anyone else for a while."

The rest of the ride rolled away quiet and sluggish, a little too sluggish. They stopped only a couple times to grab water or to rest while Adam scouted ahead. Tree Top wasn't very far away, and barring any other incidents John figured they'd get Quinn to the healer in time. Close, but in time. The steady ride gave John and Cam time to think about what had happened with Gyver, what she had said, what Sage had said, and about their current predicament.

What're you thinking, Cam?

Besides the fact that we're screwed if Gyver's telling the truth?

Yes, besides that.

Gyver's a bottom-feeding, classless psycho, but she was talking about things that shouldn't be happening, not up here.

If someone's trying to re-form the United States, that'll break cease-fire. There's no way the Colonies will let their land go without a fight.

If she right, they're part of it.

What the hell is going on?

I'm not sure I want to know.

What do you think is so important about these kids?

I wish I knew, Cam. I really wish I knew.

Well, this Seamstress has Gyver scared to death of her, because she clammed up tight, and if she's more scare of her than of you, that's bad news.

"What's Tree Top?" Quinn asked.

John shook loose from his thoughts and looked over. Quinn coughed some wetness from his lungs and pointed a weak finger toward a large, welded sign spiked to a tree on the side of the road. Symbols were welded onto it: a horse strapped down with goods, and next to that, a pole with a snake slithering up it. A trading town with a healer. On the other side of the sign was a pair of crossed rifles and a skull, identifying the local militia that protected the town.

"It's the town we're heading to, kid."

"Is this where you're going to leave us?" Sierra asked.

"If I get lucky. First we need to get Quinn to the healer."

"I thought Sage healed him. I mean, he still looks a little sick, but he's way better than what he was."

"She just put a bandage on a dike, kid. His lung infection will get worse again, and when that happens we won't be able to get him back."

Sierra looked over at Quinn, shoulders sunk, head hanging forward, eyes glued on the back of Mazzy's head. Quinn clicked his tongue and hurried her up the road away from them, following the road that led into Tree Top. Sierra leaned back and glared at John, something he was getting real used to.

"Thanks for nothing, John," she said. "You should have told us he was going to get sicker."

He knew by the look on her face that any ground he'd gained with her had been lost. He heard a muttered phrase that sounded like it ended in "jerk".

"What'd you say?"

"I said, you should have told us sooner. We have a right to know."

"No, what else did you say?"

Sierra rolled her eyes and patted the side of Betsy's neck and whispered into her ear. They clopped after Quinn and Mazzy, John watching as they shrunk toward the last bend in the dirt trail and onto the main road into the town.

Did she say I was a jerk?

Well, can you blame her?

What? So I shouldn't have said anything.

I'm pretty sure she figured it out already. Quinn's as white again as the ring around Mazzy's eyes.

I'm surprised he's done so well this far. Jane will know what to do.

You did a good thing here, John.

Tell me that when I'm back at home with my feet up by the fire.

Can we get an upgrade for Hank while we're here? Maybe trade him for, like, a Watson?

The way you've been skipping, I might have to.

That's harsh.

"IBEC, go to the tree line, camouflage, and wait," John said.

The IBEC followed John's orders, taking off fast and quiet into the woods. John turned Shadow around and scanned the blue sky-line, following the horizon as it met with the tops of the mountains and forests surrounding the town. He looked back to the road and clenched his jaw, concentrating on the twins and Adam clopping away toward Tree Top.

You okay, John?

I'll be just fine soon enough.

*   *   *

Tree Top was one of the more sophisticated trading towns in the West, and had grown from just a boomtown into one of the most thriving economies in the Free. Tree Top even came complete with thugs who had a friendly relationship with the sheriff, a merchant council that had a company of militia on speed dial, the only seamstress for a hundred miles, and, for added culture, a renowned mead maker.

The town square was made up of two- and three-story brick buildings, with smaller houses and shops shooting off onto circling side streets. Adjacent street blocks had stacks of wooden houses, more shops in smaller brick buildings, street vendors, and even a few stables. It was a mix of twenty-first century meets the Wild, Wild West.

All manner of transportation peppered the narrow streets: street cars, electric solar cars, kinetic pedal cars, bicycles, hydro-cell motorcycles, horses, carriages, stagecoaches. There was even a large hangar for a hovership, which was occupied at the moment by an old refitted war ship with what looked like circus equipment being unloaded from it.

Further clogging the streets were people busying themselves with mules, goats, cows, pigs, chickens, robotic pack mules similar to IBECs, but much more crude, and robot servants.

Wild West tech.

I'm home.

Don't get too cozy on me, Cam.

Are you really going to get me a Watson main?
If we can find one. You sure as hell earned it.
If I could breathe, I'd be hyperventilating right now.
Just try not to fry our brains, will ya?
Watson, here I come.

They rode through the crudely bricked street and past the bizarre mix of cyber world meets Hobbiton. Sierra and Quinn were wide-eyed with excitement, taking in the modern city as if they had never seen anything as great as Tree Top before.

The technology citizens in Tree Top had experienced in the last couple years had created an odd mixture like something out of a science fiction-Western novel: men and women in handmade clothing and boots, with a variety of baseball caps, cowboy hats, wide-brimmed women's hats, stocking caps, wool caps, cyber caps, all sorts of caps. Cotton T-shirts, button-up long-sleeve shirts, sweaters, patchwork britches, blouses, dresses, even kilts, exo suits, and power stilts. Almost everyone wore a small computer on their wrist, behind their ears, or around their heads disguised as spectacles.

Each building and house had a perfectly cubed, shiny black box on top that connected citizens of the town together on their own private network via an uplink to a contracted satellite orbiting far above the earth. Networks such as these were still a luxury and were found mostly in the wealthier parts of the colonies, or in merchant towns like Tree Top.

Quinn pointed to a large metal building outside the town. It was a long, rectangular structure with bay doors, topped with a black-domed roof. A metal link fence, tall enough to keep a person on stilts out, ran along the perimeter of the building, which had watchtowers on all four corners. A single improved road ran from the main gate in the fence and down to meet the town.

Quinn asked about the compound, and John explained it was an armory for the militia. There was a company of hired soldiers stationed there in case of an attack, but otherwise they kept to themselves, leaving most of the town's business to the sheriff's office, and only responding if there was something bad like a raid.

"Where are we going?" Sierra asked.

"I'm going over there, the last brick building at the end of the street." An ornate sign, "Trowley's Fabrics, Alterations, Repairs, and Seamstress Work," was painted on the side of the three-story building. "After I take you and your brother over here."

John steered them toward a white brick building that shone brilliant in the sunlight. It had blue, red, and green sticks with snakes that changed colors as they slithered up the emblazoned sign hanging over the front door.

"What's this place?" Quinn asked.

"It's a healing center. They'll have more medicine here, phages, herbs, and electrolyte fluid. They'll have you feeling better in no time." John scanned him from head to toe. "From the looks of things, we're getting here just in time."

John got off his horse, helped Quinn slide off Mazzy, and carried him to the door. He looked over his shoulder to Sierra before going inside.

"Stay."

"Why am I staying?"

"Because I'm taking Quinn inside, and you and Adam are staying with the horses."

"Oh, goodie."

"I knew you'd like that."

After a few minutes John came back out and sat next to Sierra on the bench right outside the door, where she was torturing Adam with her normal routine of affectionate fingers combing through his glossy coat.

"He pegged you and your brother pretty fast."

"It's not very hard to figure out that if you're super nice and protective, a kid is going to have a soft spot for you."

"That makes me safe."

Sierra smiled and John took that as a good sign that she wasn't hating him as much, at least not at this current juncture.

"Healer's name is Jane," he said. "She's good at what she does, best in these parts. Her and Sage worked together for a while too, so she'll have an idea of what treatment Quinn got already."

"We're just supposed to leave Quinn here with this Jane?"

"She'll take good care of him, Sierra."

"Can you promise me that?"

John nudged her with his elbow and looked her straight in her eyes. "Yes, I can. Not everyone is a killer like the company you and your brother attract."

"Like we attract? What about you and that Gyver?"

Mm, she does have a point.

Watson, Cam.

You're right. She's dead wrong.

"Look," John said. "This is a good place, and to say Jane's the best is an understatement. She's a damn good friend."

"Not an enemy?"

"Not an enemy."

Sierra looked up at him, her eyes partially hidden behind strands of scarecrow hair and heavy with exhaustion.

"I'm just tired and worried," she said. "The last few days have really sucked."

"Tell me about it. Come on, let's go see if they have your brother settled."

The hinges on the white metal door squeaked as John opened it and let Sierra in. A warm breeze followed them into the high-ceilinged entrance, making crayon-drawn pictures flutter against the bulletin board on the wall. It was a far cry from the facilities that John had been treated in before Day One, but in these parts this was the lap of luxury. Their feet clopped across the bare wooden floor as they made their way to check-in.

Now we can get a closer look at her remod.

Pretty sophisticated stuff in here, John. I bet you wouldn't be able to find hospital tech like this outside New Fairhaven.

John let out a snort. Monks.

He ran his hand along a wood and metal counter that stuck out from the wall on the left, covered with stacks of tablets, folders, and papers, and a small holo computer. The holo screen was up, and Jane, a thin, raven-haired woman, was flipping an image of a man around and around with her long, gentle fingers, mumbling to herself and ignoring her new guests. Behind the counter were racks of comp tablets, baskets of jars filled with gel-like liquids, and dried herbs. A small sitting room was adjacent to them, and past them, down the hall toward the back of the building, was another doorway.

John took a deep breath in through his nose, and then let it out slow. For the first time in days he felt he could let down his guard. He felt safe; the sight of Jane and this building radiated comfortable ease that he felt long overdue for. Jane collapsed the holo screen with a flick of her finger and then came over to the counter to greet them.

"Hello, John," Jane said.

Even in this almost magically relaxing environment, Sierra watched Jane with narrow, cautious eyes until Jane smiled at her and winked, sending her cheeks into an uncontrolled full-blown grin.

"Yes, young lady, to answer the question that was written all over your face, you can trust a good old gal like me. Even though I'm friends with a grunt like John here," Jane said. "I know he can be rough around the edges at times, but his heart is good."

"Is my brother okay, ma'am?"

"He is. You can see him for a short time if you'd like."

She looked up at John, her eyes wide. "Can we?"

John looked back at her, feigning confusion. "What're you looking at me for? I'm not your keeper. Go see the runt if you want."

"If you will, John," Jane said, waving them toward the sitting room. "I'll take a peek and see if Quinn's tucked in yet."

"Don't worry about us, Jane. We'll make ourselves at home." John pointed to a covered jar full of bite sized biscuits on a table in the sitting room. "You might have to send for some more biscuits after we're gone, though."

"Watch yourself, John. You're not getting younger and those biscuits are only going to get harder to get rid of after you eat them."

"These biscuits don't stand a chance against my high metabolism."

Jane rolled her eyes and disappeared into the hallway, her footsteps creaking up a set of stairs hidden around the corner. Sierra turned and sneered at John.

"What? Why are you looking at me like that?"

"You're acting like a kid hanging out at Grandma's house after school."

"That's not weird. Go wait on the couch with Adam, I'll grab us some biscuits."

Remember, don't eat the purple ones.

I won't make that mistake again.

It was funny though.

For who?

Me.

*   *   *

When Jane finally came back down, the trio had fallen asleep, Sierra on the couch with Adam below her on the floor, and John in the lounge chair, a mostly empty tray of annihilated biscuit crumbs in front of them on the coffee table.

"Wake up. Your weary traveler wants to see his companions."

The three stirred awake. John leaned forward and wiped some crumbs off his chest. Sierra stood, stretching, and then tried to untangle the mess of hair in her face. Adam was already up, sniffing Jane's hand for hidden treats.

"Do try to keep close, young lady." Jane turned and went down the hall to the stairs she had used earlier. Sierra and Adam looked at John.

"What? Go already," he said.

You're not going?

They need some space, and I need some air.

John waited until he saw the last of Adam's tail round the corner, and then went outside to do a quick sweep around the perimeter of the building.

You're smiling again, John.

It's a nervous twitch.

Admit it. You like them, and I think you even enjoy being here with them.

You're right, Cam. I like being here. I like being here to get rid of them.

Tell yourself whatever you have to.
Are we clear out here, Cam?
As far as I can tell, the only threat around us is your denial.
Thanks for your ongoing professionalism, Cam.

* * *

Adam barked and ran to Quinn when they got to his room, planting his front paws up on the bed and stretching his neck out so he could lick Quinn's face.

"Hold on, Adam," Quinn said. "Don't drown me in your drool right after I barely survived the river."

"Quinn! You look so much better already." Sierra rushed over and hugged him.

"All right, you two, at least let the boy breathe. He's had a rough go at it and he's bound to be sore," Jane said. "We've given him some antibiotics, fluid, and some new phages, but he has a long ways to go yet. He needs food, hydration, and most of all, rest."

"I'm okay, miss. I'm just tired," Quinn said. "Who's the lady, Sis?"

"*The lady* is Jane, and I'm the healer here."

"How'd I get here?"

"John brought you here as soon as he got to town, and he was right to," Jane said. "Saved your life."

"See, Sierra, I told you he was one of the good guys."

"Whatever, Q. You could find the best in anybody, even the Bob twins."

"Well, they weren't that smart, and they were only following orders."

"See, Q? They tried to kill us, and they were smart enough to use those exo-armor suits to do it, but you still make excuses for them."

"I remember, Sierra. I also remember John saving us."

"He's still an asshole."

"Now that's exactly what I'm talking about, young lady," Jane said, looking at Adam and Sierra. "Last thing this boy needs is you two getting him worked up. Now run along and let your brother get some rest."

She ushered Sierra and Adam out of the room, ignoring Sierra's protests.

"But who's going to stay here with him?"

"What exactly do you think my job is, dear?" Jane responded. "You and Adam can wait down in the lobby for John. There's a cocoa machine down there, and you can help yourself to the fresh biscuits on the counter."

Jane waited until Sierra and Adam were on their way, then closed the door and turned back to Quinn.

"He's really not a bad guy," Quinn said to Jane.

"You're correct, Quinn. He's not a bad guy at all; he's most absolutely one of the good guys."

"Do you know much about him?"

"I probably know more than he thinks. He's been through a lot after Day One, like the rest of us, but he had already been through worse before that."

"Was he a soldier?"

"You could say that."

"I like him."

Jane smiled, and Quinn's face flushed red.

"That makes two of us; three, if you count Adam. Now you rest. I'll be back to check on you in a bit."

"Thank you, Jane."

"You're very welcome, young sir."

Jane left the room and headed downstairs. Sierra was already asleep again on the couch in the waiting area, a half-cup of warm cocoa and a partially eaten biscuit on the coffee table next to her. John stood in the entryway, leaning on the counter with a cup of coffee, watching the girl and the dog, remembering, trying not to let himself get lost.

* * *

They're so much easier to like when they're asleep.

Just a little bit longer, Cam.

It's kind of sad, don't you think?
Like getting rid of a bee sting.
Not quite what I was thinking.
But it's what needs to happen, Cam.
Doesn't mean I need to like it.

"Never figured you'd try the family thing again, John," Jane said.

"I've heard that a lot lately."

"You saw Sage?"

"Yeah, swift-footed as always."

"That's Sage for you. Was she doing okay?"

John looked away from Sierra's curled-up form on the couch and straight at Jane.

"If you call being held captive by Gyver and two retarded exo-twins okay, then yes, she's doing just fine."

"Oh, boy, what's she gotten herself into this time?"

"Nothing that I didn't have to help her out of again."

John scanned the room from corner to corner, resting his gaze on Sierra for second, and then looked back at Jane.

"Something on your mind, John?"

"No, just tired is all. We okay here, Jane?"

"As always."

"I have a few questions that might sound odd to you."

Jane wandered back behind her counter and busied herself with organizing the comp tablets that were scattered there. "About Quinn? I'm sure he'll be fine, John. You did right by that boy bringing him here straight away."

John leaned onto the counter facing her. "No, not that. I'm glad the boy's going to be okay and all. Thanks, by the way."

She bowed her head, again studying him with her gentle eyes. "Always at your service, John. You know that."

"This is gonna sound stupid."

"Try me."

John ran his fingers through his hair and looked around the room, scanning the nooks and corners with his eyes. "Do you know anything about the United States having loyalist groups recruiting out here?"

"The United States. Now that's something that I haven't thought about in a long time. Why do you ask?"

"No reason really, just something Gyver said."

"Well, I don't think anyone out here would be interested in selling what we have to a bunch of militaristic bastards like that."

"Yeah, you're right. Probably just nonsense."

John gulped down the rest of his biscuit, and smiled, cheek half full as he walked over and gave Jane a hug.

"It took you long enough, you big sap."

"My mind gets slow when I get too tired. I'm not used to this adventure shit anymore, and Cam's not on her game like she used to be."

Hey.

Tell me it's not true.

Well, I will be after I get my Watson.

"Kids always did give you a run for your money," Jane said.

"Kids and women."

"I'm sorry about Sage, John. I know you two have had a rough go at it."

"You could say that. I still don't know how she ended up locked up by Gyver."

"I can't imagine it was easy for Gyver to get her. You said she had two men with exo armor."

"Yeah, twins. Bob and Zack," John said. "They were too dumb to have gone through any of the militias or have any prior service. I can't imagine anyone in their right mind letting them handle that kind of equipment."

"Well, a thiever like Gyver probably wouldn't have been able to attract many people to work for her. Those two were probably the best she could get."

"She had to have a sponsor or an employer. She was way too cocky to be acting on her own."

"Crap, John, what did you guys run into out there? And how did you end up with these two kids?"

John took a deep breath and ran through the series of events in his head, a sudden exhaustion sweeping over him.

"It's been a long three days, Jane."

"It looks like it."

"Do you know if Oliver's in?"

"He was with the supply group on the stage to Wenatchee."

"Do you know when the stage gets back?"

"Should be here first thing in the morning." She smiled and winked at John. "I'm sure Oliver will be excited to see you, but he'll be disappointed that you only have kids and no wine."

"I'm full of disappointment these days." He nodded his head over at Sierra and Adam. "Think you can keep an eye on these three while I go rattle some cages?"

"They're welcome here as long as they need to be. That means you too, John."

"Thanks, Jane."

John shook Sierra awake. She rubbed her eyes and sat up, still half asleep.

"Here." He handed her a microbit.

"What's this for?"

"In case you need anything while I'm gone."

Sierra started closing her eyes and relaxing her head back to her comfy spot on the couch. John smiled and then shook her again.

"I'll be back soon. Please try to stay out of trouble."

"Fine, fine, fine." She sat up and yawned, stretching her arms high above her head. "Where are you going?"

"I've got some business with an old friend," John said. "And I have to see my tailor about a new shirt."

Then we can go get my upgrades, right?

Yes, Cam. After that we can go and get your Watson.

"Your tailor?"

"Well, everyone's tailor. She's the only one in town."

"You're a dork."

"And you're swell."

Sierra rolled her eyes. "Whatever that means."

Adam came over and licked John's hand, sniffing for treats as always. Not finding anything, he went and lay by the couch next to Sierra.

Have you ever thought of changing your tactics?

No. Why?

Just wondering.

TEN

Mrs. Trowley

THE BELL HANGING OVER the door to Mrs. Trowley's seamstress shop jingled as John walked through it. Finely tailored shirts, coats, dresses, skirts, bags, hats, and a multitude of fabrics lined the shop's racks and shelves, giving the store an abstract, cluttered appearance. A small wooden counter with an old manual cash register on it separated the shop from the back room. John scanned the store and smiled when he saw the older lady peering out at him from behind a shiny chrome sewing machine.

"John. Bless me, is that you, young man?"

"I wouldn't say young, Mrs. Trowley."

She got up from behind her workbench and came through the swinging doors, arms outstretched to give John a hug.

"I missed you too, ma'am."

"I guess everyone around here is right. I do make my clothes too damn good. It's been years since you've been in here."

John poked his finger through the hole in his muddied shirt and smiled at how long ago it seemed from the first time he had noticed the hole.

"I was hoping for a little more than a new shirt this go around, Mrs. Trowley."

"More? Maybe you're hoping to find someone with information about Sage's troubles?"

"How'd you know that?"

"I always know what's going on with my clients around here."

"Damn, Mrs. Trowley, I wish we would've had someone like you in our intel section when my team was live."

"Balance to the universe, John, balance to the universe," Mrs. Trowley said. "You can't have everything."

"I'll settle for what you know."

"Sage was through here this morning." Mrs. Trowley reached below the counter and pulled out a square package wrapped in brown waxed paper. "Had me whip this up for you. Guess she figured you were due for a new shirt."

"It was the least she could do. Did she say anything else?"

"Just that she was stuck with that nasty bitch Gyver for a few days and was worried she'd never be able to wash the stink off her."

"What'd you know about Gyver?"

"I heard she was down at Ivan's a few months back throwing credits around."

"Ivan's, huh?"

"Probably a good place to start."

"Thanks, Mrs. Trowley."

"Better give us another hug," she said. "Never know when I might see you again."

John walked over and gave her another tight hug. She slipped a piece of paper into his pocket and gave him a wink.

"Just don't ruin that shirt as soon as you put it on. My fabric doesn't come cheap, you know."

"I wouldn't dare."

John headed out the door with another jingle. When he got around the corner, he pulled the note Mrs. Trowley had given him out of his pocket. There was a single name inscribed in Mrs. Trowley's perfect cursive handwriting.

Victor

Well, the reruns persist. I wish it would've been Dr. Wilcox. I'm really starting to hate this trip, Cam.

Eleven

Circus

John walked in through the healing house doors and saw Sierra watching an old movie on the holo screen from the lounge chair in the sitting room. She stuffed one more chocolate in her mouth from the bag of chocolates she held as she looked up at John, eyes wide over chipmunk cheeks.

"Where'd you go?" she asked around the chocolate.

"None of your business."

"What's in the package?"

"Also none of your business. Where'd you get the chocolates?"

Sierra smiled. "None of your business."

John clutched at his heart, and mimed a sad face. "Oh, that hurts, really stings. I'm not sure I'm going to get over that one." He shook his head at her and sat down, snatching a chocolate out of the bag and plopping it in his mouth.

"Whatever," Sierra said, but she grinned at him. "What do we do now? When do we meet this Oliver?"

"Questions, always with the questions." He moved the chocolate around in his mouth. "Mm, limone?

"Yeah, good, right?"

"It's alright."

"Are you afraid of questions?"

You're sighing again, John.

Is it too much oxygen for you?

Questions, always with the questions.

Funny, Cam.

"Oliver won't be back until tomorrow morning. He went out on a trade run."

"So what now, master planner?"

John chuckled to himself.

Slow, deep breaths, John, slow, deep breaths.

Sierra glared at him. "Are you talking to me?"

"What? I didn't say anything."

"Okay, whatever, weirdo."

"Mm, if you're joking, I'm missing the punch line. So let's stick to normal conversations for the time being."

"So what's the plan, crazy-talks-to-himself-out-loud person?"

"I was not talking to myself. In fact, I actually didn't say anything to anyone." John tensed his jaw and steadied himself. "Look, we're staying in town tonight. I still have a few cages to rattle and then I need to see a guy about some special equipment. Do you think you can handle staying here for a bit?"

"Of course." She smiled wide, showing off her toothy mouth, and batted her eyes. "I'm not quite sure why we'd ever have to leave."

He got down nose to nose with Adam and looked him straight in the eyes.

"I know it's going to be hard to convince you, boy, but I need you to stay here with them, okay?"

Adam sat up on his haunches and barked.

"You." John turned to Sierra. "Stay here and keep Quinn company while I take care of a few things, okay?"

"Can we go with you?"

"Not a chance."

"Big surprise."

"Do you have to make everything so difficult?"

"For you, *John*? Yes." She smiled another over-exaggerated smile. "Just take nice, slow, deep breaths."

That creepy?

Yes, Cam, that is very creepy.

Is she a—

Yes, Cam, she is.

"Here, weirdo." He tossed her the bag he was holding. "Keep this with you."

Sierra caught the brown bag that was holding John's shirt and put it in her satchel.

"Whatever."

She waved to John and popped another chocolate in her mouth as she turned back to her movie.

She only gets that reaction out of you because she reminds you of someone.

No, Cam, she doesn't.

Well, she reminds me of him. They both do.

Let's not talk about it anymore.

Okay, but only if we can go get my Watson now.

Not yet, Cam. Victor first.

Damn.

* * *

After getting bored with reruns Sierra checked in at the healer's main desk. Jane had her nose in a book and hadn't seem to notice her as she walked past the entryway. As she got closer to Jane, she started feeling more calm, comfortable, content even with their situation. It was much like what she had felt on her first visit to the healing house, but more visceral this time. In the core of her body she felt as if everything happening were right as rain. She caught herself forgetting why she and Quinn were even there. She shook it off, wondering whether it was the lack of sleep getting to her, and checked out Jane, who still hadn't bothered to look over at her.

Who is this woman taking care of my brother?

She could tell that Jane was older, and not just from the few silver streaks in her raven hair. It was the way she carried herself, the deepness in her dark brown eyes.

There're stories to be told in those eyes.

As she approached the counter, she felt even more at ease, and even more curious. She scanned Jane with her eyes. It seemed impossible for her to guess the healer's age or where she might have come from. Her skin was ageless, smooth milk chocolate, and without blemish. She moved with the grace of someone in her thirties, but she was older than John, so she had to be at least forty.

Jeez, she looks good. I wonder who she was before Day One. Her smile alone could have gotten her through the whole thing. Probably could have had anyone doing anything she wanted for her.

Jane put her book down and turned so she could greet Sierra and Adam with her enchanting smile.

I wouldn't say they'd do anything for me, dear.

Sierra stared at Jane, eyes frozen open, too startled to move. She had heard Jane, but hadn't seen her talk. She shook her head, trying to make sure she wasn't just too tired and imagining things.

"I'm sorry, what'd you say, ma'am?"

"Oh, nothing dear, don't you fret about it."

"Uh, okay. But did you … was I talking out loud to myself?"

"No, of course not, young lady," Jane said. "I'm surprised to see you. Did you get bored with the vid box? "

"Yeah, I think we both were." Adam was still at her side and had snuck his head under her hand for her to rub.

"Of course. Loyal Adam, as always. I suppose you both have something you'd like to check on."

Sierra shook her head as if she were trying to get weeds out of her hair. "Yeah, can we go and see my brother?"

"I was just getting ready to do that myself. I can take you right to him."

Jane came around the counter with the same grace Sierra remembered from earlier, but this time she lurched, as if her leg had gotten caught on something, and she almost fell. She tried to move it forward, but she was stuck. She lost her balance again for a split second and Sierra rushed to help her.

"Are you okay?"

Jane waved Sierra off and then thumped her leg. It made a breath-like sound, and then loosened enough to move. She took a step forward and brought her knee up to her chest and back down a couple times, a small functions check. "I'm fine, just fine. Right leg just freezes up sometimes."

"You have a cyber leg?"

"Pretty cool, huh? Got this the last time the loyalists came here and tried to turn this town into their headquarters for new U.S. colonies this side of the mountains. We ran them right out of Tree Top, and right out of the Free, but it cost us."

"Oh, I didn't notice it before. I'm sorry."

"It's not a worry, girl. Others lost more than just a leg, so I count myself fortunate. I mean, I still have my looks." She curled her lips into a sultry smile and ran her hand through her hair, flipping the silver strands away from her beautifully sculpted jaw line. Sierra snorted out a chuckle, then blushed. Jane gave her a wink and gestured to the staircase. "Now come on, let's go see that brother of yours."

Sierra followed Jane up the stairs to the ward floor and then down the hallway to Quinn's room. Her brother was still asleep, but his color was more caramel. More like what she was used to seeing. Much better than the wet white T-shirt look that he'd been wearing since the river. Jane walked over, took Quinn's temperature, and laid a soft hand on his forehead as he stirred.

"It's okay, Quinn, you're doing much better," Jane said. "You're at the healing house in Tree Top."

Jane glanced over the bed at Sierra. "His memory is still a little foggy. We've been reminding him of where he is every time we wake him up. It's nothing to worry about. I'm sure it will come back to him as he gets better."

"Where's my sister?"

"I'm right here, Q. I'm right here with Adam."

Adam pushed past both of them and jumped up onto the bed with Quinn, pawing the blankets into a padded nest beside him. He thumped his body down, as if he had just finished some sort of taxing workout, and let his head rest on the boy's chest. Quinn stuck his nose into Adam's neck and started scratching along the muscles there.

"Hey, bubba. I missed you too."

Jane glared at Adam and shook her head. "Dogs. Adam, you know better than to come in here and get up on the bed like that." She turned back to face Sierra, a reassuring smile making lines in her ageless cheeks. "Your brother's temperature is coming down, still high, but it's heading in the right direction. Sage did a good job by him, and he'll be just fine because of it. A little worse for wear the next day or two, but fine."

Guess it is good luck that John got us here.

"You're right, young lady. John got your brother here just in time."

Sierra snapped her head toward Jane, gawking. Jane smiled and gave her a wink.

You're not crazy, dear.

What's happening?

This is not the place for explanation, Sierra; that is for Oliver. This is the place to forget your worries.

Sierra was about to say something, but just as quickly as the thought had come to her, it left. She knew she and Jane had been talking about something, but what little memory of it there'd been had disappeared.

Jane stretched her mind out into the streets of Tree Top, careful to filter the coming conversation away from Sierra, her thoughts like tendrils searching for her cohort. Oliver, are you close? Are you there?

Jane, I'm here.

This is not as easy as you said it would be. A little help would be nice. Do you have them?

They are here, yes. Where are you?

I just arrived.

Good.

"Are you okay, Sis?" Quinn asked. "Maybe you need to get in bed for a while and let Ms. Jane take care of you."

"What? No, no, I don't. I feel fine. I think—I'm just tired, Q, too tired, that's all."

"Well, I can't blame you if you are," Jane said. "From what I can tell, you haven't had a good night's sleep or anything decent to eat in days, not one of you. Now where were we?"

"Is it okay if Adam stays up here, ma'am? Makes me feel better."

Jane looked reproachfully at them both. "Well, I'd be lying if I said I'd be able to get him down now anyway. He'll be fine there for a bit, but you need your rest, Quinn, so stay in bed. Your sister can come and fetch me if you need anything. I've my rounds, but I'll be back to check on you for dinner, okay?"

"Thanks, ma'am."

"Oh, boy, you two, that's quite enough with the *ma'am* business. My name is Jane and that's more than fine to use."

Jane left, heading down the hall. They were quiet for a minute as Quinn let Adam lick his face, seeming lost in thought. Satisfied with his greeting from Adam and his current surroundings, he turned to Sierra.

"Where's John?"

"Don't worry about him. I'm sure he's off figuring out ways to get rid of us if this Oliver guy doesn't want us."

"Oh. I was hoping to see him and thank him."

"Again? You don't need to thank him, Q. We wouldn't even be here if it wasn't for that jerk."

Adam whimpered and looked up at Quinn.

"John?"

"Yeah, *John*," Sierra said.

"Sierra, I'd be dead if it wasn't for John." Quinn said. Adam barked, and Quinn went back to scratching him on his neck. "You're right, boy, we might all have been dead if it wasn't for him."

Sierra turned in her chair and looked out the window at the slowly descending sun making a collage of dancing colors in the sky.

"Whatever. Q. I just want to be done."

"Done?"

"Yes, done. Done with traveling, done with getting shuffled around. Done with lies. Done with everything. I'm just done."

"I get it, you're done."

"Aren't you tired, Q? Aren't you sick of bouncing around?"

"It'll be okay, Sis, you'll see. This'll all get better."

"Maybe you're right. Maybe I'm just tired, Q. I need to sleep, that's all."

"Jeez, Sierra, you're starting to worry me, and I'm the one that's sick."

"I...do you ever feel like you're thinking something, but you're actually saying it out loud? Or that someone else is saying something, but they really didn't say anything?"

"No."

"Me either. Just ignore me, Q. I'm getting delirious."

As Sierra turned away from the window, she spotted the backpack she had set down by Quinn's bed, and smiled.

"I almost forgot, I got something for us."

"Nice change of subject, Sis."

"Just wait, Q, you're going to love this."

She picked up her pack and opened it, pulling out her cloth bag of chocolates. She took one that had a pale yellow flower on top and handed it to him.

"Where did you get these?"

"The chocolate shop. I didn't think John would mind."

"He'd probably say we earned them, even."

"Yeah, right."

They high-fived each other and stuffed down a chocolate.

*   *   *

When Jane came back into the room with a tray for dinner, Quinn and Sierra were leaning on the windowsill, staring out the open window and jabbering into the dusk, not caring that someone had just entered. Adam perked his ears, saw it was Jane, yawned, and put his head back in its position on the floor next to the bed. Jane scanned the room. Pillows were on the floor, along with the bed sheets and blankets. The footstools were scattered and turned over, and on the back of one of the chairs was an empty, chocolate-stained white bag.

"What do you think it is?" Quinn asked Sierra.

"I don't know, but it looks awesome."

Jane brought the tray of sandwich halves and milk over to a wheeled table, where she set it down with a small clang. Still not getting their attention, she coughed loudly, and they turned around.

"Hi, Jane." Sierra giggled and held out a partially melted chocolate. "Do you want a chocolate?"

Jane lifted her eyebrow at Sierra, and then studied the mangled chocolate. "Now where did you get those?"

"She got them from a chocolate shop when she was waiting for John," Quinn said.

Sierra punched him in his arm.

"Quinn, jeez."

"All right, that's quite enough, you two. You're still sick, Quinn, and you'd both do well to remember that. Now, I hope you haven't spoiled your appetites. It's not much, but the bread's fresh and so is the milk." She wheeled the table over to the end of the bed and looked down at Adam, eyes full of playful reproach. "I thought you were supposed to keep an eye on them."

Adam stretched his head up high, mouth open wide in a yawn, and rolled over, cueing anyone near him that it was time to start rubbing his chest. Quinn and Sierra both took up the task dutifully.

"But you're such a good boy, aren't you, Adam?" Sierra said.

"Oh, boy, he sure has you two figured out, doesn't he?" Jane said. "All right, all three of you over to eat your supper. It's going to be late soon, and you'll want to be in bed before the circus starts, or you won't be able to sleep all night."

"Circus?"

"There's a traveling circus that comes through town once a year or so. They arrived this morning. Whole town gets pretty festive, so it'll be loud tonight, won't quiet down until well after midnight."

"What's a circus?"

Jane cocked her head back. "You two don't know what a circus is?"

Sierra and Quinn both shook their heads.

"If you were feeling better, I'd have John take you down there," Jane said. "Some circuses aren't worth the price of admission; nothing but a few guys in tights juggling empty broken bottles and blowing fire out their mouths. I know this group though, and it's the real deal."

She looked at Quinn and Sierra, wondering whether she should go on. She tried to hold her tongue for a second, but couldn't resist. Even Adam was looking at her wide-eyed in anticipation of her telling them a circus story.

"Oh, all right then, sit down and I'll tell you about it while you eat."

Sierra and Quinn sat at the bedside table to eat their small meal, while Adam sat at their feet waiting for them to drop generous portions of food to him. Jane, taking advantage of their rare silence, got out of her chair and raised her arms out in front of her. Her voice boomed into the room like a ring announcer's.

"Barnacle and Seaweed Brothers' Famous North American Circus!"

Gauging her audience, and finding them electrified with anticipation, she started using her body to mimic the movements of things as she described them. She made a funny face and walked goofy like a clown, and then flung herself across the room, dancing like a ballerina.

"Clowns that juggle swords and flaming rings of metal while they blow balloon animals and tell jokes. Ballerina acrobats that swing from the rafters and dive two hundred feet while another one swings in and grabs them just seconds before they hit the floor." She swooped over a footstool. Sierra and Quinn roared with laughter and tried to stifle Adam, who had started barking.

Stopping for a moment, Jane swooped her hands downward to quiet the room, and then raised her finger to her lips, her eyes widening. "We don't want to wake my other patients—or the dead."

Sierra and Quinn giggled much more quietly this time, feeding into her story telling. She walked over to Quinn and reached behind his ear, producing a bright silver bit from it and whispering. "Cunning magicians that can conjure spirits from the other world and saw a woman in half and put her back together again." She flexed her muscles and gritted her teeth. "Games of strength and wit, so challenging that only the brave dare try them."

Gripping her hands together as if she were holding a sword, Jane swung a wide arc in the air, slicing at invisible enemies. "Mighty warriors from all corners of the world wage war in the unimaginably terrifying, horrific, carnage-filled *cage of doom*."

She switched in mid stride, hunched her shoulders up, and put her arms out wide. She puffed up her chest, stood on her tiptoes, and then growled ferociously.

"And you can't miss the demon of the Cascades, the Sasquatch killer, the bane of the Western colonies, *the Monster Grizzly Bear!*"

Adam got up on his hind legs, and growled from deep within his chest. Sierra and Quinn fell back onto the bed with laughter and acted like grizzly bears attacking each other, and then going after Adam. Jane relaxed and straightened to a normal posture, with a wide smile for the three travelers.

"Oh, now, Adam, no need to get scared," she said. "I'm sure Sierra and Quinn will keep you safe while you're here."

Sierra and Quinn attacked him with more hugs, scratching him behind his ears and across his shoulders.

"Yeah, don't worry, boy. We'll protect you from the Monster Grizzly," Quinn said.

"Can you take us to the circus, Jane?" Sierra asked.

"You know I can't, child. I've sick folk to tend to here, and your brother is in no shape for that kind of adventure tonight. It'll have to wait until next time, I'm afraid."

"But I feel fine, Jane," Quinn said. "I could go and Sierra and Adam can look after me."

Adam jumped off the bed and went over to Jane, nudging and licking her hand.

"No, I'm afraid I just can't allow it. Not even with all your prodding, Adam. You may be feeling better, young man, but that does not mean you are well. Even if you were, nightlife in Tree Top is no place for poorly escorted children. I'm sorry, but you will have to stay here."

Jane rounded up the dirty plates, straightened up the room, and then gave Quinn a once-over before heading for the door.

"Have you been to the circus, Jane?" Sierra asked.

"Oh, yes, dear, but it's been years since I last went. Now, you two get some rest; you'll both need it."

She turned to look at Adam and then threw a scrap of jerky to him from her pocket.

"Don't let them out of your sight, boy," she said as she walked out the door.

Sierra and Quinn raced back to the window. It was dark out, and the giant tent that was set up for the circus danced with lights, making the new circle at the end of town glow like a magical fire.

"Do you think they really have a grizzly bear?"

"I bet they have more than that," Sierra said. "Jane said she hadn't been there in years. They have all sorts of things she hasn't seen."

"I wish we could go," Quinn said.

Sierra narrowed her eyes and smiled. "Who's going to stop us?"

TWELVE

Victor

JOHN LEFT THE HEALING HOUSE and headed to the best place in Tree Top to get info, and as luck would have it, the best place to find the biggest sleazeball in town: Victor.

The tall, metal hangar stood alone on a street of broken-down, abandoned buildings. Close enough to walk to, but far enough away from the town center that the more reputable places of Tree Top could forget about it, making it the one place where the necessary evils in town could gather and close their other-than-legal deals. An old neon sign over the large wooden door blinked on and off, spelling out "The Whistle."

Ugh, I hate this place.

We shouldn't be here too long, Cam.

Don't forget to stay away from Ivan's drinks. Remember what happened last time.

I wish I didn't. Do you think Ivan's forgotten by now?

Not a chance.

John opened the door and went inside. The scruffy, square-jawed bartender drying beer steins behind the counter looked more like a chunk chiseled out of a brick wall than a normal man. He turned toward the door as the light from the opening burnt its way into the dimly lit building. He nodded his head at John, who nodded back and headed over to the bar.

"What the hell you doing here?" the bartender asked.

"Good to see you too, Ivan. Place looks nice. Have you re-decorated or something?"

"Fuck you."

"Chocolate milk, one piece of ice, please," John said without skipping a beat.

"Find someplace else for milk."

"Come on, Ivan. I'm not in the mood to hash out old hard feelings."

"You broke my nose. Now I can barely get a date."

"I don't think your crooked nose has anything to do with it."

Ivan poured a pint glass full of chocolate milk and slid it over to John.

"Where's the ice?"

"No ice."

"Jeez, Ivan. You're really letting your service slide." John put two bits on the table. "Keep the change, looks like you need it."

"What do you want, John?"

"I need to know who Gyver's been chummy with lately."

"Why'd you think I'd tell you anything, even if I did know?"

"How about for old time's sake?"

"Memory is fuzzy."

John threw a platinum coin on the table. Ivan glared at it for a second, then picked it up with his bar towel for a closer examination. His attitude changed dramatically in John's favor.

"I might know something."

"Might?"

"Depends on the question."

John took out the paper Mrs. Trowley had written *Victor* on and slid it over to him.

She's got such nice hand writing, John. He won't recognize it, will he?

No one writes anymore, Cam. I'd be surprised if he didn't just assume this was computer gen.

Lost arts, John, lost arts.

Ivan smiled, gesturing with his head toward a room at the rear, and then went back to cleaning beer steins. John chugged his milk and spun his empty glass back onto the bar.

"Thanks, Ivan."

Ivan grunted and kept busy behind the bar.

John walked casually toward the room and crept through the door once he got to it. There were six men sitting around a metal table under a cloud of cigar smoke, so focused on their game of cards that they hadn't even noticed John coming in. He changed that by shutting the door with a loud bang and flipping the lock.

A bald, thick man looked up from his cards and glared at John. He was definitely underground garbage. He wore a white T-shirt with brown suspenders holding up his gray cotton slacks, along with brown, handmade leather shoes that were kicked up on the table. He tried ignoring John by shuffling through the cards in his hand, only acknowledging him when he didn't turn and leave the room.

"John. What the hell you want?"

"Same thing I always want when it comes to you, Victor."

"Too bad, I'm busy. You wasted your time. Again."

"Victor, I've had a seriously bad day."

"Boohoo, crybaby, go tell Ivan you can have drink on me."

Trash.

You're the one who wanted to come here. I would have been happy to just get my Watson.

What's behind door number one, Cam?

Six armed men total, including Victor. No mods, but they're all armed well.

Anything behind the curtains?

Nope, just the lovely ballet dancers at the table.

Good.

John reached down and tapped one of Victor's thugs on his shoulder.

"Time to leave, cupcake."

"Hey, what gives, man?" The guy stood up, knocking over his chair, topping John by a good couple of inches. "Get the hell out of here."

John picked up Victor's thug by the coat and flung him across the room. The other four men jumped up and charged him. He dispatched them without breaking a sweat, slamming one man's face into the brick wall, and careening another man into the cement floor. He flattened the other two by grabbing the back of their heads with his giant hands and slamming them together. Blood from their noses splattered across the room and onto Victor's white shirt. Victor's bald scalp rippled with frustration. He pulled out his pistol and pointed it at John, flicking a red dot across his chest.

"You're a dead man, John."

"No, and you won't be either if you answer my questions right."

"You're crazy and stupid. Who the hell do you think you are?"

"Like I said, I'm a man who's had a really bad day."

"What'd you want?"

"Gyver."

"Never heard of her."

John kicked the table hard, sending it flying into Victor's fat gut. Victor let out a gagging grunt as he fell to the floor. His arm went limp as he hit, and the gun flew out of his hand, clattering across the floor.

"You know what, Victor, you flinch when you lie. It's why you always lose at poker. Well, at least when you're playing poker with real players."

"Screw you."

"Vic. Do you mind if I call you Vic?" John paused for a moment, giving Victor time to answer. He didn't. "Good, it's so much easier to say."

"You've lost your mind."

"Vic, I need to know how you helped Gyver."

"I don't know what you talking about, man."

If you take too long questioning him, Grandpa John, you'll have to knock out all his men again.

You think I'm getting rusty?

Um, let me think...yes.

"Now, that's not nice, Vic. I thought we could really get somewhere if we worked together." John put his boot on Victor's chest and pressed.

"So, Vic, let's try again. I could give two shits about a smuggler like you. What I do care about is how a dumb-ass gun dealer like Gyver got her hands on two fully equipped military-grade exo-armor suits." John pressed down harder on Victor's chest, making him cough and gasp for air.

"Two fully equipped suits that almost killed me." John pressed even harder. "Did I mention that I don't like almost being killed, Vic?" He let up just enough to let Victor answer.

Victor gasped with the small reprieve from suffocation that John was letting him have. "Okay, okay. I give."

John eased off a little more so Victor could keep breathing, and keep talking.

"Her and those two stooge twins came looking for some ammo for their mech suits two weeks ago. She was loaded with credits. I got her what she wanted and smuggled her some extra high-grade EP rounds."

That's why the explosion was so big.

What a couple dumbasses. How could you let them almost kill us, John?

Your bad luck, I guess.

"Where'd she get the suits?"

"She didn't tell me."

"Who's backing her?"

"I don't know, and that's the truth. Bitch had good money, paid up front. I didn't ask too many questions."

John let up, pulled one of the chairs over, and sat down face to face with the sweaty man. He picked out a new cigar that had spilled off the table and onto the floor, tore off the butt, and put it in his mouth.

"Wictor, Wictor, Wictor. Can't we at least try to be civil?" John brought a lighter out of his pocket and lit the cigar.

I think he's trying to hide that he's scared of you, John.

I have that effect on people.

"Whatta you really want to know, John?"

"What have you heard about the United States military recruiting out here?"

"Now that? That's a question I have answers to."

THIRTEEN

Dr. Wilcox

QUINN TOOK ONE LAST PEEK outside to make sure that there was no traffic. He leaned into Sierra, who was waiting, pulled back against the wall like a burglar hiding from the cops. "Do you think Jane's done for the night?"

Sierra went over to the door and listened.

"I think so," she said.

Quinn got close to Adam and looked him in the eyes. "You coming with us, boy?"

Adam whimpered and licked his face.

"Do you think he can make it?" Sierra asked.

"We can lower him down with the sheets."

"Quinn, that sounds so stupid."

Adam let out a throaty rumble and they both turned to look at him. He was holding a corner of the bed sheet between his teeth.

"That answers that," Quinn said.

Sierra and Quinn looped one end of the three long sheets they'd tied together around Adam. Quinn stood back, braced for the weight, and Sierra held Adam around the chest, easing him out the third story window.

"He weighs more than I thought," Sierra said. "It's like he's made out of metal or something."

As Adam's front paws left the sill, the sheet-rope jerked. "Grab on, Sierra. I can't let him down on my own."

"What do you think I'm trying to do, Q?" She fumbled for the sheets, but they were moving too fast. The sheet burned through her fingers and she instinctively let go.

"Sierra!"

Gritting his teeth, Quinn held on, but without Sierra's weight, couldn't keep from sliding toward the window. His feet hit the wall and he dropped with a thud, arms over the sill, chest braced. Sierra grabbed him from behind and added her weight to stop him from following Adam like a sinking anchor. His grip loosened and the sheet slid a few inches before Quinn clenched his hands in a death grip and held on; the sheet came to an abrupt stop. There was a muffled "woof" from Adam. Quinn opened his eyes slowly and then, hand over hand, lowered Adam the rest of the way. The two leaned out, expecting to get a barked reproof from Adam or a shout from some passer-by. They stared into the darkness, panicked, holding their breath until they saw him safe and alone on the ground, shaking the sheet off. He looked up at them, shadowy ears perked, tail visibly wagging in the blue-tinted night like nothing exciting had happened.

Quinn let the sheet fall to the floor and held his fingers out in front of him, staring at them and flexing his hands like they were a pair of alien creatures. "Holy crap."

"That was close," Sierra said. "I didn't know you were that strong."

Quinn kneeled down and secured his end of the sheets to the heating loop under the sill, and then started out. "Me either."

He shimmied down the tied sheets and waited with Adam at the bottom of the building as Sierra made her way down to them.

"John's gonna be so pissed if we get caught," Quinn said.

"We won't get caught, Q. Live a little, will you?"

"Whatever, Sis. Maybe we should just go back up. What if some-one see's the sheet hanging out the window and tells Jane?"

"Do you want to see the grizzly bears and acrobats or not?"

"Duh, of course I do."

"Then let's go."

They raced down the side streets toward the glowing circus top. Everyone must have been at the circus, because the town was completely empty except for the rare, passed-out drunk or stray animal. A couple of bars were open, one of them in a creepy-looking old hangar next to some boarded-up buildings. Adam barked and seemed to want to stop. Sierra and Quinn had to shush him, and hurried him past the half-lit neon light that said "The Whistle."

* * *

Light leaked through a long vertical slit at the back of the huge circus tent; they waited for one of the sheriffs to go by before they snuck through it with Adam. They blinked their eyes a few times, letting them adjust to the ever-changing light of the big top. The glow con-stantly flickered as giant shadows danced along the sides of the tent, partnered perfectly with the roar of applause and laughter. Sierra reached over and pinched Quinn on the back of his bicep.

"Ouch. What was that for?"

"Just making sure."

"Making sure of what?

"That we're awake."

The twins stood awestruck, turning in circles, taking in the mag-ical world that they had stumbled into. Bleachers were set up in sections, forming a giant circle like a coliseum around the middle of the big top. Brilliant lights lined the inside of the tent, green, gold, white, blue, red, purple, and silver. Fires glowed orange in brass pots on long metal pillars along the periphery of the giant tent. As they followed the lights and shadows from the fires, they saw the figure of a female flying through the air. Quinn and Sierra gasped as she fell like a stone toward the ground below, and then gasped again as another acrobat swept in, grabbed the falling lady by her ankles, swung with her high in the air, and then dropped her again. This time the lady stopped in midair, apparently catching something, and swung in a long arc to a tall platform at the top of the tent.

"Sierra, this is just how Jane said it would be."

"No, Quinn, this is way better."

Adam started barking with excitement. Sierra turned to scold him, but laughed instead. Adam was dancing on his hind legs, yapping and barking, making the people sitting near them throw coins and loaded microbits at him, as if he were one of the many sideshows there to keep the audience entertained.

"Are you trying to get us busted, Adam? Jeez." Quinn said.

They walked behind the stands to check out the fire-eaters, jugglers, and freak shows in a small courtyard that led to the animals. Fast-talking vendors shouted out to them, trying to get them to play their games.

"Step right up, folks... only for the brave of heart... your one chance to take on the strongest man on earth."

"This is so awesome," Quinn said.

"Want to try something?"

Quinn's eyes doubled in size. "Can we?"

"We have some money from Adam's little jig." Sierra shot him a devilish smile. "Plus I still have John's microbit. I think we've earned a little fun time."

She looked around for someplace to start. Her eyes settled on a skinny tower hovering over the rest of the booths in the courtyard. It was lined with blinking lights that ran up the sides, and it had a giant bell on top. A heavily muscled man in overalls stood next to it, holding a giant mallet and leaning on a sign that had "Sasquatch Hammer" emblazoned on it. Next to him was a much skinnier man in a worn-out, oversized suit, trying his best to round up business.

"Step right up, folks. Be the first person to swing the mallet and send the ball to the top. Ring that bell and win a thousand credits, folks. It's just that simple." He spotted the twins as they walked up.

"Step right up, kids, and take a swing." His thin lips stretched into a greedy smile. "You'll have enough money to buy up all the chocolate in town."

"Do we have to use that mallet?" Quinn asked.

"Oh, no, that's only for Brizzby there." He waved his hand at a stack of mallets in the corner of his booth. "You'll use one of these. Much easier, see, all different shapes and sizes too."

"I don't want to use any of those. I want to use Brizzby's."

"Q, just pick one of the other ones."

Quinn pointed over to the big man. "I want to use the one he's holding."

"Well, boy, you can't use that one. You have to use one of these ones." He knocked on the stack of crappy-looking mallets this time. "Besides, I doubt you could even get Brizzby's off the ground."

"I can lift it."

"Quinn. What're you doing?"

"Trust me, Sis."

Quinn walked over to Brizzby and pointed at his mallet.

"Can I use your mallet, mister?"

"Listen, kid, I don't want to get involved in your argument with Mr. Peters, okay? Just grab one of the small ones over there like everyone else, hit the base, and get your free wooden puppet, okay?"

Quinn turned to Mr. Peters. "I'll pay you double if you let me use Brizzby's mallet."

"Are you deaf or just dumb, kid?"

"Hey," Sierra said. "Watch it, mister. If Quinn wants to use the big man's mallet so bad, why don't you let him?"

"Get out of here, you two twits," Mr. Peters said. "You're wasting my time."

"Like you have so much business." Sierra glared at him and pulled out the microbit she still had from John. "We'll pay triple, for one shot. You say he can't even get it off the ground, so what do you have to lose?"

Mr. Peters scratched his whisker-covered chin, weighing his options, then nodded to Brizzby.

Brizzby set the heavy mallet down with a thud and stepped away. "Your funeral, kid."

Quinn stepped up and circled the mallet that was almost bigger than he was. Then he circled the Sasquatch Hammer, moving his head from side to side between the two. Sierra walked beside him after paying Mr. Peters and tried picking up the mallet. It didn't budge.

"I hope you know what you're doing, Q. You'll have to turn into Hercules to lift that mallet up."

"Don't worry, Sis. I hope you're ready to buy some more chocolate."

Quinn turned around and, with little effort, grabbed the mallet, swung it high above his head, and smashed it down on a crude picture of a Sasquatch at the bottom of the machine. The tower lights sprang to life, twinkling like stars as a small puck hurtled up to the top. The bell rang, fireworks rocketed into the air, and sparks flew from the lights on top as the puck and bell flew off the Sasquatch Hammer and away into the night.

"Yeah, baby!" Quinn dropped the mallet to the ground with a loud thud and turned to give Sierra a high five. She stood there, mouth gaping and eyes wide. He looked over at Brizzby and Mr. Peters, and they were wearing the same brain-frozen expression.

"Hey, Sis, you okay? Did you not just see how awesome I am?"

"Q, how did you...what did you do?"

"I told you not to worry." He walked past Sierra and over to the two vendors. "That's one thousand credits, mister."

Mr. Peters and Brizzby, slack jawed and dumb with surprise, couldn't take their eyes off the ruined Sasquatch Hammer.

"Hey, mister, sign says one thousand credits to knock the ball to the top."

"How did you...no one's supposed to be able to do that." He was mumbling, still trying to figure out what had happened. "No way am I paying some snot-nosed little whelp a thousand credits."

"Credits or cops," Quinn said.

"Sure...whatever, kid." He took a microbit out of his pocket and handed it to him.

"Pleasure doing business with you."

"Just get out of here, will ya, kid?" Mr. Peters wrinkled his hazy expression into a dangerous glare.

Sierra came up behind Quinn and grabbed him under his arm, pulling him away before he could say anything more. She hurried him away before the crowd drawn by Quinn's fireworks spectacle got any bigger.

"What the hell was that, Q?"

"What do you mean?"

"How did you lift that thing? I couldn't even get it to move on the ground."

"I didn't think it was that big of a deal."

Sierra pulled him over behind some bleachers. "Not a big deal? That was awesome. I don't think anyone here besides Brizzby could lift that mallet up."

"John could have."

"But John didn't. You did."

Quinn shrugged his shoulders. "Sometimes I just decide I can do something, and then I do it. Like with lowering Adam out the window."

People passing by were starting to stare at them, and Sierra could see in the distance that the crowd gathered around Mr. Peters and Brizzby was getting bigger. The two angry vendors were pointing at their machine and then over toward the twins.

"I think we better get out of here, Q."

Quinn looked at the Sasquatch Hammer. "Yeah, I think you're right."

They wove their way through the people and over and under bleachers, until they were far enough into the crowd under the big top that no one paid any attention to them.

"Q, that was really cool. Weird, but really cool."

"I'm not sure I could do it again. I just knew I could right then."

"Let's not do anything else like that tonight, okay?"

"Okay."

"And you have a lot of explaining to do when we get back to Jane's."

"I'm not the only one, Sis."

They came to an abrupt stop behind Adam. His fur was rippling along his back, and he let out a throaty growl as they came close to a large iron cage in a staging area at the edge of the center ring. The cage was on a huge cart with big rubber wheels. A sign read "The Mighty Thor," the letters gruesomely painted to look like dripping blood.

"Whoa, what is that?"

Quinn smiled huge and ran up to the sign. "It's the grizzlies."

"Q, hold on, don't get too close."

"He's even bigger than I imagined," Quinn said.

"It's enormous."

"Aye, he's the biggest in all the circuit."

They jumped at the voice and turned to see a tall, well-groomed man in a bright red vest and pants, black silk shirt, and ball cap. He had a curled mustache underneath a prodigious nose and a golden patch over his left eye.

"At least that's what I hear," he said.

"You scared us," Quinn said.

"Sorry about that, lad." The man took off his hat and bowed deep. "Dr. Timothy Wilcox, at your service."

Quinn reached down and petted Adam, who had his eyes trained on Dr. Wilcox and was positioned to pounce easily if he needed to.

"Do you take care of Thor?" Sierra asked.

"He takes care of me mostly."

Dr. Wilcox slipped on a pair of long rubber gloves that had been hanging from a hook on the enclosure, and then reached into a case outside the cage, grabbed a chunk of meat and tossed it inside. The giant bear pounced on it, and the meat disappeared into a mouth lined with fangs the size of daggers. In fact, Thor's cavernous mouth was so big it looked as if he could swallow a person whole if he wanted.

"Whoa, that guy is huge," Quinn said.

"Yeah, that's totally scary," Sierra said. "Are you sure that thing takes care of you?"

"More than you know." Dr. Wilcox replaced the gloves and wiped down his hands with a wet cloth from a bucket on the ground. "Now, what are you kids doing back here?"

Sierra and Quinn looked at each other, and Adam let out another low, throaty growl.

"Aye, figured as much." He scratched under his cap and smiled. "Don't worry, your secret's safe with me."

"Thank you, mister. We just wanted to see what Jane was talking about. Then I hit this puck through the bell at the Sasquatch Hammer, and now those guys are pissed, and—" Quinn shrugged, searching for his next words.

Sierra interjected for him. "We just wanted to have some fun. We didn't mean to upset anyone, honest, but I think that maybe they want their money back."

Dr. Wilcox waved his hand to stop Sierra. "Did you say Jane, the healer Jane?"

"Yeah, do you know her?"

"Of course I do, young lady." He rolled up the sleeve of his shirt and exposed a large scar that ran along his forearm. "She stitched me up and saved my arm, and my life. A friend of Jane's is a friend of mine. You'll be perfectly safe here from hooligans like Mr. Peters."

He gave them both a wink and then clapped his hands. A couple rough-looking stagehands came running up to him.

"Bert, Jonathon. I need some seats for our new guests." The two hands went scrounging through some piles of gear and brought out a couple of tall chairs for Sierra and Quinn to sit in.

"Backstage seats to the greatest show outside the States."

"This is awesome," Quinn said, as they took their new places. From the wings, they had a great view of the center ring.

Adam prowled around the cages and stagehands, sniffing and snooping, and then he came back and sat by Quinn.

"You have a mighty fine friend in that one," Dr. Wilcox said.

"He's been taking good care of us lately, haven't you, Adam?"

The tall man chuckled and then bowed low again.

"If you will all excuse me, now that I see you're in good hands, I have a show to produce."

He walked around to the front of the cage, opened the door, and went inside. Thor roared and lunged at him, making Sierra and Quinn gasp.

"Oh, stop showing off, you big lug," Dr. Wilcox said. "The show hasn't started yet."

The giant grizzly stopped, and then nudged Wilcox with his massive head. It looked as if it were all Wilcox could do to stay on his feet.

"Not now, Thor, we need to get out and do our show. We can play later if you're good." Thor growled something that sounded like an acknowledgment of some kind and then followed Wilcox out of the cage, nodding at the twins as he passed.

"Did he just smile at us?" Sierra asked.

"I think so. I'm not sure whether that's awesome or really creepy."

Sierra and Quinn watched from the staging area as the center of the ring was cleared and Dr. Wilcox's crew started lining it with his ferocious animals. Finally the workers melted back into the dark and the doctor swept a glance around the ring. He nodded as if satisfied with the exact placement of each elegant cage, exchanged his ball cap for a top hat handed to him by one of the stage hands, and then walked to the middle of the tent. The tent went pitch black. Quinn waved his hand in front of his face and couldn't even see his fingers. A single brilliant spotlight pierced the dark and encompassed Dr. Wilcox.

"Ladies and gentlemen." He paused for effect. "Welcome to the greatest show on earth!"

Applause exploded from the crowd. He let it go on for a moment and then raised his arm high. He brought it down slowly to quiet them.

"Prepare yourselves. What you are about to witness is not for the faint of heart."

Wilcox paused again, giving time for another burst of applause from the audience, this time with an undertone of rushed whispers.

"I present to you *the Mighty Thor and his Warrior Companions!*"

Thor stood tall on his hind legs and roared so loud that Sierra and Quinn worried the top of the tent might blow off. The rest of the cages rattled and the animals inside roared, screeched, and howled. The crowd did their best to repeat the sounds and beat the bleachers with their feet in anticipation of the start of the show. Dr. Wilcox bowed low and then circled the ring, signaling his crew with barked, animal-like orders and hand signals to start the show.

Wow, he's really good.

Quinn's awestruck expression confirmed his thought. Sierra thought back at him: Not just good, he's excellent.

She registered his confused look, and couldn't suppress her grin.

"Did you...did I miss something?" *Crazy, I was just thinking that.*

"I know you were."

Thor roared, shaking Quinn out of his astonishment. He looked at Sierra one more time and then shook his head, turning his attention back to the show. Thor roared again and charged Dr. Wilcox, who ran around the ring, just barely keeping out of Thor's reach. Thor would get close to Wilcox, and Wilcox would act as if he were going to get eaten. Each time, explosive fireworks went off. Swinging acrobats dressed as hunters dropped down from the rafters, acting as if they were shooting arrows and spears at Thor.

Cages that the stagehands had lined up around the arena opened randomly, and different wild animals dashed out and danced a choreographed battle under the close eye of "Maestro Wilcox." A large gray wolf came out and circled near Thor until Thor swiped his big paw out, and the wolf feigned death. Next a tiger and cougar, then a pair of vultures swooping around like birds of prey, and finally another grizzly bear. This grizzly was smaller than Thor, but still ferocious-looking. The two actually started grappling with each other in what looked like a larger version of an old wrestling match. The acrobats kept flying overhead, and every once in a while they held up a score when one of the grizzlies slammed the other to the mat. Dr. Wilcox balanced around the edge of the ring, barking orders in some grunting language, which added to the mystery of the show.

Thor and his wrestling opponent lowered their shoulders and stumbled around the arena, worn out from the long match with each other. They both stood tall and roared so thunderously that the whole arena vibrated, making the crowd shriek with excitement. They charged each other, and Thor caught the other grizzly and slammed it to the ground. Fireworks went off around the ring, and the aerial acrobats, twenty in all, floated down face-first, suspended by one leg entwined with streamers that unraveled from the ceiling. The animals roamed the circle as the crowd stood and cheered, giving them a storm of applause. The acrobats danced through the crowds and threw shirts, candy, hats, and other prizes to the audience.

Dr. Wilcox lined the animals up in the middle of the ring with the acrobats behind them and one bear at each end of the line. He barked out a few more grunting orders and each animal in the show lowered into a low bow, putting the crown of their heads to the floor, followed by bows from their human counterparts. Again the crowd's applause was so raucous that the ground itself shook.

"That was the best show ever!" Quinn said.

He got up off his chair and joined Adam, who was up on his hind legs dancing with Sierra as the line of animals streamed back to their plush cages, ushered by Dr. Wilcox, who stepped off to the side to give his stage hands a few orders before heading over to Sierra and Quinn.

"That was totally awesome, Dr. Wilcox," Sierra said. "I can't believe you got those animals to do that."

Dr. Wilcox removed his hat and bowed low again.

"Yes, Dr. Wilcox, it was a 'totally awesome show.'" Jane's voice came from behind them. "Almost as good as last year's."

Sierra and Quinn turned, and there was Jane.

"I was wondering when you would show up again, lover," Wilcox said.

"Always trying to use your animal charm on me, as if one of these times it might actually work, Timothy."

"A man does have to try."

"What are you doing here, Jane?" Sierra asked.

"I could ask the same question of you two, but I think I know," Jane said. "No one could ever resist Dr. Wilcox and his amazing animal show."

"I'm sorry we snuck out, Jane," Quinn said.

"Well, I'd be lying if I told you that I thought you'd stay in your room and get any of the sleep you needed." She studied him with her eyes. "Speaking of which, you look pretty good for a boy that was as limp as a rag doll less than twenty four hours ago."

Quinn flexed his bicep. "I don't feel like I need any sleep. I'm strong as ever. Anyways, we had Adam with us, and it's not like you didn't follow us here."

"Hmm. There is more to you children than one would perceive at first glance. Or you've just been around John too long." She turned to face Dr. Wilcox. "Timothy, thank you for taking them under your wing."

Dr. Wilcox lifted his hat and ran his hand through his hair. "Ah, how kind of you, Jane. I am always at your service."

"Your charm is only going to get you so far."

"Wait, you knew that we were going to be here, and that he would take care of us?" Sierra asked.

"I had a hunch. Dr. Wilcox has always had a sweet tooth when it comes to me, so I figured he'd try to use you two to get back into my good graces."

"Straight to the heart, dear Jane, straight to the heart," Wilcox said.

"I'd expect you'd get over that pretty soon—if you had a heart."

Wilcox bowed low again and took Jane's hand in his, kissing the back of it gently.

"Still not happening, Wilcox." Jane gave him a wink. "Well, at least not yet."

He stood up and smiled.

"As long as a speck of hope still lives, I will keep trying, my love," he said.

"See you for drinks tomorrow, Timothy," Jane said.

"Tomorrow, my dear."

With a nod to Sierra and Quinn, Dr. Wilcox stood and walked over to inspect his cages, and Jane turned and faced the kids.

"As for you two, we better get back before John finds you out of bed. I can't imagine he'd be too happy with any of us if he knew the kind of attention you two have drawn tonight. I daresay not even my biscuits could get us out of that mess."

FOURTEEN

Oliver

JOHN CHECKED IN ON QUINN and Sierra in the morning. He had spent the better part of the night talking with Victor, which had made talking to Oliver today that much more urgent. The kids were still asleep, and he had Adam pulling watch on both of them. Jane told him that they had had a long night and assured him that she would feed them and let them clean up once they were awake, so John left and made his way to Oliver's Mead and Spirits.

Sleep. That sure would be nice.

It's been eighteen hours, thirty-six minutes, and fifteen seconds to be exact, John.

Thanks, Cam. I really wanted to be reminded of that.

John went around the building to the back, where Oliver had his townhouse, and knocked on the door.

Good luck.

Why?

Because you're seconds away from being bored to death.

"John!" Oliver said. "To what do I owe this unexpected visit?"

God, he's still playing Friar Tuck.

Does that make me Robin Hood?
More like Little John.
Funny, Cam.
Do you think he changes those robes?
I've never thought about it, and I don't want to start now.

Oliver was a monk by trade and still wore a brown, hooded robe with a tattered rope tied at the waist, and leather sandals. He had a freshly bald head that crowned a pair of bushy red eyebrows, and blues eyes that contrasted with his fiery red beard. His fair skin was speckled with orange hair and freckles, and he had the giant hands of a craftsman.

"Oliver!" John said. "I wish I could say it was good to see you."

"Mm, and what a treat it is for me to see you. What can I do for you this morning, old friend?"

"More than you could possibly imagine."

"It looks like it. Come in, come in. I just made some fresh coffee."

John followed him into his surprisingly cozy home, which wasn't nearly as dreary inside as its bricked exterior suggested. It reminded John of his favorite corner coffee shop, or the local English pub he used to frequent back when such things were on every city block.

I forgot how relaxed you are when we're at Oliver's.
It smells like an old fruit shed and honey.
You say that every time.
I mean it every time, Cam.

The floor creaked as they crossed the dark-stained wood slabs. Oliver, the forever-saver of lost items, had scavenged most of the wood for the inside of the house, and the brick for the outside, from an old fruit warehouse that had been abandoned decades before Tree Top even existed. The room was furnished with two leather lounge chairs and a small lime-green sofa. Books and tablets covered a slab of tree turned into a coffee table that sat in the center of the room. An arched doorway led into the kitchen, a back room, and stairs that ran to the basement and the upper floor.

Do you think we can trust him?
If we can't trust him, Cam, who can we trust?

All right, John, but your track record isn't playing in our favor right now.
What about Jane?
That's different.
Why is it always 'different' when I'm right?
I don't know what you're talking about.
Sure you don't.

After receiving a cup of Oliver's privately roasted coffee and exchanging pleasantries, John broke into his tale. His fists clenched when he spoke of the jippers; pacing the room, he described the disaster at the river and the growling ache at the boy's illness, the fight at the brewery, and then Sage.

"So I was stuck. Should've minded my own business, damn it. I can't do this, Oliver. I'm not ready for this."

"You appear to be okay, and from what you tell me the children are fine, and more importantly they are safe—"

"You don't understand, I almost got us all killed twice. Safe! They're not safe with me. Hell, I'm not safe with them."

He sighed, and finally flopped down onto the couch, his head falling against its high back as his mind raced through the last twenty-four hours.

"Screwed, that's what I am, screwed."

"Sometimes, John, I am amazed at how long you've survived with that cloud that hangs over your head all the time."

Yes, I have to agree with Oliver on this, John.
Do you ever disagree with anyone besides me?
I disagreed with Gyver and those twins.

"I didn't have that cloud until I met people like you," John said. "Meddlers, all of you, and it's rubbing off on me. After this I might stay away from all of you for a while just to purge myself of it."

"I don't believe we're the ones who are the bad influences. I was an honest monk before you came to Tree Top, trading your wine and swindling folk with your card play. I'm sure Cam could attest to that."

Can and will, John.
Whose side are you on, Cam?

Yours.

Maybe you should try sounding a little more convincing.

"An honest monk, in Tree Top even," John said. "Now that's a line I haven't heard before."

Oliver smiled, a short chuckle escaping from his chest. "Well, one must make some exceptions, depending on circumstances. Here, I've been blabbering on, which I am sure you did not come for. So, tell me, John. What is it I can do for you?"

"I need you to take the twins, Oliver."

"The two that you say you saved from the jippers?"

"Do I have to explain this to you again?"

"I'm just wondering why they didn't try to trade the children here, like you are."

"I'm not trading them, Oliver. I'm trying to find a place for them, where they'll be taken care of and will feel like they belong."

"The jippers could have very easily gotten a decent price from Victor, or at least gotten rid of them for some credits."

He's ignoring you, John.

I know. He's in one of his Oliver moments.

"Are you listening to me, Oli? I was hoping you could take them. Help them out."

You mean help you out.

Same thing.

"Then out of all the places to squat, they chose your land, John. How did you say you decided to get involved? I never took you for the family type."

"So I keep getting reminded. Look, can you step up here or is that too much for your monkish charity?"

"Well, you're all more than welcome to stay here for as long as you need. I can use that time to see if they might like to go with me to Benedict's. The monastery has a boarding house and school that takes in lost children from time to time. I could contact them and see if they could take in a brother and sister."

"That's what I'm talking about. A boarding house thingy, that'd be perfect."

"It's not that simple, John. They have to want to go, and if they do choose to go, it's not an easy life. The journey is long and tortuous, and once there, the monks will be hard on them. You should understand what you are getting them into."

"What I'm getting them into? What about what they got me into?"

"John, listen to yourself. I'm sure out of all the choices they had, they deliberately picked kidnapping by jippers, and rescue by a man who is still crippled by the loss of his son—"

John was out of the couch the second the words left the monk's mouth and had his hand around Oliver's throat, hoisting him in the air almost to the ceiling with one strong arm, eyes glowing red like embers, fingers slowly collapsing Oliver's airway.

A choking squawk escaped Oliver as he fought against John's iron-like hold. "John, pl—" His face started turning blue and his eyes rolled back as his flailing slowed.

JOHN. Don't kill Oliver. You need him to take the twins.

John's eyes slowly returned to his normal blue, his grip lessened, and he unwrapped his fingers from around Oliver's neck, letting him collapse to his knees, then threw himself back down on the couch. "Just take the damned kids, Oliver."

Are you okay, John?

I'm fine, Cam. Oliver forgets where the tripwires are.

Does he know how close he was to dying?

Oliver cleared his throat and wobbled to his feet after a brief coughing fit, and rubbed his neck, rolling his head around to work out the knots that were now there.

I think he has an idea.

"I'm sorry, John. I shouldn't have pushed you so hard, but it is important for me to know that you are doing this for the right reason, that you are not mixed in your resolve. I am truly sorry."

"I didn't pick them up because I wanted them; but I'm not an asshole that walks away and leaves a pair of kids with those jippers. They were sadistic creeps, Oliver."

"I'm sure they were, John, but not all things are absolute, not all circumstances are under our control. Sometimes these things

178   SEIMS

happen and we don't understand them at first. Then, with some insight, we can see that there is a rough plan, a network of paths that lead us to an unexpected destination. That's all I'm saying."

Just like the network of paths that will lead us to my new Watson, hopefully. As soon as we're done here, Cam, promise.

Which might be forever the way Oliver prattles on.

"Don't start with me on that all roads lead to Ashtree crap that you and Benedict dreamed up."

"We didn't dream it up, my friend, but out of courtesy, I will leave it alone for now. So tell me more about the children. Where are they?"

"I left them and Adam at Jane's to rest up a bit while I did my poking around," John rubbed his eyes with his knuckles and blinked hard several times to clear the sleep out of his eyes.

"You look exhausted."

"I am. How about some more coffee?"

"I'll make us another couple of cups," Oliver said and got up from the stool he was on. "So you saw Sage again. How'd that go?"

"Let's stick to the material that matters, Oliver, like the coffee I'm not going to distract you from making."

"Everything matters, John."

Oliver went to the back room and banged around a bit. John stayed slouched in the sofa, too tired to get up and follow him.

"Have you heard anything about Victor getting into militia supplies?"

"I wouldn't doubt it," Oliver said from the kitchen. "He has been expanding his illustrious organization for years now, and the locals haven't done anything about it. Arms dealing, human trafficking, smuggling, moonshine, just about everything he can to shake money out of people. He's even gotten into bribing the locals and the militia to look the other way. Why do you ask?"

"I had a long talk with him last night about supplying Gyver with ammunition. He had some interesting information about the United States."

The banging and hissing from Oliver's steam espresso contraption paused for a minute and then restarted as Oliver finished
making John's cup of coffee and came back out to the sitting room.

"How about this?" Oliver asked. "I'll head down and stay with
the kids and see what I can do. You stay here and take the time to
rest up. When I get back, you can tell me all about what our friend
Wictor had to say."

That never gets old.

Wictor?

Laughing right now.

John let himself smile for a second and then got serious again. "I
don't know. This has been a bit of a nightmare, Oliver. It's weird. I
can't shake this gut feeling that I'm missing something, and it's got
my spidey sense on overload right now."

Spidey sense?

Nostalgia.

You're such a dork.

"They're just kids, John, and I'm sure this United States nonsense
is just garbage, like it always is."

"You're probably right. I'm just tired and my gut's not sitting
well."

"If you had anything at Ivan's, you won't feel right for quite some
time, I'm afraid," Oliver said. "Besides, what trouble can two children, a monk, and a healer get into?"

"Is that a bad joke?"

"Stay here," Oliver continued. "Get some rest. I'll go and gather
up the kids and Adam. If Jane doesn't think Quinn should come out
yet, I'll leave Adam there with them and come back."

John took a sip of his coffee and then waved Oliver off, realizing
that arguing was useless at this point. His eyes were heavy as he
kicked his feet up onto the footstool and let his head relax low on
the back of the couch.

"Okay, but here." He dug into his pocket and tossed Oliver a little
black square. "Press this if you get into trouble."

"Will do. Now rest, Captain. You've done a fine job," Oliver said and left through the front door.

*　*　*

John woke up to hollering and the thumping of feet. He jumped up and drew his gun, pointing it toward the noise, targeting two laughing, energized children.

"What the hell?"

Sierra held her hands up over her heart as if she'd just been shot. "Whoa, John. Don't act so happy to see us. Jeez."

Quinn nodded in agreement. "Yeah, John, chill, dude. No need to kill us yet."

"John, so glad you could join us," Oliver said. "Although I'm not sure that Sierra and Quinn were ready to play Wild West."

The twins went back to tossing the ball back and forth while Adam chased it. John looked between the two kids and then back at Oliver as his mind settled into the current scene.

Much different than the last forty-eight hours, huh, John?

He holstered his gun.

Just a little bit. Kid looks better.

That makes you happy?

Happy that they're well enough to stay with Oliver.

Whatever, tough guy.

"How long have I been out?"

"Not long, John." Oliver set a small ceramic coffee cup in front of him. "Everything's been in good order while you've been snoozing. Brilliant really."

"Brilliant? Really?"

"Sierra and Quinn are fine. They've really bonded with Adam. He seems quite fond of them, too, as you can tell."

John rubbed his head and whistled to Adam, who came over obediently and started licking John's hand.

"I'm glad someone is."

"I'd be lying if I said that he was the only one. They seem to have wrapped quite a few people around their fingers, Jane and Dr. Wilcox included."

"Dr. Wilcox?" John looked at the two, who had stopped tossing the ball, and were looking at him, innocence personified. "How'd you make that one happen?" They went to answer but he cut them off. "No, never mind, I don't want to know. You'll be someone else's problem soon enough."

A bit grumpy this afternoon, John?

How'd you think this was going to go, Cam?

You don't have to be a jerk about it, that's all.

"Ahem, yes, well, Jane said it would be fine for Quinn to come here, so I fetched them and brought them down. Quite lovely, both of them really."

"I'm sure they are. Glad you're so happy to have them. How long, Oliver?"

"You've been resting for three hours," Oliver said. "I'd say sleeping, but I don't think anyone would call your frightful fits sleeping."

"Well, time for me to get the hell out of here."

Classic John tact.

There's no easy way to do this, Cam. This is the best option for these two.

Keep telling yourself that.

Adam stopped chasing the ball and sat down by Quinn, letting out a low whimper. Quinn's expression went flat, and he tossed the ball to Sierra. He let out a sigh and put his hands in his pockets as he stared at the door, not daring to look back at John. Adam trotted over and nuzzled him to try and cheer him up. Sierra grabbed Quinn's arm.

"It's okay, Q. Don't worry about him." She glared past Oliver and right at John. "I like Oliver way better anyway."

"You can look at me like that all you want, kid. Doesn't change anything, no matter how much you want it to."

She grunted and threw the ball screaming at John. It got close enough to him he could feel a ripple in the air as it skimmed past his ear and into the wall behind him.

"Leave then already! No one here's stopping you," Sierra said. "Isn't this what you wanted, bring us here and dump us? I mean you haven't been able to get rid of us fast enough this whole trip, so leave, just leave."

"Sierra, please," Quinn said.

"Oh, get over it, Quinn," Sierra balled her fists and glared at John, her voice trembling with frustration and pain. "You knew he didn't want us and that he couldn't wait to get rid of us. What'd you think, that he was going to stick around forever? That he was going to take care of you? He doesn't give a shit, Quinn. No one does."

The lights in the house flickered slowly on and off, causing the room to fall silent.

Oliver was the first to break the silence. "Well, that's a bit odd, now isn't it? Had the generator serviced just last week."

"No one cares about the damn lights, Oli," John said. "Now listen here, kid. I never dressed it up. Leaving you two with Oliver is what's best, for everybody."

Sierra stomped off past the kitchen and into one of Oliver's guest rooms.

"She doesn't mean it, John," Quinn said. "She's just upset, that's all." He petted Adam on the head and followed his sister.

"Well, that could have been a lot worse," Oliver said.

Really, because I had high hopes that we could get those two to hate us more.

Cam.

I'm just mad, John. I'm going to leave for a bit.

To the wrist pad?

You don't have a Watson for me and it's the only place I can go to get away from you right now.

Cam?

Cam?

Damn it.

"Sorry, Oliver, but I need to check on a few things, and I don't have a lot of time. I need to get back to the house and resupply, and then I have some unfinished business with a crazy lady in a fermenter."

"Yes, I see," Oliver said. "Off to gather Gyver and see where that thread leads."

"I have other threads I need to follow too."

Adam looked to John, ears flat, whimpering.

"Go ahead, boy. Might be the last time."

Adam licked his hand a couple times and then trotted back to the guest room, to Quinn and Sierra, pawing at the door until they opened it for him. John let out a sigh and sat down, grabbing his coffee and taking long sip.

"Mm, whiskey, nice touch."

"John, do you really need to push them away like that?"

"Yes, Oliver, I really do need to, now more than ever."

"Is there something I should know about, John?"

"Just my gut feeling that something really bad is going to happen. There's something I'm missing in all this, and I'd rather have a clearer picture of what's coming this way than what I have now."

"Oh, I wouldn't doubt that. You have to trust your gut when it comes to things of this nature."

"More than. Tell me, Oliver. Have you heard of any recruiting by the United States out here?"

"I've heard some rumors," Oliver said. "But I just dismiss them as rumors."

Oliver put his coffee down on the table and sat down, leaning back in a reclining leather chair. "Do you think they could be more than rumors?"

"I think so," John said. "I don't think that the cock-up in Leavenworth was isolated. Gyver said she was on her way to recruit loyalists. That the US and the Colonies were working together."

"So what does that have to do with you?"

"Victor got her some highly controlled ammunition for some very high-end, military-grade exo suits. He said other groups besides Gyver's have been looking for those kids."

Oliver sat back in his chair and tilted his head, his gaze locked on John. "Do you really think this has anything to do with Sierra and Quinn?"

"Wrong place, wrong time. That's why I still brought them here, but if someone's looking for two kids and they find Gyver, they'll figure out where we are. Oliver, you know how this works. Someone's paying a high price for two particular kids, so every psycho out there rounds up two kids that fit the mark. They bring them in, and if they're not what the buyer's looking for, they end up in the scrap heap."

"I see."

John's vision started to blur. He rubbed his eyes to try and clear them, but they just got heavier with sleep and fog.

"God, why am I so tired?" John yawned long and hard. "Oliver? What's going on? Was there something in that…"

John's coffee cup fell out of his hands and shattered on the wood floor, the last drink oozing out and creeping into the cracked wood like blood. He collapsed back onto the couch, eyes blurring more and more.

Cam.

"Sorry, John, but I was really hoping it wouldn't come to this. I can't let you leave, not yet. Maybe after you're thoroughly rested…"

Cam.

"This is not how I wanted things to go, John. Things are set in motion now that cannot be undone."

Cam. Damn it.

"You'll see things differently soon."

Damn.

Fifteen

Death Becomes You

"I REMEMBER YOU BEING much more bold when you came to me before."

Gyver's swollen, bloody eyes blinked and cringed as her body jerked again. She swung by her feet from the rafters of the old lady's sewing shop, vomiting bile on the floor and losing her bodily functions as electricity surged through her again.

The shadow of the lady interrogating her crept forward, crouching on a knee so she could wipe the blood, sweat, and vomit from her face.

"Really, Gyver, General Murdoch gives you the opportunity of a lifetime, and this is how you repay him." She stood and paced over to the man with the electric riot baton and waved for him to leave them. "It was such a small task. Find the children and deliver them to me."

The woman raised her foot and brought it smashing into Gyver's chest, knocking the breath out of her lungs.

Gyver forced the words to leave her mouth. "I did what I was asked, I told you everything." Her body started convulsing as she sobbed.

The woman bent down and whispered to her as she placed an uplink in the port behind her ear. "We'll be the judge of that."

"Please—" Gyver tried to plead, but the link was already made. The woman was in her head.

Don't worry, Gyver, it'll all be over soon.

The memories rushed out of her. Her whole life flashed in an instant, making the pressure in her head unbearable as her brain started to hemorrhage. Gyver's recent encounter with John, Sage, and the twins flashed onto the old lady's HUD. Gyver's body convulsed again, translucent gray liquid pouring from her nose and ears, mixing with the blood and saliva dripping from her mouth.

Ah, I've found what I wanted. Dump the rest.

Dumping the rest into the main now, ma'am.

There, there, Gyver. The pain will pass soon, and your patriotism will be noted in our chronicles. You can rest now.

Gyver's body convulsed two more times and then swung lifeless in the middle of the room. The old lady slipped out of her effluvia-stained jacket as if she were simply taking off her coat after a long walk, straightened out the flat green uniform that was underneath, then moved over to the sink to wash her hands. Looking in the mirror, she traced the lines in her face with her hand, and then fixed a stray silver hair that was escaping from her tight bun. She took a deep breath and smiled to herself.

That was better than she deserved.

No one can call you heartless, ma'am.

But they can call me old.

You've aged better than most.

Send a message to General Murdoch. Let him know we're attacking tonight.

Sixteen

Reluctant Hero

JOHN BLINKED HIS EYES OPEN, a blurry picture slowly coming into focus. His mind sparked alive and tracked through his memory as the shadowy shapes of the people in front of him became more clear.

"What'd you do to him?" Quinn asked. "He looks like he's doped or something."

Cam?

"Like you know what someone doped up looks like, Q," Sierra said.

Cam?

"Well, I think he looks doped up."

Cam.

John? I'm so glad you're finally awake.

"You're a dork, Q."

I'm sorry, John. I tried to get back to you as soon as I knew what was in the coffee, but Oli had some sort of EMP nanos in it that were blocking me.

Is he still here?

Yes.

Oliver.

"Where the hell is Oliver?"

Sage walked into the room, holding a cup of steaming hot coffee. "So he's alive after all."

WTF — Sage?

Oh, and Sage is here.

How bad would it be if I killed everyone in the room right now?

I'd say go for it, but since we're in the dark here, better not just yet.

"Oliver!" The sound of his own voice felt like a salvo ricocheting inside his skull. "Oliver!"

Stop hollering.

Find him for me, Cam, and don't try to stop me from killing him this time.

"Coming, John. On my way." Oliver scurried into the room. "Boy, you're awake sooner than I expected. Dreadfully sorry about earlier. Couldn't have you leaving quite yet, you see."

"You have about three seconds to explain what the hell is going on."

Sierra giggled and then covered up her mouth.

"What are you laughing about?"

"You're so mad, and your hair is all over the place," Sierra said. "It makes you look like some kind of drugged psycho or something."

"That's what I said, Sierra."

"No, Q, you said doped up."

"Whatever, same difference."

John looked in the mirror. Under different circumstances he probably would have laughed at himself. Then he remembered he was in fact a drugged psycho right now. He heard Sage try to stifle a laugh. "What're you even doing here, Sage?"

Sage started to answer, but Oliver waved her off.

"'Fraid that's my fault too, John. She arrived shortly before you did and told me the story of your whole ordeal. I noticed some inconsistencies."

Quinn came over and sat by Sage in the worn out leather arm chair across from John. Adam walked past them, tail wagging gingerly, and laid his head in John's lap, staring up at him with wide eyes.

"Don't get too comfy, Adam. You and I have a lot to talk about when this is over."

Adam licked the hand that John had put under his chin and then trotted the few yards back over to Quinn, taking up his new favorite place by his feet.

I told you we should have never accepted him from William.

I have words for you too, Cam.

I think we should stay focused on Adam and Oliver here, don't you?

John turned toward Sage and Oliver. "What inconsistencies?"

"John, that asshole Gyver wasn't ever after you," Sage said.

"What are you talking about?"

"You see, John," Oliver said, "Gyver was excited to find you and take you to her boss. You'd be a big prize, not to mention the satisfaction of getting some payback, but who she was really after was Sage."

John looked puzzled and then turned his soured look at Sage.

"Sage, really? And why the hell is that, Oliver? How the hell are we still managing to skip over the part where you drugged me?"

"Why wouldn't he be after Sage?" Sierra asked. "You're the only one anyone can be after?"

"Oh, great, more insight from the peanut gallery."

"John, if we could all just calm down for a minute, I can finish."

"I'm done being calm," John said. "I want to know why Sage is here, why you drugged me, and why the hell Adam is so cozy with Quinn."

I say we leave him here if he wants to stay so bad. We're better solo anyway.

Adam returned to John, putting his forelegs on John's lap and stretching high to lick his chin. John tried to look cross and kept batting his head away with soft swipes from his hands.

"Nice try, Adam. Too little, too late, pal."

"All of your questions have answers, John, but you have to actually let me explain them."

"I've given you plenty of time."

"Oli, this is stupid." Sage let out an exasperated sigh. "I've been tracking Sierra and Quinn."

"What?"

"Well, that makes sense," Quinn said.

Sierra was speechless.

John was not. "In what way does that make sense, Quinn?"

"Yeah, how does that make sense, Q?"

Wow, you and Sierra just agreed. Scary.

How about you run a scan. See what you can find.

Fine, but I'm staying here, too, because this is too good to miss.

"Oliver sent me to track you after he saw the gypsy couple in town trading," Sage said.

"I knew the gypsy couple worked in trading children," Oliver said, "and I'd heard a couple of children were being held in their wagon."

"So on a hunch you sent Sage to go and look for us?" Sierra asked.

"I knew I liked you," Quinn said to Sage, eyes wide with admiration.

"Thanks, kid, you're not so bad yourself."

"Okay." John sat on the couch. "This is getting way too complicated. Oliver, you sent Sage to go after the children."

"Yes."

"Then Gyver came after Sage to get the children, and I just happened into the middle of all of it?"

"Like I said, John, there's always more going on than we realize. We're not always sure what our roles are, but we all have roles. I don't know if you happened into the middle of it all, or if you were placed into it. Only time will tell."

Adam, having given up thoroughly on John, laid his head on the ground, his body snug against John's legs. John shook his head and then let it plop into back of the couch. "I'm getting a headache. Which brings me back to you, my so-called friend, drugging me."

"Yes, about that, terribly sorry. We couldn't let you leave, because we need your help, John, so we had to take some drastic measures. We're in an awful bind, from what you've told me about Victor."

"How does that factor in?"

Scans clear for now, but your new IBEC toy is malfunctioning. It's on its way here right now.

Mm, interesting. Keep tabs on it, will you?

Got it.

"Well, if Victor supplied Gyver, then he knew about the jippers that were supposed to meet up with Gyver and deliver Sierra and Quinn." Oliver paused for a second to let the information sink in.

"He knew about the very group that I had Sage go after, and he lied to you. Are you following the events now, John?"

Eew, Wictor lied to you?

I must be losing my touch.

Or you're right, and there's someone who scares these people more.

"So you were tracking us?" Sierra asked.

"When you came into town, one of my students saw the jippers who had you, and came and got me. I had some suspicion that you weren't with them willingly and thought you could use a helping hand. Sage happened to be here also and owed me a favor, so she set out to keep an eye on you."

"I expected to get to you sooner," Sage said. "If I hadn't been waylaid by that idiot Gyver, I would've intercepted you before you got anywhere near John's place."

And I wouldn't be sitting here with drug hangover.

Bet you wish you had listened to me.

What? I'm here because I listened to you.

Don't act like you weren't going to help them anyway.

I wasn't.

Whatever you have to tell yourself, tough guy.

"So you knew all this when you helped me?" Quinn smiled, eyes wide and sparkling. "You're awesome."

"Ugh." Sierra shot a sour look at her brother. "You think everyone's awesome, Quinn."

"How does Gyver play into this?" John steered the conversation back on course.

"While Gyver and the dumb-dumb twins played captor, I heard them talking about meeting up with Mrs. Isabel." Sage turned toward the kids. "That was the name of the gypsy lady you were with, right?"

Quinn and Sierra winced a little at the name.

"Mrs. Isabel and Mr. Jorge," Sierra said.

Oliver nodded at them, acknowledging the sensitive nature of the subject. "Gyver was going to collect these two to take to her boss."

"Who was Gyver working for?" John asked.

"That part I never learned. Fortunately or unfortunately, that's when you and the kids showed up."

Lucky us.

Damn.

Everyone in the room fell silent. The fire Oliver had started earlier glowed yellow and orange. High crowns from the flames cast tall shadows on the walls of the quiet room.

"It's too dark for me to leave now, anyway." John glared at Oliver. "Thanks to you."

"Always at your service, my friend."

"Whatever. You owe me, Oliver. You too, Sage."

"I'll add it to my list," Sage said.

Quinn came up and gave John a hug.

"I knew you'd stay," Quinn said.

John held his arms above Quinn's shoulder as if he didn't know what to do, finally deciding on patting him on his head.

"Listen, kid, it's nothing personal. I'm only staying because I have to."

"What a hero. I, for one, feel like we can all sleep better now." Sierra fixed him with a glare before storming back to the guest room.

Quinn followed her, leaving Adam sitting by John's feet. Adam looked up at John with big, wet brown eyes and whimpered.

John, IBEC is here.

Great, one more problem to deal with. Have him wait out back.

"Fine, go ahead, boy, wouldn't want you to start feeling loyal all of a sudden."

Adam took off after Quinn, who had waited for him in the kitchen. John went over to a cabinet, and grabbed a flask of mead out of it. He popped it open, and filled up three pint glasses.

"You're done drugging me, right?"

"Oh, yes, of course." Oliver smiled an innocent smile. "A one-time event. Have I mentioned I'm sorry?"

"Yes, but you can say it a few more times."

"Of course."

John took a heavy swig of his mead and then pointed to Sage and Oliver. "You two are going to tell me everything you know. You won't leave anything out. And Oliver, you're going to promise never to drug me again."

"See, we're already resolving things. Don't you think, Sage?"

"Whatever, Oli. I'm so glad everyone seems to be so worried about John, even though he's not the only one that got dragged into this blindly."

"But I am the only that was drugged, so start singing, Sage."

"I've told you everything I know, John, and don't judge me for drugging you. That was all Oliver. In fact, I was trying to leave tonight too—" Sage looked as if she were trying to find what words to say next "—but Oliver convinced me to stay."

I really hate your friends.

You're my only friend, Cam.

We're screwed then.

John turned his attention back to Oliver. "And how'd you do that, Oli?"

Oliver smiled again, his thick red beard receding into the creases in his cheeks. "That is better answered with a bit more history. If you would follow me, please."

Oliver grabbed his pint glass, handed one to Sage, and then all three of them went up a set of stairs that led to Oliver's library and classroom. He pulled three chairs up around a table by one of the two windows that lit the loft. The round slab of thick oak sat on a wide iron base and was covered with tech tablets, reams of paper, and maps. One dim bulb cast an eerie light over the room; star and moon light filtered through the thin glass. The walls were occupied by floor-to-ceiling cedar shelves full of more thickly bound books, tech tablets, and photo albums. Oliver cleared off the table, walked over to the closest shelf, and pulled an old album off it.

"Please sit. We have much to discuss."

Sage and John took their seats, and Oliver set the book in front of them, flipping through it until he got to a page that looked like a school picture.

"What are you trying to show me, Oliver?" John asked.

"A very important piece of a very large puzzle."

Sage pointed to a bald man with a much thinner red beard, wearing a crisp brown robe and sandals, a thick, braided, hemp rope tied around his waist.

"Excellent eye, Sage, and of course you are correct, that's me." He pointed to the man next to him, taller but with the same striking features. "That's my brother Paul. These four were our brother monks and teachers, and the man over here on the other side of the children is our master, Benedict."

"Who are the children?" John asked.

"They're clones."

Oh, boy, this just got real.

Cam, do we have any info on the clone studies?

Not here.

Find some.

Are you asking me to hack Oliver's server?

Yes.

You sure do know how to sweet talk a woman, don't you?

Just do it, Cam.

"Clones? I thought that was illegal," Sage said.

"It is now," John said, "but it wasn't back when these pictures were taken, was it, Oliver?"

"Very astute of you, John. Of course you're right. This was at the Institute of Research and Intergenetic Study, IRIS for short." Oliver's voice trailed off as he spoke. "Back when we thought we were going to save the world."

"You worked at IRIS?" John asked.

"Yes, John, I did. I understand how awful that must be to someone with as sordid a past as you have with IRIS, but our mission was much different than building super-soldiers such as yourself."

"CyOps?" Sage looked at John. "You guys came from IRIS?"

"We did, doesn't matter anymore."

"Doesn't matter? It most certainly does, John," Oliver said. "The children in this picture were the first cloned from a combination of DNA: genetically engineered DNA and DNA from a group of soldiers, soldiers like you. They were perfect, impervious to disease, self-healing, with physical prowess beyond our wildest dreams, and they changed, John. They developed in ways we never could have imagined."

"How?"

"Telekinesis, energy manipulation, healing capabilities the likes of which we could scarcely fantasize about. They could tap into centers of their brains in ways we never thought possible. It was incredible."

"You're kind of sounding a little crazy, O," Sage said.

John, you have to see this.

Cam flashed John a small batch of files that Oliver was hiding deep in his server.

Jesus, Oli, what the hell were you guys trying to do?

John glared over the table at Oliver. "You said these were the first."

"We cloned one more group."

John, there's more.

She flipped through some more files and stopped on a single file.

Colonel Murdoch. More on him?

I already tried. This is everything he has.

Oliver flipped the page for John and pointed to a picture of himself, his brother Paul, and the man named Benedict standing in front two green, glowing cylinders, each containing an infant hooked up to tubes and respirator masks like some freakish nursery.

"Who the hell are you, Oliver?" Sage asked.

"Yeah, Oliver, why don't you explain who you are to us?"

"I...we were theologians, scientists, physicists, all working with IRIS to try and bring enlightenment to the world." He sighed and sat back in the chair. "We failed."

"The first group of children died during testing, didn't they?" John said.

"One of the side effects of the enormous power they were discovering in themselves. They suffered massive hemorrhaging."

"They all died? What kind of sick shit did you guys do there?" Sage asked.

"It's not like that. We didn't know that was going to happen. We stopped all exercises, decreased the test size, and used a more stable formula in just two clone children."

"Tell me how Colonel Murdoch fits into this, Oli?"

"Ah, I see Cam is still at her best. I knew that she would break the filters eventually."

Damn right.

"She has her moments." John pointed to the picture. "What was his role, Oliver?"

"Oversight, really."

Sage let out a sardonic laugh. "Oversight, Oli? When did the government only do oversight?"

John scanned a little more of the file Oliver had of Murdoch.

Damn.

Damn is right.

Oliver sighed. "You're right in thinking that, Sage. Oversight *was* his role until desperation made him sick for more. He's the reason why we had to run."

"He came for you, didn't he?"

"Yes, John, he did, but not when you think he did." Oliver looked out the windows and breathed heavily for a second. "The fusion matrix of small spheres called IRIS stones that gave the facility an independent power grid had inadvertently harnessed energy from the first batch of clones before they were destroyed. Murdoch knew of this, and after cease-fire, when he was near death, he had his men bring him to IRIS. He made Benedict rig him to the stones and transfer the stored energy to him to boost his nanosystems so he could heal. It worked and he became more powerful than anyone could have ever dreamed.

"The applications possible were apparent immediately, so he took control of IRIS to rebuild his army. Driven close to madness by the losses he experienced after Day One and before cease-fire, he was determined to gain back what he had lost, even if it meant making more clones and then draining them of every last drop of their being."

"Drain them?" Sage asked.

"We didn't know until it was too late. He attacked us while we were getting the children out. We were defenseless, so we did the only thing we could. We blew up IRIS."

I'm getting a headache.

I have a feeling it's only going to get worse. There's no way Oli's story checks out.

"Your story has some pretty gaping holes in it. For one, Murdoch's dead, Oliver. I saw it with my own eyes."

"You're correct that he was very near death." Oliver activated the holo deck and a green-hued screen popped to life in the middle of the table. John glared at the old man on the screen: silver, tight-cropped hair cutting an edge in his dark skin and contrasting with his much darker green uniform. Weary crow's feet radiated from the corners of his eyes and his angular jaw set tight as the AP riddled him with questions. "As you see. He is very much alive."

Cam, verify.

It's recent, John, feed's only a couple weeks old.

"So it's true."

Oliver collapsed the holo screen. "I'm afraid it is, John."

"Is he involved in this?"

"I wouldn't count him out, but right now, I honestly don't know."

Sage waved her hands in front of her. "All right, enough with the info dump, Oli. So what if Murdoch's alive. None of what you've told us explains why we're here."

"Patience, my dear." Oliver flipped to the last page in his book, where two very recognizable faces shone in the yellow light. Faces that John had seen very recently.

John pointed to the pictures. "Are you saying that you think… you're not saying that those kids are part of this?"

Please stop asking questions you don't want to know the answers to, John.

"I am saying exactly that. I am saying that they are the only two surviving children from IRIS. And I am saying that it is of the utmost importance that we keep them away from whoever is trying to find them."

John closed his eyes tight as if he could keep out the sandstorm of knowledge. He rubbed them with his knuckles and then opened them again, hoping it had all disappeared. "You're saying that those kids have super powers, Oli?" John shook his head, trying to wrap his mind around it. "Like super strength and telekinesis?"

"It's not so hard to imagine," Oliver said, still staring at the pictures. "Think of the open mind drug and the nanotech boom. Remember what telepathic powers and super strength those gave people. " He looked up and pointed to John. "What about your enhanced strength, endurance, the nanotech and cybernetics that you and your team have, that General Murdoch has?" He paused and looked back down at the pictures. "That Jane has."

"Jane?" Sage stood up from her chair, shaking her head. "This just keeps getting better. Look, Oli, I didn't sign up for this. What the hell did you get us into?"

"I'm with Sage," John said. "I'm not sure what you're trying to do here, Oli, and I think my mind is still a little foggy from you drugging me, but I'm out."

Sage squeezed John's shoulder, her intensity cooling a little as she grinned. "How much of that did you use anyway, Oliver?"

"Enough to tranq a horse. Taking his increased metabolism into account, I thought it was an adequate amount." He turned back to John. "I'm actually surprised you woke up so soon."

"You tranq'd him with horse tranq. Good job, Oli. I wish I would have thought of that."

This is a nightmare.

John. You might want to check on IBEC.

Why?

Oh, just because his weapons system came online.

Piece of crap. Shut it down, and I'll go check on it in a second.

"Well, this has been fun," John said. "Thanks for inviting me to your little party, but I think I've done enough for you and your misguided adventure, Oliver. I'm going to rack out and then I'm leaving first thing in the morning."

"Me too, Oli. This is all a little too weird-sounding and way over my pay grade."

"Please, just let me finish. You must at least help me get the kids to the monastery. Benedict will know what to do once we get them there."

"Sounds like a lot of fun, Oli, but I'm sticking with John on this one. I've had enough fun."

John.

What, Cam.

I can't shut IBEC down.

SEVENTEEN

Mirror, Mirror

THE OLD LADY TOOK ONE LAST look in the mirror and shook her head, then stalked out of the room.

Three guards standing outside tightened up their bodies and gave her a salute, which she returned with crisp precision.

"Ma'am," one of the guards said.

"Get me to the armory, Sergeant. I'll need them to turn a blind eye for the next twenty-four hours."

And I can finally get out of this God-forsaken town.

The guard smiled and fell into step in front of her. "Roger that, ma'am."

He led her out the back of the building to the up-armored, all-terrain rig waiting there for them.

She turned sharply and gestured to the other two guards behind her. "When the fighting starts, I want you to burn it."

They looked at each other and then back at her. "The building?"

She smiled as she looked up at the sign hanging above the door. "The town."

Their salutes were particularly enthusiastic. "Roger that, ma'am."

Her crisp salute back was deadly, arm slicing through the air like a blade, hand at a perfect forty- five degree angle as it came to the corner of her eye. "Do try not to catch yourselves on fire while you're having your fun, boys."

Her men were laughing as she got into the waiting rig. Giving a go-ahead nod to the driver, she pressed her palm to the transmission device in front of her. A holo screen popped open, a dark-skinned, black-haired man appearing in the middle of it. His eyes narrowed as he peered into his holo deck screen.

"Colonel, what a pleasant surprise to hear from you."

"Major." She gave him the barest nod of recognition. "Did my AI get the details to you?"

"It did, but are you sure you can contain this? We cannot afford any mistakes."

"Just let your monk friends know that we won't need them anymore."

"I'm sure nothing would please you more, but we will wait to see how things play out."

She rolled her eyes. "Do what you want, David. You won't be smirking so big when I get back."

David smiled. "We'll be glad to have you back. Good luck tonight, Colonel."

I won't need luck.

Of course not, ma'am.

"Thanks, David, just have my ship ready. I won't be able to get out of this insect-infested wilderness fast enough."

"Copy that. We'll be expecting to hear from you."

With that the screen blinked out.

The sergeant shifted in his seat and looked over his shoulder at her. "Ma'am?"

"What is it, Sergeant?"

"Look on your holo screen. You'll want to see this."

She flipped her holo screen back on and clicked on the feed from the cameras outside Oliver's townhouse. Her eyes narrowed and her jaw tensed as if she were trying to break her own teeth.

"Ma'am?"

Her head snapped up. "What the hell is it?"

"The militia's moving into the town."

Damn, damn, damn it.

"Get me down there now!" She shut the screen down with a flick of her fingers. "With any luck we can salvage whatever the hell shit-storm just started."

The rig jerked as it banked into a sharp turn and sped back toward the town.

Eighteen

Glass House

What do you mean, you can't shut it down?

I mean you should hit the floor. NOW.

High-explosive rounds from the IBEC's cannons rocked the building like a hundred men taking sledgehammers to Oliver's townhouse. John grabbed Oliver and threw him to the ground. Sage had been blown to the other side of the table, but she was moving for cover already. The rapid hissing thud of heavy pulse fire started hammering the front of the house. The building shook again and again as the storm of explosive gunfire burst against it.

Shut it down now, Cam!

I can't. It's been hacked. Damn good too.

You think?

Maybe if I had a Watson.

Not now, Cam.

Just saying.

John drew his gun and pushed Oliver closer to the floor; Sage dumped the table over to protect them from the flying glass. The building shuddered from the percussions, and dust from the holes being blown in the walls flooded up the stairs. Sounds of panicked people from the streets flowed in from outside, and heavy-wheeled vehicles could be heard surrounding them.

I still can't scan outside the building, but I think that's more than just the IBEC now.

Do you have any news that might be helpful?

The guest bedroom hasn't been hit.

Sierra and Quinn are safe then?

Cam put the kids' heat sigs up on John's HUD. They were huddled in the corner of their room, maybe a closet, he couldn't tell for sure, but he could tell they were alive and safe.

They heard a loud explosion from where the IBEC was, and then the pop-fizz of Oliver's electric security field going up around the townhouse and entrances to the building.

Possible hostile entered through the breach.

Damn.

Rapid footsteps echoed on the stairs. John rolled out and aimed his gun to meet the intruder.

"Jane, what the hell, I almost blew your fucking head off!"

She completely ignored him and ran to Oliver.

"They're here, Oliver. We have to go now!"

"Get the children—they're in the spare bedroom in the closet—and lead them into the tunnel," Oliver said. "I'll be right behind you."

Now how did he know that, John?

Fucking Oliver.

Jane took off at a run.

"Uh, Oliver, what's going on?"

"No time to explain now, Sage. We have a limited escape window."

Cam, Oliver's ESF is up. Can you see with the thermals?

Oh, just the entire militia and their armory of gear.

How many?

Fifteen at least, and two APCs with quad REP cannons.

Not bad odds.

If you want to die.

"We wouldn't need to escape, Oliver, if you had been up front with us," John snapped as Jane, Adam, and the children scooted past, heading down to the cellar.

"Well, I figured poorly." He smiled another innocent smile. "I'll have to catch you both up a bit later."

"Oliver, quit prattling and get us out of here," Sage said.

"Right. If you would please, John, grab that book there and throw it in your bag. I have already taken the liberty of having your things removed to the cellar."

Incredible. Never again, John.

Finally you agree with me.

"Got it," John said. "Now, lead the way, monk."

"Monk, very nice of you, John. Chop-chop, time to go. You first, Sage; then me, and then John."

She bumped past him. "This is bullshit, Oli."

"I know, Sage, terribly sorry, had it planned a little differently."

They ran down the stairs as sporadic gunfire and explosions raged outside. Orange glow fought its way through the blinds, and John caught a quick glimpse of the destroyed IBEC through the blown-out rear door as they rounded the corner.

I really wanted to keep that.

Jane versus IBEC. Jane kicks IBEC's ass. She might actually give you a run for your money.

Let's not find out.

"John, no time to delay, my friend," Oliver said.

John shook it off and followed Sage and Oliver down the stairs to the cellar. He heard the front door explode open and the electric barrier hiss, frying the first person through the door. Oliver slammed the cellar door shut behind them, tapped a code into the pad on the side of the door, and then turned back to the open tunnel door that had been behind a mead rack, which was now lying on the floor amongst a cemetery of broken bottles. Honey sour vapors flooded their nostrils as they crunched their way over the jagged glass and concrete.

"Oops, watch your step now. Shame to see it go to waste."

Sage went through the door first, followed by Oliver and John. The tunnel was well built, narrow, two shoulder breadths wide at best, but it was a clean tunnel that was lined with brick and smelled like a dank Seattle dock.

This thing must have taken years to build.

Thirteen years to be exact, if Oliver's files are correct.

"Where does this tunnel lead, Oliver?"

"It comes out of the mountain by the river about five miles outside of town, by a small forest trail that only myself and the two other monks that were here before me know about."

"Won't they find us in here if we have to take it that far?"

They lurched forward and against the tunnel walls as an explosion rocked the entrance to Oliver's tunnel.

"Ah, that takes care of that," Oliver said. "Not to worry, those were mine. There'll be no coming after us for a while."

They caught up with Jane and the kids, who looked equally disturbed, in a larger room off to one side of the tunnel. Jane raced over to them, relief painted over her face.

"Good to see you made it, Oli," she said.

John brushed past Oliver and Jane, making his way over to Adam, scratching him behind his ears and looking him over to make sure he was okay.

More lives than a cat.

Okay, so it's kind of a relief to see that he's okay.

Wow, someone might think you like him.

I'm already erasing that from the record.

"Good to see you too, Jane," Oliver said. "We can rest here for a bit, but we'll need to get moving again soon. Jane, did you bring the provisions?"

"I got all of them, Oli, but should we really rest? It won't take them long to get through that rubble."

"It'll take long enough." He smiled gingerly. "So, children, how are you? Sorry about this mess. Terrible, isn't it?"

John turned from Adam, scanning everyone in the room before settling on Oliver. "I'm with Jane, we have to keep moving."

"Can anyone explain what the hell we're going to do now?" Sierra asked.

"Take a rest," Oliver said.

"No. We're moving, now."

"Please, John, just trust me. I have contingencies. We'll be safe for a moment or two. Now, let's catch our breath, and assess our current situation."

Sierra stomped her foot on the hard-packed rock, and let out an almost comical grunt. "You're driving me crazy. What are we doing here?"

"We're running from the guys that are trying to take us away, like Mrs. Isabel and Mr. Jorge, like what you were telling Sage and John before they started bombarding the town." Quinn looked at Oliver and took a loaf of bread and meat from him. "Right, Oli?"

"Splendid, brilliant. Now tell me, Quinn, how did you know that?"

Quinn smiled but didn't get a chance to answer.

"We heard you guys earlier when we were eavesdropping," Sierra said.

John and Sage shared a laugh at Oliver's disappointment.

Not the telepathy he was expecting, eh?

I guess not. Get some bearings for us down here, Cam.

I'll try. Lots of interference.

Understood.

"Oh, I see," Oliver said. "Well, quite brilliant by all accounts. Yes, we are running from people who, for reasons not fully understood, want to take you."

"Way to sound dark and mysterious, Oliver," Sage said. "Now, you want to explain what crazy little plan you got us all into?"

"Wait. Did you hear that?" Jane asked.

She grabbed her rifle and went around the corner to check it out. The tunnel lit up with fire and a crack like lightning striking a solar panel. The explosion from deep in the tunnel sent her flying back into the small cove, her body crumpling like a soda can.

John looked up through the dust, his ears buzzing, movements sluggish, and saw flashlights coming down the tunnel.

Jane's down. Maybe the others too, John. How'd they'd get through?
They have help.

John's training kicked in, and he rolled to his side, pushing himself up.

You have to move faster, John.
I'm moving, aren't I, Cam?
They're one hundred feet away. Hurry.

He grabbed his assault rifle and turned the corner. Gripping the handle tight, he fired a single shot into the first stooge that came around the corner. He ran forward and caught him, thrusting the dead man's body into the next person and firing another single shot into his head.

Scrambling their links now. Targeting is up, John.
I wonder how many I'll have to kill today.
Ten at least, if you want to clog this artery. Or was that a rhetorical question?

"Fall back, fall back!" voices shouted from the entrance of the tunnel.
Mm, they're trained better than militia.
Soldiers?
Mercs.

John grabbed a smoke grenade off the vest of body number one and chucked it down the tunnel. The rest of the tunnel rats started coughing.

I'm still trained better.
And you have me.
And I have you.

John fired laser-fast, computer-accurate rounds into the heads of the intruders. He breathed slow and steady. A mix of endorphins coursed through him, relaxing his nerves and steadying his shot. Advanced adrenaline took up the slack and raced through his muscles, helping him rip through his assaulters.

"Fuck. Radios are down. Kill those assholes. Stop falling back, jackasses," one the men called into the chaos.
It's too late, tunnels too small, and you're too slow.

John kept firing into the smoke. The tunnel had become a gateway to hell for the unfortunate souls who entered it. John lowered himself onto one knee, dropped his magazine, and quickly replaced it with one from the dead mercenary below him.

John. His pulse grenades.

A grenade hung in one of the men's hands. John took it from him, pulled the pin, flipped the drop button on the top, and threw it past the mound of bodies. The explosion drowned out the cries of the last few live members of the tunnel rat team, turning them into part of an impassable obstacle.

They won't make it through that anytime soon, John.

Good. Cam, check the cove for vitals.

On it.

John checked the obstacle to make sure it would hold and then set up a quick thermal trip wire.

One last hang up, just in case.

John, you need to get back.

What's up?

Oliver's unconscious, but he'll live. Sage is tending to him.

Adam, the twins?

They're all fine, but Jane...

She's dead.

It was instant.

John walked back to the cove. Cam put the bioscanner on his HUD as she swept the four surviving members of his crew and Adam to make sure there weren't any injuries they were missing.

All clear. We better get moving, John.

"We need to go," he said.

The three conscious members of the group gawked at him as he started gathering what supplies were still intact.

"HEY! Wake up, we have to move. NOW!"

"We can't go, John," Sierra said. "Oliver's hurt, Jane's dead, and you're creepy killer guy again."

"Sage, can he move?"

"I think so," she said.

"Get 'em up, get 'em moving."

"Did you not hear me?" Sierra asked.

John put on his chest rig, which thankfully Oliver had made sure to bring, and dug a thick, gunmetal-gray collar out of his pack. He went over to Adam, crouched low by him, and connected it around his neck.

Cam, link with Adam's collar.

On it—okay, I'm linked, John. We'll be able to see wherever he goes.

"Go scout it for us, boy. Go all the way through."

Adam took off faster than anyone had seen him go, heading down the open part of the tunnel. John picked up Oliver, tossed him over his shoulder like bag of sand, and followed Adam out.

Quinn looked over at his sister, blinked his eyes a few times, and got up, holding his hand out to Sierra. "Come on, Sis. John's right, we need to keep going."

"Are you nuts? This is getting crazy! What are we doing here? What is that crazy guy Oliver talking about half the time? We can't just leave Jane. Can anyone answer me?"

Quinn stood over her and smiled, still holding his hand out. She took it and jerked herself up.

"We just need to keep moving." He let go of her hand and walked after John into the tunnel.

Sage grabbed Jane's bag and tossed it over her shoulder, then came up behind Sierra and put a hand on her shoulder.

"Come on, Sierra. Sometimes when you don't have any answers, you just have to keep moving until you find some." She dug through the satchel, pulled out one of Jane's purple biscuits, and handed it to Sierra. "Try one of these. It'll make you feel better."

Sierra took the biscuit and gobbled it down. Within minutes she couldn't shut up. "And Sage, I'm going to figure you out. This sneaky loner business won't last long. Oh my God, Q, get one of Sage's biscuits. They are so good. Sage, do you have a biscuit for Q?"

"What did you feed her?" John asked when they caught up with him.

"You're not gonna complain, are you? I did get her to follow us."

"I'm not sure it would have been worse leaving her."

"Leaving who?" Sierra asked.

John, Adam's sensors say the tunnel's clear. No contact, and the path on the other end looks okay, no heat sigs.

How long do we have left?

An hour, maybe less, if we don't stop.

John felt Oliver's body start to squirm on his shoulder.

Oliver groaned. "Ugh, what's happening?"

Oh, and Oliver's waking up.

"Hey, Sage. Let's hold up a minute."

Sage stopped moving and came back down the tunnel to where John was letting Oliver down, sitting him against the tunnel's wall.

"What's up? Everything okay?" Sage asked.

"Yeah, Sleeping Beauty's waking up."

Oliver's head was wobbling on his neck. He blinked his eyes open, adjusting them to take in his surroundings. "What happened? Sage?"

"Bad guys came into the tunnel. Big boom knocked you out and killed Jane. John kicked their asses and resealed the tunnel. We're about hour away from the end." Sage looked over at John. "Did I miss anything?"

"No, that's pretty good."

Except the part about Cam being awesome.

"Oh, Cam was helpful too."

Thank you.

"The twins?" Oliver asked.

John pointed over to a dark corner of the tunnel. "Over there. They're still in shock, but they're making it."

John just could just see their shadowy hands waving to Oliver.

"Hi, Oli," Quinn said.

"Thank God you two are safe. Should be over soon, just a bit farther. Keep up your spirits." His fake smile faded and he turned back to John. "Jane. She didn't make it?"

Sage knelt down and grabbed his shoulder. "Sorry, Oli. It was fast, if that's any consolation."

"It is, Sage, it is. She knew what she was getting into. Brave woman, brave indeed."

"You good to walk, Oli?"

"I think I can manage."

"Then we need to go."

"Of course. Onward and upward then." Oliver used his hands to help himself to his feet. He felt along the side of the tunnel for a second before speaking again.

"About an hour, you say?"

"About."

"Very good, very good. Then I think we've delayed enough. Lead on please, John."

Cam?

Still clear. Adam should be back soon.

John looked over at Sage. "You heard the man. Onward and upward, Sage."

"Onward and upward, great."

*   *   *

They trudged on quietly, the sound of gravel beneath their feet the only whispered echo in the moist tunnel as they went.

"John, is it getting lighter up there?"

"Good, maybe we don't have too much farther to go."

Adam came scurrying down from the light and bee-lined straight for John, putting his front paws on his chest.

"Hey, boy! I missed you too. Did you find anything?"

Adam barked and pawed the ground twice, letting him know it was clear, and then licked John's face and nuzzled him.

"Good boy, good boy!"

Adam got back to the ground, and trotted past them to Quinn and Sierra, who smiled for the first time since they escaped from Oliver's.

"Hey, Adam, where'd you go, boy?" Quinn asked.

Adam barked and trotted around both of them, pushing off them with his paws and making them chase him.

"Come here, boy." Sierra got down on her knees and grabbed him around his neck. "Let's just stay together from now on, okay, boy?"

"Come on, Sis, we better get moving again."

Adam barked again and started nudging her back to her feet.

"Ah, nice, right to it as always, Adam. See, John, here we are. Just around the corner and we'll be home free."

"Somehow I'm not comforted by that."

Sage laughed. "I second that, John."

Third.

NINETEEN

Home Free

AS HE CAME OUT OF THE TUNNEL, John squinted and held his hand up to shield his eyes from the fresh morning sun. "Oliver, where the hell are we?"

Just be thankful we're out of the god-awful tunnel.

John looked around at the trees, the mountains looming high above, the creek, and a cabin on a low hill ahead, partially hidden behind the trees.

"Yes, some explaining is in order, but all in due time, all in due time," Oliver said, and continued up the trail toward a small stream. He pointed to a fork of paths that led farther up into the mountains. "All these trails lead to our little-known pass through the mountains. We'll find some extra supplies up there at the cabin. Fresh food, water. Maybe rest awhile, resupply, and catch our breath."

"I'm so thankful, Oli, for your always lengthy, yet un-insightful explanation."

"You are very welcome, John."

Sage came out of the opening, followed by Quinn, Sierra, and Adam. Sierra stretched her arms out wide and put her face to the sun.

"Oh, yes, finally, sunshine!" Sierra said. "I think I would have gone mad if I would've had to be in there one more second."

"Yeah, feels amazing," Quinn said.

Sage came to a stop near John. "I think your sarcasm is lost on Oli right now."

Maybe we should make a run for it while we have the chance.

John sighed, dropped to one knee, and surveyed his companions. No one had rested since the fight in the tunnel when they'd lost Jane. Their dirt-covered faces were pale with weariness, and their shoulders slumped from exhaustion. They'd all been carrying more than just the baggage they had on their backs.

They need a break, John.

They need to keep moving.

They need a break. Damn, John, we need a break, a chance to remember Jane.

Give me a quick scan while we break then, Cam.

John pulled a leathery meat stick out of one of his pouches and held it out for Adam, "Here, boy. You did good in the tunnel today, yes you did. One more scout, then we can get out of here." Adam licked John's hand and chomped down the jerky before taking off into the woods.

What are Sage and Oliver talking about, Cam?

Convincing you to stay the night.

No way that's happening.

Good luck. I think you might have a mutiny brewing.

"Where's Adam going?" Quinn asked.

"He's going to check ahead, make sure it's safe."

Sierra glared at him. "It's sick, you know—using him to do the dangerous stuff you don't want to do all the time."

I'm getting a headache.

I can tell.

Really, Cam?

It's my head too.

"Well, I guess I'm a sick guy then."

"Whatever."

She dropped her pack and stormed over to a fresh stream that ran out of the rocks and along the trail. Quinn followed her, willing to let Sage, John, and Oliver decide on what to do next.

John shrugged and turned to Oliver and Sage. "We'll rest here, do some recon—need to check our stock anyway and see what we have left, then we need get some miles in before nightfall."

"I understand your point, John, but let's stay here for the night. We have to eat, and we have to restock, take time to recover. All things we can do safely at the cabin."

"Safe? Safe like your house, safe like your tunnel."

"I think you're being unreasonable, if you would just—"

John held his hand up, palm flat to Oliver to cut him off. "Thirty minutes, Oliver, then we have to keep moving."

You know he's right, John. This is probably the safest we've been the whole trip.

We're never safe.

I said "safest".

If we rest now we might never get moving again.

Sage cleared her throat to get their attention. "I can see how standing out here and discussing going to a cabin that's only a couple hundred yards away might make sense to you two, but I think while you do that I'll head up there and check it out."

Oliver and John looked at each other and then stared after her as she turned and strode up the trail toward the cabin.

Now I remember why I like her so much.

"Oliver, when we get up there, you owe us more explanation."

"Of course, of course. I'm sure this is all a little much." Oliver nudged John's arm and wiggled his eyebrows up and down at him. "That Sage sure is a fiery one, isn't she."

"Let's not make this more of a nightmare than it already is, Oliver."

"I'm not sure if nightmare is the correct term, but you're right, it has not gone exactly how we planned."

"There was a plan?"

"Of course there was a plan."

That's good news, John.

Are you kidding me?

Imagine if there wasn't a plan.

Never again, Cam. I'm never getting involved again.

So you keep saying.

I mean it this time.

Sure.

Sierra came over, pack on, hair wet and pulled back, and nudged John in the ribs. "Are Mommy and Daddy fighting?" She reached over and grabbed something out of John's bag. "Oh, look, a choco bar, dibs!" She grabbed the bar, took a bite out of it before stuffing it in her satchel, and started toward the cabin.

Are you going to let her know what those are?

Not a chance.

"Oliver…"

"Right on it, John. I'll fetch Quinn."

They hiked up the rocky trail, surrounded on either side by a picket fence of trees and rocky mountain. The cabin overlooked the stream and the hidden tunnel.

"How long have you had this cabin here, Oli?" Quinn asked.

"Oh, it was here before we got here; in fact, all this was. It was just forgotten about until the right people came around."

John snorted. "So it's still waiting then?"

"Ah, very funny, John, and maybe too true."

"Are we going to be able to, like, sleep and clean up there?" Sierra asked. "I feel gross and I'm exhausted."

Oliver raised his hand and was about to say something, but John interrupted him.

"No."

"Well, we might have a little time to freshen up," Oliver said.

"No."

"Of course not," Sierra said. "Why would I think you would let us get comfortable and actually rest?"

"Oh, I don't know. Maybe because last time this group decided to rest, one of us died. Or did you forget that little piece of information already?"

The mood darkened, and the four of them got quiet.

Damn, John.

Really, you can't tell me you're not thinking the same thing.

I'm just saying try something different for a change.

What's the sit-rep on the lodging, Cam?

You really do know how to change subject, don't you?

Cam.

Cabin's clear, John, and so is the trail.

What about the tunnel?

No one's triggered the wire you left, and from what I can tell, there's no other way here.

Good, maybe we'll have a chance to get some distance between us.

"Let's just make it to the cabin for now. We can figure things out from there."

Oliver nodded his head, as if shaking off the thought of Jane's death. "Right, onward. A short bit of regrouping and remembering should be just the right thing."

They got to the cabin and dropped their gear in the front room. It was a cozy little place, one room with a small kitchen, dining area, and sitting area. A black iron stove sat in the corner on flat, broken stones. A small ladder in the middle of the main room led up to a sleeping loft that looked as if it had a couple of sets of bunks. A door at the back of the cabin had a carving on it of a bear sitting on a toilet reading a newspaper.

Well, that's something you don't see every day.

I might've liked the original owners of this place.

You don't like the current one, John?

I'm reserving judgment.

Quinn was rummaging through the kitchen and stopped to scan the occupants of the room.

"Where'd Sage go?"

The group stopped and looked around at each other. Oliver turned to John and shrugged his shoulders.

"Maybe she's in the toilet," Sierra said.

"I'm not in the toilet." Sage came through the door and nudged past them, walking over to the kitchen counter and dropping a couple of rabbits onto it.

Damn, she's good.

She's not that good.

What, we've been out of the tunnel for all twenty minutes and she already has dinner.

Lucky.

No, she's good, John, even you have to admit it.

Sage started skinning them and gutting them, nodding her head to John. "Want to start a fire in that tin can over there?"

"Sage, we don't have time."

"John, we'll never make it on the provisions that we have left from Oli's. If we don't eat something, rest, and take whatever stores we can from here, we might as well go back into the tunnel and return to Tree Top."

Told you she was good.

"Doesn't sound like I have much of a choice."

"No, John, you don't, not unless you want to carry us all on your back."

I could do that.

I think you'd get more of a fight than you bargained for.

This is why I always hated working with her.

Because she's right.

Because she's intolerable.

You didn't think that the other night.

Sierra sneered at him. "Yeah, John. I'm going to wash up and get some rest." She went over to the door with the bear on it and headed inside.

Never again, Cam.

Keep telling yourself that.

Oliver smiled and walked over to the wood stove, where he started loading logs into it from a small stack on the stone tile.

"No worries, my friend. I've got a smart cabin really, solar panels, fresh spring well, compost bathroom, and this—" he gestured to the stove "—completely smokeless, this one. Pipes right into the rocks behind it." He smiled even bigger. "Previous occupant must've been a bit paranoid."

"Did you know whoever lived here, John?" Quinn asked.

"Why would you ask that?"

"It just seems like someone you'd know."

"The other people out there like me aren't ones we want to meet, kid."

Sage bagged up the rabbit's innards and hung the skinned and trimmed bodies above the sink to bleed. "I think he meant paranoid, John, not smart."

Ouch, John.

"Well, I guess smart *too*, but paranoid, that's a good word for it," Quinn said.

Sage and Oliver burst into an overtired laugh that had a slight ring of hysteria to it.

"What?" Quinn asked. "Did I miss something?"

"Do you remember the last four days, kid? There's a reason people like me live alone in the woods." John ripped his pack open and dug through it, jerking a couple of extra pulse magazines out of it, and then stormed toward the door. "I'm going up the trail to check it out and see what's taking Adam so long."

Showed them, didn't you.

I want my lonely life back.

Sure you do.

Where's Adam?

Cam showed him Adam's heads-up display from the collar.

About a mile north of here.

Good, that should be far enough.

* * *

"Are you going to tell me what Jane died for, Oli?" Sage asked.

John was still gone. The twins were sitting up in the loft, their feet dangling between the rail posts as they listened to Sage and Oliver. The smell of gamey rabbit and stale rosemary saturated the cabin. Oliver looked up at the twins, eyes glazing over as if his mind had flashed him a thousand memories all at once. He shook himself out of it and turned back to Sage, exhaustion changing to recognition.

"You all deserve to know what you are involved in," he said. "Benedict, I, and a few others at the monastery who were originally tasked to take care of the children at IRIS found and built many places like this around the old country: the United States, the Colonies, and here in the Free, in hopes that we would be able to find our two IRIS children."

He looked back up at Quinn and Sierra. "You two."

Sierra looked at him, eyes narrowed, lips tight. "There're other places like this, other monks like you waiting for us?"

"You've known about these two this whole time?" Sage asked. "You knew and didn't think it would be a good idea to share the information?"

"As you remember, I was trying to catch you and John up on events when things went a bit south."

"A bit south? And the way I remember, you weren't doing much explaining—"

"I think I know why," Sierra interrupted. She stopped kicking her feet and leaned her head out between the posts. "Why Jane died trying to protect us. Why you couldn't tell us everything right away. When I met Jane—I don't know how to say it, but she could, like, talk to me without moving her lips. I could hear her in my head, and I think she could hear me back." She looked at Quinn, who smiled and nodded at her with encouragement. "Quinn can hear me too."

Oliver stood up and looked up at both of them, a huge smile of relief breaking on his face. "Yes, Sierra. Jane was a telepath. She could read minds and share simple instructions or sentences with someone." He switched his gaze to Sage, who shook her head and slumped back into her seat as if she were exhausted from the shock. Oliver sighed and looked back up toward the children. "You are too, Sierra. In fact, you have many powerful abilities that you are very much unaware of, both of you."

Quinn stuck his head out by Sierra's and blurted, "I broke the Sasquatch Hammer." He smiled proudly. "And I can lift really heavy things sometimes."

Oliver laughed, looked over at Sage, and shot Quinn a sardonic smile before getting up to stoke the fire. "You see now, Sage, this is what Jane died for. She died for these two beautiful children."

"Just remember she died, Oli, that's all I ask."

The group got somber and Oliver sat back down. "Never. Never would I forget her. Or you, Sage, or John for that matter."

The door opened just then, letting in the last shred of light from the descending sun as John came in. Adam squeezed between his legs and trotted over to Sierra and Quinn, as if their sole purpose had been to wait for him to get back.

John slammed the door and turned to face the room, bringing in more tension like a sledgehammer breaking ice.

"Hi, John!" Quinn said.

"Don't start, kid." He faced the room and let out a grunt. "Well, isn't this cozy?"

Nice entrance, John. I think you're giving off a strong sense of warmth.
I'm tired, Cam, I don't feel like warmth.

Sage glared at him. "You're a ball of sunshine. So glad to see you too."

"You should be glad it was only me, seeing as you're all so alert."

Quinn spoke up again, as if he had no idea John was irritated at all. "You missed all the good stuff."

John shook his head. "I'd say I don't care, but I'm sure you're going to tell me anyway."

"Sage is mad at Oliver for keeping us in the dark about Sierra and me being really important, and about his secret bases all over the world."

"So I didn't miss anything worth hearing. That's good."

Adam went over and sat under Sierra and Quinn's dangling feet, head tilted, ears perked and tail wagging, thumping hard on the floor.

"What? You can't get up here, boy?" Sierra asked.

Adam barked and danced on his hind legs. He jumped up and tried to catch Quinn's foot, but Quinn pulled it back just in time and made him miss.

And you keep saying he's smart.

He has his moments.

"John…" Oliver started to say.

"Trail's clear. We can go when everyone's ready."

Sage shook her head and went over to turn the rabbits in the fire. "We've already talked about this, John. We're staying the night."

"She's right, John," Sierra said.

It's too late now anyway, John, and unless you spotted something that my brilliant self didn't, there's no shelter out there past this.

You know this big happy family is temporary, right?

So you keep saying.

"So what do you two geniuses have planned?"

"Four geniuses—don't forget me and Sierra," Quinn piped in between giggles, as he pulled his feet back from Adam again.

John looked around the room. No one was budging.

Looks like everyone's minds are made up, John.

"I'll take first watch." John walked over and grabbed his bag from where he had left it earlier. "Adam. Let's go, boy."

Adam stopped playing and turned to look at him, head cocked as if trying to decide whether he should go or stay.

"You don't have to do this, John," Sage said. "Rabbits are almost ready."

"I'll come wake you when it's your turn."

John won the stare down with Adam, and they were out the front door before anyone could say anything more.

Showed them again.

Shut up, Cam.

* * *

John snuck back into the cabin after nightfall with Adam beside him. Adam perked his ears and trotted silently over to the table to look for scraps.

Everyone good, Cam?

Everyone's sound asleep, John, very sound asleep.

Good. They really must've needed rest, eh?
Really, you're going with that now?
Just saying.
John checked the fire and threw on another log.
"Come on, boy, time to go back up."
You know Sage was right. You don't have to do this.
Yes I do, Cam. It's better this way.
You're the only one who thinks so.
This isn't going to last forever, and you know that. We need separation.
They left and stalked up the rocks of the mountain behind the
cabin. They got to the top of an outcrop and perched themselves
under a camo sheet that John set up. John leaned up against a tree,
feet kicked out, and Adam lay next to him, both of them facing the
stars that poked through over the western skyline.

Adam let out a whimper and nuzzled closer to John.

"I know, boy. They're growing on me too. But we have to leave at
some point. Maybe not now, but at some point." He rested his head
back and watched the clear sky twinkle.

It's beautiful, isn't it, John.
I wish you could see this through your own eyes, Cam.
This is pretty damn good for now.
Sorry I didn't get you a Watson.
It's okay. I'm sorry about Jane.
Me too. You got this.
I got it. Get some sleep, grumpy, you need it.
John smiled and closed his eyes, letting the night sweep over him.

TWENTY

Self Destruct

JOHN SHOOK OLIVER AWAKE. Sage was already up, prepping her things for the next leg of their journey. The kids came down, slow and tired, making their way into the room like zombies.

"I thought you said you would wake us for our watch," Oliver said.

"I said I'd wake you if I needed you," John said. "I didn't need you."

"John doesn't need us when he's got Cam. Do you, John?" Sage asked.

"Aha, you would know better about that than I would, Sage."

I so need a different partner.

Like you have better options, Cam.

I wish I did.

Liar. How's the trail look?

No changes. Heat sigs are clear, no EM fields, should be safe and sound.

Should be.

John went over and made himself a coffee with his small contraption, while Sage handed out rations from the boxes of provisions that Oliver had stored at the cabin. John passed his coffeemaker around and let Sage and Oliver make a cup, since Oliver had provided an over-abundant supply of coffee. The three conferred with one another while the kids ate and played with Adam.

"We have about fifteen miles to go today, give or take," John said. "I figure we'll want to avoid Leavenworth this time around."

"I second that," Sage said.

Third.

John heard Adam bark, and he turned to see Sierra and Quinn playing keep-away from him with a jerky stick. Quinn turned and waved, a perfect childish smile on his face. Sierra did the same, smile and all.

Did she just smile?

Creepy, huh?

John, I don't want to do this.

Noted already, Cam, but it's not open for discussion.

"Oli. We'll follow your trail for now, but once we get close enough, Adam and I are splitting off to go home."

Sage looked at John, eyes concentrated as if she had a question to ask. She opened her mouth to say something but then turned back to her coffee and stuffing her pack.

"Very well, John. Looks like you made up your mind," Oliver said. "I wish it were different."

"It's not."

"Then we better get to it," Oliver said, "while I still have your services."

Sierra came over, Adam and Quinn right behind her. "So what's the plan?"

"Hit the road hard," Sage said. "Put as much distance between us and this rock as possible."

Quinn nodded his head up and down in agreement. "All right, let's do this then." He headed out the door.

"He can be a dip sometimes." Sierra grabbed her bag along with his and followed him out. "Plus I shouldn't have given him any coffee."

"Right," Oliver said. "To the road less traveled, then."

Adam trotted out behind them, followed by Oliver.

Sage looked back at John. Once again words were written on her face that never left her mouth.

"Not now, Sage," John said. "Let's get this over with, okay?" He waved his hand toward the door for her to go.

Cam.

Timer's already on.

Good.

They got exactly a mile down the trail when the hillside erupted like a small volcano, sending everyone scattering off the trail except for Adam and John. The explosive charges John placed the night before had gone off, blowing the rock face off and burying the tunnel entrance.

Sage stood up and dusted herself off. "What the hell was that?"

Sierra and Quinn crept out of the bushes they'd thrown themselves into, an exasperated look of surprise on their faces.

"Did they find us?" Quinn asked.

Sierra nodded her head. "How are we ever going to get rid of them? Jesus!"

Oliver looked at John, who walked past them and up the trail as if nothing had happened.

"He's awfully calm," Sage said.

Oliver nodded. "Obviously he knows something we don't."

"Have to be his," Sage said. "What an asshole."

"So we're not going back that way ever," Quinn said.

Oliver wiped himself off and started back up the trail himself. "Apparently not."

It's the small things in life, Cam.

Or the extremely large explosions.

Yes, or that.

They crept along the trail until it came to an intersection where Oliver halted and inspected his map. Instead of following the trail straight on, Oliver led them down through a thicket and into the forest until they came to a creek bed.

"Ah, here we are."

"Uh-huh, where are we exactly, Oli?" Sage asked.

"A supply depot."

"I don't see anything," Sierra said. "Hey, where's Adam and Quinn?"

"They're over there." John pointed to a group of boulders that looked like an old rock slide. "Inside Oliver's cave."

Sage searched the trees and rocks. "Sneaky."

Sierra put her hand above her eyes to shield them against the glare from the sun. "I still don't see them. All right, Q, fun and games are over, where are you?"

Quinn stood up on a group of tall rocks and waved to them. Adam jumped up beside him, barking as if urging them to follow.

"I'm over here, Sis. You guys got to see this. It's so cool!"

Sierra started hopping over to him on the boulders. "Not a good idea to go hiding when we're being chased by crazy people, Q."

"Aha, well done, Quinn!" Oliver started over toward him.

"How did he find that?" Sage asked.

John smirked at her. "Jealous?"

"You're a jerk."

"I'm glad that's finally catching on for you."

Sage punched John in the arm before heading over to the others.

"You're all gum drops and candy canes, aren't you?" John said.

"I was never able to hide my true self from you, John."

You two need to get a room. This is getting seriously disturbing.

What are you talking about?

Really, are you flashing back to high school or something?

You're weird.

You're weird.

John caught up to them and slid through a small separation between two giant boulders. A set of carved stairs led into a decent-sized cave.

"It's too dark to see anything in here," Sierra said.

"John, don't get any ideas," Sage said.

Really gross, John. You could at least try to not to think of things like that.

Oh yeah, sorry, Cam.

A cranking noise came from the back of the cave, and a small string of lights illuminated the space.

"Wow, nice job, Oli," Sage said. "What do you think, John?"

"Real cozy."

John surveyed the cave, which was lined with metal racks full of dry goods, canned goods, boxes of small packaged rations, and water. Toward the back stood a rack with some hydro cells and some regular lithium batteries being charged by wires that disappeared into the cave wall, probably linked to a solar panel camouflaged on the boulder. John followed the string of lights to the back of the cave where another tunnel led farther into the rock.

"Where does this go, Oli?" Quinn asked.

"A small stable. Unfortunately, we only have a mule back there; just got her up here two days ago. She goes by the name of Esmeralda." Oliver pointed to a dark area even farther back. "Then it leads back out to another trail on the other side of these boulders."

At least this mule won't try to blow us up.

I really wanted that IBEC.

"You're just full of surprises, Oliver."

"That means a lot coming from you, John."

John followed the rest of the crew as they went through to the tunnel. Sierra and Quinn had already raced to the far back of the cave and were expertly investigating the dark cavern and Esmeralda. Sage finished stuffing her bag with food and water, and threw on a large medical vest that was full of supplies.

Quinn ran his hand along Esmeralda. "She's so shiny, Oliver."

"She might be a mule, but she's one of the best." Oliver threw a blanket on her back and then a load-bearing harness. "I've actually grown quite fond of her."

"She's so pretty," Sierra said.

"I think she's awesome, Oli," Quinn said.

Sage came over to John, who was dropping some hydro cells into his pack.

"They do know that thing's only a mule, right?"

"Beats the hell out of me." He threw his pack over his shoulders and checked to make sure his magazines were full of pulse rounds. "You ready?"

"Always."

Oliver finished loading the supply boxes onto Esmeralda with Sierra and Quinn's help.

"I think that's the last of it," Oliver said.

Cam, how we looking?

Still clear, John, but if we keep going the way Oliver's taking us, we're going to run right into our house.

Interesting.

More like creepy.

John checked Oliver, Quinn, and Sierra's gear to make sure they had all the supplies that they needed. He went over to check Sage's, but backed away when he got a harsh glare from her.

"Trying to get your hands on me again, John?"

"Yeah, keep dreaming, sweetheart."

Her glare let up into a wry smile. "Why don't you focus your hands on something useful, like a map, so we can get out of here?"

"I am focused."

"Sure you are."

You two are weird.

You're weird.

Since the routes are clear, Casanova, how about you take her advice: focus on a map and get us out of here.

Shut up and show me the damn grid, Cam.

As you wish.

An overlay of their current position, and the route to the flashing grid Oliver had provided, popped up on John's HUD.

"All right, Cam says the road's clear. We have about ten more miles to go today, according to Oliver's grid." He whistled to Adam and headed out the back of Oliver's secret cave, the dog right on his heels. "Try to keep up. We won't be resting again until we've reached Oliver's next camp."

* * *

"My feet are killing me," Sierra said for the thousandth time.

Sierra and John were in the lead, with Oliver and Quinn in the middle and Sage pulling up the rear. Adam was done scouting for now and was walking back by Sage.

John let his head fall back and looked toward the sky, soaking in the blueness.

Looking for divine intervention.

Or an asteroid to hit me.

"No way we're stopping, kid," John said, "and no way I'm carrying you, so I suggest you deal with it."

"Like we think you'd ever go out of your way to be nice," Sierra said.

"How much farther do we have to go, John?" Quinn asked.

"Not much farther. According to Oliver's map, maybe a mile or two at most."

"Good," Oliver said. "I think I've become too accustomed to carriages while in Tree Top. This walking has done me some good." He looked at Quinn. "Always a positive out there if you search for it, eh, Q?"

Adam stopped and sniffed the air. The hair on his back raised and he growled, curling his lips up and baring his usually hidden fangs.

John, we are literally only like half a kilometer from the house, and I'm tracking four heat sigs heading there right now.

Coincidence?

Really, John?

Wishful thinking.

"I know, boy, I know," John said. "Stinks, doesn't it?"

"What's wrong with Adam, John?" Sage asked.

"He senses that we're about to kill Oliver."

Oliver's face turned red and he cleared his throat. "I'm sorry, what was that last part?'

"Oliver…"

Quinn walked up and started petting Adam, instantly calming him down.

That's something new.

No one but you has ever been able to do that once he's in beast mode.

"It's okay, boy, it's okay," Quinn said as he petted Adam. "Where are we, John?"

"Close to where we started, kid, too close."

Yeah, no doubt about it, John. They're heading to the house.

Damn it.

"Oliver, you have about sixty seconds to explain why you've been slowly leading us to my house."

"What do you mean?" Oliver asked.

"You've been leading us to John's house this whole time?" Sage said.

"Yes, John, one of our alternate routes is apparently very close to your property," Oliver said. "I thought you would have realized that by now with Cam's help."

Oh, no he didn't.

Yes, yes he did.

John looked at the sky and then the mountain, kicking the dirt a little.

"You knew exactly where we were going this whole time."

Sage scooted in closer to Oliver, hand on the hilt of her knife. "Oliver, why *does* your secret trail lead to John's house?"

"Like I said, easy to get disoriented out here, and I didn't exactly remember that we would be so close."

Sage let out a snort. "Are you ever not full of complete bullshit, Oli?"

"I never once said that my plan was perfect, Sage. To tell you the truth I'm much more suited for books and lectures than I am for things of this nature."

"Well, next time, save us all the trouble and stick to the books; leave the strategy to someone else."

John, we should go.

I have to make sure Oliver isn't setting us up before we do anything, Cam.

Well, that's easy, I can just…

No, Cam, not this time.

Your funeral.

John moved past Sage, confronting Oliver, his eyes flashing red. "Why are we so close to my damn house?"

"Will you trust me, John? Please."

The kids stared back and forth at the three of them, Sage positioned behind Oliver, John staring him down, looking as if he might leap at him at any second and rip his head off.

John. Goldilocks. With multiple heat sigs.

Damn, damn, damn.

"We don't have time," John said. "They're heading to my house, Oliver. To my house."

John took off into the trees, Sage and Adam right behind him. Oliver and the kids stayed farther back, just close enough not to lose sight of them. They made their way down and down, cutting through the underbrush like a wildfire. By the time they got to the trail leading to the house, everyone but John was exhausted.

"Sage."

"Got it, John."

Adam froze at the base of the last hill before they had a clear shot at the house. John snapped his pulse rifle to his shoulder and flipped the safety off. Adam got onto his belly, inched forward to the top of the hill, and waited. Sage took the kids and Oliver, went down the trail, and then peeled off behind a large boulder for cover. She gave John a thumbs up, and he crawled up the hill beside Adam.

How many, Cam?

Two five-man squads

Why, why did I get us into this?

You're a bleeding heart?

Yeah, not that.

Then Adam, it was definitely Adam.

John's house was infested with militia. They had to have gotten there in the last few minutes, because they were still unloading personnel to set up a perimeter, and unpacking large cargo boxes of equipment.

"Damn, Adam, sorry I got you into this boy."

Adam put his paw on John's hand and wrinkled his nose, curling his lips up to show his teeth.

"Good idea."

He slid the un-lock on his wrist computer and keyed in a code.

It's all yours, Cam. We only have energy for one shot at this.

Sorry, John, I know what this...

Just do it, Cam.

He turned to Adam and scratched his head. "Sorry about your bed, Adam, but we'll get you a new one, okay?"

Adam put his paws over his eyes and whimpered. John buried his face in the dirt and waited. A loud pop came from the house, followed by a high-pitched buzzing sound, screams, and the roar of fire. Adam and John were safely hidden behind the hill, but the heat could still be felt rolling outward and over them, like ocean waves rolling up onto the beach.

John wondered what the people inside the house were thinking as they died, wondered what was on their minds the split second before Cam activated the EMP that sent their equipment into disarray, the split second before the lasers focused from every corner of the house had sent a volcano-strength flare that enveloped the people, left his house a skeleton, and cannibalized itself until nothing was standing.

Well, shit.

John slid down the hill and ran around to where it hugged up against the back of his now blackened skeleton of a house. With Adam stalking just behind him, John crested the hill, his weapon trained in front of him.

Cam.

Three bodies.

Damn, it reeks.

He circled around the far side of the house.

Two more, John. I have some vitals coming from that one.

Cam magnified the image so John could see one of the charred bodies trying to claw to the trees. John raised his weapon a centimeter and shot a single burst into the man's head.

Six down, four more to go.

John came around the front, Adam still on his heels, and saw them creeping up in formation toward the still smoking remnants of the house. Cam sighted each of them on John's heads-up display and locked on. He squeezed the trigger smooth as a panther four times, barely moving as four bursts came from his REP rifle. The assaulting force fell, each one with a new smoking hole where their left eye used to be.

John stalked forward like a predator, only lowering his weapon enough to see whether there was any more movement.

No more vitals, John.

Safe to bring 'em up?

Safe.

He clicked his tongue twice. Adam took off over the hill and starting barking. John went over and looked at the rig. It was military grade, high end. *Militia. What were they doing here?* He heard Adam barking at the others, urging them to hurry up.

Bossy dog.

Sounds like his owner.

You're just jealous you can't be bossy.

Adam came back over the hill with Sage, Oliver, and the twins, each of them gawking at the destruction John was capable of in just a matter of minutes.

"Anyone else getting tired of this?" Sierra asked.

"Whoa, what happened here, and what's that smell?" Quinn asked.

Oliver, looking a bit green, shuffled his way through the mess. "Those young men, I would imagine."

Sage came up and ran her fingers through the fur on Adam's head as she made her way to John.

"You boys are always so messy."

John didn't take his eyes off where his house used to be. "We don't know any better."

"Sorry about the house, John. I know how much it meant to you."

"No time for that now, Sage. There'll be more coming."

John turned and faced Oliver. He always knew the man had secrets, but now those secrets were turning his world upside down. He raised his REP, pointing it at Oliver's chest, and Oliver's hands shot up over his head.

"Now, John, wait a second—

"Oliver, I want some answers. You have about ten seconds before I blow a hole in you."

"Just give me minute, I can't think with that thing pointed at me."

"Deal with it." John flashed the laser dot onto to Oliver's chest for effect. "This team isn't normal militia, they're too high tech, too organized. How did they find my house? How'd they get here so fast?"

"It's a bit complicated."

He moved his REP around, making the laser dot dance in a circle around Oliver's heart. "Try me."

Remember, bossy is what you're going for, John. Please don't kill him before we have answers.

No promises.

Quinn and Sierra were sitting on the charred steps, shell-shocked at the events of the last few days, and looking at Oliver as if they were wondering what was so important about them that people were dying because of it.

"I didn't know, John. I don't know who they are or how they got here so fast. Things seem to be moving much more quickly than anticipated." Oliver wiped his brow and looked over at Quinn and Sierra, his face softened. "Plan a lifetime and it's still not enough."

Sage got close to Oliver and snapped her fingers in front his eyes. "Hey, don't get lost in there, Oli. We just need Cliffs Notes here."

"Oh yes, sorry." He looked back at John and pointed at the REP John still had on him. "Do you have to keep that damn laser dancing around my vital organs?"

"Until I start liking what I hear, yes."

Oliver let out a sigh and then continued. "Well, let's sum it up. We rebuilt that tunnel to the old Native's trail that led past your house just in case we needed a fallback option."

"Just in case," Sage said. "That's quite the emergency plan."

"Thank you, Sage, but as I said, I hadn't quite counted on that band of mercenaries. They must've been paid rather handsomely. Quite good, weren't they?"

"Oliver, stay on track. What do you have planned now?"

"John, there are things going on now that I am not aware of. I'm missing something. We have to make it to the pass and over to the monastery at Galbraith. Benedict will know much more than I."

John, we don't have time for this.

We never have time.

We need to go.

"If this is your short version, cut it more."

"Right, right," Oliver said. "John, I simply need your help, along with Sage's, to get these kids to Benedict at the monastery. It is the only place we will be safe now."

John and Sage looked at each other. Sage raised her arms and shook her head.

"Great, at least it's that simple," John said. "Just like all the rest of your plans have been. Everything on this whole damn trip has been one cluster fuck after another, Oliver. How the hell can you think it's all so simple, let alone safe?"

"Never simple, John," Oliver said. "But it would be manageable with help from both of you."

John, they wouldn't make it two seconds without us.

They'll have to at some point.

But not yet?

Not yet, Cam.

Great. Now we really need to go. I got APCs coming this way. Maybe fifteen minutes out.

Sage walked over and got her face so close to Oliver's he had to lean away from her so their noses wouldn't touch.

"Tell me why John and I should help you anymore, Oli."

"You probably shouldn't."

Sage's voice was escalating. "But it's too late now, isn't it, Oliver?"

"Never too late, friend."

John stormed past Sage and Oliver and up to his ruined house.

"It is too late, you two. They're on their way." He stopped on the steps and turned toward the hatch in the floor of what used to be his kitchen. "I'll get you as far as I can, Oliver, for old time's sake. Then you're on your own."

Twenty-One

Bumpy Ride

JOHN WALKED INTO THE WRECKAGE that was his house, cleared off the rubble over the hatch on the kitchen floor, and lifted the hidden trap door.

Cam, can you link?

To dumb-dumb? I'll try.

Of course.

"We'll take everything we can load," John said.

"Load? Load onto what, us and Esmeralda?" Sierra asked.

"Esmeralda stays. Oli, unload her and the gear, and then get the kids over to the garage."

"Stays?" Oliver raised his hands in exasperation. "Leave her here so she came become game for someone, food for some predator?"

"She stays."

Probably get eaten by the same thing that ate our bull the other day, John.

Not helpful, Cam.

"Well, at least let her into the garage with some food and water."

"No way, are you kidding me? It's a mule. No way she's staying in my garage."

"John—"

"She stays. She stays outside, Oliver. That's it."

Sage stepped between them, arms outstretched and one index finger on each of their chests, and turned her head to face John. "Great, now that we've settled that the mule is getting its freedom, can we get on with our escape plan?"

John winked at Sage and lifted up his arm, swiping the top of his wrist computer again. He keyed in another code and the garage door opened, revealing a hydro-celled, armored SUV.

A smile stretched across Sage's face. "Keys?"

"Cam."

"Nice, I'll take these three and start the prep."

John, I'm linked.

Great, dump and jump. I need you helping Sage get Brutus up.

On it.

Sierra finished the chocolate bar that she had snagged from John earlier, and made a snotty half smile at Sage as Quinn and Oliver followed her over to Esmeralda.

"You and John have romantic history?" she asked.

"We have history." Sage hefted a crate off the pack mule and gave it to Sierra. "Here, take this over to Brutus." She pointed over to John's gun truck.

"Who made you boss?"

"Just do it, kid."

Sierra nudged past Sage with the crate and headed over to the rig. She caught a glimpse of Quinn smiling from ear to ear and stuck her tongue out at him.

"Sweet kids you got us wrapped up with, Oli," Sage said.

"You'll warm up to them, I'm sure of it," Oliver said.

"Whatever. Here." She tossed Oliver an earpiece. "Cam's starting the systems up on her. Finish loading, and then keep the kids entertained."

Sierra turned sharply toward Sage, eyes narrowed. "Wait, where are you going?"

"To help John."

John brought up two large cases from the control center under his house and loaded them in the back of his rig with Sage's help.

John, we have to go.

On it.

Now, John.

"Time to pop smoke," he said.

Sage looked at John and raised her eyebrows.

"Driver?"

"Not you, you're in the gun hatch."

"Not a very lady-like place."

"You've never been lady-like."

"Isn't that what guys like you are into?"

Oh, please stop before I throw up.

You can't throw up, Cam.

"You know the answer to that." He gestured to the small hatch leading to the gun turret. "Ladies first."

Well, I sure as hell want to throw up.

Sage got behind the gun and John behind the wheel. Oliver was strapped in on the passenger side, and Sierra and Quinn were in the back.

Cam?

What do you need first, John?

Put the APCs on the HUD.

"What is all that back there?" Quinn asked.

"Really, right now, kid?"

"Just asking," Quinn said. His eyebrows rose up to his scalp, eyes wide and twinkly. "Hey, do I get to have one of the pulse guns too?"

John looked over to Oliver, jaw set, eyes narrowed. "Oliver."

"Right." Oliver turned to the back seat to face Quinn. "Uh, Quinn, now's not the best time. Maybe we should let John and Sage work, eh?" He glimpsed Sierra's head hanging limply, involuntarily rolling to her shoulder. "Is your sister asleep?"

"I know, right," Quinn said. "She's totally gonna miss all the fun."

"Well, strap her in, and then get strapped in yourself. I have a feeling this ride will get a little bumpy."

"Uh, John, we got company," Sage said.

"I know." He looked to the back seat and saw Quinn finishing with his strap. "Hang on tight."

John pulled up the computer pad on the middle console and slid through a couple screens until he had all the APCs on one screen. Four fast-moving, highly armed vehicles coming their way. He moved the information over to his HUD and pulled back on the driving console.

Was Sierra already sleeping?

Fast work, huh?

I wish I could sleep like that.

You do, Cam, every time I eat a choco bar from Jane.

John hit the accelerator pad below his foot, and Brutus sped backward through the trees. Sage's eyes went wide as the militia's four HAMRRs came into view.

"John!"

"I see them, Sage."

John pressed two buttons on his steering wheel, releasing a string of land mines that dropped and exploded as the first two HAMRRs drove over them. They went flying, tumbling over each other and crashing into the ground, turning into a smoking heap of crunched-together armor. Cam lit targets in red on Sage's HUD and she opened up with the REP cannon mounted on top of John's rig, finishing off the wrecked vehicles.

"I only see one, John," Sage said. "I don't know where the other one went."

They're trying to cut us off, John.

I got it.

"Hang on."

John flipped the rig around, and Sage spun the gunner's hatch so she was facing the rear again. Cam adjusted the targeting on her HUD so she could open fire on the approaching HAMRR.

"Oliver!" John said.

"I am well aware that you are mad at me for this predicament, John, but do you really feel that this is the appropriate time?"

"Really, Oliver? Try not being a putz for a change. I need you to get into the fight."

John pressed his palm against the dash in front of Oliver, and it opened with a hiss. A butterfly controller came out of it, with double triggers and a heads-up halo imager. The halo screen popped up with views of their rapidly passing surroundings, including their pursuers.

"Touch the vehicle on the screen to select your target," John said. "Cam will help you lock on and track it after that."

John jerked the steering wheel to avoid a deep drop off and then straightened out. The sharp turn left made Oliver even paler.

"The green square over the HAMRR will turn red when the system's ready to fire. We can only take one shot at a time, so fire fast. Shit…"

John slammed on the lock pad and slowed the vehicle down. He jerked his console to the left and hit the accelerator again, sending the rig spinning sideways. Cam changed everyone's HUD instantly to the new direction. The vehicle rocked as it took a direct hit from the HAMRR's more advanced REP gun.

We're not dead; they must want a few of us alive.

Their mistake.

"Sage!"

"I'm good, John, but the other two are just about on top of you."

John pushed in the console and the rig sped forward while Sage blasted at the HAMRR that was behind them, making it back off.

Cam flashed John a view of the red targeting icon blinking on Oliver's HUD.

"Oliver, fire, damn it."

"How would I know how to do that?" Oliver said.

"The triggers, Oliver. The damn triggers."

"Oh, right, brilliant."

Oliver pulled both triggers. Three mortar rounds launched from tubes on the back of the rig, making it rock slightly. The rounds raced toward the HAMRR behind them, cutting and weaving through the air, chasing their target. The explosion shook the earth, and the HAMRR that had been there was instantly engulfed in an orange and black cloud of fire and smoke.

Last one, John.

Cam spun Sage's hatch to the side and targeted the last HAMRR. Sage lit it up with heavy bursts from the REP cannon. Their rig lurched to the side from the HAMRR's returning fire.

Sage ducked down below the hatch. "We can't take much more of this," she said. She looked over at Quinn, still smiling from ear to ear. "Jeez, kid don't act scared on our account."

"You're totally awesome."

"You're weird."

"Oliver, we'll only have one good shot at this," John said.

"The little bugger won't turn red!"

John, we need to get closer.

John hit the stop pad again and jerked the driving console to the right, this time sending the vehicle straight for the HAMRR.

"Sage?"

"I'm fine!"

She jumped back up into the hatch and started firing at the HAMRR they were jetting toward.

John, we're getting dangerously close.

Tell me something I don't know.

"Oliver."

"Almost, John."

Two hundred meters.

John's fingers tensed white on the steering console. "Oliver!"

"Almost."

Fifty meters, John!

"Oliver!" Sage and John both yelled.

The square turned red on Oliver's HUD and he pulled the triggers. John hit the stop pad and turned the rig around, almost tipping it over.

The HAMRR lurched back up off the ground, billowing smoke and flame, and slammed into the rock wall behind it.

The firing mechanism sunk back into the console.

"What happened?" Oliver asked.

"You finally fired and blew the shit out of the bad guys," John said.

John, we have another inbound.

How far?

Fifteen hundred meters.

Put it on everyone's HUD.

"John. Are you seeing this? We have to get out of here fast," Sage said.

"John?" Oliver prompted. "Is that another one?"

"What'd you think, Oli?"

"Then I have to agree with Sage. Let's get the hell out of here."

"Shut up, Oliver. I'm not running again today." John slammed on the brake pad, bringing them to a halt in a cloud of dirt. "I'm tired, and I haven't had my coffee." He climbed out his door and walked to the back of the rig. Adam was back there, scrunched up with barely enough room for his wagging tail among the boxes. "I'm still damn hungry."

He opened the back hatch, let Adam out, and then opened up one of the crates to get his sniper rifle. He cocked the bolt back and pulled a forearm-length round out of the bin, slammed it into the chamber, and rode the bolt forward. He stepped back to the side of Brutus, took a knee, and steadied the rifle. Adam sat beside him, tail wagging, tongue hanging out the side of his mouth, his snout almost in a smile as he waited patiently for John to fire.

"And I just had to blow my house up. I want some damn answers!"

Cam.

Not close enough yet.

Lock me in when they are.

"John, I can take them out with the REP."

"No, Sage, I want at least one of these bastards alive."

Cam flashed John an image of the man driving the new HAMRR and a tiny icon on his scope flashed red. He pulled the trigger twice before the HAMRR was even visible. They heard a small explosion in the distance and shortly after saw a small stream of white smoke heading toward them.

Direct hit to the driver and their hydro cells, John. They should be limping into view in a second.

The smoking HAMRR crested a small hill and veered away, running into a mountain of a rock.

John went back the rig and put his long rifle away, and then loaded up with EP rounds for his assault rifle. He grabbed a small pulse gun, made sure it was ready to fire, and walked back around to the front of the rig, opening the door and tossing the handgun to Oliver.

"If I don't come back, get these kids out of here."

Adam whimpered and paced, nudging John with his muzzle.

"Not this time, boy. I need you to stay with Oliver and keep the twins safe, okay?"

Adam barked twice and jumped through the open passenger door, right over Oliver's lap, and back next to Quinn.

"Hey, boy, you were so good back there," Quinn said. "Were you scared? Oh no, you weren't; me either."

"Sage, cover me with the REP."

"Not a chance, John. I'm coming with you."

"Sage…"

"John, there's no time to argue, so deal with it."

She's right, John. I'm picking up vitals on at least one person in the rig.

"All right, Sage. If we're gonna do this, let's do it now."

Sage jumped down, grabbed another REP rifle and chest rig from the back, and then went around to link up with John. They started away from the rig when Quinn peeked his head out the door, Adam's right above his.

"John, Sage?" Quinn said.

"What is it, kid?" John said.

"Be safe."

Damn he's good.

"Oliver?"

"I've got it, John, but I don't think I will need to leave."

They headed toward the wrecked HAMRR, circling slowly toward it until they were only a few meters away. John looked over at Sage and signaled that he was ready. She signaled back that she had him covered, and he moved in, weapon to his cheek, ready to drop anyone who dared open the door. He got up beside the rig and kneeled, setting at an angle from the rear hatch.

"Clear," John said.

"Clear," Sage repeated. She glided up to him the same way he had made his way there. "Where is it?"

"Rear pouch."

Sage unzipped a pouch on the back of his chest rig and pulled out a blister pack with a small cord twined up inside. She handed it to John and then stepped back to pull security on the rig. John slung his weapon over his shoulder, popped open the blister pack, and lined the door of the vehicle with a thin thermal cord. He and Sage backed away a few feet, keeping their weapons trained on the rig the whole time. The rope worked fast, melting a line in the door until all that was left was a red-hot outline around a dark, empty space. John and Sage crept forward and waited. And waited. Nothing.

Cam?

I still have one vital onboard, John.

We're going in.

John, I don't think you should. I can't tell what's inside there.

Only one way then, isn't there, Cam?

Don't say I didn't warn you.

John signaled Sage that he was going to close in on the door. She staggered behind John slightly, and they moved in. John started inside the HAMRR and ran into what felt like a battering ram. A giant leg came straight into him, sending him flying backward. Sage glanced at John's form sailing through the air. By the time she turned back to face the oncoming assault, it was too late. A giant woman was on top of her, ripping her weapon out of her hand and tossing her to the ground. Sage wobbled to her hands and knees to get up, but the giant woman kicked her hard, sending her reeling against a tree. Sage crumpled on the ground, holding her ribs and coughing as her whole body shuddered.

Quinn gasped and Oliver gripped his gun, gawking at the scene unfolding a hundred meters away from them.

"Damn," he said.

Adam howled from the back seat and paced from door to door.

Oliver crawled over into the driver's seat and started eyeing the controls.

"Damn again."

"We're not leaving them, Oliver," Quinn said.

"Of course not, but how are we to help if I can't figure out these damn controls?"

"I watched John driving. I think I can remember what he did."

John's body went flying by them and rammed into a tree behind their rig. Oliver looked over and saw the giant pick Sage up by the throat.

"No time."

Oliver pulled the console backward and put his foot on the accelerator pad. The rig propelled backward, and John had to jump out of the way so he didn't get hit. He looked up and glared at Oliver.

"Oops. Maybe you should come up here, Quinn."

Oliver got back in the passenger seat and let Quinn get behind the wheel. Brutus rocked and they looked out at Sage, who had just been thrown over the hood and was now slithering to the ground unconscious.

John was already trying to hammer away at the iron lady, ducking and weaving, attacking her with blows that would have crushed a normal person's bones, but she didn't seem fazed. John came flying over to the rig again and landed on the windshield.

Oliver and Quinn looked wide-eyed at each other.

"We better hurry," Oliver said.

"Looks like you got her on the ropes, John," Oliver said. "Just keep her distracted a moment while we get oriented here."

John snarled at Oliver and then took off to face steroid lady again.

Quinn smiled and adjusted his seat. "Hold on, Oli. This is going to be fun."

John, she's AMP'ed, she can't feel anything you're doing right now. Can you jump?

The giant lady came speeding toward him. He leapt to the side, making her miss, and then used her momentum to slam her into the ground. He grabbed her from the back and swung her into the HAMRR.

Damn it, she's cyborg, John. She's got me jammed out of the rig.

That would explain things.

Quinn hammered the accelerator down, sending Brutus leaping forward. John watched as his rig plowed into the giant lady, slamming her into the HAMRR she'd escaped from. Quinn put the gun truck in reverse and peeled away, coming to a screeching halt right before hitting a huge tree. Adam barked and paced in the back, barely keeping his balance.

"Yes, very nice, Quinn." Oliver smiled nervously at Quinn, his knuckles white as he gripped the roll bars. "Thank you for not killing all of us."

Cam, can you jump now?

Yes, but John…

Damn it, Cam, Jump.

"Oliver, Quinn. Can you hear me?"

"Cam?" Oliver asked.

Quinn tensed his forehead. "Hey, it's that voice from John's house."

"Both correct. Oliver, you need to go now."

"But we can't just leave."

"John wants you and the kids out of here now."

"No way," Quinn said. He opened the door and hopped out to go over to John. Adam leapt out behind him.

"Quinn, wait. Not yet." Oliver undid his straps and went after him.

As Quinn ran over to John, Adam went to the cyborg, barking and growling at her motionless form.

"John!"

"What're you doing, kid? Get back in the rig." John saw Oliver coming up behind him. "Oliver, you have to go."

John.

Why aren't you getting them out of here?

A screeching, metal wrenching sound came from where the cyborg was buried into the HAMRR. She stood up, tearing the rig in half, and gave them a broad smile, like some flesh-eating, soul-devouring demon looking down upon fresh meat.

Damn, damn, damn!

Definitely steroids.

The cyborg scanned over all of them and then made a beeline for Quinn and Oliver.

"Run, Quinn, run!" John said.

Quinn turned to run, but he wasn't nearly fast enough to get away. Adam howled and ran between the cyborg's legs, trying to slow her down without getting crushed. He barked and snapped at her, biting where he could to get her to misstep, to fall, anything to give Quinn and Oliver more time to get away.

John took off at full speed and slammed himself into the cyborg, sending her flying back. He jumped on top of her, grappling with her as she stood and darted forward again toward Quinn. Adam kept on her with quick bites to her legs and arms. John grabbed, pulled, and hit everything he could think of to get her to go down, but she kept running. His arm could barely wrap around her neck as he struggled to get a hold there, to get leverage, to get anything.

It's like she's growing.

Her joints, John.

What'd you think I'm doing?

Can you get to her neural link?

He ripped open a box under her skin at the base of her skull and pulled everything inside out.

She's still going. She's too AMP'ed.

John, you can't stop her until she shuts down.

John wrenched the cyborg's head toward him, making her lose her balance and finally getting her back to the ground, but he gave up all his leverage to do it. She grabbed him and tossed him sideways into a tree. Adam roared viciously at her and bit onto her wrist. She flung him away like a swatting a fly.

Damn it. Can you hack her?

Sorry, John, there's nothing to hack, she's all borg right now without the cy.

John charged at her again, managing to slide under her legs and up on her back again. He fought frantically, trying to find the cyborg's weak points.

"Oliver, shoot her!"

"But you're too close. I can't get a good shot."

"Damn it, Oli, just shoot."

Oliver emptied his rounds into her torso, shredding what was left of her uniform and ripping away skin, leaving her underlayer of cybernetic-enhanced muscle exposed. She roared with pain and charged Oliver. He fired again, but it was too slow. She reached out and crumpled him with the back of her hand. John tried to jump down to help him, but his arm had gotten wedged between her cybernetic muscle and the hardware on her back.

I'm stuck, Cam.

Well, that was dumb.

Not helpful, Cam.

Quinn ran up and kicked her shin, making her stagger backward. "Leave them alone, bitch." The cyborg turned, grinned, and stalked toward Quinn.

Damn, John, that kid has one hell of a kick.

Great, you can sign him up for soccer.

Adam backed him up. He was limping and bleeding, but he growled deep, rippling the fur high on his back to make himself look bigger than he really was.

John tried to wave him off. "Quinn, NO. Adam, get him out of here, NOW!"

Adam snapped at Quinn, grabbing onto his pants legs with his teeth and tugging at him, trying to get him to run.

John.

"QUINN, RUN."

I'll have to light us up, Cam.

Do it.

John stretched his arm behind his back and grabbed the explosive disc he had there.

Last one.

Only one we need.

Adam stood in front of Quinn, growling deep and vicious, teeth bared fully, hair on his back straight up. The cyborg just laughed and kicked at him. Adam dodged and attacked the cyborg's leg. The laughing stopped, and her expression changed from sick satisfaction to annoyance. She pulled at John, trying to get him off her back, and kicked her leg until she caught Adam, sending him flying back into the hillside. John pressed his thumb on the imprint button to start the timer on the explosive, and slammed it on her back.

Ten seconds. John—

I know, Cam. Me too.

Nine seconds.

Quinn ran over and grabbed Oliver's weapon.

Eight seconds.

John, he's got Oli's gun.

Seven seconds.

"Quinn, NO!"

Six seconds.

The cyborg saw the weapon and lumbered toward Quinn.

Five seconds.

John, do something.

I'm trying, Cam.

"QUINN, RUN DAMN IT. WE'RE GONNA BLOW."

Four seconds.

John wrestled with the charged disc that was ready to blow them all to dust, but it was wedged too tight. Quinn's eyes got wide with understanding. He dropped the gun and ran, sliding under the cyborg's legs, her outstretched arms missing him just as he got within reach of John.

"Get the hell out of here, kid. What are you doing?"

Three seconds.

Quinn jumped and clung to John's side, pressed his feet flat against the cyborg's back and pulled him and John free. They fell flat on the ground ten feet away from the monster that was turning

to chase them down. John covered Quinn with body to shield him
from the impending blow.

Two seconds. It's too late, John.

Sorry, Cam.

Me too, John.

There was a deafening scream from Sierra. The cyborg froze. A
hot blinding flash filled John's field of vision, and then everything
went black.

TWENTY-TWO

Natives

QUINN, RUN!

John was trapped in some sort of dream, arms and legs held to the ground by giant roots from a tree.

Quinn, no...

The more he struggled, the tighter the roots got. He flexed and strained against them as they cut into his skin like razors.

Quinn, RUN, damn it! We're gonna blow!

John looked over and saw Sierra get out of the rig as if in a daze, her eyes on the scene in front of her. She opened her mouth again and her eyes glowed like orange embers. An even higher pitched scream came from her mouth, growing in intensity until all that could be heard was a drawn-out shriek, like finger nails on chalkboard, and then nothing but ringing. Sparks went flying from the two vehicles and gathered into a glowing ball of white energy above Sierra. She spread her arms out wide and then clapped her hands together. A burst of wind that sounded like a sonic boom came from her, flattening everything between her and the cyborg.

The ball of energy above her grew bigger and started crackling, sizzling, convulsing like hordes of animals trying to fight their way out of a sack. Then the ball turned solid and glowed brilliant white. A single blinding bolt of energy shot out from the ball and straight at the cyborg, hitting her, freezing her in place; she lit up like a light bulb, growing brighter and brighter as the bolt flooded her with energy. The cyborg let out one last murderous cry and then exploded in a bright blue flame. John was blown free of the roots as the aftershock from Sierra flattened every inanimate thing within a two hundred-meter circle, including half of the giant boulder that stood at the very edge of the damage.

*   *   *

John's dream loosed its hold, and he opened his eyes, gasping for air. He blinked slowly to try to clear the blinding white that was all-encompassing, and then held his arms up in front of him to make sure he didn't have tree roots trying to hold him down.

John?

Cam?

Pretty impressive, you having a nightmare within a nightmare.

Something tells me it wasn't all nightmare.

I take we're still alive and we didn't just get a fast track to hell?

Run the systems just to make sure.

John sat up, every movement burning like someone was sticking needles into his nerve endings. The world around him started coming into focus. He stared at his arms and legs, moving them to make sure he wasn't being dragged into the ground by living roots.

What happened?

That girl of yours gots skills.

What girl?

Oh boy, you were hit a little too hard.

Cam. Sierra's not mine.

There's the John I'm looking for.

He stood up and surveyed the area. Burnt ground, trees shredded to black smoldering stumps. A half blown-away boulder. Two rigs torn apart, down to the tires. Surprisingly, Oliver, Sage, and Quinn were alive from the looks of it, and stirring awake too.

But where . . .?

We're alive, John. Heat sigs all accounted for.

"Adam." He scanned in a circle, trying to locate him. "Adam?"

Cam, locate Adam, now.

I told you, John, everyone's alive. Including Adam. He's right over there.

Cam brought up a small overlay map of the blast zone, showing him where they were, and highlighted Adam's location. He was making his way back.

"Adam." John got up and ran to the edge of the blackened ground and through some bushes, where he found Adam limping toward him, head high, tail wagging, and tongue hanging out of his mouth.

"Oh, good boy, you're such a good boy." John slid down onto his knees, hugging his dog, his best friend, and burying his face deep in his neck. "You are such a good boy, aren't you. Yes you are, a very, very good boy."

Adam licked John's salty, sweaty face and chin, sitting on his hind legs and putting his good paw up on John's shoulders.

All right, Cam. Let's run a sweep on everyone else and make sure there are no other surprises.

On it.

"Come on, boy, let's go find out what the hell just happened."

* * *

"Sierra, Sierra! Please wake up, please," Quinn said.

Sierra opened her eyes. She was looking up directly at Quinn's worried face. She put her hand up to her forehead and rubbed the bridge of her nose.

"What are you yelling at me for, Q? My head is throbbing," Sierra said.

John, she's waking up.

Who? The human lightning cannon?

Yes, Sierra is waking up.

John got up from where he was wrapping Sage's ribs and splinting her arm with some of the medical supplies from her vest. Oliver was already bandaged. Surprisingly, he wasn't really hurt, just a head laceration, some bruising and abrasions, but nothing more than that. Quinn and Sierra didn't look any different than the dirt-covered kids they had been before the chase. In fact, he couldn't tell from looking at them that anything had happened at all.

I'm surprised we're not all deaf, John.

Our filters protect us and Adam.

What's their excuse?

Good question.

He came over and looked down at Sierra.

"Well, you don't look too happy to see me," Sierra said.

"I'm not."

John helped Quinn sit her up and gave her a once-over, and then walked off, kicking through the scrap heaps on the ground. Oliver came by and handed out water and what was left of his biscuits. Adam, front leg taped with a compress, trotted around Quinn and sat beside Sierra, head high, ears perked, and tail wagging as he took up sentinel duty for her.

"Oh, don't worry about John for right now, Sierra," Oliver said. "He's just mad about the way things have turned out so far. Well, and about losing his anonymity, his house, his rig—actually, we might very much have to worry about him."

"What about his rig?" Sierra looked sourly at him. "Last thing I remember is waking up alone and then…"

Sierra looked around, her eyes searching their surroundings as if she were expecting a monster to come barreling out of the underbrush at any minute. Her eyes got wide as they took in the charcoaled ground, the deadened trees, destroyed rigs, and the half blown-away boulder.

"Didn't there used to be an egg-shaped boulder there?"

Sage came up behind them limping, with her own water and biscuit and some jerky for all of them.

"Before you, there were a lot of things here," Sage said.

"That giant lady, I thought she was going to crush Quinn, and then me." She hugged her brother, tears streaming down her dirt-crusted face. "What happened? How are we still alive?"

"Cyborg," Sage said.

"What?"

Sage gestured to the darkest area on the black ground, where the cyborg had been when Sierra toasted her.

"She was a cyborg. Human with shitty black market enhancements, and amped up on steroids." Sage glared at Oliver. "Someone really wants you kids."

Sierra's forehead wrinkled, showing her growing frustration. "Will someone please tell me what the hell is going on?"

"You screamed real loud and about sent us all mad," Quinn said. "Then this big ball of light formed over you, and the REP guns blew up on the HAMRR and Brutus. Everything started crumpling and this huge bolt of electricity shot out at the cyborg lady. She disintegrated, the rigs blew up, then the trees and the boulder. You pretty much fried her and everything around here but us." Quinn smiled. "It was pretty cool."

Sierra was starting to understand now. "I fried John's rig?"

Adam whimpered and lay down flat, nuzzling Sierra's hand.

"Yes, unfortunately," Oliver said. "But let's look on the bright side of things: we're all safe for the time being, and in some ways closer to our objective."

He smiled broadly at Quinn and Sierra, and then a bit more sheepishly at Sage.

"I'm not going over there," she said.

"Well, you do know him best."

"No way, you go."

"I should really stay here with the children," Oliver said. "And he's a lot less likely to hit a woman."

"Nice, Oli, real nice. Have you seen him mad?"

"You mean this isn't mad?" Quinn asked.

Sage shook her head, then shot a nervous look over at John, who was still checking on his burnt-out rig. "Not a chance."

"Sage, I am sure he would agree that we have to keep moving, all things considered."

"I know, Oli, I just don't know if he's going to be ready to hear that yet." She looked down at Adam. "If I'm going, you're coming with me as insurance." Adam buried his face under his paws and whimpered.

"Not working, Adam. Come on, tough guy, let's go." She nudged his butt with her foot, and then they both limped over to John.

"That's the spirit. We'll be right here prepping to leave," Oliver looked at the twins, and realized they had nothing to get ready. "Or we'll just sit here and wait to see how he takes to talking with you."

Sage rolled her eyes, took a deep breath, and set her jaw.

Sage is coming.

Can I shoot them all now?

No.

Should I really be listening to you, since you're the reason we're in this mess?

I thought we agreed it was Adam.

I'm blaming all of you right now.

Sage coughed behind him to get his attention.

"Don't even think about it, Sage, I'm not in the mood."

"John, no one meant for this to happen."

"Sage, I mean it, not now."

"John."

Adam trotted over and sat down by him, pawing his knee with his bandaged leg. John's expression changed, softened even, and he bent down to eye level with Adam, putting his forehead to his for a moment.

"Sage, I've lost my house, my rig, and my favorite hat. We all just almost died, and Sierra, the ball of lightning fun, just about made me deaf. How did you expect me not to me out of my fucking mind and pissed off right now?"

"You're a dick, John. I didn't want this either." Sage looked down at the destroyed wreck. "You two deserve each other."

Dick? How am I the dick?

Well, they almost died too, John. Everyone here has lost a lot on this trip already.

Damn it.

Sage stormed back to the group and left John and Adam lingering in the dirt. He looked over at Oliver who was with Sierra and Quinn, acting as if he hadn't been watching what was going on, and then down at Adam.

We really aren't going to get rid of them, are we, Cam?

I knew you'd come around. Oh, and we've got company.

William?

Bingo.

Took him long enough.

"What'd you think, boy, should we still help them?"

Adam barked and started licking John's neck and chin. He got down and trotted, limping, back to the small group.

All right, Cam, let's get this over with.

John ripped the only good hydro battery out of his rig and walked over to the group.

"Do you know where we are, John?" Quinn asked.

"Yeah, I know."

"Well, let's have it then," Oliver said. "How bad off are we?"

"Pretty bad off, I'd say." John looked over at Sage. "Wouldn't you, Sage?"

"Depends on how bad your last card game with him was, and what kind of back up you'll need." Sage nodded her head toward her immobile arm, and then gave John a wink. "Not really in fighting shape."

"What is that, some kind of code?" Sierra asked.

Oliver squinted his eyes at the two. "I believe we're missing something, children."

John pointed to the tree line past the fallen debris. They all looked up and saw about sixteen fighters moving toward them. A man as tall as John's rig used to be, with a warrior's jaw, tanned skin, and long, braided black hair led the group out.

Quinn rolled his eyes and slumped to the ground. "Oh, great, probably more people who want to kill us. This is getting so old."

Sierra's crossed her arms and she let out an exhausted huff as she sat down next to Quinn.

Wow, that left her speechless.

Maybe we should overwhelm her more often.

Good luck with that, John.

"Ah, of course, Indians," Oliver said. "I should have seen that coming."

"You mean Native Americans," the tall warrior said.

Oliver shot him a nervous smile. "Yes, Native Americans, that's what I meant." He turned to John, anxiety still written on his face. "Friends of yours, I hope."

"Something like that." John headed toward the hulking leader. "Hi, Will."

"Friends of John's?" Sierra asked. "Makes perfect sense."

"Oh, yes, we're old friends, aren't we, John?" Will said.

Maybe we can get him to fix Adam.

I didn't know you were so worried about his injury.

His injury? I just want someone to make him smart.

"Excellent. You are friendlies, what a stroke of luck," Oliver said, holding out his hand. "My name is Oliver."

Before he was close, he froze, hands hovering in the air, outstretched, waiting for a hand that didn't come. Will's figure blurred as Oliver focused his eyes on the men behind the tall native, men who now had their weapons trained on his chest.

"We're not that good of friends," Will said.

"Oh, I see. Well, if you don't mind, we'll be on our way then," Oliver backed off slowly, waving at them as if he were surrendering. "We have a tight schedule to keep."

One of the men flashed the laser sight on his weapon, and the other men followed suit. A flood of red dots showed on Oliver's chest and on the ground in front of him.

Um, did you do something I don't know about?

How could I possibly do that, Cam?

So he's just posturing. He does know we were joking, right?

He knows, Cam.

"I suggest you shut up and stop moving, Oliver," John said. He turned toward Sage and let his eyelid fall down into a wink, and then nodded to Will. "Listen, Will, I'm sure you can see that we had no other alternative here."

Quinn whispered to his sister, "Sierra, what's going on?"

"Shut up, Q!"

John shot them both a look that might as well have been daggers.

"What's going on, kid, is that John here has been warned about coming this side of the rock giant," Will said. "He's been warned that he'd risk his life, and the lives of those he brings with him."

He always did like to put on a show.

I think he'll get along great with Oliver.

"You mean the giant boulder my sister blew up?"

John turned his head sharply at Quinn and glared at him. "Quinn!"

"Yeah, Quinn, way to sell me out."

Will looked at Sierra and started walking toward her, moving his eyes up and down, scanning her as he went. She stood up to try and back away from him, but John shook his head, warning her not to move.

Adam growled at Will, deep and full of warning. He was wounded, crippled even, but still ready to protect the kids if they needed him.

"Easy, boy, easy," John said. "Will, the kid really doesn't know what he's talking about. Head concussion from the wreck back there, I think."

Yeah, tell him, John.

Will stopped in front of Sierra and circled around her, looking her over from different angles.

"I might let you live if you let me keep this one," Will said, looking straight into Sierra's eyes. "She would make a good squaw."

"Oh boy, here we go," Sage said.

Oliver shifted toward John, concern and confusion written on his face like graffiti. "A little explanation might be helpful here, John."

"We crossed into Indian land when we passed that big rock that Will called the Rock Giant, the one Sierra just blew up. The last time Adam and I were here, I promised never to come back."

"Adam?" Will looked toward the dog. "At least he gave you a strong name. Your training seems to be lacking though. I would have done better—and taken better care of you, from the looks of it."

Sierra kicked a plume of dirt at Will.

"Stop talking to our dog," she spat. "I am not going to be some old man's squaw. I'm tired, and hungry, and my head is throbbing. In the past three days we've been beat, kidnapped, chased, shot at, blown up, lied to, and starved. I'm not doing one more thing until someone explains to me what the hell is going on!"

A splash of sparks flew from the charred wrecks behind them as Sierra plopped down on the ground, stubbornness winning out over grace, and glared at anyone who dared make eye contact with her.

Will bent forward with a roar of laughter, and his men followed suit.

"John, you finally found someone who will give you a run for your money." Will headed down the small hill toward John, his arms spread wide. John smiled back and walked to meet him.

"Yeah, she's a real spark," he said.

Real spark? That was horrible.

I thought it was pretty damn good.

Keep trying.

They gave each other a quick hug and a handshake, knuckle bump, back hand slap combo that confused everyone, but that dropped the tension between the two groups like sunshine in the middle of a gray January day.

"Why do you have to bust my balls about the rock giant thing all the time?" John asked. "It was that damn smoke out with Bert. I would have believed anything you guys told me."

"That's true, but you did run naked from a giant rock because you thought you made it mad by pissing on it, and promised you and Adam would never come back."

There was muffled laughter from Sage, Oliver, and the twins, which earned them a small wink from William.

One word John, legendary. You're legendary.

I thought it was a damn God.

Keep trying.

Sierra glared at him so hard that John felt like she might somehow penetrate his layers of body armor.

Oliver leaned over toward Sage and mumbled out the side of his mouth. "Um, a bit of enlightenment might be helpful. I'm not sure if I should be laughing or crying."

Sage smirked and brushed past him, bumping him with her shoulder.

"Doesn't feel good not knowing what you're getting into, does it, Oli?"

"Right, I see your point. I'll just stay here with the children then."

"You do that, Oli."

Quinn sat down beside Sierra, let out a long sigh, and watched John, Sage, and Will all embrace one another like old friends.

"At least it's better than the jippers, right?" Quinn said.

Sierra glared at him. "Not a good time, Q."

"Yes, better than jippers is right," Oliver said. "Very good, Q. Way to look on the brighter side of things."

Sierra turned her soured look toward both of them. "You two are going to make me gag." She got up, shaking her head, and stormed over toward John and Will.

"It might best to stay here, Sierra," Oliver said. Sierra flipped him off and kept walking. "All right, looks like it's just us then." He turned around to pat Quinn on the shoulder, but he wasn't there either. He looked up and saw Quinn following his sister, and got up to go after them. "Very well then, let's go over, shall we?"

John smiled as he watched Will petting Adam behind the ears, until he spotted Sierra coming over, Quinn and Oliver in tow behind her.

"Who's the baggage?" Will asked.

"Just some road warriors we got roped into helping."

"That girl sure does like to glare at you, John."

Sage smiled as she turned to look at Sierra. "I think she might have a little crush on him, Will."

"Oh, poor girl."

"Poor girl? Poor me," John said.

Will smiled and narrowed his eyes, looking at John as he stood back up. "Be careful, John, you don't want to get zapped by her laser eyes."

John scowled back, meeting his stare without a flinch. "Yeah, right."

"Didn't take you for a family man, John," Will said.

"I'm not."

"I'm glad you're all having a fun time," Sierra said as she came up to them, "but would anyone like to explain this little meeting to me?"

John tried to ignore Sierra, but she slapped him hard on the arm.

I wish I could shut her down.

You could if you fed her another choco bar.

John smiled at the thought.

"What are you smiling for?" Sierra said. "Aren't you forgetting a key element here?"

Will and Sage looked at John, stifling laughter as his smile faded.

"And what element would that be?"

Sierra pointed to her and her brother. "Duh, us?" she said as Quinn and Oliver walked up behind her.

"Sorry, John, terribly impatient, that one," Oliver said.

John looked at his motley crew and let out a deep breath. "Will, meet Sierra, Quinn, and Oliver."

"Oliver. The monk Oliver?" Will held his hand out to Oliver.

"Yes, that'd be me." Oliver shook his hand. "I don't recognize you. Have we met?"

"You know each other?" Sage asked.

"You might say that," Will said. "Oliver the tunneler, the trail breaker. Oliver the mead maker."

Recognition shown on Oliver's face. "Aha, I see." He smiled over at Sage. "They've gotten their hands on some of my mead."

Will whistled. One of his men dug through the satchel on his horse and produced a clear glass bottle full of golden liquid. He held it up and tossed it to Will, who in turn showed it to Sage. Oliver's likeness was displayed on the label in bold black ink. Sage looked between the bottle and Oliver, who was beaming with pride.

"See?" Oliver said.

"I do see, Oli." She waved the bottle off. "Hide that thing, please. I can only stand one of him for now."

Will laughed again and tossed the bottle back to his man. "A good bottle of bad decisions you make, monk."

"Well, thank you. Thank you very much. You know, I don't think people understand just how much goes into making a real quality bottle of the stuff."

"Okay, okay. Oli, we know you make a good bottle of mead," John said. "I don't think we need to find out your whole process right now. Will, are you going to let us through?"

"Are you guys Indians?" Quinn asked.

We'll never get through here.

They're your friends.

"Yes, young man, we are the scary Natives." Will put his hands out in front of him and wiggled his fingers at Quinn. "Not as spooky as you pictured?"

"Way better," Quinn said.

"Great, I'm glad we're all becoming buddies," Sierra said. "Are we going to actually do something here? I mean, we did almost die, and I'm sure that they aren't the only ones trying to kill us."

"If you're looking for help with her, John, I don't think I have any," Will said. "But if you want to get up to the pass…"

"Yes, we do."

"Then," Will continued, "it'll cost you a good story. One that *sparks* the imagination."

"It's a very long one," Sage said.

"Even better."

"What is he talking about?" Sierra asked.

"Nothing you need to know about," John said without taking his eyes off Will. "Oliver, can you take them over there and get them ready to move?"

Oliver waved his hands in front of him. "We actually don't have anything to get ready, John. Even if we did, I'm not sure that any of us is ready for a long travel yet."

"I'm fine, Quinn's fine, we're all fine," Sierra said. "So can I please have some idea of what's going on?"

"No," John said.

Sierra crossed her arms and gave John her back.

John looked at Quinn, who just shrugged his shoulder. "She's always been like this."

"Great help you are," John said.

"I'm her brother, not her keeper."

Will patted John on his shoulder.

"Good luck," Will said. "I can only spare two horses, but that should get you to the village." He turned and looked at Sage.

"You remember the place."

"Sure do; we'll be right behind you, Will."

Cam, run everyone's vitals again. I want to be sure they can make it.

Got it.

Sage followed William up the hill to gather the horses, while John organized the others.

"That went much better than I anticipated," Oliver said.

"We're on foot for the next fifteen miles, Oliver," John said. "Oh yeah, it's going real swell."

"I knew you'd see the upside."

John rolled his eyes and went over to horses that Sage had come back with.

John.

Give it to me, Cam.

The nanodoctors you bought for Adam are already working, as you can tell.

John heard him barking and smiled, relieved when he spotted him running around Will's men, chasing a ball.

Worth every penny.

That's up for argument.

John whistled loud and waved everyone up to the trail so they could leave. William's crew teased Adam one more time with ball before getting back on their horses and riding away. Sierra and Quinn mounted the two borrowed horses and started up the trail behind Oliver and Sage with John pulling up the rear.

Go on, Cam.

Sage has it the worst: cracked ribs and sprained arm. She should be riding.

Go ahead and try it; see how that works for you.

Right. Oliver has absolutely nothing wrong with him, but I could have sworn that he had at least a head laceration before.

What about the kids?

Nothing. Not even a scratch. It's like they weren't even there.

Interesting.

No, that's just freaky. Not interesting.

Freaky doesn't even begin to describe it.

Twenty-Three

No Rest for the Weary

My god, John, I'm so glad we're done with that.

You didn't like our beautiful little hike.

I didn't mind the eight-mile scenic mountain hike—I still can't believe you told them it would be fifteen miles.

Well, can't say I didn't wish they had to walk fifteen miles today.

If Oliver says one more thing about the power of the universe, and just asking for what we want and we'll get it—you might just have to kill him for me John.

You don't like his theology.

If it was that easy, why didn't he just ask for us to be teleported to William's?

Want me to ask him?

Do, and I'll shut us down right now.

John smiled and looked back at his gang of tired, dirty misfits. Oliver was walking beside the horses carrying Sierra and Quinn, who were half asleep in the saddle. Sage was right behind them, and when she saw John she put her hand into the shape of a gun and acted like she was blowing her brains out.

How's Sage?

I've been running her vitals every half hour or so, she's doing fine. Her mods are normal Army, so she's healing, but it's really slow.

Straight legs never got much more than the MC booster. Keep an eye on her for me, will you, Cam?

What'd you think I'm doing? Anything else you want while I'm doing all the work for this group?

Yeah, find us the town center.

As you wish.

Just get to it, smart ass.

Cam displayed the map of William's town on John's HUD, highlighting the spot where Will had told them to meet.

Head that way, Prince Humperdinck.

Really, Cam?

Well, I never got my Watson, so deal with my poor attitude until you find me someplace I can dump.

What about the wrist comp?

Full.

Damn. I'll find out from Will if they have a system for you here.

As you wish.

Oh boy, this is going to be a long stay.

After showing his troops to the town square, John walked back through the small Native town of White River. The village he remembered had grown into a small city since he was last here. Snaking roads paved with river rock wound through town. The bumpy road was fronted by rows of wooden and stone buildings, small earthen huts, and even dome-shaped pods. Other stone paths led away from the square to small residential areas, where dwellings ranged from large, multistory stone and log structures for larger families, to one-bedroom cabins for singles or the occasional visitor. Each structure had its own wind turbine or solar panel wired to a generator the size of a bicycle tire that powered the house. John stood for moment, closing his eyes, breathing slow, deep breaths, and listening. He let the hum of the river, the croaking toads, and the whispering trees of the forest wash through his senses and steel his resolve.

He marched up the front steps and into the guesthouse where Will was waiting for him. John took it in quickly: sitting room off the main room, fireplace surrounded by old but comfortable-looking couch and chairs, a galley kitchen, complete with wash basin and trestle table, and a flight of steps to a second story.

He's concentrating, John.

He's trying to think of how to tell us no.

Oh boy, here it comes. It looks like he's going to break up with us.

"I'm sorry, John, we can't help you."

It's not me, it's you.

I knew this wouldn't work.

"You're sorry? You can't help me? You owe me, Will."

"I know, but I can't help you with this. The elders don't want to get involved. Whatever Bert saw in the smoke, it wasn't good."

If you get me close enough, I can make Bert see whatever we want him to see.

"You know what was going on back there. Someone with a lot of weight behind them is coming after these kids, and we're not even close to where we need to be."

See, Bert's the problem here, John. We just need to figure out how to fix that.

"What are you even involved for, John? Leave all this to Oliver and Sage. The kids will be fine."

Bert's not stoned enough. That's it, John. We just need to get him to smoke more, maybe lace his pipe.

Not helping, Cam.

"I won't leave them. Whoever these guys are, whatever their plan is, they've made it personal."

"John, I can't…"

"Will, I had to blow up my house to eliminate a couple of squads. You could try a little harder."

"All right, John, all right. You can stay here for now." He looked around as if he were taking stock of everything. "It's not much, but it'll do while I see what I can do to help you, but I'm still not making promises."

"That's all I can ask for."

Are you listening to me, John?

Cam, none of that could have waited?

What? Was I interrupting something important?

Will walked out, leaving John to his thoughts. He looked down at Adam, who had been sitting next to him as if he had been an integral part of negotiating with Will.

We can't stay, Cam.

Not the way you're trying.

"What do you think, boy?"

Adam tilted his head, barked once, and nudged at John's legs with his nose.

"I know, I know. Go ahead, go check things out. I'm sure everyone is anxious to see how well I've been raising you."

Adam stood up and put his front legs up on John's chest, licking his face and letting out a quiet growl as if letting John know that he still loved him, and then got back down and trotted outside.

After seeing him, they'll never let you have another dog again.

They shouldn't have the first time.

John went over to the wash basin, splashed cold water over his face, and dried himself with a coarse towel that was hanging on the wall.

At least for the time being we're safe, Cam. That counts for something.

You don't think the militia will find us?

Not any time soon. Besides, this town's been hidden from everyone for a decade, don't think they'll find it unless we stay too long.

You're not going to give it a chance.

We can't stay, Cam.

Just being wishful here.

I know, Cam, but you don't even have to run a tac analysis to put that one together.

I said I know, you don't have to rub it in.

Ease up, Cam, or I'm going to send you to your room.

Don't have a room.

John looked into the sitting room of the guesthouse. It was a solid little cabin, probably a lot nicer than what most visitors got when they came to town. In the main room, he ran his hand along the smooth log walls, ingesting the scent of pine and cedar.

Kind of like home, huh, Cam?

Kind of.

Sorry I had to blow it.

Me too.

He traced the room, looking from wall to wall, imagining Sierra and Quinn sitting by the stone fireplace, listening to stories from Oliver. He rested his hand on the soft animal-hide furniture that Will had made himself, one of the many things Will did in his spare time. The walls were dotted with beautiful scenic art Will's wife had painted, giving the room the feeling of a comfortable family dwelling. John would have let the small group stay, maybe even leave them here, if he could be sure they wouldn't be found. But he wasn't sure.

Should we check on our wayward companions?

If that entails fresh air and campfire stories, then yes.

John walked out of the house and down the steps of the porch, sucking in another big breath of fresh Cascade air.

We're lucky to stay the night. Do you think Will can get them to help us?

Don't be too hopeful.

They're right about us, Cam, we're too dangerous to keep here. Do you want whoever is after those kids to come and ruin this?

No.

Then we have to leave.

I hate it when you're right.

Ditto.

On the other side of the small river that flowed through the town was a group of wooden buildings that served as the schoolhouses. Playgrounds surrounded an ancient evergreen tree, and rough grass fields behind the schoolhouses were ready for soccer, rugby, and baseball. John could almost imagine the recess sounds of kids laughing and yelling for the ball, of adults whistling and trying to maintain order, and of bells chiming for them to return to class.

At the center of town was a longhouse made of huge logs, topped with a shiny copper roof. It had a small utility building beside it that housed storage for the power provided by the river, which supplied the town with all of its backup electricity through an underground network of fibers.

Pretty complex for this size of town, even one in the States.

They've come a long way.

Hey, maybe they have a Watson here you could barter for. Maybe a game of chance?

Cam.

You can't tell me not to wish.

Stop wishing.

Okay.

Hearing the raucous sound of a crowd laughing and clapping over by the town square, John turned to see whether he could spot the rest of his group. The town had started to gather around the huge nighttime fire that was crackling against the sides of the giant stone fire circle. Wooden bleachers surrounded the circle that the tribe used for seating during the evening's dramatic story sessions. He walked over and stood on the outskirts of the circle, waiting and watching. He spotted Quinn and Sierra, playing with Adam and some other children from the town. The older men and women were already gathered, watching Oliver from the bleachers and laughing at his storytelling.

You have to admit, John, it is nice to see everyone so relaxed for a change.

I don't have to admit anything.

Killjoy.

Sage came up behind John and nudged his arm. "Big change from this morning, huh?"

"You mean Oliver being an even worse storyteller than before?"

Sage shot him a half smile, lingering and staring into John's eyes. "How's the arm?"

She held up her new leather sling and wiggled her fingers. "Almost don't even need the sling; if it wasn't so nice I would've ditched it already."

"Good healers up here."

"Damn good. I might let you guys finish this journey without me."

John glared at her and they both started laughing. She held her ribs and groaned, coughing as if she had some water go down the wrong pipe.

"Ouch, don't make me laugh like that or you will be going the rest of the way alone."

"Almost forgot you were beat up so bad." He pointed toward Oliver and the kids. "They got the same treatment and right now it looks like they're doing better than they have the whole trip."

"Bastards."

"I think Oliver has a little more telling to do."

Sage bumped his shoulder again with her good one. "You think."

John took in a long breath through his nose and let it out.

"What are you doing here, Sage?" he asked.

"I thought you looked lonely."

"Not right here, I mean *here*. What are you doing *here* mixed up in this mess?"

"Oh, you mean that *here*. Oli asked for my help, so I helped. Now I'm stuck in the rabbit hole. How'd you get involved?"

"I kicked a jipper couple off my property and ended up being a babysitter."

Sage's head fell back and she let out a guarded laugh while John scowled at her.

"Fuck, John, I told you not to make me laugh."

"Serves you right."

She punched him on his arm, and when she had her laughter under control, smiled at him as if she wished they had something special planned for later.

"So Quinn was telling the truth," Sage said. "Did you really tell the wife to leave her husband's body so you could use it as a warning?"

John relaxed, letting out a long chuckle as he thought of Quinn recounting the tale of their rescue.

"It really wasn't as glorious as it sounds."

"Now that's something I haven't seen in a while," Sage said.

"What?"

"A genuine smile from you." Sage got close and started inspecting his face.

"What're you doing?"

"Checking to make sure you didn't break anything."

"Funny, Sage." He smiled again and looked back at the two twins by the fire. "Did he really tell you that?"

"Oh, yeah. You became an instant hero to him after that. Doesn't think you can do anything wrong, that one."

Poor kid.

"That's a dangerous position to hold."

"Probably, but I have a feeling you won't disappoint him," Sage said. "So what did Will say?"

"We can stay tonight, but they're not going to help us past that. He's going to talk to them again to see if he can do anything to change their minds, but I wouldn't hold my breath."

"At least we can sleep easy tonight."

"Do you ever really sleep easy, Sage?"

Sage looked at him again and gave him a wink. "You know the answer to that."

They got caught in each other's gaze for a second, and then she turned and walked over to the fire, taking a seat next to Sierra and Quinn to listen to some of the Friar Oliver's stories.

You're hopeless, John.

Aren't we all.

I'm not.

Oliver told stories of giants and monsters, heroes and villains, of times long past, and of myths long forgotten, carrying on the proud tradition of his order. He only stopped when dinner arrived. Stacks and stacks of vegetables, bread, fruit, and turkeys were brought and set on low tables by the fire.

Two muscular women, tall as any man, cranked a large handle that was attached to a thick chain that went into a large pit. As they cranked, John could see a container starting to rise up out of the ground, steam rolling off it like tendrils from a ghost. Two work-chiseled men opened it and started unloading cedar racks of cooked salmon, distributing the smoke-scented fish to the crowd.

A group with flutes, drums, mandolins, rattles, and sticks started playing music by the fire as the tribe ate. After dinner, cases of Oliver's mead were brought out and opened, and the dancing started. The celebration would go on far into the night.

John came up behind Oliver, who had taken up playing mandolin with the fireside musicians, and held up his clay glass full of mead. "No wonder Will knew who you were."

"Yes, I guess I am somewhat of a celebrity here."

"That's what happens when you put your face on the bottle, Oli."

"Not my idea at all, but it did boost sales for the monastery."

"Sure, Oli, tell yourself whatever you have to." John slapped him on his back and wandered back over to the bleachers. He climbed up to the top and sat alone, watching the fire dancers, music makers, and children playing tag in the dark, and let himself relax just enough to realize he was relaxing.

Cam?

Yes, John.

How are we doing?

So far so good. Nothing has come up since we've been here.

Good. I think it's time to round up everyone.

John, let them have a little more fun.

Show 'em to me.

Cam showed John the surrounding area, and then did an overlay highlighting the twins, Oliver, and Sage in red.

Okay, a little longer. We'll give them until I find Reet.

Wow, really? Maybe you are getting a little soft.

It's because of you.

What?

Just find Reet for me, will you?

Cam highlighted Rita, Will's wife, on his grid. He sat and soaked in the ambiance of the night for a bit longer, and then he left the fireside party to go to join Rita. He didn't have to go far;

she was waiting for him on the porch of the small cabin they were
using. The obsidian-haired woman, who looked much younger
than Will, had caramel skin and shimmering brown eyes. She
smiled when she saw him and walked to the top step to give him
a hug.

"Hello, long lost brother."

"Hi, Reet."

God, Will's wife could have been a supermodel before Day One.

She's one of a kind, that's for sure.

She's like a sexy huntress or something.

Wow, Cam, a sexy huntress?

That's not weird, is it?

Sure.

"Thank you again, Rita." John bowed his head slightly.

Rita bowed her head in return. "We wouldn't have you accept
any less, John. Will and I both wish we could do more."

"No worries, Reet. We'll be fine. Where is the bastard anyway?"

"He's still boxing it out with Dad and Bert. I'm sure he'll be by in
the morning."

"Tell me again how he suckered the daughter of the chief into
marrying him?"

"I'm not sure I really remember," Rita said. "Might be the shaman
he hired to put a spell on me."

"That would make sense."

John turned his head and surveyed the quiet outskirts of the
town, the small glow and rumble still going strong in the square,
and then turned back to Rita.

"What do you think about all this, Reet?"

"I think that Elizabeth and Adam are proud of you right now."
She smiled and stepped closer to him, placing her hand on his shoulder. "How else do you think you've made it this far?"

John smiled, his eyes threatening to overflow. He cleared his
throat and blinked a couple of times, making the wetness disappear
before it could pour out.

"Yeah, we'll see when this is all said and done."

"It's happening exactly the way it's supposed to, John. Don't fight it." She adjusted the collar of his stitched-up, sun-worn gray shirt. "You're exactly where you're supposed to be."

"You and Oliver must have been talking."

Rita gave him a hug and then kissed him on both cheeks. "Always the skeptic, but then you wouldn't be the man Will and I love so much if you weren't, would you?"

"Someone has to be."

"I better get back to the house, check on our little prince and princess."

"With Will's DNA running through their veins, you might not have a house to check on."

She chuckled and waved him off. "I've learned not to linger away too long, that's for sure. Still, they haven't burned down the house yet."

Ouch.

Reet caught her breath. "Sorry, John. Will told me." She squeezed his shoulder. "If you need anything, you know where to find us."

She started down the trail and then turned her head and waved at him. "Goodnight, John."

"Goodnight, Reet."

Oliver, Sage, and the twins, with Adam in tow, came up the rock trail leading to the cabin, waving to Rita as they passed her.

"Decided to call it a night, huh?" John asked.

"I believe that we've all had our fill of the party." Oliver pointed over to Sierra and Quinn, dragging themselves up the steps, yawning, eyes heavy with sleepiness. "What'd she say about Will?"

"We won't see him until morning."

"Smoking the wrong stuff with that Bert fellow, eh?" Oliver nudged John's arm and wiggled his eyebrows at him. "If you know what I mean."

"No one ever knows what you mean, Oli," Sage said.

"Well, it's very simple. See, I was making a joke as to the fact that they're smoking the wacky stuff instead of the seer herb they're supposed to be smoking…"

Sage put her hand on his shoulder and interrupted him. "Oliver, we know. God, you're a dork sometimes."

"Oh, I see, of course. I'll just make my room upstairs then."

They entered the cabin, and Oliver headed over and up the short stairs to one of the rooms in the loft.

"We'll take the other room," Sierra said. "Come on, Q, I'm beat."

"Top bunk." Quinn raced past her up the stairs.

Sage turned toward John and pointed to the last room on the main floor. "Room?"

"All yours. Adam and I will take the couch."

"Are you sure?" Sage pointed to Adam gimping his way up the stairs. "What?"

No loyalty. Aren't you glad you at least have me?

Overly excited, Cam. Every day.

"I guess it's just me on the couch then."

Sage made her way to her room, looking back over her shoulder just long enough to shoot John another wink.

"You should be more careful what you wish for, then."

Damn, she's good.

Hold steady, John. Hold steady.

*   *   *

"John! Help us, John!"

John scanned the battlefield for his wife and son, squinting to see through the smoke and debris of the war-scarred city.

"Elizabeth! Adam!"

"John! John, help us, we're burning."

John ran to where he thought the voices were coming from, but it was another dead-end alley. He searched frantically for them, turning over cars, ripping apart walls, nothing.

"Dad, please! Hurry, she's dying!"

John ran back down the alley and out to the road. The scene changed, and he was staring at his house engulfed in flames. Shadows that loomed behind the burning house circled toward him. The screams got louder as the dark shroud closed on him.

"Why didn't you save us, John? Didn't you love us enough?"

"Why couldn't you save us, Dad? We needed you. We were dying. Where were you?"

John collapsed on his knees, screaming in agony at the pain searing through him as the darkness overwhelmed him. The voices got louder and louder until all he could hear and feel was their death all around him.

"John! John! John! John…"

*   *   *

He woke up at the first touch of wetness, grabbed his gun and had it jammed against flesh in seconds.

John, wait.

"Bad move, asshole," he said.

John, wait a second, big guy, relax.

"Oh. God, John, go easy." Sage took a breath and changed her voice to a whisper. "Go, easy, John, it's okay. It's me. Sage."

John shook his head, trying to clear the visions of his nightmare from his mind. He blinked his eyes, open, shut, open, shut, until he was aware enough to know he was awake.

It was a nightmare, John. A nightmare. You're safe now.

Cam.

I'm here.

"Sage?"

"I'm here, John. Everything's okay."

"What the hell are you doing here, Sage? I almost blew your fucking brains out."

"Your 'thank yous' always did suck."

Sage pushed her hand against his forehead, making him lie back down, and then took the wet cloth she had dropped and wiped off his forehead.

"You look like shit. Must have been a bad one. How long has it been, John?"

"None of your business."

"You can't go this long between re-orgs."

She's right, John. We have been feeling a little frazzled.

John set his jaw and glared at Sage. "I'm fine." He put his gun back in his holster and sat up. "I need some fresh air."

"Classic John tact. Run away, it's what you're good at."

"Look who's talking."

Sage curled her lips into a sneer. "Good luck, John. I hope you choke in your sleep." Standing, she threw the wet cloth at him and then headed to her room.

Anyone tell you that you need a little help when it comes to relationships?

No, and don't you start either.

John grabbed his pulse rifle and headed out the door.

Twenty-Four

Fight or Flight

JOHN SNUCK BACK INTO THE CABIN early in the morning, did a quick check on everyone, and then washed up. He slipped on a new blue T-shirt and a fresh pair of pants that he had gotten from Reet, and then met Will at the stables to prep the horses Will had procured: one for each of them, and the pack mule Esmeralda loaded with supplies, which one of Will's patrols had found wandering in the woods.

Will removed the saddle from Sierra's horse, leaving just the bridle, remarking "You sure that's what she wants?"

"So she says."

A teasing smile crossed Will's face. "Oh, okay." He scanned the horses, smile fading, voice turning serious. "I'm sorry, John. This is the best I could do."

"It's more than enough, Will. Good chow, fresh water, weapons, ammo, and clean clothes: what else does a crew of rejects need?"

"Yeah, right," Will's eyebrows scrunched together and his eyes narrowed. "Listen, are you sure you know what you're getting into?"

John grimaced. "No idea, actually."

"That's what I thought." Will looked at his friend and shook his head. "Listen, the elders are saying that some sort of dark spirit's after those kids. They say there's a death spirit attacking anyone who tries to help them, but if they aren't helped, the darkness will consume everyone."

"That's about as reassuring as a nightmare."

"It's probably all bullshit anyway, like his stories about meeting some Sasquatch chief. Sometimes Bert smokes too much spirit weed. Either way, someone with some major power is after those kids, so watch yourselves out there."

Told you we should have laced Bert's pipe.

"Damn monks and pipe-smoking elders, right?" John said.

They both laughed, giving each other a hug.

"I wish you luck, old friend," Will said.

"And you too, William."

"Hey, tell Sage and Oliver bye for me. I would stay longer, but I promised to take the kids down to fish, and if I don't there's no way Rita will let me live through the night."

"Don't sweat it. I'll tell them, and you tell Rita thank you for me."

Will made a sexy wiggle, clapping his hands to his hips. "I'll tell her a couple of times."

Gross.

We need to get some of that smoke.

Will gave him one last look, like maybe he would never see him again, and then turned and walked toward the other side of the town.

* * *

"Wake up, sleeping beauty," John said, so close his heat and breath brushed Oliver.

Oliver woke up, eyes open wide and bloodshot, and pushed his head back into his pillow to get some distance from John.

"What the...John? You scared the piss out of me. What is it? Is there something wrong? Are the kids okay?"

John leaned back, smiling a nice, toothy smile.

It's the small things, Cam, always the small things.

Worth their weight in gold.

"Everyone's fine, Oli. Time in Pleasantville's up though. We gotta hit the road."

"Oh, right. Fantastic," Oliver said. "I knew they would help us over the passes."

"Not quite. Will says the twins have some sort of death force chasing after them, so they won't have anything to do with us."

"Oh."

John slapped Oliver hard on the shoulder. "But Reet cleaned your stinky robe and Will procured us some horses and supplies, enough to get us as far as we need to go." John got up to leave, but then looked back. "Oh, and I'll give you until tonight, Oliver."

"Until tonight?"

"I want to know everything by tonight, or I leave you stranded on your own in the mountains, all alone with the Sasquatches."

Do you really think he'll tell us everything?

They always do. Eventually.

John stared straight at Oliver for a minute and then headed toward the door. "Wake the kids up and get 'em ready to go."

They were getting loaded up and onto the horses when Sage came out, eyes tight, jaw tense, a well-rested Adam right on her heels. She looked freshly showered and wore new clothes: a green T-shirt under a thick grey cloak and a pair of brown cargo pants tucked into her combat boots. She walked dangerously close to John, nudging him hard as she headed to her horse.

"Morning, Sage. Looks like Adam woke you up, and got you straightened up, too."

"It was better than waking up to you."

"Thought you liked it when I woke you."

"Keep dreaming, John."

Oh, great, this is going to be just like high school.

You don't know what high school's like, Cam.

Thank God. You need to talk to her, John.

I'm done talking.

You're a child.

You're a child.

"What's the holdup, Oli? You think we got all day to dillydally?" Sage asked.

She hopped onto her horse and clicked her tongue against her teeth twice, heading up the road that led out of town.

"What's gotten into her?" Sierra asked.

"She and John had a fight last night." Quinn climbed onto his coal black horse with some help from Oliver.

Sierra scrunched her lips and eyebrows in thought. "Really? What were they fighting about?"

Adam nudged Sierra and barked to get her to mount the dark chocolate horse she'd be riding.

"All right, all right. Take a chill pill, Adam, jeez." Sierra looked at Quinn. "This isn't over, Q. I want details."

Sierra and Oliver looked over at John, who just smiled at the red-cloaked twins and mounted his own horse, clicking his tongue twice and following Sage down the road.

They look like two little red riding hoods, John.

Two little red riding pains in my ass is more like it.

Sure tough guy, sure.

On that note they left White River behind and headed into the mountains.

*   *   *

"Where are we going?" Quinn asked.

"To Galbraith Monastery, at Old Fairhaven," Oliver said. "It's where I made my home after Day One. I think you and your sister will find it comfortable enough, always plenty to do around the grounds and the town there. An over-abundance of food, I might add. The land and soil are very fertile, plus the school system you will be attending is second to none."

There was a short silence as Sierra and her horse, which she found was aptly named Spitfire, clopped up beside Quinn and Oliver.

"It's not like we get to decide, do we, Oliver?"

"I guess we haven't given you children much of a choice, have we?" Oliver said. "But there really hasn't been much choice to give unless you wanted to stay back at Tree Top."

Sierra huffed and trotted up behind Sage, leaving Oliver at a loss for words. "Really, you'll like it all immensely, even though you didn't—oh, never mind."

"You're pretty cool, Oliver," Quinn said.

"Thank you, Quinn. Can I ask where that came from?"

"I just wanted to tell you before you change your mind and leave us because of Sierra."

"No worry about that. I'm afraid we are all joined at the hip for the duration."

"Well, just in case, I think you're really cool, and your stories are awesome."

Oliver smiled, sat up triumphant in his saddle, and looked over at John, who grinned back at him.

"Thank you, Quinn," Oliver said. "Did you hear that, John? I'm awesome."

"Sure, Oliver, you're one of a kind."

We'll never hear the end of it, John.

I'm sure we won't.

Then why do you encourage it?

The small things, Cam, the small things.

Adam marched alongside them for a while until John whistled a short burst of a tune, signaling it was time to start his watch. At the end of John's whistle, Adam tore off through the thick trees, training and instinct taking over.

You linked with Adam?

Tight as fiddle strings. As far as I can tell we're clear for miles. Like really clear.

Maybe we'll catch a break.

I'll believe that when it actually happens.

Yeah, right.

They clopped on for hours along the pine-scented dirt and rock trail. Winding up and up, the trail looked as if it might take them to the clouds. Then they would descend into a valley, only to start going back uphill again. John had Cam scanning constantly but there was nothing to find besides the indigenous wild life. There were no towns or villages up here, and only very few people could be found this deep in the wood. Mostly scavengers, people who had gone a little too wild for everyone else's taste, and who, for whatever reason, decided to live up here on their own. Luckily they hadn't run into any of these hill people yet, and the way things looked on the scans, they wouldn't.

Every once in a while they crossed a torn-up section of earth and a root-covered remnant of a concrete road, reminders that these mountain passes, now deserted for longer than most could remember, had once been the only connections between one side of the state and the other. Even though the Earth had long since taken this land back, it was easy to follow the concrete swath of the old I-90. It was still slow going in places where hard pavement turned into a bumpy, pothole-filled, bombed-out skeleton of its former self.

They rested very little, stopping only at swiftly flowing freshets to water the horses and refill the water bladders. The day wore on, and as the sun dipped, the wind began its steady assault on their bare skin, penetrating the cloaks and jackets like ice picks.

Damn, eight Celsius, John. That's cold.

It's always cold up here, Cam.

Feels too cold for spring.

You don't actually feel, Cam.

I sense how you feel, same difference.

Sure you do. Anything from Adam?

No, but I think he'd agree with me that it's colder than usual.

Cam.

His feed's clear, but I'll check.

Cam brought up Adam's vid feeds and an overlay of the countryside. They were already crunching though a dusting of snow that was settling onto the path like powdered sugar on a brownie. The trail that came through on Adam's feed showed heavier downfall and an accumulation of at least a foot.

More snow up ahead, John.

Used to be waist-deep up here, if not more.

Remember when there was no snow?

Let's not remember that.

Let's not. Looks like Adam will be back to us soon. Oh, and he found it. We're actually pretty close.

Thank you, Cam.

I really don't know what you two would do without me.

We sure as hell wouldn't know if it was cold or not.

If I had a tongue I'd stick it out at you.

"How long until he lets us stop?" Sierra said between her chattering teeth. She pulled her cloak tight against her and put her hood up. "Doesn't he know it's snowing?"

"I'm not so sure that would make a difference," Oliver said.

"He'll stop," Sage gritted her teeth and put a hand her hand on her ribs, checking her splint and guarding against any movement with her arm. "He's just waiting for the right place."

"It's freezing," Quinn said. "I hope he finds someplace soon."

Oliver looked over at Sage, a gentle smile on his face. "Are you doing okay? We can stop if you need to, Sage."

Sage bore down on her horse and glared at him. "I'm fine, Oli. I might not heal as fast you, but I have my own tricks."

Adam found his way back to his companions, appearing from between the trees as though he'd been on a fine afternoon stroll. He'd been gone long enough this time that the sun was dipping behind the tall peaks of the Cascades. He barked and spun in circles as he got to John, who threw him a piece of jerky and continued on the trail. Adam demolished it and then fell in line with the group.

"We're almost there."

You'll be able to see it soon, John.

"And where would *there* be?" Oliver asked.

"An old building that was part of the modified military outpost up here. Cam and Adam both say the area's clear, so we'll be able to start a fire and bed down there for the night."

"Finally," Sierra said. "I'm not sure my numb body could take much more."

Sage brought her horse up alongside her. "Don't worry, kid. Numbness won't last that long once we get some heat on you."

Sierra glared at her and pushed her horse to go a little ahead of Sage. "Duh, I know that already. I'm not a little kid."

John laughed as Sage came up beside him. "Having fun?" he asked.

"Looks like you're having more fun than me."

"It's nice to see someone else on the receiving end of her charming attitude."

"I'm glad you're enjoying it."

"Thank you." He glanced over her and cocked his lips up into a smile. "Looks like you might have taken your sling and rib swathing off a little soon."

He was about to say something else, but Sage swatted his horse hard on its rear end. The horse reared up, threw him from his saddle, and then sprinted up the trail until it was out of sight. John rolled onto his back in the ankle-deep snow and looked up from his new position at Sage as she went on with a satisfied smile on her face.

"You're very welcome," she said.

Oliver and Quinn trotted their horses over and smiled down at him as they passed. "What was that about? Horse giving you a run for your money?" Oliver asked.

John hollered after them. "We're going on foot from here anyway."

See, this is what happens when you seclude yourself. You get out of practice and give Sage the upper hand. Then again, I think she's always had the upper hand.

Shut up, Cam. Obviously I haven't secluded us enough.

You know, we don't have to go on foot from here.

They don't know that, and they need to get warmed up anyway.

Oh, yes I'm sure you're thinking of them getting warm.

It's only half a click.

Bully.

Whatever.

John dusted the snow and dirt off his clothes, and smiled at Sierra's grumbling as his four companions dismounted. He jogged to the head of the line, and led them on foot, trudging through the snow as the icy wind chapped their faces. Up and up they went, as if there were no end to the forested road snaking up to meet the sky.

Sierra kicked a rock and it went tumbling down the hill until it disappeared into the trees below. "Is this the only way?"

"Yes."

"What happened here?"

John looked back just in time to see Quinn jump over a large part of road that looked as if someone with a fist the size of the Hulk had punched a hole in it.

Be patient, John.

I'm trying.

"The military blew it up before cease-fire to disrupt supply shipments over the mountains."

Quinn stopped for a minute and looked up at John. "Weren't you military?"

"Different part of the military, kid."

"But you were part of that military?"

Almost there, John.

"Yes."

"So what happened?"

How much farther, Cam?

Quarter click, why?

"Cease-fire happened, Quinn, and now we're all safe. So how about you stop jaw-jacking."

John glanced through the large gaps where mountain and road fell down the steep rock-and-tree-covered descent into the forest below.

Just thinking we better get there soon—before I jump.

Funny, John.

They left the road, John taking them onto an overgrown trail leading to an old lodge.

"What is this place?" Quinn asked.

Sierra repeated the question, as if she knew it would drive John crazy. "Yeah, what is this place, John?"

John looked back, eyes wide with exasperation, jaw clenching, and then smiled as he settled on Oliver. "You know what, kid, Oliver's been up here the most; why don't you ride next to him and ask all about it?"

Quinn's forehead wrinkled as he thought about it, then he nodded his head and slowed his pace so he could be next to Oliver.

Oh, you're so smart, John.

Just using the tools I have, Cam.

Adapt, overcome, and improvise.

Exactly.

You're a dork.

But I'm your dork.

Lucky us.

John didn't quite catch what Quinn had asked but he heard Oliver go into instant story-telling mode.

"Oh, yes, of course, I guess I have been up here more than most." He answered every question the twins asked about the area: how it had been transformed from an old ski resort to a military compound, one that changed hands between the resistance fighters and US forces several times. Then, after a long and tedious description of what skiing was and why it had been something fun to do, Oliver explained why the area had been converted to military use, and why it had been abandoned almost intact.

"People who came up here to scavenge for supplies after cease-fire started disappearing. It was easy to disappear in the chaos, but these ones disappeared never to be seen again."

The twins looked to Sage and John as if they were checking Oliver's facts. Both nodded in agreement.

"How were they disappearing?" Sierra asked.

John shrugged. "Some people came up with stories of Sasquatches coming down to take people. There weren't any signs of them being taken by other humans, so people became desperate for anything to blame the mysterious vanishings on."

Oh boy, you're not going to start that are you, John?

It'll make for better campfire stories.

"So they blamed Sasquatches?" Quinn asked.

"They did, and because of that fear of getting taken by the horrible Sasquatch, people stayed clear of this entire area. Soon the only way to the other side was far north, far south, or in the sky. The woods and the compound were slowly forgotten, except by a few people."

John looked back and saw Quinn smiling from ear to ear. "People like you right, John?"

He couldn't help but grin. "Something like that, kid."

You are such a big child.

You like it just as much as I do.

You only say that because you know I'm a sucker for campfire stories.

John led them first to an old maintenance building, where they left the horses and pack mule with the majority of their gear. It would be a cold night for the animals, but they had food and water, along with heavy blankets to help keep them warm.

He let everyone select the bare minimum of gear before leading them to another small outbuilding that was made out of logs and cement. The windows were still intact, which was a rarity up there. Snow covered the roof, a good sign the building was still sturdy. The walls and doors were in one piece; the place should hold the warmth from the wide stone fireplace inside if they could get a fire lit.

They made camp, pushing rotten, moth-eaten furniture aside to make space to sit by the hearth. John secured the entrances—the door at the front that they had come in through and a well-covered exit at the back—while the others took out rations and started eating as they laid out their gear and chose where to rack out. Adam curled up in front of the fireplace next to where Quinn had laid his claim for the night.

"Hey, boy," Quinn said. "Do you think it's true what they say about the Sasquatches that live up here?"

"Sasquatches don't exist, Quinn," Sierra said.

"They do too. If they didn't exist, why are there so many stories about them? About how they ate up all the travelers that came up here after Day One, the ones trying to go across the mountains to hide?"

"Whatever, Quinn. You stay in your little fantasy world if you want to."

Sierra got up and went over to her bed. Adam whimpered, pushing his body closer to Quinn.

See what finding someplace warm does to them, Cam?

You like it.

Like I'd like an ice pick in my eye.

"I believe you, Quinn," Oliver said.

Oliver had been sitting on an old steel stool, drinking some water he had steamed by the fire.

"Don't encourage him, Oli," Sage said. "You'll give the boy nightmares."

Quinn looked sideways at Sage, a quizzical look on his face. "Really, you believe me?"

Sage rolled her eyes. "Good going, Oli."

"I do believe you, Quinn," Oliver said. "In fact, when I was on my second trip to the monastery, I met a man who told me a story about how he barely survived a Sasquatch attack."

This is going to be good.

You ready, Cam?

What, we can't wait and hear Oliver's story?

You've heard it before.

But it's cold out.

You can't feel it, Cam.

But we already scanned and it's clear.

Yes.

And you want to a quick scout anyway.

Yes.

In the freezing cold.

Yes, Cam.

Damn it.

John headed out the back door, waving to Sage, who nodded her head in recognition. As he slid the door shut he could hear Oliver starting in on one of his stories, and smiled.

*   *   *

Oliver told them of a man he ran across who had been part of a scavenger party. "Early on, you see. There wasn't much organization, and small groups would form up together and try to go it on their own. This man was in one of those groups.

"They were on their way to Leavenworth because word had spread that a strong free colony was flourishing there. The land in most of the coastal cities had been swallowed by water, and what was left of the peninsula had either been wiped bare or turned into wetlands. So they were heading over the pass in a small caravan of vehicles, back when most everyone still had such things.

"This man and his band of scavengers holed up close to where we are now, up at the main lodge. Even though people still had vehicles, few had come over the passes in a long time, and the lodge, just recently closed, had a good chance of still being intact. The scavenging party was counting on this, and hoped to find an untouched trove of supplies.

"This particular group hadn't seen anyone else yet on their trip and felt safe in just having one person at a time pulling watch shifts, but one of the watchers fell asleep, and as they all slept an ancient evil crept down from the tallest peaks of the mountain to the small mound of red hot coals that the watcher had left without tending. They crept like two-story tall Indians through the trees, and over the rocks and rivers to the tiny light that burned gold.

"When the man I met woke up, he saw a giant, fur-covered monster, with fangs like a saber-toothed tiger's and claws as long as samurai swords, stuffing his cohorts into a giant sack. He could hear their blood-curdling screams and see them struggling as the hideous creature poked and prodded the sack, laughing a deep and sickening laugh at their pain."

The light from the fire flickered violently across the room and over Oliver, making him look like a mad magician instructing his pupils as he paused to take a drink out of his flask. Sierra got up and looked out the window. In the light of the full moon, a hollow-looking structure stood high on the mountain's slope. Sierra's eyes went wide with a queasy terror.

"Is that the building up there?" she asked.

"You're correct, Sierra, the building they sheltered in is that very building up there. I imagine if any Sasquatches were up there, they'd have noticed our presence by now and started our way to investigate…"

John came in right at that moment and everyone in the room but Oliver jumped. Sierra let out an uncontrolled shriek, and Adam howled toward the ceiling as the gust of wind that had followed John inside whirled through the room until he slammed the door.

He caught a ratty old pillow Sage had thrown at him and coughed from the small cloud of dust and dirt that exploded from it.

"Jeez, John, you scared the crap out of us."

He dropped the pillow and smiled at the glare he was getting from Sage. "You have everyone scared with one of your Sasquatch stories already, Oliver?"

Adam lay back down and tried covering his eyes with his paws.

"You should cover your eyes, Adam," John said. "You didn't even try to scout outside with me, and now you're acting scared like a toddler."

Adam rolled over halfway onto his back and nudged Quinn's hand with his nose, and then his paws. Quinn laughed and started scratching his chest and belly.

"Don't listen to him, boy. I think you're brave, and I'm glad you stayed here to protect me from Sasquatches."

"Looks like you've effectively turned Adam from a military Shepherd into a pushover," Sage said.

Everyone in the room laughed. John rolled his eyes and did one last check around the room as Oliver started up his story again.

Your dog has no shame, John. No shame at all.

Reminds me of someone else I know.

Oliver.

Sure.

"Did they eat them?"

"Sierra, shut up," Quinn said.

Oliver smiled at the two squabbling siblings. "The truth is the man didn't know what happened. He did what I expect most humans in his predicament would do. He ran like mad out of that lodge and into the woods, without so much as a bottle of water. By the time I found him, he was hardly coherent from exhaustion, hypothermia, dehydration, and starvation.

"I fed him, gave him drink, and tried to get him to leave with me, but he would not go back to the trail because he was so terrified. So I got him drunk one night until he passed out, and I hauled him myself all the way to Tree Top.

"At the time I still believed the man to be mad, but he never changed his story, not once. It drove him to drink his life away, and he died from a knife wound after picking a fight with some other drunk. All because they told him his story was only the ravings of a crazy man."

Damn, he tells a good story.

You scared, Cam?

I can't get scared.

You can't get cold either.

"Has anyone else seen the Sasquatches?" Sierra asked.

"There are stories, rumors, a rare whisper on the occasion some-one catches sight of something moving in the trees below them, or sees something when they've traveled deeper in the woods than they were supposed to."

"Is it true what they say about them eating your insides, and using human skin for their shelters?" Quinn asked.

"I imagine not but—" Oliver looked over at Sage and John, who were sitting much closer together now, and gave them a wink "—there are the stories of the missing children that always worried me."

Quinn and Sierra's eyes got wide, and Adam tried to cover his eyes again and whimpered.

"What children?" Sierra asked.

"Most of the merchants these days live in or near the towns they make their living in, but a small few still choose to live out in the woods. As with our good friend John here, they live deep in the woods, not believing the stories of children getting snatched up by Sasquatch hunting parties in the dead of night, and taken deep in the mountains where no one can hear their screams."

He is joking, right?

I thought you couldn't get scared.

I can't. I'm just curious.

Sure, Cam, sure.

"Alright then," Oliver said. "Off to bed now."

Sierra looked at him as if he'd just asked her to stick her hand in the fire. "Now, really?"

"Yes, now." Oliver raised his arms above his head like an ape and charged at the twins. "Before the Sasquatch comes for you!"

Sierra shrieked as Oliver tackled her and Quinn. "Oliver!"

"Get him," Quinn said.

The two of them started on the offensive, sending Oliver onto his back and bombarding him with their tiny camp pillows. Adam growled playfully, grabbed Oliver's robe between his teeth, and pulled on him so he couldn't escape.

"Kill the Sasquatch!"

"Don't let him eat the children!"

Oliver peeked out from under Quinn's arm at John and Sage. "I might need a little help here."

"I think you're doing just fine, Oliver the Sasquatch. Don't you, Sage?"

"Yeah, don't worry, Oli, you got this."

"Wait, don't leave me to these Sasquatch killers," Oliver said as John and Sage made their way to the back of the room to lay out their sleeping bags.

*   *   *

Sierra picked up her pack and sleep gear, and moved over to an open space by Quinn. "I better come and sleep by you, Quinn, just in case you have a nightmare."

"Good idea, Sierra," Quinn said. "That way when a Sasquatch comes, I'll make sure he takes you first."

Sierra flicked him behind his ears with her finger.

"You're a jerk, Q."

"I love you too, Sis."

"Good job, Oli," Sage said. "Scare the kids half to death and then tell them it's time to go to sleep."

"I'm not scared at all," Sierra said. She glared at Oliver. "I don't believe in Sasquatches."

Sierra turned over and pulled her sleeping bag over her head.

"Do the Sasquatches really eat the kids?" Quinn asked.

"No one knows, Q," Oliver said. "The children are never seen or heard from again."

He unpacked his bag and flung out his sleeping bag.

"So they might still be alive," Quinn said.

"Or they might not."

Quinn lay on his back and stared at the ceiling, arms behind his head as if lost in thought. Oliver looked at him one more time for good measure, and then tucked himself in his bag for the night.

"Goodnight, Q," he said, "sweet Sasquatch dreams."

John and Sage lingered awake for a little longer, making sure everyone got off to sleep okay; only Quinn was still awake. John figured he'd have the gears of misadventure and imagination turning in his mind for a while yet.

"First watch?" Sage asked.

"Rock, scissors, paper?"

* * *

Sage grumbled as she got ready for her first sweep around the perimeter. "I should call cheating. Who even uses dynamite anymore?"

"The same people that use a handgun to try to win Rock, Scissors, Paper," John said.

He wrapped himself up tight in his sleeping bag and rolled over onto his side. "Enjoy your patrol. Might want to dress warm. It's pretty cold out."

"Jerk off," Sage said.

She opened the door and let an extra-long, cold gust of wind in as she headed outside.

Thanks for flashing dynamite to me, Cam.

Dynamite gets them every time.

Amateurs.

"Was Oliver telling the truth about the Sasquatches, John?" Quinn asked.

"I didn't figure you'd let a story like that keep you awake."

"But are they real?"

"I don't know, kid. I bet there's a lot of stuff up here that we don't know about. It's wild in these parts anymore, so I guess Sasquatches could be real. But don't worry, we'll feed them Oliver first."

Quinn laughed and petted Adam, who was still curled up near him.

"I bet Adam would save us, wouldn't you, boy?"

Adam rolled over into Quinn and let him rub behind his ears.

"Looks like you've made yourself a pretty loyal friend. He must really like you."

"I think he does."

"He always did have bad taste," John said. "Now shut up so I can get to sleep."

John caught a small smile from Quinn before the kid rolled over and pulled his sleeping bag back up over his head.

"Goodnight, John," Quinn said, voice muffled.

"Goodnight, kid."

TWENTY-FIVE

Sasquatch

"Wake up, sunshine," John said.

"It's too early for milk, mommy," Oliver mumbled.

Mommy?

Opening his eyes slowly, blinking a few times, and then a bit wider, Oliver sat bolt upright. "I mean, right away, of course, sorry."

I think he's a cute beardy man.

I don't think cute is the word for it.

"Don't worry, sweetheart," John said, "your secret's safe with me."

"Right, thank you."

"Can you get the kids up and get them moving?"

"Gladly." Oliver looked around. "Any news from the front?"

John leaned back against the wall, smiling, and took a deep breath.

"No, all clear so far. Sage's out getting the horses ready, so you better put a move on it."

"Brisk start this morning; I like it. Let us get marching then."

"Yup, we have to get a head start on your Sasquatch friends, don't we?"

Oliver smiled, a bit more nervous than John had anticipated.

Aren't you chipper this morning.

That's me, Mr. Chipper.

Eew, that sounds kind of creepy.

"Yes, of course, funny. Sasquatches. Very good." Oliver crawled out of his sleeping bag and walked over to Sierra and Quinn, prodding their small forms to life. "No rest for the weary. Up and at 'em, you lollygaggers."

Sierra and Quinn moaned but stayed in their caves. Oliver nudged them with his toe a little harder, and then bent down and uncovered them.

"Rise and shine, children. Time to hit the open road."

"Really, Oliver?" Sierra said. "It's still so early."

"Yes, really. No time to waste, long day ahead of us, up with both of you."

The twin zombies named Quinn and Sierra started moving and with no great speed, finished climbing out into the light in the matching black T-shirts and blue jeans they'd gotten from Will and Rita. They slouched on one of the benches and slugged down their breakfast before gathering up supplies and stamping out the fire.

"Why do we always have to leave so early?" Sierra asked.

John finished checking out Quinn's horse and started his inspection of Sierra and her horse, Spitfire. He nodded: Sierra had everything she needed. He hadn't been able to convince her to use a saddle, but after Quinn's swim in the river she was at least using reins.

"Because we have to."

"That's a brilliant answer."

Quinn looked over to Oliver and Sage. "This is going to be a long day."

Do we always have to start off like this?

It seems to be the routine.

Ugh.

They rode for most of the morning, John in the lead and Oliver in the middle, playing his mandolin and singing old ballads of wayward travelers for Sierra and Quinn. Sage brought up the rear, and Adam ran up and down the line, checking on his companions.

"How many days is it going to take us to get to your monastery, Oliver?"

"Five days if we don't run into trouble, Q."

"Are we going to like it there?"

"Oh, indeed you will, Q. It was built out of the ashes of a gated town up on a mountain. Its white-stoned walls are strong and majestic, towering over the endless ocean."

He should be a vendor.

He is a vendor, Cam.

Oh, yeah, I forgot.

Quinn saw Oliver gaze far past the trail they were on. Past the trees and stone that surrounded them. Past everything.

"You really miss it, don't you, Oli?"

"I do, Quinn. It's a wonderful place, and I am anxious to get back."

Sierra came up behind them and sneered at Oliver. "Is it just a monastery? Sounds boring."

"Monastery, and a small village. It's become a hub for anyone traveling the coastal areas, really." Oliver smiled proudly. "Its keeper is my master and teacher, Benedict. He will know how to help us."

Almost as good as our place, John.

As our place was.

Sorry.

Don't worry about it, Cam. Maybe we'll end up staying with Oli.

Don't play with me like that, John.

Sierra leaned back in her saddle and looked straight at John. "It does almost sound as good as your place was, John."

She winked at him and then clicked her tongue, speeding her horse up past them to the front of the trail, where she couldn't hear anyone.

Where'd that come from?

Who knows.

They get weirder by the second.

John whistled and Adam took off after her.

"Did we miss something?" Oliver asked.

"Don't worry about her, Oli," Quinn said. "She's almost always like that."

"Yes, I'm starting to get a grasp on her subtle tendencies."

"Good luck. She's not so subtle."

"So what's the name of your monastery again, Oli?"

"Galbraith, in the coast city of New Fairhaven. That was the name of the last city below the mountain before it was swallowed by the ocean."

Sage came up behind them on her way up to John. "Telling more horror stories, Oliver? One might think that you never want the boy to sleep again."

"I wasn't scared last night," Quinn said. "I was just worried about Sierra, that's all."

"Of course, Q. I'm sorry, I was so mistaken."

"We're going to need to rest soon, Sage," Oliver said. "I know of a place a bit farther down the trail that would be suitable. Could you tell our silent, fearless leader for us?"

"I'll try."

Sage spurred her horse into a trot to catch John.

"Quiet today, big fella," Sage said.

"Something's been tracking us."

"I know. I can't tell if it's just curious or waiting to eat us."

John looked at Sage, eyes wide. "*Sasquatch*," he said.

Sage laughed, making her cough a little, and she punched his arm. "I told you, don't make me laugh, this shit still hurts, John, Jesus."

"I'm sorry, I just keep forgetting you're not as strong as you look."

"And here I thought you had lost all your humor when you were born."

"Nice."

That's a good point, John. Maybe you were born without humor.

I evolved.

Thanks to me.

In spite of you.

"Our senses are a little high right now. It's probably just some wolves, curious about what a rag-tag band like us is doing up here."

"Yeah," John said, "or wondering which one of us tastes the juiciest."

"Look at you," Sage said. "All worried about your new friends."

"Worried about getting rid of them, that's all."

John heard the clopping stop behind him and turned to see who had stopped. Quinn sat in his saddle, tense and glaring at John.

Damn.

Damn's right.

Sage scrunched up the side of her face and looked at John as if he'd just spit on the kid. "Good work, John. Never disappoint, do you?"

John sighed and rubbed his temples hard with thumb and forefinger, and then pulled his hand down his road-weary face.

"Hey, kid, I didn't mean it like that."

"You don't have to lie, John. You'll be rid of us soon enough, and then your life will back to normal."

Quinn steered his horse back toward Oli, who waved helplessly to John.

No way to sugarcoat that one, John.

Damn again.

John's horse reared its head up, snorting and neighing, trying to turn in the middle of the trail. John looked at Sage; her horse was doing the same. He tugged on the reins, fighting to keep the horse grounded, and win back control for the moment. "Sage. Better go check on Adam and Sierra."

"Yeah, I'm on it."

Sage sped off at a gallop.

John looked back at Oliver, who was talking to Quinn, trying to convince him that John wasn't a complete asshole, when he heard Adam start howling.

John, big heat sig bearing down on Sierra and Adam right now.

Is it the wolf pack?

No, this is way different, and way bigger.

John pulled his REP rifle off his back and kicked his horse into a gallop toward Sage, Sierra, and Adam.

"Climb, Oli. Climb!"

Oliver heard John yelling at him and wasted no time grabbing the reins of Quinn's horse and leading them over to a giant boulder. Oliver jumped off the horse onto the rock and helped Quinn up after him. They climbed, higher and higher, until they weren't obvious targets from the road.

John saw Sage's horse speed past him and into the trees. He dug his heels deep into his horse's ribs, leaned low, and urged it forward. He reached Sage and Sierra and dismounted, letting the spooked animal run loose back down the trail. Sierra was on the ground, her horse long gone. Sage was helping her up, and guarding her own ribs, out of breath already. Adam was howling at something John couldn't see yet, fur rippling along his back, lips furled up to show his blade-like fangs. John took a knee by Adam and scanned the trees.

What've we got, Cam?

Grizzly, has to be. It's huge, John.

Are you sure it's not a Sasquatch?

Really, now you want to be funny?

"What is it?" Sierra asked.

Sage pulled her close to her weak side and held her handgun with her good hand. "Don't know, but it's big if it's got Adam spooked like this."

"It's my fault. I shouldn't have let myself get distracted, then maybe Spitfire wouldn't have gotten distracted…"

"No time for that now, kid. Get up slow and move back to John, okay?"

Sierra started edging toward John. He looked over his shoulder, and was just able to spot Oliver boosting Quinn up to a ledge above a near-vertical pitch.

Almost out of sight, John.

As close to grizzly-proof as they're going to get.

If there is such a thing. You sure grizzlies don't climb?

We'll find out soon enough.

Now he only had to worry about Sierra and Sage. He waved at Sierra, letting her know that he and Sage had her covered.

"We're going to have to make our way back to Quinn and Oli," John said. "Just stay calm and follow my lead, okay?"

Sierra nodded and kept creeping toward him. Sage got up slowly, holding her ribs with her healing arm and the gun with the other, and followed Sierra. John, keeping a close watch on the area, saw Sage freeze as an earthshaking growl came from the trees, making John's stomach churn and his skin prickle as if he'd just walked into a freezer.

John, now might be a good time to run.

The ground shook again as an even louder growl blew out of the forest. The trees and underbrush exploded with movement, sending debris flying toward the three of them. Two giant grizzly bears came barreling out at them, thick saliva hanging like vines from their cavernous, fanged mouths, their muscles rippling under their brownish-red fur like white caps on the open ocean.

Too late.

"Sage!"

"On it!"

Sage emptied her handgun at the closest grizzly, and then let the weapon drop to the ground. She unslung her pulse rifle, movements smooth and trained, her injured arm moving as if totally healed, and fired blasts that would have flattened an entire squad of well-armed men, but the grizzly bears barely skipped a step.

Uh, John. They're not slowing down.

Not helpful, Cam.

You should've have gotten a cannon from Will.

John fired more rounds, and slowed the bears down enough to buy them some time to fall back.

Great idea; remind me before the grizzlies next time.

Sage grabbed Sierra and ran for the rocky peak twenty yards away that held Oliver and Quinn. John got down on one knee, pulse rifle steady and trained on the bears, as if he were waiting for an inevitable demise, but when the grizzlies got close, he threw himself in the air and shot bolts of amplified electricity surging toward the assaulting monsters at such close range he could smell the scorched fur on their backs. They roared with a horrific fury and scrambled after John as he landed behind them and sprinted into the trees. John's shots didn't slow them down as much as he'd hoped.

Damn, they're fast.

Are you even trying to give me something useful, Cam?

They're like evil mutant grizzlies.

He slung his rifle as he ran to a tree and jumped twelve feet in the air, catching a branch and swinging forward onto a boulder as the tree burst into splinters behind him. He felt the outcrop he had landed on tremble under the thunderous assault of his pursuers.

We're dead.

If you keep stopping we are. Move, old man, MOVE.

John leaped for another tree and felt his side split open and his lungs catch fire. He careened through the air, crashing into branches that felt like baseball bats pummeling him, and landed on the ground like a sack of bricks.

Ground feels harder than I remember.

We're dead.

He tried to get up, but daggers sliced through his arm, and then he was flying up into the air again. He kissed the side of the mountain with his face and slithered down to the ground.

Tenderizing me. I hope they choke on my bones.

Why can't they choke before they eat us?

He heard the two grizzlies tussling with each other, a quick squabble over who gets first meat, then felt more daggers in his leg. He readied himself for the last blow.

I'm going to pass out soon.

Bye, John.

Bye, Cam.

John…

I know, Cam. Me too.

They waited, lying on the ground in agony, bleeding onto the forest floor. They waited and waited, slowly dying, expecting the final blow.

It didn't come. John lay there, limp, feeling the warm trickle of blood leaking out of his many open wounds. A roar twice as loud as what he had heard earlier shook the mountain, and he sensed that the grizzlies had stopped toying with him. The ground shook like a trampoline, and trees sounded as if they were being ripped from the earth. John thought he heard a cry of pain come from one of the grizzlies.

He forced his eyelids to open and blinked the blurriness away. He saw two massive, shaggy-haired monsters tossing the grizzlies aside like bags of garbage, and then proceeding to pound on them with their fists and feet. When they were done with the grizzlies, they turned and lumbered toward him. He felt his body shake with every one of their footsteps. A big hairy hand lifted his hollow, blood-drenched body, raising him high into the air. He saw a sliver of blue sky peeking through the forest canopy before he closed his eyes and let everything disappear.

TWENTY-SIX

Ashtree

"Hello, John."

John blinked his eyes clear, trying to focus on where the voice was coming from. He saw a wall of white light and moved his arms, swimming through air to get to it.

"Hello, handsome," the voice said.

He drifted, floated, gliding toward the brilliant light. Closer and closer, until he could make out the naked form of the most beautiful woman he had ever seen in his life.

"Elizabeth?"

"It looks like you found more trouble than you knew what to do with this time, husband of mine."

John reached out to touch her, but his hands went through her body.

"What is this? Am I dead?"

"Not yet, sweetheart. It will take a lot more than a couple of giant grizzlies to bring you down, apparently."

"Where am I? Are you real? Where's Adam?" John started feeling as if the air were getting sucked out of his lungs.

"There is not enough time, John," Elizabeth said. "You need to go back to your unlikely band of heroes, sweetheart."

"I'm not ready." John reached for her, clawing at the void of space with his bare hands, trying to get closer to her, trying to move his immovable body. "I won't leave you again!"

"It is not your choice, darling man of mine. Besides, my John wouldn't desert the people who need him most."

She started floating away from him, disappearing into a blinding light.

"Save the children, John."

"No!"

John tried to escape his worthless body and chase after her, but she was gone, and he was anchored to whatever he was lying on.

"NO!"

John sat straight up, breathing hard, his chest heaving and wet with perspiration. Every movement burned through his muscles, and when he moved it felt as if it took every cell in his body to make it work. He scanned his surroundings and got even more confused.

Maybe I am dead.

No such luck, cupcake.

Cam?

Hi, handsome. Nice dream.

Dream?

Never mind.

His head turned side to side, eyes darting from item to item, trying to gather as much information as he could. He was in a sun-lit room. The walls were made of what looked like enormous horizontal logs, whole trees maybe. Branches grew up from the floor to the high ceiling, nine feet tall at least, John guessed. Leaves were scattered in the winding growth. He could hear birds hopping and fluttering outside from branch to branch, humming and chirping. Crickets sawed their legs together, and toads croaked in dark corners, out of sight.

He pressed down with his fingers into the soft, feathery surface beneath him. It felt as if it were made out of the same clouds that he saw outside the windows. Windows. There were four of them, more or less just clear, sealed breaks between the branches of the tree walls. He worked his way to the side of the bed, threw his feet off the edge, and let them dangle to the floor. He wiggled his toes to make sure they worked, and then—carefully, slowly—got up, stooping a bit, and walked toward the nearest window, but had to stop by a bedside dresser. The room swayed back and forth, making him queasy. He hugged his sides, the searing pain stretching like cracks in broken ice through his chest and stomach. His vision tunneled, and he gripped the dresser with white fingertips to steady himself.

Yep, I'm totally dead.

Don't you think death for us would be a little hotter?

Funny, Cam. Where are we?

Well, I've been working on that, and I couldn't capture the full dramatic presentation, so I'll let Oli fill you in.

I don't think I can take Oliver right now. Just give me the info, Cam.

No way. I want to savor this, things are just getting interesting.

I can't handle more interesting.

He made his way to the window, fighting for air, and gasped. Blue sky and giant, wispy white clouds as far as he could see, the sun shining brilliantly against the blue and white canvas. John felt so close that he reached out as if he would be able to cup the brightness in his hand.

If I'm not dead, Cam, where am I?

I've been trying to scan, but this place is like static to me; I can't pick up anything.

"Welcome to Ashtree, John," Oliver said from the doorway on the far side of the room. He had a small teapot and a mug in hand as he headed over to John.

"Ashtree?" John asked. "Oliver, are we dead?"

The monk set the cup and pot down on the bedside table, and then stood in front of John, examining him. "No, my friend. We are very much alive."

"I don't feel so good."

"You do not look so good either, John." Oliver guided him over to the bed. "Here, have a sit."

"What happened, Oliver? Where are we? Adam!" John's eyes went wide and he tried to get up, but he half fell over on the bed. Oliver helped him to sit back upright.

"Why're you laughing at me?"

"Adam is fine, more than fine, to be exact. I think he believes he has found heaven, but one thing at a time, John. Everyone else is safe and no worse for wear. There will be plenty of time to answer all of your questions later, but for now you must rest. You've quite a bit more healing to do."

"Quinn, Sierra, Sage."

"Safe, safe, and safe. Now rest, John. I have brought you something that should lift your spirits."

"I don't drink tea, Oliver, no matter how hard you try."

"Not tea, John."

Oliver grabbed the pot, poured the steaming black drink into the earthenware cup, and handed it to John, who stuck his nose over the cup, eyes closed tight, nostrils flared. The fresh-roasted aroma melted his senses at once, flooding his body with delight, and he took a sip.

Coffee!

You still might want to kill him after his story.

What do you know, Cam?

You'll see.

John went to take another taste when the door burst open. He just had time to set his coffee down before Adam leapt in and tackled John to the bed. Quinn followed Adam with his own acrobatic smothering.

"Whoa, whoa, whoa," John said. "Let a man get some coffee in him before you get him killed again." He winced as they squeezed and crashed against his tender ribs. "I think those might be broken still."

"They are broken," Oliver said. "Now please, Adam, Quinn, off. We talked about this."

Sierra walked in behind them and squeezed in between the two boys to give John a hug.

"If you weren't such a jerk, you'd probably be dead." She rubbed her face on his white shirt, smearing snot and tears on him. "Thanks for being such a jerk, John."

Wow.

I know, jeez.

"What is this?" Oliver asked. "Has everyone decided to completely ignore me? I strictly forbade you to come in here until John was feeling better!"

He pushed them away from John. "What are you two trying to do, kill him?"

"Yeah, what're you trying to do, kill me?" John asked.

Sierra wiped her eyes with her knuckles and looked over at Quinn. They grinned at each other before tackling John again.

"Oh, Oli, calm down, it's not our fault," Sierra said. "Adam took off running when we were playing and bee-lined straight for here. So we followed."

"Yeah, calm down, Oli," Quinn said as dug his head into John's armpit.

Ow, ow, ow, ow.

Love hurts, doesn't it.

Very helpful observation, Cam.

"Ow." John tried peeling them off him. "You know, being broken really does hurt. Jeez."

"Come on now, get off him. All of you, out," Oliver said. "Out, out, out. Out with you too, Adam." He started prying their hands from each other's grip and separating them from John, who was grinning between grimaces. "Quinn, let go, it was very nice of all of you to think of him, but this is too much too soon, please and thank you!"

John scratched behind Adam's ears, and patted Quinn on the head as he always did when he really didn't know what else to do.

"It's okay, Oli," John said. "No one spilled my coffee, so no one will die yet." He winked at Sierra, who blushed bright red.

Sierra hugged John tight one more time and gave him a kiss on the forehead. This time his face went beet red, and he looked over at Oliver, sending a plea for help.

"Don't look at me," he said. "No one spilled your coffee, so you're right as rain, or so you said." He finished pulling the kids away. "It is your own fault for saving everyone's life. Again."

John limped his way out of bed and patted Sierra and Quinn on the shoulders. They seemed different to him, rested, cheerful, endearing even.

Crap.

See, this whole thing is your own damn fault.

Don't think I've forgotten your part in this, Cam.

Crap.

"Saved everyone's lives again, go figure," John said. "Okay, Oliver's right, everyone out. I need to talk to our dear monk alone."

He gave Adam one last good pat-down and then let Oliver send them all out of the room.

"I knew it would be a bit much," Oliver said. "I tried, I told them that you would need more time, more rest."

John's smile disappeared, replaced with the stern glare of determination. "Oliver. Answers."

Oliver gestured to the bed again and John grabbed his coffee and sat.

"As I said, you're at Ashtree, or basically, the tree that connects all things, quite literally. Do you remember any of my stories, John?"

"I try not to."

"But you do remember some of them, maybe some of the details?"

"Yes."

"Ashtree is a wormhole, John. A fold in time and space that connects us to the network of the universe."

"I'm getting a headache."

"Stay with me just a bit longer, John. It will be clear soon."

"A wormhole? On Earth? How could that possibly work? The ISA would have found it. And even if they hadn't, all the ones they did find were too unpredictable to use. Hell, even the military stopped trying to send people through the one by Pluto because of all the losses."

"Unstable when not anchored, yes. After my encounter with the man from my story on the pass, I researched every tale, every myth, tracked every fantastical journey, and then went searching in the mountains for any evidence that would corroborate his tale. I journeyed a little too deep in the woods, and ended up here. I've been studying the wormhole ever since.

"It seems that when a fold in space is anchored to a world, even if it is in a different space and time, it can remain stable. Opening and closing just like any ordinary door, until that door gets locked from one side."

"What happens then?"

"Whoever is on the other side is stranded."

"That stranded Sasquatch tale you told me years ago."

"Exactly."

"Holy hell, Oli. How? I mean, I've seen a lot of weird shit, been in the middle of some crazy places that no one would ever believe existed if I tried to tell them, but this—this is crazy."

"Crazy, yes. But very real, my friend."

"Friend, that's a funny word coming from you. Do you even know what that word means?"

"I do, and I feel proud to call you one."

"Yeah, not sure how I feel about that yet. I knew you had secrets, man, but this is over the top. How did you come up with the cover stories? Why'd you choose Ashtree, and all the myth?"

"Adaptations to old stories, and a sprinkle of more modern stories our hosts here put together, ones that have grown in myth and legend over the years. All designed to keep people away. Fantastical, brilliant *creatures* really."

"*Creatures*? Wormhole? Have you drugged me again already?"

"Ah, you might want to take another drink of your coffee."

John swirled his drink and sniffed at the lip of the mug, scowling over the top of it at Oliver.

Cam?

Surprisingly, it's plain coffee, no tranquilizer, no drugs at all.

I might need some.

"Are you going to look at me like that every time I offer you something to drink?"

"Yes."

"You are a child sometimes. I am sure Cam has told you it's perfectly safe."

"She has."

"Then why are you still looking at me with such distaste?"

"I just wanted to see you squirm a bit longer."

Oh, you're good.

Thanks, Cam.

John winked at him and then took a long swig of his coffee, holding it in his mouth and savoring it. Oliver sighed deeply and waited until John waved to him to continue.

"All right, then, are you sure you're ready to hear this? You've had enough tease from your coffee?"

"Sure, Oli. Try me."

"When the Norsemen came here in search of Yggdrasil, the Natives brought them here, to Ashtree, to meet the guardians of the gate."

John groaned. "Guardians of the gate? I can't take much more, Oli."

"Please. Let me finish."

John nodded his head, and went back to sipping his coffee.

"The Norsemen thought that they had found the giant green Ashtree from their legends and named the inhabitants Skellring, but the local people had already given them a different name."

Oliver continued, but John completely ignored him, distracted by the towering fantastical *creature* that had just walked into the room. John sat blinking, ears buzzing, trying to make sense of the curious-looking fur-covered giant that was staring back at him. It was about six and a half feet tall with golden fur covering most of its face, very much resembling a heavily bearded, square-jawed human. Its fur puffed out from under its black velvet vest and the bottom of its dark brown pants, and over its shoeless feet. His eyes—the creature seemed to be male—were blue and very human, which was unnerving. It was even more unnerving when Oliver's new furry friend smiled at John and started talking.

"You fight with a true warrior spirit, friend of Oliver. You almost died, coming to the aid of your friends. If not for your unique construction and the first aid skills of your lady friend, you would not have made it to us. It is an honor to meet you."

Oliver looked between the two, smiling from ear to ear and looking very satisfied with himself.

"As I was about to say, John, welcome to the home of the Sasquatch, watchers and guardians of the gate at Ashtree." He went over and shook the Sasquatch's hand. "And, more specifically, the home of my good friend Balder, war chieftain of this branch."

"You're a Sasquatch?" John asked.

Told you, unbelievable, right?

A bit of an understatement.

The Sasquatch walked over to John and put his hand out to him. "Just Balder."

John grasped the hand and watched in awe as his own was engulfed. Balder's palm felt like sand paper pillows stretched tight under his fur-covered fingers, of which he had five. The Sasquatch's arms were muscular and his forearms and biceps attempted to bulge out of his tight fitting shirt.

"Thank you, Balder," was all John could manage before he passed out hard onto the bed.

*   *   *

Oliver looked up at Balder, a forced smile stretching across his face like a showman whose show had abruptly folded.

"He's had better moments."

"You will need those better moments on your journey to Galbraith."

"He will be fine. His biotech is impressive, to say the least. That, along with the upgrades and treatments from your surgeon, and he'll be better than ever." Oliver sighed, and put a hand on Balder's arm as he turned to walk back to the door. "And I'm afraid he has to be. I'm certain we will need his services again before the end of all this."

Balder walked with him, opening the door when they got to it and allowing the monk to go out first.

"You think more trouble comes to find you?"

"I'm sure of it, Balder. Which makes our travel to Galbraith all the more urgent."

"Njord will help however he can, as long as help will not expose our existence here."

"Transport is all we need, Balder. The faster we can get to the monastery the better. We will be safe once we get behind her walls; Benedict has promised as much."

"I hope you speak rightly, old friend, for all of our sakes."

"Me too, Balder, me too."

TWENTY-SEVEN

Smash and Boom

"SO, SASQUATCH, HUH, OLIVER?" John asked.

You need to stop passing out like a sissy, John. It's starting to give us a bad rep.

"Afraid so."

I'm getting too old for this shit.

Oh, brother.

"How long have you known?"

"They'd been watching me since my first time across the pass. After my encounter with the gentleman from my story, I came up searching for the rest of his party. That's when they found me. I thought I was hallucinating when they came in those ten-foot-tall Sasquatch walkers of theirs."

"What about the guy you brought back from Galbraith that died?"

Hope you're seeing the pattern here.

Don't trust Oliver.

Bingo.

"Yes, but he's not dead. In fact he has been a great friend to me. I just added that to the story for effect, you see. His group was attacked and he did escape, though the Sasquatches wouldn't have hurt any of them. Just wanted to give a little scare to keep them away from the gate."

"Sasquatches."

Yeah, Sasquatches, John. Honest-to-God Sasquatches.

"Yes. Quite brilliant too; well, most of them anyway."

"And the mandolin music?"

"Ah, I thought you might come to that. It is my way of saying, 'Hello, I'm passing through.' They sure do love string music and a good hymn."

"Oli. I'm really, really tired of getting my ass kicked."

Oliver smiled and clapped him on his shoulder. "That's the spirit!"

Wincing, John glared at him and lay back down on the bed.

"Now, you get your rest. I have some things to tend to, and information to gather."

John was almost unconscious before Oliver finished his sentence.

*   *   *

"John! John, time to wake up, buttercup."

John blinked his eyes open and lifted his head up off the pillow. He saw Sage's head blocking the light, her hair pulled into a clean braid hanging over her shoulder and her ageless caramel skin stretching into a smirk on her face. She looked fresh and well fed, no more sunken lines or bags under eyes. She wore a tight black shirt and loose cargo pants. He turned away from her and scanned his room, remembering where he was, and then let his head drop back onto the pillow.

"Sasquatches?"

"Sasquatches," Sage said, "Vikings, and a giant tree that's a wormhole."

"That's a good touch."

"I know. Half of them are named some sort of Norse or Native American name. Damn Vikings and Indians made a lasting impression."

"Who knew?"

"It's crazy, but for once, Oliver was telling us the truth. And he's right about them being brilliant, John. Their tech is amazing."

"Tech?"

"Yeah, crazy, huh? Damn good fighters in those giant Sasquatch suits, too. I think you better get up and take a walk with me, John."

John threw his feet over the side of the bed and wiggled his toes on the floor.

"How long have I been out?"

"Three days."

John rolled his head from left to right, stretching out his neck.

"What happened?"

"You took off like an idiot and almost got yourself killed again." Sage raised her left eyebrow and gave him a skeptical look. "This time your luck almost ran out, tough guy."

"At least I tried. Doesn't anyone know how to say thank you around here?"

"No." Sage tossed him a pile of folded clothes.

John slipped on some pants, a white T-shirt, and a pair of canvas kicks, and then checked out his bundle of repaired gear from Will's, his chest-rig, and his REP rifle. All was in good order; he left it where it was and gestured for Sage to lead the way out of the room.

"Age before beauty," she said.

"Funny. Where're we heading?"

"To meet the Chief."

Looking down over the rail, John judged that the base and height of the tree was just the right size to fit hidden, nestled between the volcanic mountains that encompassed it. Each branch he could see was as big as ten full-sized trees and supplied the town of Sasquatches with areas for living, eating, building, and trading.

John and Sage strolled down the walkway, which was made out of sort of wood composite material. It was big enough for three humans to walk side by side, or one, maybe two Sasquatches. It wound like ivy, snaking to the few routes that led to the different areas on this side of the tree.

Variously furred Sasquatches—black, gold, red, brown, white, spotted, tiger-striped, gray, orange, and green—lumbered around the small town on Ashtree; there were even some shorter ones that looked like children. He peered closer: some had long shaggy fur, some had short fur that had a fine sheen in the light. Most were dressed in overalls or pants and T-shirts; in fact, the attire was so non-descript that there was no way to tell gender from their dress at all. Making a best guess, the females seemed to be taller on average than the males, and their faces were completely devoid of hair, while the males were shorter by a few inches, and stout, with facial hair that fell into beards of various shapes and sizes.

"Where are all those giant Sasquatch walkers?"

Sage smiled and gave him a wink. "Not scared you're going to get tossed around by grizzlies again, are you?"

"Ouch, too soon, Sage, too soon."

"There aren't very many of them, and they're not allowed over here. This is the residential side of Ashtree, They're limited to the other side; we haven't been there yet."

"There's another side? How do they hide all this?"

"They have some cloaking mechanism built into the generator that keeps the whole valley concealed. Like I said, their tech is pretty impressive."

I guess the branches are like the homes, huh?

I wonder if they send their kids door to door to sell cookies for the soccer team?

We should send Sierra and Quinn out.

They'd have too much fun.

Oh yeah, can't let anything like that happen.

Have you been able to pick up anything on your scans?

Nothing. Sage is right, their tech is outstanding. I haven't been able to hack in yet.

Giant gears and wheels, well-greased and tuned to perfection, turned and pulled small platforms made out of the same wood composite material as the walkways, moving without so much as a sound.

Sage pointed to the heart of Ashtree, which was responsible for the ever-changing landscape. "The whole thing is full of mechanisms like that."

"How do they power it?"

"My read on it? It's a non-Earth technology. Every moving part creates kinetic energy that they capture and reuse, which means the efficiency has to be phenomenal. That's supplemented by a source they won't talk about. Something to do with the wormhole is my bet. The power system has been around since before Ashtree was a twig. Some of the living area was here already too, for travelers coming through the gate, but most of what you see is what this group built after they got stranded here." She smiled, a mischievous look shining through her eyes. "And that's all just the boring part."

John, this place is pouring out energy. I have no idea of anyplace outside of the US capital in Colorado that puts out energy like this place.

Where's the source?

All over; it's all over, John.

They stepped onto a perpendicular stub and Sage pressed a button. Their chunk of the walkway swung away and sped toward the middle of the giant tree. They were lifted to a platform, and were caught by a magnetic clasp that held their chunk tight, slowing them as they connected again to the closest walkway.

"I take it the Sasquatches aren't the dim-witted animals they have been made out to be?"

"Not even close," Sage said.

She looked around for a minute and spotted one of the only other humans inhabiting the tree at this time, and started toward him. Oliver waved to them and waded through the narrow stream of Sasquatches. He held his hands out and greeted them both with vigorous handshakes and a jovial smile.

"They are actually a very advanced society," Sage continued. "Oli here thinks they've been coming around since before humans even existed, until a group got stuck got stuck here in the mid 1800's. They've been trying to get back home ever since."

I have a feeling we have no idea who Oliver really is.

No, we don't, and I'm not sure I ever want to know.

"They really started to expand by leaps and bounds when we stopped bugging them so much," Oliver said. "Since they didn't have to try to keep us away as much, they built better walkers and machines to protect and study Ashtree."

"This place is awesome," John said. He felt as if he were a boy again, and wanted to explore the new world that he found himself in, but he wasn't a boy and he had business to finish. "I can't believe it's been here this whole time."

"They've been fortunate on more than one occasion. I'm sure Sage has told you about their cloaking mechanism. It predates even this group, been here to shield Ashtree from discovery. Since the gate's been closed it's been running on borrowed time. They believe they have a fix, but if that doesn't work, this whole valley will be naked for discovery. However, I believe they are running out of resources."

"Running out of resources? You didn't tell me that earlier, Oli."

"It's a touchy subject for our hosts, Sage."

"How can they be running out of resources? This place looks stacked with resources."

"True, John. But their technology requires energy and goods specific to their home world, expendables that they have not been able to reproduce here. There is a time limit on everything, and theirs is coming up."

"I'm not getting involved any more than what I already am, Oliver."

Sage cleared her throat. "I think he's just trying to fill you in on as much as he can, John."

Oliver nodded at her. "Sorry, John. Maybe a bit much for now. Bits and pieces, smaller crumbs maybe. Now, if we continue, I believe there is a dog and a couple of kids waiting to see you."

"And where exactly is that?" John asked.

"With the Sasquatch leader, Chief Njord. A valiant warrior, the oldest living Sasquatch, and wise beyond anyone else here. He will hear us, but there's no guarantee that he will help us more than they already have."

Jealous, John?

Of a giant, furry Sasquatch chief? No. Relieved is more like it.
I can tell.

"Why are they with him?"

"He was having so much fun watching them and Adam play that he may well try to keep them."

Sage chipped his side with her arm. "There's your out, John. If you still want it."

"I could only be so lucky, but he can't keep Adam."

When they came into the main chamber, two of the Sasquatch walkers stood guard by a set of large wooden doors. John traced the patterns carved into the doors with his eyes. Large ships manned with Vikings sailed over wooden waves. A group of Viking explorers traded with a group of Natives. There was a carved scene of some type of war, Sasquatch walkers towering over a band of fleeing warriors. In the middle was a carving of Ashtree itself, branches reaching to what looked like other planets resembling Earth.

The two walkers opened the doors and let them enter the main chamber, the heart of Ashtree. John heard a crash and heavy, thumping footsteps. He turned and saw a Sasquatch in a walker suit playing keep-away from Adam and the kids. He heard a roar of laughter and looked a little farther down the large hall. A silver-furred Sasquatch watched from an enormous wooden throne, his long white beard flowing over a red robe, and his belly rolling with laughter.

While they made their way toward the throne, John searched for intricacies on the walkers. The frames were ten feet tall, as Oliver had said, but anything of value was well hidden under swaths of fur.

Cam, can you scan the walkers? See what's under the fancy coat?
That I can do. Putting it up on your HUD right now.

He watched the schematics rotate in his peripheral vision. Some sort of carbon-metal framework made up the skeleton of the walker. Tiny, whirring gears were designed into every joint. The torso was an armored plate with side compartments. The back framework had more whirring gears under broader armor plating. The precision with which the Sasquatch operated the suit was impressive, to say the least.

The Sasquatch chief saw them and waved to Oliver with arms twice as thick as Balder's.

"Oliver, glad you are here."

"Chief Njord," Oliver said, waving John forward, "this is my friend that I spoke to you about."

Njord gestured for John to come closer. "Friend of Oliver? Then you may very well be friend of mine as well." He gave John a gentle hug.

He's a hugger?

Could be worse, Cam.

Yeah, he could be naked.

Not sure I'd be able to tell.

Njord smiled as he sat down in his large wooden chair and gestured to the sentry playing with the kids. Saluting, the sentry dropped the ball they were playing with and resumed his post by the large main door, while the twins continued to play with Adam.

Do you know how to address a Sasquatch chief, Cam?

Let me check: uh, no.

"We see few humans on our trails. Even fewer friendly humans." Njord shook his head and watched Sierra and Quinn, a look on his face as if he were watching his great-grandchildren play. "I trust Oliver. So I trust that you are friendly humans."

He's kind of like a sweet old grandpa, John.

He might come off like a sweet old grandpa, but he's shrewd. Look how easily he separated us, and then made us wait before coming here, to give him time evaluate our intentions. No, Cam, this one is deliberate and smart.

I like him.

Of course you do.

Njord turned back to Oliver. "I checked, Oliver, as you asked, and no persons from Galbraith have been seen in many weeks."

Oliver rubbed his thick red beard, his forehead wrinkled in thought for a moment. John cleared his throat, and Oliver shifted his gaze between the members of the small group.

"Mm, as I said before, most likely deep in study and training at the monastery, I would suppose. Not much reason to come over the pass, I guess. The walls always need to be protected against those who would rather loot and murder than live at peace; it wouldn't take long for the order to run short on numbers."

This sounds like more Oliver BS to me, John.

Is there anything that he says that isn't BS?

Good point.

"I'm not sure you are convincing even yourself with your explanation, Oliver," Njord said smoothly. "Either way, we can talk more of it at council. I was happy to hear word of your mandolin song on our road; it was by good luck my scouts got to you in time."

He must mean you, John.

I'm so happy that it looks like I'm the only one who needed saving.

Uh, we did need saving. Or did you already forget death asking us if we wanted a one- or two-bed suite?

I hate it when you're right.

"I still feel that timing," John said. "Thanks."

"You are welcome."

A small silence followed and John looked at Oliver, who shrugged his shoulders as if he didn't know what to do next. John let out a sigh and got a bit closer to Njord.

"I'm sure Oliver has filled you on his little mission and the heat it's brought."

"He has informed me of your mission, yes."

"Not my mission. I plan on leaving from here and heading back home."

Oh boy, here we go.

Cam, I'm sick of almost dying. I thought you'd be with me on this.

"I hear you have no home left, and in fact, you are needed to help Oliver and these children, on which so much depends."

John turned and looked at his small band of misfits and then turned back to the conversation.

John, don't get us kicked out of the most fantastical place on earth, please.

"Look, Chief Njord, I don't know what Oliver told you, but this isn't my mess, and I'm not worried about a few militia punks. After the way I whipped their asses, they won't be bothering me anymore."

He looked sternly at Oliver, and then back to Njord. "I plan on leaving tomorrow. What you guys want to do after that is your business."

Njord laughed a hearty laugh and slapped John on the back much harder than John had expected, making him cough and grab his ribs.

Damn, he's classy, John.

I'm glad you think him making my whole body ache is classy.

And he called Oli on his bullshit.

Oh yes, he's super.

"You told me right about this one, Oliver. Worry not, friend John, do as you must, but I am feeling you might change your mind by morning. I have seen to the provisions you asked for, Oliver." He pulled a long, thick rope, and a brass bell clanged. The two sentries came back in the room.

"Smash and Boom will show you to the staging area. As for accompanying you, we cannot risk much. Transportation, with a small detail, but I can do no more, friend Oliver."

"Chief Njord, that is more than I could have ever hoped for."

"That's settled then. Now, I must meet with our other chieftains. After a short rest, you will join us; just a small gathering for introductions." He grimaced a little and let out a long sigh. "If I manage to keep politics out."

Oliver bowed his head slightly. "Of course we will be there."

"Good, Balder will see it done."

With that he was off, and the crew was dismissed from the hall.

John turned to Oliver, frowning. "I feel like I just missed something very important, Oliver."

Bingo.

"No worries. I will bring you up to speed before we head out tonight."

Fat chance.

"I'm heading home tomorrow, Oliver. Nothing's stopping that. And you if you think for one second I trust one goddamn word that comes out of your mouth, you're wrong."

Njord seems to think you'll change your mind.

"Yes, of course, I am sure of that, John. I wouldn't want you to go out of your way anymore than you have; it's only the entire Free that's in jeopardy. Sage, children, time to go."

I'm going to kill him one of these times, Cam, I'm going to choke him to death.

So you keep saying

I mean it, Cam, and there is no way I'm changing my mind. First thing tomorrow, we're gone.

I keep forgetting, you're an oak.

Adam came running up to John, barking and pushing off him until John gave him some recognition.

"I missed you so much, boy! Were you working hard playing keep-away from the Sasquatches, huh?" He buried his face in Adam's neck, pulling Adam's thick fur with one hand while the other arm braced his sore ribs. "Yes, you're a good boy, Adam, such a good boy. I missed you too."

He stood up and looked over at the Sasquatches in the two walkers chuckling amongst themselves as they waited for them.

"What? They don't have dogs around here?"

Oliver smiled and put his hand on John's shoulder. "They just wonder what such a smart dog is doing with you."

Sage and the kids roared with laughter and started following the giants across the main hall and into a large, open causeway on the other side from where they had entered. Adam got up and ran after them, walking right between the twins.

Oliver smiled and patted John on the back. "Can't win them all, now can we, John."

"Exactly why I'm leaving."

Adam might just have to stay here, I guess.

Nice try, Cam.

I just don't want to break his little heart, that's all.

I'm sure.

This side of Ashtree was scaled much bigger than the smaller residential side. The causeways were larger to accommodate the

Sasquatch walkers and heavier traffic. In the middle of the platform they'd just walked onto, two tracks carrying small wooden cars full of Sasquatches from other parts of Ashtree were speeding in opposite directions. In the middle of the huge space was a giant tram power machine slightly different than the large cog and crank that supported the rest of Ashtree. Oliver explained that it ran off the same kind of kinetic energy that the rest of the tree did, with a backup wind-and-crank machine to maintain the movement of the mass transportation system if the power ever went down, which had never happened.

This place is fantastic, even better than Disneyland.

You never went to Disneyland, Cam.

You did, so it's like I did.

"This is awesome!" Quinn said.

Adam barked and paced between the two Sasquatch suits, trying to follow all the moving parts.

"You guys haven't seen this yet?" John said.

"No, John. Our movements were somewhat limited until you met with Njord and he felt that all of us were okay," Sage said. "It's been loads of fun."

"Balder took good care of you," Oliver said. "He is the chieftain of that war branch, and quite the hero among the Sasquatches. It is an honor to be there."

"You really love these guys, don't you, Oli?"

What's not to love?

I like their suits.

Oliver smiled big and chuckled. "I believe they have grown on me, much like all of you have."

"Well, this conversation's getting awkward," Sierra said.

"Rad, it's totally rad," Quinn said. "Hey, Oli, what's Smash's real name?"

"Thorsgard. He's been tasked with seeing to our provisions and travel."

"Thorsgard." Quinn nodded his head. "Cool."

Sierra rolled her eyes at him. "You are such a dork."

Quinn, Sierra, and Adam followed the two giant walkers, with Oliver, Sage, and John not far behind, as they made their way across a bridge and onto another causeway that was a bit smaller. The walkers, Smash and Boom, waved to a couple of other Sasquatch suits that were rambling by. They went over two more bridges and took one of the bigger wooden swinging pads until they came to a large hangar.

"What is this place?" Quinn asked.

"Our hangar," Thorsgard said.

Sierra looked at Thorsgard as if he hadn't quite heard him right. "Hangar?"

"For our rotor ships."

The large door opened and John couldn't believe what he saw. The bay was lined with a small blimp, a row of six rotor ships that looked to be made of some sort of hardened wood, and group of four smaller, winged gliders. In the far corner was a squad of four mid-sized vessels with oval fuselages, four rotors on short wings that jutted out from the sides, with small REP rifle gunner's stations port and starboard. The small band gathered at the entrance, taking in all the things they'd thought were impossible before they had come here.

John, look at that helo ship in the corner.

Bet Sage could fly one of those.

Like she'd know how to fly a Sasquatch helo ship. Stuff's not even from our dimension.

Good point. Any luck with the hack?

I'm completely blocked out here; it's like we're in a black hole for our tech.

John craned his head up to look at Thorsgard. "Why do you need these?"

"How else could we make so many Sasquatch sightings around the West Coast?"

"You guys fly those suits all over?"

"No, we have small outposts, places to gather supplies, study technology, keep humans guessing. We travel on six-month tours."

"What about those ones with the pulse rifles on them?" John asked.

"Those are our *just-in-case* suits and ships."

"Just in case?" Oliver asked.

"Just in case humans find the Ash, and try too hard to be humans." His voice was serious and flat, and even though it was hard to see behind Thorsgard's beard, John could tell his expression matched his voice. "You know better than most what I speak of."

Okay, that makes pretty good sense.

They definitely won't be giving us one of those.

John and Oliver were about to ask more questions, but the two giants started walking down the middle of the cramped hangar. Quinn and Sierra went running after them with Adam right beside them.

"We love this place!" Quinn said.

The three adults walked slowly after them, watching the three best friends run between the enormous suits, bouncing and squeaking as if they were in the world's biggest toy shop.

"I'm not sure we're going to be able to get them to leave," Sage said. "Why can't they stay here, Oliver?"

"I asked Njord that already, if they could stay at least until we could get to the monastery and get help so that we could travel safely, but he said that, among other things, the risk of Ashtree being discovered while they're here is too great. I am surprised he is helping us as much as he is, considering what humans have done to the Sasquatch in the past."

Why do we always have to leave?

Not much longer, Cam. I promise.

"Awesome!" Quinn's voice echoed from the other end of the hangar. They went to see what was going on.

"This one is totally ours," Sierra said.

Sage walked up to her and pinched her arm.

"Ow, what was that for?"

"This is the best spirits I've seen you in since we met," Sage said. "I just wanted to make sure you were real."

"You just wanted to pinch me."

"That too."

Quinn turned in circles, eyes wide like a kid in a store full of free toys. "Aren't you guys excited to fly in one of these babies?"

Oliver and John walked around to the other side of the ship and saw the two sentry suits already loading boxes into the small open cargo hold. The oblong hull was made of sheets of some wooden composite material that looked almost like leather scales, sealed together with gold joints. It had two broad, short wings with large rotors in the middle of each. A cockpit on the top of the bow had multiple windows, allowing the pilots to have full view of everything. More windows ran along the port and starboard sides above two door-mounted, double-barreled REP cannons.

"Now that is a thing of beauty," John looked over his shoulder to Sage. "Feel nostalgic?"

"My ship was better."

"Yeah, in your dreams."

Sage smirked at him. "Saved you enough times, didn't it?"

"Depends on who you talk to."

"Whatever, hotshot."

Maybe this is what Njord was talking about.

What do you mean?

He knew you wouldn't give up a chance to fly in one of these babies.

Damn.

"How do you build so much? You guys have got to be the most technological group this side of the Rockies."

"This old one Chief Njord brought with him through Ash gate, before it locked down. We update it as well as we can to keep it air worthy. Most of the rest were built as materials came ready," Thorsgard said. "We manufacture a newer composite in the old cave sublevel. Supplies not available to us here are procured off the market."

"Off the market?" Sage asked.

Thorsgard looked at Oliver and smiled.

"I might have arranged a few things here and there for them, through contacts and back channels," Oliver said.

How is this here, and no one knows about it, John?

If we stay too long, there's going to be a whole list of bad guys who know about it.

Quinn popped his head out from the loading ramp, followed by Adam's, who barked loudly to get the attention of the crew below.

"There's more under the ground?" Quinn asked.

"There's more everywhere." Thorsgard said.

"We don't need more right now, Thorsgard. Why don't you tell us what we have on board." John said.

"Princess Sophia is fully stocked."

John looked up at the Sasquatch, a contorted look of confusion on his face. *"Princess Sophia?"*

Thorsgard let his head hang as he explained. "Chief Njord let his granddaughter name this one."

The small group broke out into muffled chuckles while Thorsgard showed them around to the ramp.

Nice.

Princess Sophia. Has a ring to it.

Thorsgard looked down at them as he continued. "The cargo hold is loaded with rations, hydro cells, supplies for weeks, more than enough to get to Galbraith."

"Nice," John said. "Oliver, does Benedict know we're coming?"

"I thought you weren't coming," Sage said.

Damn.

They got you pegged, John.

"And miss out on flying in the *Princess Sophia*? No way."

Sap.

Tell me about it.

Oliver smiled and then continued.

"I sent word to Benedict two days ago. He will know we are coming. If there were any trouble we would have heard by now."

John took a deep breath in, ran his hand along the ship, and then turned to face his fire-tempered companions. "After dinner we'll sleep down here on the ship, and then we'll leave first thing in the morning." He turned and walked up to the end of the ramp to talk to Quinn, Adam, and Sierra, who were racing around the passageway of the ship, playing tag.

"Hey, twiddle-dumb and twiddle-dee." He looked reproachfully at Adam. "And you. Want to come down here so we can go get you ready for tonight?"

John caught Sage mocking him out of the corner of his eye, making Sierra and Quinn giggle. John looked back up at them and tried to make his look as stern as he could, but all that formed on his face was a sour smile.

"What was that?" Quinn asked.

"Yeah, are you constipated, John?"

Adam jumped over, pushed his front paws up onto John's chest, and started licking his grimacing face. "Ow, Adam. Gotta go easy, pal."

Ow? That still hurts? Our bio looks good. I'll run a diagnostic.

No, I'm getting over the hump. Adam's paws don't feel like baseball bats to the chest anymore.

Thank god for nanotech.

And Sasquatch pain shots.

"And no, I'm not constipated. Just get down here, will you? We've got things to do." He scratched behind Adam's ears and then nudged him back to the deck.

I think Thorsgard's laughing at you.

John looked up and caught the Sasquatch chuckling as he said something to the other Sasquatch.

"Hey, Thorsgard, any time you're ready, we'd like to head back."

The sentries' laughter stopped and Thorsgard grunted directions at Boom. They led them to the doors and to one of the small wooden carts that would take them back to their branch. It was a short, quiet ride, except for Adam, who was racing around the inside of the trolley-sized transport, jumping up to look out the windows and barking at every new thing he saw.

Balder was at the platform waiting for them, wearing a stiff, silk jacket similar to a karate gi. He escorted them to the quarters they had been provided before, and stopped outside their door.

Balder turned to Oliver. "The branch Chieftains are gathered, Oliver. You can find your way on your own, yes?"

"No worries, Balder, we'll be fine."

"Good, what you requested waits in your lodging. I will see you at the council chambers, if I survive the branch politics." Balder waved his furry hand at them and then left the room.

Oliver waved and then turned to his friends. "Lots of political undercurrent between the different chieftains right now. Balder isn't very fond of it."

"Any chance of getting out of this meet-and-greet, Oliver?" John asked. "We need to be getting prepped to leave."

"It's too late, I'm afraid. Balder has already made arrangements for us."

Oliver smiled and opened the door. Four Sasquatches dressed in red, green, gold, and purple overalls stood in front of six different racks of clothes. An older gray-furred Sasquatch held out her hand; a long measuring tape uncurled from her palm.

"You've got to be kidding me."

"It's no joke, John," Oliver nudged him forward. "They are here to whip up an outfit for us for tonight and get measurements to throw together some fresh clothes for our journey tomorrow."

"I am Skadi, and these are my sons," the gray Sasquatch said, and then bowed low. "Tailors to chief Balder and this branch. We are pleased to serve you." She snapped her fingers and her sons moved forward and started pulling and pushing John and his companions into awkward positions, using the measuring tape to measure inseams, outseams, chests and waists. While they measured, the younger Sasquatches spouted numbers to Skadi, who scratched them into a notepad.

The three Sasquatches scrambled through shirts, pants, dresses, ties, vests, coats and hats, holding them up in front of John and company while Skadi watched and nodded her approval or disapproval.

After some time they were each outfitted for the evening. John looked at himself in the mirror. Much to Skadi's disgust, he had only allowed them to dress him in a black T-shirt, grey linen pants, and his own boots. Sage, on the other hand, was drop-dead gorgeous in a cream floral lace gown with a silk slip dress underneath, her hair pulled to the side in a large braid.

Oliver made a few last minute adjustments and added a red bow tie to his black velvet vest and matching pants, grey long-sleeved button up and his own slightly repaired leather sandals.

Have you ever seen him out of his robe?

First time.

He almost looks normal.

Weird.

Sierra was dressed in a gray skirt, white, short sleeved button-up, and black buckle shoes. Quinn was poured into a pair of black cotton pants with a bright red shirt.

"I feel like we have made art out of you finally." Skadi laughed and clapped her hands; her three boys gathered up their things and headed out the door. "We will have the clothes that you requested waiting for you on your vessel."

At that she waved and whisked her company away, while Oliver finished getting everyone ready to go to the great hall.

John went over to his pack and riffled through it until he found the singed, torn, brown wax-paper bundle from Mrs. Trowley that Sierra had saved for him, one of the only things he'd managed to salvage through this whole shit storm. He took a small pocket knife out, sliced through the twine holding the bundle together, and pulled out the gun-metal grey, long-sleeved shirt, smiling as he slipped it on over his T-shirt.

"Is that all you're going to change?" Oliver asked.

"Something wrong with that?"

Oliver smiled and shook his head. "No, John, nothing at all."

"Good, I'll meet you outside." He whistled and Adam left the serious work of clothing Quinn to follow John out the door.

John leaned against the railing of the small walkway outside their room, watching the slowing activity of Ashtree. The day's light faded with every minute, and soon Sasquatch-made lights were popping up here and there, like someone was turning on the stars in the night sky one by one.

We so have to come back here.

You think they'll let us?

Maybe if we come with Oliver.

I'm not sure it's worth it then.

Funny, John, real funny. You do know that we have a few more days with him, right?

I thought that's what you wanted.

You made the right choice.

I hope so, Cam. I really do.

TWENTY-EIGHT

Mixed Reception

AN ECHO REVERBERATED THROUGH the council chambers as a beefy Sasquatch fist pounded on the table again. "They cannot stay. We do not know the source of the new energy at the main Ash, or why Oliver has brought these humans here, or even where the children come from. Whoever, or whatever, is after them could search the forest until they discover our presence," a silver, male Sasquatch in a red gi said. "How can you even be thinking of holding them here?"

A taller, obsidian Sasquatch female wearing a purple gi took a deep breath and stared down her nose at the speaker. "With the events that have transpired at the main Ash, I cannot believe that we would be thinking of allowing them to leave. Not to mention the fact that we have no idea if they will keep our secrets. There is no alternative, Dane." Irritation and arrogance lingered in the air after she spoke.

This isn't exactly what I had in mind when Oliver told us about his meet-and-greet.

Fucking Oliver.

John scanned the council chamber; the walls of the tree were lined with shelves filled with volumes and volumes of books. In the middle of the room sat a group of thirteen Sasquatches around a U-shaped table. John could tell that just over half were female; all wore gis, like Balder, but each gi was unique in color and pattern.

Centered in the middle of the U, a large glowing orb hovered above a holo box. The orb shifted and morphed, changing from an image of John's face, to Sage's, the twins, Oliver's, and even Adam. John's eyes narrowed, and his jaw tensed as he listened to the arguing Sasquatch chieftains. Oliver caught his eye; he appeared to be trying just as hard not to break any of the teeth in his mouth.

I'm not sure if I'm relieved, or nervous, that Oliver looks just as surprised and pissed as we are.

If I wasn't thinking of roasting this nasty female Sasquatch, I might actually be smiling at that.

Balder stood between the two Sasquatches, shaking his head. "Dane, Tyra. These are not just any humans, they are honored guests, and Oliver has been a loyal friend for years."

Tyra glared at him. "We know this human, Balder. We know all your humans. What my branch cannot understand is council's ineptitude in allowing them in without proper security measures, and now, in allowing them to leave, flying them to the bottom of the mountain even, at the risk of our very survival." At this last statement she glared directly at Chief Njord, whose affect had been flat during the entire discussion.

Oliver leaned into John and whispered into his ear. "Tyra is Njord's oldest daughter. She's been gunning for his seat for the last couple years, thinks he's senile."

Remind me to decline an invitation to dinner at Njord's house, Cam.

If Tyra has it her way, we'll be gutted before we make it to dinner.

"I remind you, Tyra," Balder said, his voice saturated with frustration. "This meeting is not to discuss their presence, only for introductions and to discuss the existence of an anomaly since their arrival."

Her steely gaze met Balder's. "We will discuss what this council needs to discuss. Or is this ruling party so totalitarian they would allow no discussion? Risk the same fate that sealed the gate and got us stuck here in the first place? We have the right to challenge this chief's decision to aid their mission. To challenge any decision."

"You speak out of ignorance and you offend the guests of Chief Njord! This matter has been discussed and decided in the Security Council—as a non-member, your approval is not required. Or did you forget how our government works?"

Tyra looked like she might jump the distance between her and Balder and strangle him, but instead she reluctantly sat down, steaming.

How did we let Oliver wrangle us into coming to this meeting, John?

He's sneaky.

More like snaky.

That's probably more accurate, but I have a feeling Oliver is just as surprised as we are this time.

John turned to glare at Oliver, and caught Sage kicking the monk's shin under the table, making Oliver grimace. Sierra and Quinn were the quietest he'd ever seen them, slumped in their chairs, yawning, almost as if they were bored with the current events. He looked down at their feet and spotted Adam comfortable as ever and licking himself.

I tell you, John. I think Adam's getting dumber.

So you two are probably pretty even now.

Ouch, that stings, John.

Don't be so dramatic. Can you tell me what that thing is that keeps displaying our images?

Some sort of holo device.

Thanks, genius, big help.

Like I said, I can't really scan in here. I feel like we're blind.

We are blind.

"Excuse me." Oliver had risen, and spoke as he approached the table. "Excuse, me. I think that my friends and I are at a loss as to the true meaning of this gathering."

Holy shit, is Oliver doing what I think he is?

Yes, I think he is.

I might have heart attack.

You can't have a heart attack, Cam.

Well, you might, and then I will; so same, same.

Balder stared blankly down at Oliver, as if he had forgotten the monk was in the room. John looked at Tyra and noted her lips rising into a smile as murmurs welled up from the chieftains. Balder banged a fist on the table, trying to bring order and quiet the growing uproar.

"If I may be so bold," Oliver said. "I was under the impression we were coming here as a simple meeting to introduce my friends. I am completely baffled by the conversation that has transpired. Changes to the main Ash, where do the children originate from, who is responsible for our 'intrusion' into Ashtree? These are all questions that I am surely misunderstanding."

At this Chief Njord stood, causing the voices to fall silent. "I understand your confusion, Oliver." He gestured for Balder to sit and then took a chain from around his neck that had what looked like a data stick hanging from it. He inserted into a port in front of him. "Forgive me, this change to the discussion is last minute, as the information was delivered to me within the last hour. If you would pay attention to our viewing sphere."

The orb swirled, and the image morphed into a picture of Ashtree, dull and leafless. Njord stood at the head of the table, his hands behind his back, his face wrinkled as if in deep thought. "This is the future of our home. A barren, dead tree. It will not happen in my lifetime, but maybe in this council's, should they be blessed with long life as were our forebears. The decline started when the gate from this planet to our home world got sealed, although we did not notice it for decades." He flicked his hand across the orb and a picture of a planet that looked identical to Earth appeared. "The gate has been bound to both our worlds since blossoming from barren rocks. If Ashtree dies, the gate dies, and so does any hope of us ever returning home." He waved his hand again and the image changed to a picture of Ashtree, bountiful and full with life. "Since our guests have been here, the main Ash has shown signs of new growth and power. That new vitality has effectively reset the clock to our benefit by some years already."

Njord scanned John and company, who were now fully paying attention, even Sierra and Quinn.

I'm completely lost, John.

You're not the only one. This is not what I expected at all.

John leaned forward on his elbows. "So, what exactly are you saying, Chief?"

"That for whatever reason, since your presence here, Ashtree has started to rejuvenate itself."

Did he say rejuvenate?

Yes.

Because of us?

Unless it's our winning personality, I highly doubt it. Probably coincidence.

Oliver walked toward the orb. "Are you sure? Has your data been verified?"

Balder cleared his throat and raised his hand. "I checked the numbers myself, Oliver. They are all correct."

"Then there must be an oversight, a mistake somewhere in the data collection."

Njord walked over and put his hand on Oliver's shoulder. "There is no mistake, friend. It is happening even as we speak. I can feel it throughout this room. A young energy, one that has long since been absent here."

John leaned over close to Sage's ear. "Are you following any of this?"

"You're not?"

"Funny."

Sage smirked at him. "I'm getting the gist of it, but I have a feeling the Chief's going to get interrupted again. Tyra looks ready to blow—look at her."

John glanced over at Njord's daughter. She was already on her feet, her face like thunder.

"Yeah, we should get the kids and get out of here before she nukes us."

Sage rolled her eyes at him. "Real mature."

"What, you don't think this is all bogus?"

Sierra cleared her throat, and they both looked over at the twins. "Why does everyone always act like Quinn and I aren't here?"

This time John rolled his eyes. "This one's all yours, Sage."

Tyra slammed her fist on the table, interrupting all conversations in the room. "We are speaking too freely in front of these humans. Once again, I ask: why are they being permitted so deep into our society that we can divulge generations of secrets to them?"

Njord's flat affect held. He merely paced around the globe, which was now a vision of two identical worlds connected by a single tree, roots entwined into both worlds. He settled in front of John and let out a long controlled sigh. He looked straight into his eyes, then into Sage's, and finally at the twins. Adam, who had been quietly resting at Quinn's feet got up and trotted over to Njord, who patted him on the head, then took Adam's paw and put his forehead to it.

"Tyra, your question is moot. As for helping this band of Oliver's, there is no choice. They will receive our help. The discussion of energy anomalies happening at the main Ash will be postponed until more data is collected. This forum is closed. You are all excused."

Tyra let out a squeal of outrage, and then raised her head as if to speak again, but Chief Njord silenced her with an outstretched hand and a stern look.

John glanced over at Oliver, who just shrugged his shoulders, then over to Sage and the twins, who were trying to get Adam to come back to them from Njord's side.

There was some angry murmuring around the table as the council members started rising from their seats. Tyra glared as if she might stay to fight, but instead whispered quickly to some of the chieftains near her, and then hurried out of the chamber. John and Sage got up to leave, but Njord gestured for them to sit.

"Please, if you would indulge me a bit longer."

John exchanged a confused glance with Oliver before he and Sage sat back down.

Well, this is getting even more uncomfortable, John.

I'm so ready to get out of here.

Just one more leg.

Damn.

Njord watched the council leave, one by one, but stopped Balder. "I need you to keep an eye on these chambers. No one is to enter—no exception."

Balder bowed slightly, and then followed the last of the council members out through the only door into the chamber. Njord waved to Oliver to come sit, and then slumped down in a chair close to Sierra and Quinn.

"Forgive me, children. I am sure that your adult companions can attest that politics is a delicate thing. Once a meeting is derailed, there is little to be gained from continuing."

"Uh, sure." Sierra said. "I'm don't think we really understand what just happened, but we really weren't paying attention until the end when it got exciting."

Quinn smiled big. "Yeah, you were like 'You're dismissed.' That was awesome. I wish I was in charge."

Njord laughed hard and leaned forward to pat Quinn on his shoulder. "One day maybe, you will regret you ever said that." He looked over toward John, Oliver, and Sage. "I did not want for this to go on as it did. My deepest apologies, to all of you. Things around here have been tense, and there is a large part of the council, including my daughter, that would see me...retired."

Did we just wander into another place of crisis, John? Maybe we should just go home.

Too late, and remember, this is all your fault.

Sure, like you were ever going to leave these two.

Agree to disagree.

Uh-huh, that's what I thought.

"I am at a loss, Chief," Oliver said. "I don't understand how Ashtree could be gaining its old strength just by our presence. It has to be coincidence."

"I thought so too, but it is no coincidence, my friend. I have seen Balder's calculations. It started the minute you arrived." He turned back to Sierra and Quinn. "When you brought these two magnificent children here."

John found himself clenching his fists. "What are you trying say, Njord? Listen, pal, I don't care who you are, if you're planning—"

Njord starting laughing again, cutting off John's next words. "Before you finish, let me tell you, no, we do not plan on stopping you from leaving. In fact, I want you to leave first thing in the morning. If you stay here, I believe you would be in grave danger."

Sage narrowed her eyes and sat up in her chair. "Danger? From what?"

Putting his fingers on the bridge of his nose and pressing hard, Njord shook his head. "Tyra and a group of her supporters would most likely try to manipulate the situation to take control of the twins, and of Ashtree. It is something I cannot allow." He looked at the twins, a fond smile in his eyes. "If indeed you are the reason for the Ash's new found exuberance, I still would not hold you captive. I believe you must continue your journey. If Oliver says that you will be safest at Galbraith, then that is where you belong."

Wow, I like this guy, John.

I think I'm starting to also.

"Uh, thanks," Sierra said.

Quinn got out of his chair and took Njord's hand and put his forehead to it. "I learned how to do this from my mom and dad, Sam and Jean. I don't know if they knew you, but it seems to be the right thing to do."

"I did not, but if they taught you this simple gesture, I believe they had some contact with my people that they were not supposed to have, that has been kept secret for a very long time. It is of no consequence now, though. You will be safe, and you will be looked after."

"Chief Njord," Oliver said. "I have no words that would be enough to thank you."

"Just say 'thank you', Oli, jeez," Sierra said.

Again Njord laughed. He walked over to a small cabinet and pulled out a bottle that everyone recognized. "A bit of mead to seal our pact. I would ask that you speak of our talk to no one, but I do not believe that is necessary." He poured glasses for everyone except the twins, who received spring water. "To Ashtree."

"To Ashtree."

"Now, I understand that you will be sleeping in the hangar tonight after you gather your belongings from your lodging?"

John looked at him quizzically. "Yes, we thought it would make for a speedy exit in the morning."

How'd he know that, John?

Probably knows a great deal more than that.

"You are correct. Besides, there are some dock workers who are waiting for you, Oliver. Apparently you lost a bet last time you were here and they feel you owe them some drinks." Njord pushed the rest of the bottle across the table to him.

"Ah, yes, Thorsgard. I believe he could best even you, John."

Not likely.

Let's not find out tonight, John.

Good idea.

"So you're letting us go?" Sierra asked.

"Yes."

Sage finished her glass and clanked it back down on the table. "And you're still providing us with transport to the base of the mountain."

"Yes."

"And how does this benefit you?"

"Sage, it does not."

"I'll drink to that." Sage took the bottle from Oliver and poured another glass.

Njord stood, and John, Oliver, Sage, and the twins all stood too. Njord smiled and waved them to sit. "I must go, but I am not far away, if you have troubles. Balder will see to your final provisions; and I will be there to send you off in morning. Until then, may Ashtree keep you safe." With that Njord waved goodbye to them and walked out of the chamber, stopping for a brief talk with Balder before disappearing around the corner.

* * *

Sage and John walked Sierra, Quinn, and Adam to the hangar, leaving Adam with the kids in their quarters on the ship. Oliver stayed to have a nightcap with a couple of cheery Sasquatches down at the hangar entrance. Figuring everyone was safe enough, John and Sage walked back to their quarters to grab the rest of their things.

"Are you glad you got mixed up in all of this, Sage?"

"I don't know: maybe. I guess I'll only know if I live long enough to remember it when times are better." She grabbed John's arm again and leaned into him as they walked. "I'm liking my choices right now."

John, we're getting dangerously close to me being completely grossed out again.

She opened her door and led John inside.

"I didn't take you for someone who'd pick up someone else's cause so fast," John said.

Don't worry, Cam, I got this.

Sage winked at John and then grabbed her T-shirt and cargo pants off the bed and walked behind the wall to change. "Like I said, Oliver can be convincing. If he had told me you were going to get involved, I would have skipped out on the whole thing."

"Nice. I'm glad I can contribute to your experience. Makes it that much more worth it."

She came back around the corner, looking more like what John was used to, grabbed her go pack, and headed toward the door. John snatched up the large duffle bag that held the rest of their gear and then reached for her bag, their hands resting on each other's for a moment before she let him take it from her. John was going to say something—he wanted to reach out to her and grab her—but he held himself in check this time, and just like that, the moment was gone.

"Uh, we better get going."

Sage rolled her eyes. "Yeah, we better."

"Good." He gestured to the door and smiled. "Ladies first."

She narrowed her eyes at him and headed out. "Oh so charming, aren't you, John?"

See, told you, strong as an oak.

I've heard that before.

* * *

When they got back to the ship, they found Sierra and Quinn sound asleep in the main cabin, with Adam vigilant at their feet. Oliver and his friends were still going strong by the hangar door, shouting and laughing.

John shook his head. "Who knew he could hold his liquor so well?"

"Who knew that they could hold their own against him so well?"

They both laughed, the stress from the last few days leaving a little more with the passing hours.

"You want to take the cabin with the kids?" John asked.

"I'm not sure Adam will make any room for me."

John whistled and Adam came trotting out to sit on John's foot.

"No excuses now."

I stand corrected.

I can't believe you doubted me.

"Such gentlemen," Sage said. "Goodnight, boys."

Adam barked twice and nuzzled John's leg.

"All right, all right. Let's go get some rest before Oliver sees us and decides to come over."

* * *

"Do you think they will make it without you?"

John opened his eyes and saw the blurry image of his wife surrounded by a brilliantly gold light. A white dress clung to her like milk being poured on a naked body. Her eyes were as bronze and bright as the sun that shone daily upon the world.

"Elizabeth!"

"Checking in on you again, darling. Your heart needs to be lightened. You will need to ask much of it if you are to complete your journey."

"I don't want a journey. I just want to be with you and Adam. I don't want anything else."

She cocked up her left eyebrow and smiled, a look that always drove John crazy with love. "I know, but your duty comes first, darling John."

She started floating away from him. He jumped to his feet and followed her, but she was moving too fast.

"Don't go! I don't want to do this without you anymore. What am I supposed to do?"

She tilted her head slightly, and reached her hand out, as if she could touch his cheek. "Protect the children, John."

"NO! Don't go..."

He ran after her, but she floated through the cargo bay door, just out of reach. He jumped to grab her, a full body stretch—and fell flat on his face on a stack of supplies below the airship.

Morning, graceful.

Thanks for warning me before I jumped off the damn ship.

I tried. You didn't want to wake up.

I don't think you tried hard enough.

Probably not.

Adam came running out with Sierra, Quinn right behind him. They stared down at him from the bay door as Adam stood barking at him.

"What are you doing down there?" Quinn asked. "Were you sleepwalking or something?"

John rolled onto his side to get up and let out a dull groan.

What time is it, Cam?

0700.

"Yeah, something like that," he said.

"Who were you screaming at?" Sierra asked.

"Screaming? I wasn't screaming, just having a dream, is all."

We need to get in the air.

You're the one holding us up, sleepwalker.

Sage looked at Quinn and circled her finger around her ear, signaling to him that John was going crazy.

Adam barked again and ran to the boarding ramp to go down to him.

"You know, I'm really thinking about leaving you with them when we get to the monastery, Adam."

I don't think we'll have much of a choice. So sad.

I know you're real broke up about it.

Adam whined and trotted over to him, nudging him sideways with his strong body.

"Don't listen to him, Adam," Quinn said. "He's just having another crazy spell."

Crazy spell?

There's been talk.

And you listened?

Sierra rolled her eyes and tapped Quinn on his back. "Come on, Q, let's go get ready to leave."

They walked off, and John heard them giggling as they left. Adam barked up at them and then whined at John.

"I'm not crazy," John yelled after them. "And if I am going crazy, it's because of you two."

Adam barked again.

"I know, boy, you don't think I'm crazy, do you."

"Ahoy down there," Oliver said. "Are you okay?"

"Just fine, Oliver."

"What's going on, Oli?" Sage asked. "John having another crazy spell?"

"Man overboard," Oliver hollered.

Sage peeked over the side of the airship and smiled.

"Thrown over the side already, and we haven't even left port yet."

"Funny. You're all damn comedians. Can we just get some breakfast and get this ship in the air?"

"You're the only one holding things up, sleeping beauty," Sage said.

She and Oliver left the hold, laughing, and headed toward the small space behind the bridge, where the Sasquatches had set up breakfast. Adam didn't even look back at John before he raced to catch chow with the rest of the crew.

So loyal.

Sage is right. Not even in the air yet and you have a mutiny on your hands.

Hardy-har, Cam.

John got up and dusted himself off before heading back up to the ship. A couple of the looming Sasquatch workers laughed heartily as he walked by. John kicked a box under their legs, sending them toppling over each other.

See, Cam. Simple pleasures.

You're so mature.

The ship was to be manned by Thorsgard and a crew of five Sasquatches who would fly John and the group to the base of the mountain, where they would take a couple of the Sasquatches' Big Dawg carriers to the monastery. He could drop the kids off with whoever this Benedict was, and then he could figure out where to go from there.

After breakfast Balder and Njord appeared to see them off.

"This is too radical!" Quinn said.

"I'm starting to think that's the only word you know how to say right now, Q," Sierra said.

"What? It's radical, isn't it?"

Oliver came up behind them and put a hand on each of their shoulders. "It has been very radical, Quinn, but you and Sierra might want to take your seats in the passenger hold. It can be pretty bumpy going up."

The two of them jockeyed each other to grab the best seat as the ship rumbled to life and got ready for takeoff. Oliver checked the twins' safety harnesses and then hooked himself up.

"It is truly fantastic, isn't it?" Oliver said.

John and Sage helped the Sasquatch crew secure anything loose on the ship while Adam trotted around, sure-footed, getting attention from his new friends and distracting them from their work whenever he could.

"Come on, Adam. Time to get comfy." John secured him into a safecage, then strapped himself into a seat next to Sage. Thorsgard's voice came over the commlink, instructing everyone to brace themselves for takeoff, and the ship began to lift.

The clouds wisped past them as they made their steady ascent over the giant Ashtree and up through the cavernous valley it was hidden in. Then the upward momentum ceased and they started their slow progress toward the drop off point.

"The sky looks like it could go on forever," Sierra said.

"In a way it does," Oliver said. "What we see is just the reaction of particles to the light of that golden sun over there."

"Brilliant," Quinn said.

"Science is one of the many things you will be taught by the teachers at the monastery."

"Are you going stay there with us, Oliver?" Quinn asked.

"Yes. Now that you are found and you're safe, we can start to give you more of a normal childhood experience." Oliver exhaled a light chuckle, a smile showing despite his overgrown beard. "Well, as normal as can be expected these days."

Sierra unhooked herself and wandered back over to one of the windows on the port side of the ship. "Do you really think that our lives will ever be normal again, Oli?"

"What do you mean?"

"Do you think we'll be safe with you, with your friend Benedict?"

Quinn unhooked and walked over beside her. Oliver looked at the children, and then at John and Sage. John shrugged his shoulders and whispered "good luck" to him.

Oliver shook his head and got up to join the children. "I don't know, Sierra. I wish I did. I believe that we will be safe. If not, at least we'll be with Benedict. He is the wisest man I know, and I am sure he will know what to do."

Sage and John came up behind them, the five of them there, along with Adam, who had his paws up on the wall as if trying to see what Sierra saw in the ever-changing skyline.

"I hope you're right, Oli," Sierra said.

"Me too," Sage said.

John smiled at her and felt a pang in his gut. He looked at each one of his companions, his growing family, and felt something inside him, something he hadn't felt for anyone since Elizabeth and Adam. *Love:* he felt love for each of them, and it scared him to death.

Me three.

EPILOGUE

Unsavory Alliance

THE SHIP SOARED ACROSS THE BAY, creating a white wash over the already violent waters. On the holo screen the old lady's face held a flat affect as she updated General Murdoch. The picture fizzled in and out with the turbulent movements of the hover craft.

Murdoch's lip twitched as he gathered his thoughts. "He wiped out your whole team, including the cyborg?"

"Yes, sir."

"And your attempts to trace his movements since have been futile?"

She lifted her chin up as if to try and loosen the tightness of her collar. "As I said to you in my report, they were more resilient than we expected."

Murdoch leaned in close to the image of her face; she flinched. "I am disappointed, Colonel."

"Sir, I understand if you want my resignation."

She could still be useful to us, sir.

If she can locate the twins, or find out where any resistance to our occupation may come from.

We could always hack her AI if needed, control her that way.

Yes, we could. Messy business, though.

Just a suggestion, sir.

A good one.

"No, I do not. In spite of your failure on this mission, I may have need of your services again." He leaned back in his chair, scratching his chin. "Do the good citizens of Tree Top suspect you?"

"I have no reason to think that they do."

"Then stay with them, help them migrate when they evacuate the city after our little invasion. Find out where they're going. I will contact you if I need you."

"I won't fail you again, sir."

He glared at her through the screen, the cybernet behind his eyes flashing red. "No, I don't suspect you will."

The screen flickered out and he turned his chair to face the pilot. "How long?"

"Fifteen minutes, sir. You can see the lights of the monastery now if you look."

He stared out at the firefly-sized lights burning against the deep blue night.

"Ah, Galbraith. It has been too long." He leaned back in his chair and smiled. "Take us in slow, Captain. We don't want to spook our resident traitor, now do we?"

The pilot smiled and went back to his controls. "Slow and smooth, roger that, sir."

*   *   *

"Why didn't you tell me they were coming?"

"We didn't know they were coming until Charles's man saw them heading in over the water."

"Over the water? Did anyone else see them?"

"I don't think so."

"It had to be Charles." The old monk grunted as they raced down the halls of the monastery, their leather sandals slapping, echoing in the night. "Did he ask questions?"

"Of course he did."

The monk paused in the hall at the head of a descending stair-case. Gnarled fingers from one hand clenched the railing while the fingers of the other dug hard into his forehead.

"Sir, we need to hurry."

"Why did they have to turn up? Now of all times." He regained his composure and started down the stairs, moving quickly. "We will have to come up with something to tell him."

"We can make Charles understand. Surely he of all people would see this is the only way."

The older monk glared at his most trusted abbot. "He will not. He is like Oliver. Inclined to wishful thinking and soft-handedness. They have no backbone for what needs to be done to heal this world."

"Then we could…"

"No." The monk cut him off. "Michael, I am telling you right now that we will not even think of taking his life until all other options have been exhausted."

Michael stared past him out into the blue night.

"Do you understand me, Michael? I need you to say it."

Michael bowed and pulled his pitch-black hood over his head. His faced flickered out of view, like a candle extinguished in a cellar, until only his pale, snake-like lips were visible.

"As you wish."

"We will handle it by other means."

The two monks hurried down the steps of the south entrance to the monastery, and made their way to the ocean gate. A tall monk came out of the shadows of the vines that crawled up the white walls of the city, his intent evident in his gait.

"Brothers."

"Ah, Charles," the older monk said. "I am glad you could join us in meeting our new guests."

"Do we know who they are? How did they cross the ocean?"

The older monk looked at Michael, nodded, and then turned his gaze back to Charles as Michael stepped to the side of him.

"I'm sorry about this, Charles. I should have explained all this to you."

"Explain it to me now." Charles pointed out to the obsidian-dark waters. "That's a military vessel out there; if they're friendly, then I'm the President of the United States."

"Charles, there's no time. You'll have to trust me."

"What are you talking about? Make time right now—I am the Abbot of the guard. If something is going on, I need to know about it."

"I don't like this anymore than you will, but I see no other alternative. It is what we must do to bring order back."

"Damn it, what have you gotten us into?"

There was a blur of movement as Michael attacked him. Three rapid bursts with his bladed hand, and Charles let out a gasp, then fell limp to the ground, still straining for air. Michael glared at his dark form writhing in pain and whistled a few short bursts. Four black-robed figures came out of the shadows.

"Michael! What are you doing?" the old monk said. "This is not how we handle such matters. He is still one of us."

Michael bowed, his pale lips spreading into a thin, sinister smile. "I misunderstood, I am sorry. What would you like for us to do now, sir?"

"I would like for you to be more patient." He shook his head in exasperation. "It is too late now. The damage is done. Take him to the basement cells in the main guard tower, and do be gentle with him. We will talk of this later."

"Of course, sir."

Michael gestured to his men. They bound Charles quickly and carried him off to the base of one of the watchtowers, disappearing through the entrance.

The two monks made their way across the small rear courtyard and out the south gate.

"This partnership is turning into a nightmare." Almost as if speaking to himself, the older monk repeated fretfully, "Why did they have to come here?"

"Sir," Michael said, "we won't have to wait long to find out."

Two groups of soldiers dressed in military armor and fatigues flowed up the trail that led from the water. One group took the left flank and dropped to their knees, weapons trained on the two monks. The other stayed to the right of the trail entrance, staggered weapons sighted to cover anything that might approach from the other direction.

"Easy, men, easy," a deep, commanding voice said out of the shadows. "We're all friends here."

The two squads relaxed a little, but not much, as the man commanding them came forward. The monks took this as their cue and hurried toward him.

"I did not expect you so soon, General. May I ask the purpose of this unexpected and, might I add, ill-timed visit?"

"Ill-timed?" The general's form grew larger in the dark, his broad shoulders made even more ominous by his V-shaped body armor. Laser-red eyes shimmered over an arrogant nose and a chiseled chin. "Interesting choice of words. Now, Mrs. Trowley told me a different tale. I was hoping you might be able to enlighten me."

The monk tensed, and he sensed Michael doing the same. He placed his hand on Michael's arm, reassuring him that this was not the time.

"Of course I can, General Murdoch, of course," he said. "We are but humble monks trying to save the world for you. In fact, maybe you could help us with a few problems of our own."

"Good, Master Benedict. Real good," Murdoch said. "I had a feeling you'd say that."

News Clippings

Day One: A New Beginning for Americans!
End of World War in Sight

April 26, 2080 — While skirmishes rage in the North between a depleted Canadian military force and American troops, the rest of the world has voted for peace. President Powell has declared an end to all hostile engagements outside the North American continent and has restored the Treaty of Mexico, originally signed in 2055. He has officially dubbed this Day One, calling it "A new beginning in human history." World leaders will gather in VR Switzerland to sign the accord that will bring an end to the nearly twenty-year conflict that has spanned every continent and territory.

Sources close to the president confirm that American forces have been withdrawn from overseas posts and recalled to the North American continent, which will be governed jointly by the United States and Mexico. Canadian forces continue to fight and Canada has not agreed to sign an accord with any country, refusing to attend the VR treaty summit in Switzerland. Newly starred general of the US Army, Wilson Murdoch, hero of the battles in South Africa,

Australia, the Pacific Islands, and South East Asia, victories that led
to Day One, has been charged with clearing out the rebel military
forces in Montana and helping the newly installed governor restore
peace for the Canadian people.

Polls show that Americans across the nation support the new peace
accord by a staggering eighty-two percent. While President Powell's
approval rating is still low, a new poll shows that his appointment
of General Murdoch has helped his position. This couldn't come at
a better time for the president. Weather disasters linked to global
warming are at an all-time high, the jobless rate is a staggering
thirty percent, and resources, both monetary and physical, are at an
all-time low. A statement from the Joint Chiefs of Staff concluded:
"The American public is ready for peace and prosperity again. With
General Murdoch in charge we can be assured the American people
will be safe, and the hostilities will soon be over, paving the way for
a lasting peace."

Promise of Peace Not Fulfilled

December 26, 2081 — Despite the signing of the peace accord in
May 2080, US forces still battle insurgents in the American North
and West. The self-named Colonies have sent a declaration of independence to General Murdoch. While Canadian forces have been
driven back and the Montana territory regained, the cost has been
high in troops and materiel. Continued migration west from the
New England states due to killing swings of temperature, and the
swarms of refugees from Canada, have taxed an already belea-
guered infrastructure. Now, with talk of secession brewing in the
South and forces stretched thin on the northern front, it is said that
the General will sign the declaration from the Colonies so he can
focus on the stability of the portion of the United States controlled
by his forces.

CEASE-FIRE!

September 21, 2083 — Three bloody years after *Day One*, when President G. Robert Powell of the United States famously declared "A new beginning in human history" just days before his own assassination, a cease-fire has been declared between the forces of the United States, Canada, the Colonies, and the Free.

With General Wilson Murdoch on life support following the August insurrection within his own forces and the threat of a coalition amongst the separatists, the senate agreed to demands from separatists for independence. President Cole has assumed the General's responsibilities until such time as the Joint Chiefs of Staff can appoint new leadership for the martial rule that has been in effect since the series of bombings that killed the President, Vice President and the Chief of Staff earlier this year. Polls show that even with such turmoil, the nation is optimistic about the cease-fire, hoping this resolution will bring peace after the long, exhaustive, twenty-plus years of conflicts that have left the country broken and depleted.

ACKNOWLEDGMENTS

While creating this tale, I benefited greatly from the guidance and mentoring of Cindy Wyckoff: without her this story would have been shelved countless times over. Many thanks also to Jennifer Gilbert and Jesse James Freeman for giving me this great opportunity at Booktrope, and to my team at Booktrope: Gerald Braude, Greg Simanson, Melissa McCarter, and Ruth Silver. Many thanks to my writing group, Dan Gemeinhart, Pat Rutledge, and my author mentor Kay Kenyon. I owe a special debt to my local writing association, Write on the River. Without such a group to hone my craft and practice my pitch, I would have never been a part of the wonderful team at Booktrope. To my coworkers in the Heart CATH lab, who have put up with my distractions into whimsical stories: you are brilliant and ILY more than you know. Love and thanks to my wife Patricia and our three sons, Andrew, Tanner, and Michael, and to Bam Bam, our five pound Yorkie hero. You have been my biggest supporters and foremost readers through many drafts and derelictions; you are better than any story I could ever write.

About the Author

Benjamin Levi Seims lives in Wenatchee, WA with his wife and their three teenaged boys. He works full time as a cardiac nurse and is an officer in the Washington Army National Guard. *After Day One* is his first full length novel, and is the first book in a planned trilogy.

MORE GREAT READS
FROM BOOKTROPE

Undersea by **Geoffrey Morrison** (Science Fiction) In a world flooded and irradiated by a nearly forgotten cataclysm from generations past, all that remains of civilization clings to life in two war-torn, city-sized submarines. For fifty years, the only peace between them had come from separation — that is about to change.

Parallel Extinction by **T.R. Stevens** (Science Fiction) Two interstellar soldiers race to a far-flung planet of ice and phantasms to rescue a marooned scientist who might hold the key to defusing the next Big Bang.

Mission Veritas by **John Murphy** (Science Fiction) Black Saber recruits must qualify on Planet Veritas, where the air makes them reveal their true selves. Vaughn Killian must hide his past as a rebel fighter — a hard thing to do on a planet of truth.

Daimones by **Massimo Marino** (Science Fiction) Nothing could have prepared them for the last day. Explore the future of humanity in this apocalyptic tale that feels like it could happen tomorrow.

Ouroboros by **Christopher Turkel** (Science Fiction) In a dystopian future, Thomas the assassin is about to face the job of his career — and his life.

Discover more books and learn about our
new approach to publishing at **www.booktrope.com**.